ONE CLEAR CALL II.

TIMELINE

World's End	1913 - 1919
Between Two Worlds	1919 - 1929
Dragon's Teeth	1929 - 1934
Wide is the Gate	1934 - 1937
Presidential Agent	1937 - 1938
Dragon Harvest	1938 - 1940
A World to Win	1940 - 1942
Presidential Mission	1942 - 1943
One Clear Call	1943 - 1944
O Shepherd, Speak!	1943 - 1946
The Return of Lanny Budd	1946 - 1949

Each book is published in two parts: I and II.

ONE CLEAR CALL II.

Upton Sinclair

Simon Publications

2001

First pub lished in Au gust 1948

Re print 2001 by Si mon Pub li ca tions

LCCN: 48008056

ISBN: 1-931313-26-1

Dis trib uted by Ingram Book Com pany

Printed by Light ning Source Inc., LaVergne, TN

Pub lished by Si mon Pub li ca tions, P.O. Box 321 Safety Har bor, FL

An Author's Program

From a 1943 article by Upton Sinclair.

When I say "historian," I have a meaning of my own. I portray world events in story form, because that form is the one I have been trained in. I have supported myself by writing fiction since the age of sixteen, which means for forty-nine years.

... Now I realize that this one was the one job for which I had been born: to put the period of world wars and revolutions into a great long novel. ...

I can not say when it will end, because I don't know exactly what the characters will do. They lead a semi-independent life, being more real to me than any of the people I know, with the single exception of my wife. ... Some of my characters are people who lived, and whom I had opportunity to know and watch. Others are imaginary—or rather, they are complexes of many people whom I have known and watched. Lanny Budd and his mother and father and their various relatives and friends have come in the course of the past four years to be my daily and nightly companions. I have come to know them so intimately that I need only to ask them what they would do in a given set of circumstances and they start to enact their roles. ... I chose what seems to me the most revealing of them and of their world.

How long will this go on? I can not tell. It depends in great part upon two public figures, Hitler and Mussolini. What are they going to do to mankind and what is mankind will do to them? It seems to me hardly likely that either will die a peaceful death. I am hoping to outlive them; and whatever happens Lanny Budd will be somewhere in the neighborhood, he will be "in at the death," according to the fox-hunting phrase.

These two foxes are my quarry, and I hope to hang their brushes over my mantel.

Author's Notes

In the course of this novel a number of well-known persons make their ap
pearance, some of them living, some dead; they appear under their ow
names, and what is said about them is factually correct.

There are other characters which are fictitious, and in these cases the autho
has gone out of his way to avoid seeming to point at real persons. He ha
given them unlikely names, and hopes that no person bearing such names ex
ist. But it is impossible to make sure; therefore the writer states that, if an
such coincidence occurs, it is accidental. This is not the customary "hedg
clause" which the author of a *roman à clef* publishes for legal protection;
means what it says and it is intended to be so taken.

Various European concerns engaged in the manufacture of munitions hav
been named in the story, and what has been said about them is also accordin
to the records. There is one American firm, and that, with all its affairs,
imaginary. The writer has done his best to avoid seeming to indicate any ac
tual American firm or family.

...Of course there will be slips, as I know from experience; but *World's End*
meant to be a history as well as fiction, and I am sure there are no mistakes o
importance. I have my own point of view, but I have tried to play fair in th
book. There is a varied cast of characters and they say as they think. ...

The Peace Conference of Paris [*for example*], which is the scene of the la
third of *World's End*, is of course one of the greatest events of all time.
friend on mine asked an authority on modern fiction a question: "Has any
body ever used the Peace Conference in a novel?" And the reply was: "Cou
anybody?" Well, I thought somebody could, and now I think somebody ha
The reader will ask, and I state explicitly that so far as concerns historic cha
acters and events my picture is correct in all details. This part of the manu
script, 374 pages, was read and checked by eight or ten gentlemen who we
on the American staff at the Conference. Several of these hold important po
sitions in the world of troubled international affairs; others are college pres
dents and professors, and I promised them all that their letters will b
confidential. Suffice it to say that the errors they pointed out were correcte
and where they disagreed, both sides have a word in the book.

Contents:

BOOK SIX: MUCH HAVE I SEEN AND KNOWN

BOOK SEVEN: HUMANITY WITH ALL ITS FEARS

BOOK EIGHT: ACTION IN THE TENTED FIELD

BOOK NINE: FEATS OF BROIL AND BATTLE

BOOK SIX

Much Have I Seen and Known

16

California, Here I Come!

I

SO NOW Laurel and Lanny were going to have a honeymoon, nearly two years after they had been married in Hongkong. Maybe their trip through China had been a honeymoon, but it had been hard to enjoy while escaping from the Japs. A bride is supposed to have a veil and a train, orange blossoms in her hair, a trousseau and a going-away dress; but all Laurel had had was a pair of Chinese trousers and a loose jacket, and such belongings as could be stuffed into a duffel bag; that, plus deadly fear.

Now they drove back to New York and got their belongings. Laurel wouldn't let her husband bring the trailer into city traffic on his first trip, for she imagined all sorts of complications. They loaded up the trunk of the car with suitcases and bundles, and piled the back seat with clothing for both winter and summer; they were starting out in the midst of a chilly snap, and later on they would be crossing hot deserts. They made arrangements with Agnes to take care of the baby, whom she adored as her own; she had a friend who would serve as baby-sitter now and then. Lanny said, "It is not the American custom to take babies on honeymoons."

They returned to Newcastle, and one of Robbie's welders put the ball on the back of their car, the smooth steel ball over which the trailer hitch is fastened, leaving the trailer free to turn on it. Their clothes were packed in drawers or hung in the small closets; the suitcases were tucked away under the two beds—one bed at each end of the vehicle, crossways. It wasn't quite as if they were going through darkest Africa, Lanny mentioned; there would be towns on the way, and they could buy what they needed. So off they went, right after lunch on a Monday that happened to see the first snowfall of the season. Esther stood and waved good-by to them, along with her butler and her parlormaid and the governess of some of her grandchildren.

It was a new way of life, of American invention. It had become popular before the war and now was spreading fast; every workingman who wanted to move to higher wages wanted a rolling house to move in and to live in when he got there. Some who couldn't find one took the chassis of an old car and built a wooden box on top. Arriving at a new place and unable to find even a chicken house to live in, some would build themselves a shack in trailer shape, hoping to put two axles and four wheels under it later on. Trailer parks and "motels" sprang up all over the country, some of them a new sort of slum, and others with modern conveniences and even luxuries—swimming pools, dance floors, playgrounds for the "kiddies."

II

Neither one of this bridal couple had ever tried this new way of life. They discovered to their relief that the trailer followed right along behind and didn't jerk or otherwise misbehave; soon you came to take it for granted. The only difference was that rounding corners in a city you had to clear the curb more widely, and when you wanted to stop you had to put on the brake a few feet sooner. The trailer didn't slide off the road in the snow any more than the car did. Observing this, Laurel consented for the expedition to cross the George Washington Bridge; but they must approach it from the north, avoiding the city traffic, and they must find a secondary road westward, and not venture on a main highway between speeding trucks loaded with heavy goods.

So began a six-thousand-mile journey that might have been faster if they had wanted it so; but Laurel was seeing her native land for the first time and didn't care to rush past it at a mile a minute. They crossed New Jersey and a corner of Pennsylvania, finding their way by less-frequented routes. They avoided the mountains, keeping in the Atlantic plain until they got to the southernmost tier of states, and thus had little snow and cold. They started early and did their traveling by daylight; when darkness approached they didn't worry about finding a resting place, for any good farmhouse would do. They would pay for the privilege of running their electric light cord to a connection, usually in the barn. A bucket of water was the only other thing they needed.

Trailer life had its drawbacks, they learned. The little room was crowded, and when you started off in the morning you had to stow everything away, otherwise you would discover that it had slid off the shelf or the table, and maybe had skidded under the bed where it was difficult to reach. Trailer builders had learned this sliding business, so all the drawers had little notches which kept them from opening until you lifted them a quarter of an inch or so.

The apparatus for cooking and washing dishes looked most attractive, but this couple decided that they would have one hot meal in a restaurant in the middle of the day, and for breakfast and supper would make out with bread and milk and fruit, so they could use paper cups and plates and spoons and throw them away. On trailer trips you rarely saw the same people for long, so you didn't have to dress—that is, you put on clothes for comfort and not to demonstrate your social position. The name Budd was a fairly common one, and nobody guessed that these were *the* Budds; so Laurel could wear a sweater and skirt and Lanny didn't have to have his trousers pressed.

This was really seeing America. They could get out and look at the landscape, climb a hill, gather hickory nuts and wild persimmons in a wood, or buy cider from a farmer. They could stand and talk when they met an amusing character, and then move on to the next adventure. Goods were scarce in the city department stores, but in general stores at country crossroads you would still find things that had been made before the war, and these were the best. If you liked plain food well-cooked, you could find it, and after a few mistakes they learned how to judge eating places. When they had got settled in the evenings they would stretch out and indulge in the greatest of all luxuries, reading a good book. They had accumulated many and never had time for them before. They would take turns reading aloud, or read separately, and during the long drives tell each other what they had found.

Also, there was the radio, a powerful instrument of culture sadly misused. But you could learn to dodge the commercials and get the same war news anywhere in America, and the same commentators to tell you what it meant. The Russians were pressing steadily on, taking German fortified positions or by-passing them, chewing up German manpower and resources. There was the continuing clamor for a second front by the Russians and their friends, and the same secret fear in many hearts that the Soviets might make another deal with the Nazis and get out of the war. Lanny said, "Our salvation lies in the fact that Hitler has shown himself a man whom nobody can trust." He didn't have to say more, for Laurel had been in Hitler's home and knew him as a woman knows a man who has offered her the supreme insult.

That had been only four years ago, but it seemed ages away from these peaceful American scenes. Crimes were committed in this country too. Lanny had a Budd automatic in the car and took it into the trailer at night, just on chance; but no such chance befell. It was a grand country if you had a little money, and pretty nearly everybody had it now. That was the irony of the free enterprise system, so ardently praised by the enterprisers; the system could keep the people in comfort so long as the energies of the community were being devoted to killing other people; but the moment they settled down to enjoy the peace their valor had won, they found themselves heading into another depression, with breadlines and apple-selling on the streets and boondoggling and leaf-raking on the country roads.

III

Down through the middle of Virginia, and then, avoiding the crowded Highway Number One, along the coast of the Carolinas and into the land of palmettos and magnolias and live oaks draped with Spanish moss. It was warm; they dug out their summer things, and strolled in the moonlight and listened to the mockingbirds—a honeymoon according to the tradition of all romantic novels about the Old South. How long would they be able to enjoy it when they read in the newspapers and heard over the radio about American boys fighting in the rain-filled trenches in front of Monte Cassino, and in the terrible jungles of the Solomon Islands, where it had always been believed that no white man could survive?

From Savannah they cut across to the western part of Florida and along the Gulf Coast. Laurel had got used to the trailer now and was no longer afraid that some truck was going to crash into the back of it. When they got a flat tire, it was a sociable truckman who stopped to help them out of their trouble, and tried to refuse the dollar bill which Lanny handed him. Now they rolled comfortably on Highway 90, dining on freshly caught shrimp and crabs, and forgetting that there was supposed to be a food shortage. Baker had supplied them with gas coupons, and Robbie had added more. To Los Angeles and back the trip would take less than four hundred gallons, which was only a small part of the "tank-car" full that Lanny was said to have earned.

This was the land of the "Tin-Can Club," as the trailerites playfully called themselves. They had worked all their lives on farms in Illinois or Minnesota, and in their old age had retired on a small competence and wanted to spend their days where it was easier to keep warm. They got their tin-can, old or new, and drove as far south as they could without wetting their feet. They lined up in rows in a camp—first a trailer, then a car, then another trailer, and so on. They put up an awning on two poles in front of the trailer to make a porch, and set flowerboxes along the edges to make a garden. The women sat in canvas deckchairs and told one another about their families up north, while the men pitched horseshoes in the vacant space alongside. Every Saturday night they had a country fiddler and danced the Virginia reel to the tune of "The Arkansas Traveler," and on Sunday mornings they read a Hearst newspaper, printed a day earlier, and then attended a Four Square Gospel Church.

To Laurel Creston, brought up in the secretiveness, called reserve, of the wealthy, this was a delightfully different way of life. So easy for a novelist, where characters revealed themselves in a half-hour's conversation, and a whole family saga could be gathered in an evening! But there would be another camp just like it at the next stop, and so they moved on—along the Mississippi Sound, and across Louisiana and into Texas, which is an empire in itself and was preparing to win a war all by itself. As the motorist clocks it on his speedometer, Texas is eight hundred miles across, and there is every kind of scenery and climate and people. Most of it is outdoors, and the people are glad to show it and tell strangers about it. They are especially proud of their distances, and like to recite a jingle on the subject: "The sun has riz, the sun has set, and here we is in Texas yet."

IV

So they came into southern New Mexico, a land of tumbled mountains and clear blue skies, of hot days and cold nights. Rain fell in winter, but mostly in the high mountains, and filled the dry arroyos with raging torrents. The mountains were bare, and the rocks of every color—gray, yellow, red, brown or black. The deserts were endless-seeming; with irrigation they could be turned into prosperous farms. Jack rabbits fled from you and coyotes kept up their shrill barking at night. If you turned over a stone you might see a centipede waving his tiers of legs like fringes, or a yellow scorpion threatening you with his claws and long inverted tail carrying a deadly sting. When these inexperienced tourists sat down on a rug for a picnic they discovered that little round-bellied ticks had crawled up their ankles and settled themselves for *their* picnic.

There was a new town called Budd. The road to it turned north off the highway—a paved road, and there was a spur railroad near it, both climbing between almost white rocky mountains to a high plateau. Trucks roared past them, just as if it had been U.S. 1 between New York and Washington. The war had come to this land of sagebrush and Indian reservations, and wherever the war came there was hurry, hurry, hurry. The leisurely tourists climbed until there was a crackling in their ears; then suddenly a landscape broadened out, and there was the top of the world spread before them, miles and miles, and painted hills all around, a blazing sun and a sky without a cloud.

There was a roadblock, and soldiers on guard, with side arms. Lanny gave his name, but it didn't impress anybody. "This is the Army, Mr. Jones!" Contrary to what the song says, they had telephones, and a sergeant called the office. Then the barrier swung back, and a soldier on a noisy motorcycle led the way to the administration building. Lanny had heard all about this dream town of his father's, but even so astonishment seized him. Two years ago there had been only sand and sagebrush, jack rabbits and coyotes, and now there was a settlement scattered over the landscape for miles.

This had been the way of it: Robbie Budd had got what his associates called a "bug," a stubborn determination to find out about jets, and what were then called rocket planes. The British were doing it, and why should America wait upon them? Everything the British had was available, and Robbie had sent for it. Because he wanted to experiment with hundreds of the most dangerous chemicals known, he had sent his men to find a tract of land where there was nothing to set on fire and nobody to kill but the scientists and technicians whose job it was to take risks.

They had told him about this plateau that had water and power available from a government dam, and Robbie had bought it without ever seeing it—he hadn't seen it yet. He had paved a road and built a laboratory and about a hundred little cupola structures of concrete, in which to keep the fuels, far enough apart so that one could blow up without hurting the others. There were concrete sheds where such things as eighty per cent hydrogen peroxide as oxidant and methyl alcohol and hydrazine hydrate as fuel could be slapped together and burned, with measurements made of the "thrust" they developed.

And then, all of a sudden, somebody in the Planning Board in Washington had waked up to the fact that the Germans had jet engines actually in production; presently they would have jet planes flying in combat—planes that couldn't be flown economically at less than four hundred miles per hour, and might go to six hundred. What then would become of our air supremacy, so painfully won only this year?

What would happen to the flights of daylight bombers we were sending over Berlin and Bremen and Hamburg, figuring that we could stand a five per cent loss but not a ten per cent loss on each expedition?

The Army had stepped in and insisted on buying for Robbie about ten times as much desert as he had expected to need, and on running a railroad up to Budd. They sent in a swarm of workers to live in tents and lay out a city and build it in a few weeks. There was nothing new about any of this, it was being done all over the land, and the more remote and unlikely the place, the more important it might turn out to be. Had not Presidential Agent 103 sent in word about the V-3 which the Germans were planning and perhaps building, and which would carry many tons of explosives a distance of five thousand miles and drop them where it was told to?

Disperse industry, was the Army's word, and here Robbie Budd had gone and done it. The town of Budd was ordered not merely to test jet engines, but to make them, and more important yet, to think them up in somebody's head. To that end hundreds of scientists were assembled from all over the country, and some from England, plus refugees from Germany and France and all the Axis lands. Trainloads of cement were brought in, and as for sand, you didn't have to look far for that in New Mexico. Laboratories and machine shops of concrete arose, almost literally overnight, and homes for the scientists and the workers. So here was a jet-engine center, and soon it would be a jet-plane center.

V

Robbie had written that his son and daughter-in-law were coming as his representatives, and to show them the works. That meant they were not merely VIP's, but VGDIP's. The manager of the plant took personal charge of them, and wanted to move somebody out of one of the best houses for their comfort. But Laurel laid down the law; this was a camping trip, and they had everything arranged in their little aluminum trailer, named Bienvenu. There was no opposing a lady's will, and no accounting for the whims of the rich. A place was found for them among the workers, and they carried their trays in the cafeteria like everybody else.

It was good food, served hot and in a clean place—for everybody had to be well and happy. They had crèches and kindergartens so that the wives and mothers might work in the plant; they had movies every night, and community singing, and athletics, and dances, and home-made churches—everything that anybody could think of to keep workers contented in a desert wilderness. To keep them from packing up their belongings and driving down the trail! And better yet, to cause them to write to their relatives and friends, saying that Budd, New Mexico, was the best war town yet!

The visitors were put into a jeep and driven around to inspect the wonders of the place. Everybody vied for Lanny's favor, for it was important that his report should be right. They had expected to meet a playboy, and were surprised to find that he knew something about jet propulsion and could ask intelligent questions. He didn't tell them that he had been coached on the subject off and on for a year, and had been boning up as hard as any would-be college students preparing for entrance exams. The scientists, old and young, took an interest in him and showed him what they had got from England, and what they had designed themselves; what they had on the drawing boards, and then what they had in action. After talking and thinking about jets for so long Lanny found it thrilling to observe one develop its "thrust" in actuality. There was a tremendous "whoosh," but no sign of flame—the combustion was so perfect that the flame was all inside. The blast of hot air was terrific, and if you had stood within twenty feet of it you would have been burned to a crisp.

The P.A. sat in at conferences in which the top men discussed in highly technical terms what they were doing and hoped to do. They reported that the Germans had been two years ahead of us in getting the first jet plane into the air, and were now two years ahead of us in production. The Heinkel concern was putting out an engine with a straight-through combustion system with downstream fuel injection. The Junkers had in production what they called the Jumo 004B, with an eight-stage axial compressor. The German Army now had in service a jet interceptor plane called the Viper, which was launched by rockets and was capable of rising to thirty thousand feet in less than one minute.

Lanny asked, "How do you know these things?" And the answer was, "The OSS sends us information." Lanny felt chagrined because he had not been able to get any of this; but he reflected that General Donovan's organization no doubt had scores of men working on the subject in the enemy lands. He had contributed his mite, and once or twice the scientists gave him items which he recognized; but he said nothing about it, and nobody in this place ever knew that he had been inside the Kaiser Wilhelm Institute Physics Building in the winter and again in the summer of this year.

The American Armed Forces were preparing to spend twenty-five billions of dollars during 1944 on airplane production and development. It was a scientist's dream of heaven, for he could have anything in the way of resources and facilities that he called for—provided only that he could show the possibility of getting something new. Lanny met elderly bespectacled gentlemen who had spent all their lives in laboratories and had thought they were lucky if they could get a few hundred dollars for an experiment, but who now asked for tens of thousands and got them. He met young chaps just out of college whose eyes shone with excitement as they explained some oddly shaped piece of steel.

In the not very elegant language of the time, the town was lousy with new ideas. There was the "Jato" rocket unit, that could be mounted on the outside of a plane's fuselage, and be easily detached. It would "boost" planes to get them off the ground, and thus enable them to carry twice the loads they had formerly taken; or it would enable them to rise from half the flight space, which would mean smaller carriers, or that large carriers could utilize more of their flight deck for storing planes, and thus keep more planes in the air. There were blueprints for "composite-engine" bombers, and "jet-cum-propeller" fighter planes for carriers. Lanny listened patiently while a youngster who looked like a school kid explained a "reaction engine," as they preferred to call the jet, that was so beautifully simple you could cry over it, he said. It had only one moving gear, the compressor and the turbine being on the same shaft; it had no vibration and very little noise to warn the enemy, it used little oil and needed no warming up, but could fly in thirty seconds; and, best of all, in peacetime it could use the cheapest fuel, even kerosene. The only trouble was it went so fast that you were liable to be blacked out on the slightest turn; also, they had had to put wire gauze over the air intake, because birds got sucked in out of the sky!

VI

The inspecting team spent a week at the plant, and so far as either of them could see, everything was all right. Lanny air-mailed a report, saying that all the people were wrapped up in their work, and their ideas appeared to be excellent. Laurel, who had spent her time among the wives, both in the trailer camp and in the villas, reported that there was the normal amount of backbiting, but none of the women knew what their husbands were doing—which was as it should be. Lanny knew that this would please his father, who was surely no feminist. Robbie's pride in life was his ability to find the right men and then give them a chance to show what they could do. Women made good stenographers and filing clerks, but nothing else.

The tin-can Bienvenu rolled again, and came into Arizona, which was like the rest of the Southwest, except that more irrigation works had been built and more crops were being grown. The valley in which lay Phoenix, the state capital, had grown so fast that the highway was like a city boulevard. The trailer camps and motor courts were crowded, so they had to spend the night by the roadside; because they had neither radio nor lights, they went to a movie, and discovered that many other persons were in the same fix and had found the same solution.

More mountain passes to wind through, and they came to a long bridge over the Colorado River, and on the other side was that dreamland of movie addicts all over the world—California. Seeing was believing, and the addicts all knew that in this Golden State everybody's kitchen was the size of a large drawing-room and had all the latest fixtures made of chromium; also, that boys who were poor but honest and handsome invariably married the daughters of millionaires. Animated by this certainty, thousands of new people were pouring into California every day, and a lot of them had come by Highway 80 on the same day as Lanny and Laurel. All had to sit and wait, and then turn out the contents of their cars and trailers, for the state authorities took strict measures to prevent the importation of infected fruits and plants. It didn't constitute a cordial reception, but you could feel sorry for the poor inspectors, who worked long hours and still couldn't keep up with the procession of cars.

More mountains and deserts; it was Mary Austin's "land of little rain." A huge dam had been built on the Colorado, and an aqueduct brought the water some two hundred and fifty miles to the Los Angeles district—just in time to get the swarming new populations clean. Lanny told his wife about the political war going on over the name of the dam; the Democrats called it Boulder and the Republicans called it Hoover, and it was like casting a ballot every time you spoke the name. Lanny said that if the Japs were able to do a bombing job in this neighborhood, all they would need was to destroy a couple of aqueducts, and Southern California would have to be evacuated; quite probably a million or two persons would perish while trying to get out.

They came to the Coachella Valley, the date country, and Lanny, who had been through here before, told the story of how a few shoots of date trees had been smuggled out of Arabia long ago—with difficulty, because the natives guarded their secrets closely. Now there were miles and miles of stately trees, each one resembling an enormous royal crown, and planted in rows as exact as a checkerboard. Dates require an immense amount of water, but it has to be underground and not in the air; they were told that the general irrigation of Southern California might change the climate and make date growing impossible.

They spent a night at Palm Springs, which had once consisted of a hotel and a few villas nestled in a niche of mountains and was now a spreading town, with factories and trailer camps like everywhere else. Next morning they drove up a long pass and into the orange country—a highway through fifty miles of orange groves, now loaded with blossoms and at the same time with ripening fruit. It was rapidly becoming a roadtown with "hotdog stands" and "eateries" and "realtoriums"—you could learn a whole new language on the way. The traffic was heavy, and you had to watch out or you would end up in the hands of a "mortician."

With every mile as they approached Los Angeles, this traffic grew worse, and it was well that Laurel had got used to the trailer by now. From Pasadena it was one continuous city, whatever the name. Industrial plants had sprung up everywhere, and many thousands of them were discharging smoke or chemical fumes into the atmosphere. The result was an extraordinary phenomenon, a dense gray haze that sometimes made it impossible to see more than a few hundred yards. The plain was bordered on the east by a long chain of high mountains, the Sierra Madre, and apparently this "smog" couldn't get over them, but piled up against them, and from the ocean to the foothills people coughed and sneezed and wiped their eyes. Lanny said, "It's the price for licking Hitler."

VII

They had taken it easy on the way, and came into Hollywood toward sundown, the worst traffic hour. They found it as had been foretold; everything was packed to the doors. Lanny tried one hotel and was told that people were sleeping on the billiard tables and in the chairs of the lobby. He went to the telephone and tried half a dozen other hotels and got the same response. They drove to a few of the trailer camps and found that these had illuminated signs: "No Vacancy." The visitors didn't have to worry, for they could go a bit out into the country and camp by the roadside; but first they would have a meal, and do that in style.

They parked on a side street and made themselves as presentable as could be done by the light of a candle. Then they strolled on Hollywood Boulevard, and into Sardi's, one of the smart restaurants. They had to wait their turn, but they didn't mind, for this was one of the sights of the land; people came from all over, even in wartime, just for the privilege of glimpsing in real life some of those faces and figures they had seen magnified and glorified upon the screen. The food would be good when they got it, and meantime it amused them to watch the flashily dressed crowd. They had no forewarning that it would be the beginning of an adventure.

In due course they were seated at a table, and it happened to be near the door. They had finished studying the menu and deciding what they wanted when they saw a woman come in and join the waiting throng. She was clad in a full-length mink coat, which tells the world that its wearer is at the top of the heap, at least financially; she was a large woman and it took a lot of minks, even without the hat to match. She had some jewels too, and anyone could be sure that she was able to pay for her dinner. She was alone, which was unusual. Lanny glanced at the full and rather florid face and it seemed familiar, but he couldn't place it. The headwaiter came in the nick of time to spare him embarrassment; the man bowed and said, "Just a few minutes, Miss Rector." Then Lanny caught the woman's eye and he saw that she recognized him. Good manners required him to make the first advance, so he rose and said, "How do you do, Miss Rector. I am Lanny Budd."

"How pleasant to see you here!" she exclaimed, her face lighting up. They shook hands—it was the custom for ladies to shake hands with gentlemen here in the West. "We are a long way from Paris," she added. "And it must have been ten years ago."

"This is my wife," said Lanny. "Laurel, this is Miss Roberta Rector, for whom I had the pleasure of selecting some paintings in Paris."

"A pleasure to meet you," said Laurel cordially. "Won't you join us for dinner?" She couldn't say less, since otherwise she would have left the lady standing.

Roberta Rector sounded like a movie name, and Laurel guessed that she must be an actress—one of those who have passed the ingenue age and have to take roles as mothers and aunts. But no, there were other kinds of people in Hollywood. Lanny said, "Miss Rector is a cattle princess," a remark which would have been crude in the extreme, except that Lanny knew his princess. He said it with his smile, and she took it with a still broader one.

"No," she explained. "No more cattle for me. I sold out and put my money into tax-free government bonds; so I have nothing more to worry about in this world."

"You are wise," commented the man. "What have you done with the Monets and Cézannes?"

"Oh, I got tired of them and gave them to the County Museum. I was living in the Beverly-Wilshire Hotel and had to have a separate room for them, and I was afraid the place might burn up or somebody might steal them. And then, you know how it is, so many people heard about them and wanted to see them; I was always being bothered with letters and telephone calls. So I said, 'I'll put them where everybody can see them without having to see me.' "

"Mostly people wait until they are dead before they are that generous," remarked the art expert, who had known the rich from babyhood.

"Oh, well, I get tired of things, and I want something new to look at. I keep hearing about Detazes, and perhaps I might like to own some. Is there anywhere I could look at them?"

"I showed you quite a number in Paris, Miss Rector."

"Oh, did you? I had forgotten. I see so many paintings. People try to sell them to me."

"Fortunately the Detazes are in this country now—what we have left. They are in charge of my old friend and associate, Zoltan Kertezsi, in New York. You met him, a Hungarian."

"Yes, I remember; he had a lovely soft brown mustache."

"It is gray now. He'll be happy to show you the paintings whenever you are in New York."

"I expect to go this winter. My life seems so restricted since Paris or London are out. I do hate this war. Don't you, Mrs. Budd?"

"I hate all wars," said Laurel. She had realized by now that here was a "character," and as a novelist she took out her mental notebook and sharpened her pencil.

"I had covered my signs with slogans against war," continued the retired cattle princess, and a stubborn look came into her gray eyes. "Everybody objected to them, but I kept them, even after Pearl Harbor. Then people splashed tar on them, so I had to change them."

Lanny explained to his wife. "Miss Rector owns a hill in the heart of Hollywood, and on all four of her street corners she has billboards with her political opinions on them. You remember, you noticed one about India."

"I hope you agree with me," said the propagandist lady. "I ask the world, what right have the British to talk about freedom when they refuse freedom to the people of India? Don't you think I am right, Mrs. Budd?"

"It's a complicated question," responded Laurel. "I am troubled by the possibility that if the British set the Indians free, they may soon be flying at one another's throats."

"Well, let them; that's their business if they want to."

"Don't you believe in a police force, Miss Rector?"

"Yes, but I wouldn't want a British policeman in my home and neither would you, I am sure. I see that you haven't thought these matters out, Mrs. Budd. You must let me introduce you to some of my Hindu friends and let them explain their cause."

VIII

This meal was served and eaten—with great gusto by Roberta Rector. Lobster à la Newburg, and a pitcher of buttermilk, and then a *coupe glacée*—neither Lanny nor his wife had ever seen such a meal, and they observed with quiet amusement that the lady let the gentleman take the check without protest. Perhaps she was one of those many rich people who are extravagant in large matters and penurious in small. Certainly she was one of those many stout people who reiterate that they are "small eaters"; they want you to believe that they are able to manufacture *embonpoint* out of water and air. "I only eat one meal a day," said Roberta, and failed to mention that she kept chocolates in her room and took a nibble every now and then, and visited her refrigerator for both buttermilk and beer.

This meeting solved a problem for the two travelers. When they mentioned that they were living in a trailer and had been unable to find a place to keep it, their guest said, "For heaven's sake, come and park it on my grounds. There is all the room you want, and I'll be delighted." They accepted, and the woman took them out to her big limousine with a waiting chauffeur, and drove them to the place where they had parked. They followed her car, and on the way Laurel exclaimed, "What a curious human! What do you know about her?"

Lanny said, "I know that her father was one of the big cattlemen in Texas. You see the signs 'Rector Ranch Products,' and he was it. Also, I know that she bought half a dozen paintings that cost ten or fifteen thousand dollars each. I was told that she has never been married, but has a grown son."

"What did she do that for?"

"I don't know; probably she's a feminist and thinks the child should belong exclusively to the mother. She consorts with anarchists and other radicals, and no doubt is considered a dangerous character out here."

"I'm curious to know what's in her mind," declared the novelist; to which the husband replied, "That ought to be easy. She's certainly a free enough talker."

After they had climbed "Rector Hill" in the heart of Hollywood, they parked their trailer alongside Roberta's house and connected up the electric light with her back porch and their water line with her garden hose. They went inside and were shown through the house and were besought to occupy one of the guest rooms. But Laurel said no, they had promised themselves that this was to be a camping trip and they didn't want to spoil their record. They were told about the house, which had been designed by the man whom advanced and art-loving Americans considered the greatest architect of the time; the roof was so built that water didn't always run off it, and the chimneys smoked, and the kitchen was inconveniently placed—but it was one of the most original and beautiful of designs, and everybody wanted to come and see it.

Roberta said this without the faintest trace of a smile. Whatever great architect had designed her mentality had left out the sense of humor. If you made any sort of joke in her presence, she would stop and look disconcerted, as if you had stuck a stick between her legs while she was walking. Then she would resume the conversation as if nothing had happened. Her manner of talking seemed to say that she had always had money and therefore other people had to learn to listen.

First she told about her house, and then she told about her hill. She had deeded it to the city for a park, and the mansion on top for an art museum; but the city had not kept its part of the bargain, and now she was bringing lawsuits, and was tied up in quarrels with the politicians; she talked at length about these most evil men. Then, too, she had the problem of her dogs; she had eighteen water spaniels—they kept multiplying, after the way of nature, and what could she do about it? The dogs raced all over the house, and when they were turned outside they bit somebody, and that, too, was a cause of lawsuits, and Roberta had had to appear in court, and worse yet, in the newspapers.

One more proof of the ancient thesis that the possession of wealth multiplies cares. Everybody knew about those tax-free bonds, and all wanted some of them, or at any rate some of the interest. In the beginning Roberta had been generous, but gradually she had come to realize that nobody was interested in her for herself, only in her money, and that hurt her feelings; so she had made up her mind to refuse all requests. It had become a sort of phobia with her, and she said no even before she was asked. Certainly neither Lanny nor Laurel had any idea of asking her for money, but she appeared to be including them when she sounded her defiance. "It's no use to ask me, for I won't give! I am sick and tired of giving! My father killed himself earning that money; he broke his heart valves. He left it to me, and I am guarding his fortune and his good name!"

IX

The Budds retired to their tiny nest and sat for a while discussing this strange human soul which had fallen, as you might say, like a ripe peach into a novelist's lap. They spoke in whispers, for they were sure that curiosity had not been left out of the make-up of this intensely personal person, and it might be that she was standing in her garden trying to hear what these suddenly acquired friends might be saying about her. In the morning they were invited in to breakfast—anything they fancied, for there was a Chinese cook whom Roberta described as "the dearest old thing you could imagine," and a Filipino boy who was too delicate for the Army and who watched everything that went on with a pair of quick dark eyes.

Lanny went off in the car to look up a couple of his clients and tell them about art works he had discovered in London and Stockholm and Rome, for the Americans were soon going to take that last-named city and perhaps the Nazis wouldn't have time to sack it. That left a woman writer to pursue the subject of psychology in what might be called field work. When Lanny came back toward evening he found that Laurel had decided to move into the house. The two women had become fast friends and were deep in a conference, which consisted in the cattle king's daughter telling everything that had ever happened to her, and what she thought about it, and what she knew, or thought she knew, about life. There were men, and a few women, who called themselves psychoanalysts and would charge you as much as fifty dollars an hour to let you do that; but here was a highly intelligent woman who would let Roberta do it free of charge—or so Roberta hoped and believed. Laurel Creston Budd hadn't said much about herself, and surely not a word about being Mary Morrow.

The session went on for two days and might have gone on forever if Lanny had consented. This woman of "independent wealth" was independent of everything on the whole earth; she had no obligations, no ties, and apparently no friends; she was frantic with loneliness, yet afraid to meet anybody, because that person, male or female, old or young, rich or poor, would sooner or later try to get her money. The poor would want it for themselves, and the rich would want it for causes, charities, ideas, whatever it might be they were interested in and desirous of promoting. Roberta Rector lived alone with her Chinese cook and her Filipino houseboy and her eighteen water spaniels, and apparently she saw nobody but her lawyers and the people who served her in restaurants, stores, and banks.

X

Driving with her husband, Laurel retold a pitiful story. Roberta Rector had not had a baby in order to defy society; just the other way round, she had defied society because she had a baby. A rich man's daughter whose mother had died young, she had been brought up in a splendid but lonely home. She had been a beauty, and Laurel said, "She really was, for she showed me the photographs; and you mayn't believe it, but I do, she hadn't been told a thing about sex and hadn't the remotest idea what it was. At the age of eighteen she came here from Texas, and she met a Russian stage director, a brilliant and fascinating man, who seduced her. She was mad about him, and thought he loved her, and found out little by little that all he wanted was to get her money to finance the world's most startling stage productions. When she learned that she was going to have a baby she was terrified; but then she happened to meet Emma Goldman, who talked Anarchism and Libertarianism, and advised her to make having a baby into a crusade, and say that she had done it as an act of defiance. She said that, and so the radicals all thronged about her and got her money; but she doesn't really understand any social theories—she just accepts what the last person has told her, until she decides that that person, too, has had too much of her money."

"What became of the man?" Lanny asked.

"He has his career, and once in a while he shows up here. Roberta is still in love with him, but she also despises him. She used to give him money, but now she has shut down on him as she has on everybody else. She has never loved any other man, and never could; she fears them, because they all want her money. She gets something over thirty thousand dollars a month and hasn't any idea in the world what to do with it, but she can't bear to give it away; she wants to be loved for herself alone, and she can't find anybody who will do that."

"What about the son?"

"The son is like everybody else: he wants money, more and more of it. He was sent to a so-called "progressive" school, and was allowed to do whatever he pleased because the head of the school wanted money from the mother. The son ran off with one of the girls in the school and married her and got a baby; then he couldn't get along with the girl, so he divorced her and married another girl, and both girls and the boy are living in the same house—one of Roberta's. When I asked her about that she said, 'What can I do? The first girl has no other place to live.' She summed up her maternal feelings in one sentence: 'I wish the whole lot of them would go to China and stay there.' "

So there was the story of a retired cattle princess who had an income of nearly half a million dollars a year, tax-free, and was the most frustrated and unhappy human being the novelist Mary Morrow had ever described. She was in a position to gratify her every whim, and got up every morning with no idea what she was going to do with herself that day. She would employ a name architect to build her a lovely home, and when she had got tired of it she either sold it or just left it; she had done that half a dozen times, and gone to live in a hotel. She had had a fine sailboat built on one of the mountain lakes in Southern California, and when it sank at the dock, in a storm, she hadn't troubled to have it raised. She had taken up "causes," and then decided that they were mistaken. She had put up a fortune to help free Tom Mooney, labor leader jailed on a frame-up, and when he had got out he divorced his loyal wife and married a younger woman—and had come to Roberta Rector for more money!

Said Laurel, "Someday she will die, and then I will write the story. She is a living sermon on the evils of wealth inheritance."

Said Laurel's husband, "It wouldn't do any good, because nobody would believe it. They would say you had made it up to fit your propaganda."

XI

Lanny took his wife to meet his old friends, the De Lyle Armbrusters, wealthy people who had a sumptuous villa on a hill slope above Hollywood. They were the opposite of Roberta Rector—instead of shutting themselves off from all the world, they gathered all the world about them and aspired to be everybody's best friends. They were rather commonplace middle-aged people who sought distinction by surrounding themselves with celebrities. Lanny had known them of old on the French Riviera, and two and a half years ago, when he had come to Hollywood for the first time, he had made something of a hit with them because he had met Hitler and Göring and was able to tell about the private lives of these undoubted celebrities.

When they heard where Lanny and his wife were staying they were somewhat shocked. "Why do you tie yourself to that dreadful woman?" And when Lanny pretended not to know what they meant, De Lyle went on, "A woman who consorts with Reds and Pinks, and Hindu and Irish revolutionists, and all sorts of riffraff. Why don't you come and stay with us?"

"We are traveling in a trailer," explained the son of Budd-Erling apologetically.

"But that's quite all right, Lanny; people do what they please nowadays."

"But it's such a wee little trailer, made of aluminum."

"That's all right too; we can put it behind the garage." De Lyle, like Roberta, talked without the faintest trace of a smile. He had a round, bland face, and was stout and growing stouter; he was just as money-conscious as the cattle lady, but had much more than she, and he was willing to spend it for value received, that is to say, for social prestige and publicity in the society columns.

Lanny had expected this invitation and forewarned his wife. One of his jobs was to watch these people, so he would play his role of near-Fascist, and the thing for Laurel to do was to be a little mouse wife, with no ideas on the war or politics, just listening respectfully to the famous ones. Everybody in this town was playing a role, on and off the screen, and what Laurel as a novelist wanted was to store up material without giving any hint that she possessed a critical mind. They went back to the retired cattle princess and told her they had to be on their way; her chauffeur hitched up the trailer, and the P.A. drove it up into Benedict Canyon and deposited it safely out of sight and out of mind on the Armbruster estate. Then he drove his wife to the shops in Beverly Hills, for she couldn't appear at "Genie's" parties in the clothes that had been all right in the company of eighteen water spaniels.

XII

The screen people you met at the Armbrusters were all very rich; the poorest of them earned more than the President of the United States, and they all knew what the others were earning and talked about it frankly—and often. People were graded in importance according to their salaries, and if you dropped from the five-thousand-a-week class to the two-thousand-a-week class you were relegated to a different social group. There were many who would deny that this was true, but meantime it would be happening automatically, for if you had only two thousand a week you couldn't live like those in the higher class; your liquor wouldn't be so choice or your swimming pool so roomy. There were some who talked about saving their money and retiring to do something worthwhile, but few indeed were able to achieve this, for the pressure to spend money like your friends and associates was irresistible. Here and there were little groups that got off by themselves and talked about "art," but as a rule that would be considered pretentious, and even a bit unkind, a criticism of your profession and your friends.

This Hollywood world had grown up in the course of some forty or fifty years, and money was what had made it and now maintained it. Money had brought talent of every sort from all over the world; money love and money glamour had put its stamp on them and on every product they turned out. In the last great panic "the industry" had been on the rocks and Wall Street had stepped in and bought control; now it exercised its silent but firm say-so, as everywhere else in American big business. Pictures were produced to make money and no nonsense about it, and if you didn't like that you could move out to the Mohave Desert and raise chickens, or up into the bare hills and walk behind a flock of sheep.

The couple from the east found the movie stars for the most part kindly and likable people. There were some among them who had a social conscience in spite of their high salaries. They defended the New Deal, and this was considered a sign of a disordered mind, for why shouldn't they be grateful to a country which paid them so extravagantly The mass of the "colony" were normal Americans who wanted two things: to get more money, and to be allowed to keep it and not have to pay it to the government in the form of income taxes. There were some who were rabid on this subject. They damned the bureaucracy which spent their money for them; and, above all, they damned "That Man," who was the "master mind," to use one of Hollywood's own phrases.

It was these people whom one met at the Armbrusters' cocktail parties and evening affairs. They had no idea that the Budds were or could be any different from themselves. Lanny discovered that now, with the country at war and the Soviet Union an indispensable ally, they no longer expressed the hope that somebody "would shoot 'That Man.' " What they wanted was to get rid of him at the next election, less than a year away. They agreed that a fourth term would be absolutely fatal to American liberties; they rejoiced in every mistake that Roosevelt made, even when it was one which might be costly to the nation.

What these near-Fascists wanted most of all was to revise and remodel the war, and find some way to get the Germans on our side and the Russians off. They had given up Adi Schicklgruber as being a hopeless bungler; they wanted to get rid of him at the same time they got rid of the Squire of Krum Elbow, and they questioned Lanny, knowing that he had been in Germany and actually knew the Nazi leaders. He was able to please them by revealing that many of the Wehrmacht officers wanted to oust Hitler and take over the government. These were the natural-born leaders of Germany, and Hollywood actors who had enacted their roles on the screen thought that was an ideal solution. They urged the son of Budd-Erling to stay and join the society they had organized to combat the many Red agents who were trying to seduce Hollywood and turn it to the ends of Moscow.

XIII

After a few days Lanny sent a telegram to the lord of San Simeon, reminding him that he had asked Lanny to bring him information whenever he could, and added, "I am here at your disposal. My wife is with me." It took no more than a couple of hours for a reply to arrive, saying that the lord would be pleased to receive them at any time. They could be flown from the Burbank airport in his plane if they so desired. Lanny replied that they would motor up the next day.

To bring a tiny trailer to a place where sumptuous accommodations were prepared for a couple of hundred guests would have been rather absurd; so "Bienvenu" was locked up and left behind the Armbrusters' garage, and Laurel took her best clothes in suitcases. The coast highway had been opened up all the way to the north, and through the San Simeon property in spite of the lord's most strenuous opposition.

The highway was costly, winding along the sides of cliffs; the scenery was of the finest, but you had to watch out with your driving or you'd find yourself in the Pacific Ocean.

Lanny warned his wife, "I have been asked to find out what this old man is doing and planning; so you have to be a Fascist for a while longer. Of course you call yourself a democrat, but you don't work at it. You mustn't say anything impolite about Hitler, or even about Mussolini; even though he's been kicked out he's still a great man, and he made the trains run on time."

"I've been reading the *Examiner*," said Laurel, "so I know his ideas."

"No, that's a mistake," replied the husband. "What the old man says in the *Examiner* is what he wants the public to believe about him. He calls it Americanism, and it sounds fine, but what he actually believes is something out of the Middle Ages. It will be wiser for you to keep quiet and watch me draw him out."

He told about the life of "Willie"—so his parents had called him, but now even his most intimate friends called him "Mr. Hearst." He was the son of a gold-mining king who had bought himself a seat in the United States Senate and had sent his only son to Harvard. Willie had got himself expelled for indecent behavior, and from that experience he had conceived a bitter hatred of the so-called respectable world, and a determination to "show them." His father had bought a derelict San Francisco newspaper, and Willie's way of "showing" had been to fill it with crime, sex, and sensation. "Yellow journalism," it was called, and by appealing to everything base in the nature of the masses Willie had collected their pennies by the billions.

He had come to New York and bought a small paper called the *Journal*, and had set out to conquer that most haughty and sophisticated part of the world. He had built up an empire, with newspapers in a score of cities, including the most proper Boston which had kicked him out. Then he had taken up the idea of "showing them" in politics; he had dreamed of being Mayor of New York City, Governor of New York State, President of the United States. To accomplish that he had become a "radical," espousing the cause of the masses and calling himself their friend and champion. But he found that while the masses would read his papers, they wouldn't trust him and didn't vote for him.

So William Randolph Hearst had become an embittered man, turning against all the causes he had espoused in his younger days. He had built himself the palace of an emperor, and retired to sit on his heap of gold and use it to dominate the lives of other men. In his heart he despised these men because they took his money and wrote not what they believed, but what he commanded. "All his life he has done that," Lanny said. "He would come into the office of the *New York American* shortly before midnight and throw out everything the paper had prepared in reference to some politician; because that politician's wife had just insulted Hearst's lady friend, Hearst would order a cartoon portraying that politician in prison stripes. In politics, as in every other phase of life, he has been cynicism incarnate, and I think he has been the most demoralizing single force in American life."

Laurel said, "What an introduction to a host!"

XIV

There were gates, and a porter's lodge, and apparently a list of names which the porter consulted; then they drove on a winding road to the hill on which this economic emperor had erected a monument to his own glory. There was a vast main building and half a dozen villas, each with a fancy Spanish name. A majordomo received them, much as if it had been a smart restaurant; a servant brought in their bags and another took their car. The place looked and felt just like a de luxe hotel; you had a suite with a sunken bathtub, and you found a list of rules on the inside of the door, telling you among other things that if you wanted meals you must come on time. Exactly like the Berghof, except that in this place you were allowed to smoke, and there was a bar where you could drink all you wanted, but you were not allowed to take anything to your rooms.

San Simeon resembled Karinhall in that it was an art museum as well as a residence. There were cellars, occupying the entire space under the main building, packed with art works, most of which had never been uncrated. Hanging on the walls of the rooms were paintings enough to keep an art expert happy for weeks. The "Yellow Kid," as Hearst's enemies had called him during his early days, shared the blind passion of *Unser Hermann* for collecting for its own sake. Everything that anybody else wanted very much must belong to them, even though they had no use for it and hadn't time even to look at it. In Hearst's case it included everything from Egyptian scarabs to a twelfth-century monastery, which had been taken down stone by stone, boxed, labeled, and shipped to New York, but never put together again! San Simeon differed from Karinhall in that it was also a zoo, with a great number of wild animals from all parts of the world, in cages or fenced enclosures. It was also a gym, with provision for a variety of games:

handball, tennis, and squash courts, indoor and out, and swimming pools of fresh and salt water both warm and cold.

The Budds had arrived in the middle of the afternoon, and after they had freshened up they went down to the main rooms. Several guests were there, chatting, and Lanny introduced his wife to Miss Marion Davies, retired motion picture star, who was made-up as if expecting to be called before the camera. Laurel had been duly posted—this was their host's special friend and much depended upon her favor. In her company they strolled and looked at old masters, and Lanny poured out a fund of information surprising to people who had never realized that the history of art is a subject of study, just like the history of politics, or warfare, or other human activity.

In one corner of the great hall sat a large, tall, extremely wrinkled old man with gray hair and a long face which had been a boon to cartoonists for more than fifty years. He was diligently writing with a pencil on a pad, and it was one of the unwritten laws of this place that nobody ever disturbed him at such times. He was laying down the policies of the Hearst newspapers for the next day, and thus determining the thoughts of some ten or twenty million Americans for that period and longer. He didn't bother to retire to his study, but just sat in any chair that happened to be handy and set down whatever occurred to him. It might be a headline, or a directive for the handling of some news item; it might be an editorial idea for one of his many writers to elaborate, or it might be a proclamation to be signed WILLIAM RANDOLPH HEARST.

When the writing on the pad was completed, a secretary would type it, if there was time, and then it would be "shot" from the telegraph office in this building. It would go to the nineteen Hearst newspapers in leading American cities, and in due course the air mail would bring copies of each of these papers, and "W.R." would check carefully to be sure his instructions had been followed. If it hadn't been done he would "shoot" a wire to the offending person, telling him in the plainest language what mistakes he had made; if that happened more than once or twice there would come a wire saying, "Your services are no longer required."

Such was the life of an eighty-year-old journalist-emperor. This was what interested him, and if he ever talked or thought about anything else, it was just play, or politeness to some guest. His right to manage these papers in this precise way was what he meant by all the noble phrases he used: the free enterprise system, freedom of initiative, the American way, the Constitution, the Flag, and the Christian Religion.

Above all, this was democracy, spelled with a small "d"; for now the Democratic party was a prisoner of the New Deal, and the Hearst newspapers, calling themselves "Independent," gave their support to Hoover, Coolidge, and Harding.

XV

At the beginning of December President Roosevelt at last accomplished his desire to exercise his charms upon Marshal Stalin. Churchill had already been to Moscow, but Churchill's charms were of a different sort. Stalin had a good memory and knew that Britain's Tory leader had been calling for war on Bolshevism from the moment it had lifted its head in 1917. But the Squire of Krum Elbow was the author of the New Deal, the friend of the common man, and the enemy of the economic royalists; more than that, he was the inventor of lend-lease and was shipping hundreds of millions of dollars' worth of supplies to the Soviet Union every month. Money talks, and F.D.R. was talking world order, peace, and prosperity in a voice loud enough for even the people of the Soviet Union to hear.

Stalin had been too busy to come to Allied lands, and they had compromised upon Teheran, the capital of what had once been Persia and now was Iran. There, in the Russian Embassy, the three top leaders had a four-day conference, and now as it came to an end a formal statement was issued. That was what Mr. Hearst had been so busy with; and when he had finished he strolled over and welcomed his new guests, and after chatting for a few minutes took Lanny off to his study and spent the rest of the afternoon with him. On Lanny's earlier visit to San Simeon he had received the handsome offer of fifty thousand dollars a year to become one of this imperial person's political scouts, and to report to him privately what he could learn about the insides of world affairs. Now the lord of San Simeon had a chance to get some of it free of charge, and he wasn't failing to take the chance.

He talked about the news which had come over his private wire, and to which some of his guests were now listening over the radio. The statement issued from Teheran brought no satisfaction whatever to the owning and directing head of a great newspaper chain. It consisted of the vaguest and most empty generalizations. Complete unanimity had been reached on military plans, unity was to be maintained in the making of peace, and all freedom-loving nations would be invited to lend their aid in meeting the world's future problems. "Bunk!" exclaimed William Randolph Hearst. "Pap for infants and imbeciles! How much of Poland are they going to leave to Russia, and how much of Germany are they going to give to Poland to make up for it? And what are they going to do with Austria, and all the Balkans? Are they going to let Russia bolshevize them, and if not, how are they going to prevent it?"

Lanny didn't have the answers to any of those questions and could only say that the situation looked dark indeed to him. There could be no question that the Russians were on their way to Berlin and would get there in a year or two, especially if the Allies attempted a Channel crossing next spring. Lanny could say that the Allied armies invading Italy were not being reinforced, and were even losing some of their bombing units and landing craft; and this was a sure indication of a projected landing in France. The military men in Berlin, the really competent ones, were becoming hopeless as to their chances.

Naturally a large-scale vendor of news pricked up his ears. How did Mr. Budd know these things? When Lanny said that he had recently been in both Berlin and Rome, he was free to talk as long as he pleased and be sure of close attention. How in the world did he manage such a trip? Lanny replied that it was his father's influence; beyond that, unfortunately, he was not free to say. But he talked about Ciano and Badoglio and Count Volpi, and then about Hitler and Göring and their entourages, both in Berlin and in Berchtesgaden and Karinhall; he made it plain that this was no fairytale he was making up. He told how Hitler had promised a competence to Kurt Meissner to compose an opera about the collapse of National Socialism, which showed what was going on in a Führer's secret soul.

Adi, unrelenting opponent of the Reds, had sent Lanny Budd a special message to his American friend and colleague. What Herr Hitler wanted was to get rid of Herr Rosenfeld as quickly as possible and by any means possible. The Hearst newspapers were doing everything in their power to accomplish this by the constitutional process; but that wouldn't be soon enough—the election was eleven months off, and there would be two months more before a new President could be inaugurated. By that time the Russian barbarians might have nearly all of Eastern Germany—and would they ever get out until they had established a Bolshevik regime over all the territory they held? Hitler wanted the job on Roosevelt done by some quicker process and had commissioned the son of Budd-Erling to consult with all his friends in America and try to arrange the matter.

Lanny said he was doing his best; there had been a lot of talk about the idea, and now, apparently, some action was going to be taken. He dangled this bait before the publisher's nose, but the cautious old fellow behaved like a fat trout that doesn't rise to a fly. All he said was that the situation was desperate, and he personally could see no basis for hope. He went on to ply the high-class messenger with questions about conditions in the Axis lands, and at the conclusion of the talk he tried once more to get the messenger into his service. If fifty thousand dollars a year wasn't enough, let Mr. Budd name a price.

Once more Lanny thanked him and said, "What I am doing, Mr. Hearst, is for the cause of free government and the American way of life. Any help that I can give you is free of charge." Speaking the words, he wondered: Would Mr. Hearst decide that he had met a social equal at last? Or would he conclude that the visitor was an FBI agent trying to get something on him? Lanny talked the problem over with his wife, and that observant lady said, "This is a child who has been hopelessly spoiled and will never grow up in this life."

17

Always to Be Blest

I

TELEPHONE service was slow and tedious in wartime, but Laurel had made it her practice to call Agnes once a week to make sure the baby was all right. Back in Hollywood, Lanny got his father on the phone and told him they were ready to start for home. How was everybody and how was business? This last was meant for a joke, since never in anybody's memory had there been such business as Budd-Erling was doing.

Robbie had an item of news. "Hansi and Bess are back." Lanny exclaimed, "Oh, good! How are they?" Robbie reported that they claimed to be well but looked undernourished; they were staying with Johannes Robin, Hansi's father, until they could get the tenants out of their home.

Lanny's half-sister, Bessie Budd, and her husband had been in Russia for more than two years, and Lanny hadn't seen them since he and

Laurel had passed through Moscow twenty months ago. Then the war situation had been black, and these musicians, friends of the Soviet people, had been heavy of heart. Now the tide had turned, and they ought to be happy; but what had this long sojourn in a foreign land done to their minds and bodies, their musical technique and their careers?

"Bienvenu" was hitched up and the Budds set out on the return trek. It was the second week in December, and they would stay in the south to avoid snow in the mountains. But they chose a different highway for the sake of variety. The novelty had worn off, and they traveled longer hours, to get it over with. Long ago an English poet had remarked that "man never is, but always to be, blest"; and this pair who had everything to make them content spent their time counting the miles and the hours. They talked about the things they were going to do when they got back to the crowded city—their baby, their musician relatives, and what they were likely to hear about the new world overseas, the Soviet world, in which they were trying so hard to believe.

II

They were almost home, Trenton, New Jersey, when a snowstorm hit them; impossible to see anything out of their windshield, and there was nothing to do but put up their trailer and car in a garage and themselves in a third-rate hotel, the only room they could get, small, dingy, and without a bath.

In that unpromising place they had an experience. They were tired of looking out of the window and seeing the soft silent flakes drifting down; they had heard all the war news several times over on the radio; they had read until their eyes hurt; and then had taken a walk and got lost for a while. Back in the room again Lanny suggested, "Let's try a séance."

They had about given up their psychic researches, for the husband had got tired of the fashionable banter of Otto H. Kahn; that important gentleman either couldn't or wouldn't oblige them any more, and he had a tendency to repeat himself. Lanny had the persistent idea that some tidings might come from or concerning Marceline or her Junker lover; he asked about them, and about other friends who were or might be in the "spirit world." But each time, when Laurel came out of her trance, he had to report to her that he had got nothing of significance.

Infinite patience is the number-one lesson that has to be learned by every investigator in this strange underworld of the mind. Laurel said, "All right," and stretched herself on a bed which was covered with an old-fashioned crazy quilt. Lanny put out the light, and sat and listened to her heavy breathing, and then to the stillness which meant that she was in her trance. The husband waited for more conversation of the Algonquin Hotel type, but nothing came, and he thought that Laurel had missed the bus again and fallen into ordinary slumber. However, he said, "Is anyone there?"

Then came a voice, a woman's, low and gentle. As a rule the imitation of voices is the weakest point in the case of these mysterious entities; but this time there seemed to be something vaguely familiar in the tone. "Is that you, Lanny?" And Lanny, being of long acquaintance in this other world, did not ask rudely, "Who are you?" but considerately, "How are you, my dear?" Love appears to be the prevailing temper in that environment, and since there is supposed to be no marrying or giving in marriage, there can be no harm in endearments.

The voice said, "I have just arrived, and am a little confused." To this the obvious reply was, "No harm can come to you here, and I hope you will stay and talk to me."

Lanny was thinking of Marceline, thinking of her intently, with the idea that this might have some effect upon the séance. But no, it wasn't Marceline; there was a decided foreign accent, and he thought of Hilde, Fürstin Donnerstein, who might have got into trouble on Lanny's account. As the conversation went on he decided that the tone was that of an older woman, and he thought of Hilde's mother, who had been killed in the heavy bombardment of Berlin last March. She had hated Americans and had hardly been able to endure having one in her home. Strange indeed if she were to make her first appearance in a cheap hotel in the capital city of the State of New Jersey!

Lanny followed the line of conversation which he had learned from long contact with mediums and their "controls." "You are not in any trouble, I hope," and "You will soon find friends where you are," and "Do come and talk to me whenever you feel able," and "What can I do to help you?" This last brought a response that gave Lanny a jolt. Said the voice, "Deliver a message for me. Tell Baby Marcel that he is the one I miss the most."

Baby Marcel! Lanny's mind leaped to the Hotel Mamounia, where he had spent a night only four months ago. The voice was that of Madame Zyszynski, the stout and amiable old Polish woman who had been the cause of Lanny's taking an interest in psychical matters. He had been too rushed to have a séance with her on that last trip, and his conscience troubled him for fear that he had hurt her feelings. She had adored him as a son, and had been so pathetically happy whenever he told her that her work was good and that he had learned much from his sessions with her; apparently it was necessary to her success that she should believe this. And now she had passed over into this new world, peopled with the beings who had used her voice, but of whom she had had no conscious knowledge. Would she know them now?

III

Lanny recognized this as an event of importance to him, and he handled it with tact acquired during a lifetime of diplomacy. "Madame," he said, "this is the first word I have heard about the change in your situation. I am glad, because it saves me having to grieve about you. Can you be my friend in the new world, as you were in the old?"

"I will try, Lanny." The voice was clearer, perhaps under the encouragement of love. He talked to her as he had done in real life, gently, affectionately, as to a second mother; with a little humor, just a trace of skepticism, to stimulate her and keep her on her mettle. "Perhaps you will be my control now," he said; and when she promised to try, he added, "I wonder if you will be able to find Tecumseh." Lanny would be sorry to lose that old Indian chieftain who had been Madame's "control" for most of her life and had carried on queer arguments and quarrels with the son of Budd-Erling over a period of fourteen years. Many people had told Madame about him, and she promised now to try to make contact with him.

One question more: "Have you seen or heard anything of Marceline?" The voice expressed surprise at this idea; had Marceline passed over? Lanny explained that he did not know, but that she had been in trouble when he last spoke to her. He didn't say where or how—that would be for the "spirits" to report. Madame Zyszynski had lived in the household with Marceline off and on for years and knew well her virtues and her faults. How she would find her was a question that Lanny did not ask. Madame had passed away of a slowly creeping anaemia, she declared, and she still felt a confusion of mind. He replied that he would not press her any more. The voice died away, and Laurel began that quiet moaning which indicated her coming out of a trance.

He had a story to tell her now! She too had visited Bienvenu and knew the simple-minded, rather dull old woman, an ex-servant who had married a butler, and who was wholly incapable of making up or even understanding the strange communications which passed her lips. If Lanny had been conducting a psychic investigation, he wouldn't have told Laurel what had happened; but he wasn't trying to convince an uninterested world, he was dealing with the wife he loved. So he told, but of course without mentioning Marceline.

IV

The storm let up next day and they drove to New York. Robbie sent a man with a car to get the trailer, and the very next day it would become the home of a family which had come from Quebec or Oklahoma to put rivets in the newest Budd-Erling model. Meantime the traveling couple had hugged and kissed Baby Lanny, and grown-up Lanny had danced with him to music which magically filled the air or the ether or whatever it was, all over the North American continent. The same Toscanini and the same Bing Crosby, the same Major Eliot and the same H. V. Kaltenborn, and the same Franklin D. Roosevelt, followed always by the same "Star-Spangled Banner"—of which everybody knew the first three lines and the last two, but few knew the rest.

Laurel presented her faithful friend Agnes with a beautiful Navaho blanket which they had picked up on the outskirts of the town of Budd; they had used it on the last stage of the journey, but that hadn't hurt it. They had bought Indian products for all the Budd tribe and for Laurel's relatives, none of whom needed anything; also for the Robin family. The first telephoning they did was to the Hansibesses, who came in to town the next day, and what a time they had exchanging reminiscences!

Hansi Robin was now thirty-nine and Bess was thirty-five. They were a pair of finished musicians, and had played together in concerts in most of the capitals of Europe and in cities and towns all over America. They were devotedly in love after some eighteen years of married life, but they had been through a period of desperate strain because of their disagreement over the political problems of the time. The only daughter of Robbie and Esther Budd had become, to the utter dismay of her parents, a stern and Calvinistic member of the Communist party, while her husband was a gentle soul who demanded a kind and decent world right away and could not face the grim realities of the class struggle. They had been wearing each other out with arguments when the attack of Hitler upon the Soviet Union had solved the problem for the time being.

Of course the Russians had to defend themselves, and every right-minded person had to help them. A violin virtuoso and his accompanist wife had betaken themselves to this land of music lovers to play for them and express the sympathy that was in their hearts. For more than two years they had been doing this, all the way from besieged Leningrad to Vladivostok and back; from the mining and factory towns of the Urals to the camps of the Red Army behind the front, where you could hear the guns day and night. And what had the experience done to them? The P.A. and his wife were most eager to find out.

The first thing was obvious, the pair were thinner and paler. The lad whom Lanny had called a shepherd boy out of ancient Judea was a man, still slender and sensitive, with pain, his own and mankind's, written all over his features. The news of what the Nazis were doing to wipe out the Jewish race had been reported everywhere, but it was something so monstrous that most people in America were unable to believe it. Hansi knew that it was true, and there was death in his soul; in Russia he had put such sorrow into his music that tears ran down people's cheeks as they listened. He didn't know if that would happen in America, and talked sometimes of playing only for Jewish audiences. Only a people which had been persecuted for a score of centuries could understand what he was saying. "Even Bess cannot understand," he said.

V

This was meant half playfully, but Lanny guessed that it was half true. The attack upon the "Soviet Fatherland" had brought this pair together intellectually; and now, what had been the effect of actual daily contact with that country over a long period? Neither Hansi nor Bess mentioned the subject, and Lanny waited until he got Hansi alone; the man would tell the man and the woman would tell the woman.

The violinist revealed that the breach had opened again and was as wide as ever; they never spoke of politics to each other. "I love the Russian people," he declared; "they are a great people, warmhearted and generous, and their response to music is instinctive and overwhelming. But I can't bring myself to tolerate their government."

"Would you like *any* government, Hansi?" asked the brother-in-law.

"You have to be there to understand the difference, Lanny. It is not like anything in our world. You meet some official, you visit in his home, you like him, and play music for him; and then someday you go to his office and find his desk vacant; you ask where he is and nobody knows; you discover that you are troubling them by your questions. You go to his home and learn that he has disappeared off the face of the earth; his own family doesn't know what has happened. You can see that they have been weeping, but also you see that they wish you wouldn't press them; they are afraid to talk to you. You discover that they are afraid to be known to associate with a foreigner; they are embarrassed to say so, but they don't invite you to their homes any more. All their lives are dominated by fear."

"I have been told that, Hansi; I thought it was explained by the national peril."

"America is at war too, but I meet all sorts of foreigners here in New York, and I hardly know the difference. In Russia I was welcomed by tumultuous audiences—you can hardly imagine such scenes; but I had very few friends, and I had the feeling that most of those were selected persons. They were Bess's sort of friends, not mine; they were the party-sort of people, who could not be corrupted by any unorthodox thing I might say. Some of them pretended not to be party members, but I had the feeling that they were playing a role, and of course I didn't enjoy that. Even your Uncle Jesse did not talk frankly to us; and then he went away to Irkutsk, and since then has not written us a line. He too feels himself distrusted, I am sure."

Such was Hansi's story; and Lanny argued with him, not for the sake of the Communist government, but for Hansi's marriage. "This war is a grim and terrible thing. It is my hope that when it's won the pressure may be relaxed. I have recently been rereading Lenin's argument that under Socialism the state would wither away in the end."

"It may be, Lanny, and I hope so. But the way I see it, when men get power, they hold on to it; they come to like it, and think they are the only people who are really capable of using it; if anyone suggests otherwise he becomes an enemy, and he disappears off the face of the earth. I do not care about waging a war to remove one kind of totalitarian government and set up another. I think it is just as wicked to liquidate the bourgeoisie as to liquidate Jews and Poles."

VI

Lanny got Bess's side of the argument from his wife. Bess had spent the time trying to persuade Laurel to become a Communist. There was no other road to freedom for the workers, and it was childish to imagine that the capitalists would ever consent peacefully to giving up their grip upon the workers' lives and fortunes. Of course the Soviet government used force; all governments used force, whatever amount was necessary to preserve their own power. The amount and kind of force depended upon the resistance the government had to meet. The American capitalist class didn't need much because they owned practically the entire press, screen, and radio, from which the masses derived their ideas. But how long would the American political system endure if ever the workers made up their mind to break the chains of the profit system?

That was a subject for argument, and the two ladies had it. Bessie Budd Robin had never heard, or had forgotten, that Karl Marx had admitted it might be possible for Socialism to be obtained by parliamentary means in the Anglo-Saxon lands; when she was confronted with this citation from the gospel, she took the argument back to Russia, where the people had never been accustomed to the use of the ballot and would have to learn by slow stages. Or to Spain—the classic example of what would happen when big business and the landed interests was threatened by a political protest. The Spanish people had trusted to the ballot and had won their freedom and set up a people's republic—and what happened? With the tacit consent of the world democracies the capitalist groups of Italy and Germany, acting through their Fascist agents, had sent in gangster armies and destroyed the people's government of Spain, and had committed cruelties exceeding anything ever charged against the Soviet Union.

"I had to admit that she has a case," said Laurel, and her husband asked, "Are you going to let her make a true-believer out of you?"

"What I am going to do," said the wife, "is to wait and see what happens. Bess is sure of her formula; she insists that after this war we shall see a dozen small nations having to make a choice between a murderous White government and a Red government. I asked her if that too would be 'murderous,' and she answered that it would do whatever was necessary to protect the workers trying to break their chains. You see how it is, each side applies all the bad words to the other; neither side will hear anything of the other side's case, and if you try to present it you get called the bad names—a Red or fellow traveler on the one hand, a reactionary or Social-Fascist on the other."

Lanny replied, "I am putting my hopes in Roosevelt. He's been trying his charm on Stalin, and I'm eager to hear what happened."

Said the wife, "The man in the middle gets the bullets from both directions; but I suppose we have to take our stand there all the same."

VII

Lanny Budd had business of his own to attend to. The art center of the world had removed itself from Paris to New York, and the town was full of painters who wanted to earn a living, and of patrons who were making money by the hogsheadful. They wanted to decorate their homes, and at the same time make a shrewd investment, and they were willing to pay for the advice of an elegant and plausible gentleman who could talk about paintings in the same fluent way that they could talk about the food-packing business or the razor-blade business or whatever it might be. There were others who lived in Kokomo, Indiana, or Horsehead Gulch, Montana, who hadn't time to visit the metropolis but would look at photographs of paintings and pick out something that appealed to them. The fame of an art expert spread in mysterious ways; letters would come, and Lanny would be surprised to discover that these people didn't mind paying thousands of dollars for a painting that had a proper certification.

With his wife and his old-time colleague Zoltan Kertezsi, he visited the exhibitions and inspected what the dealers on East Fifty-seventh Street had to offer. They knew him, and greeted him with carefully modulated cordiality; it was a pleasant way to earn one's keep. Lanny would jot down the data he wanted, then stroll in the crisp wintry air to his home, and there dictate a few letters to a stenographer. Everything would be fine—until he turned on the radio and was reminded of American boys dying hour by hour in trenches on the rain-swept hills of Southern Italy, of helpless Poles and Jews being packed into cattle cars and carried to some destruction camp, to be locked in a poison-gas chamber and then burned in a furnace.

Every night the couple tried a séance, hoping to get Madame again; but, alas, it was only Otto Kahn, urbane and friendly but vague. When they asked about an old Polish woman named Zyszynski, he asked what was that, a sneeze?—which was good fun but didn't advance the cause of psychical research. Lanny had sent a cablegram to his mother and received no reply, which did not surprise him, for he knew that there were censors who took their time and were suspicious of anything the least bit out of the ordinary. He was sure that Beauty would send an air-mail letter if anything had happened to Lanny's old friend.

Sure enough, a letter came, and he read it to his wife: the old woman had passed peacefully away just two days before the séance in New Jersey had occurred. Lanny said, "There you are! Another case that we can have printed in one of the journals and bound up and put away to gather dust on the library shelves." He was pessimistic about the matter because he had read hundreds of such cases and knew from the books that there were thousands and tens of thousands recorded. But who would pay attention to them? The learned ones, the literati, had their formulas, their systems of thought, and were by no means to be persuaded to revise these. Huxley said that Herbert Spencer's idea of a tragedy was a generalization killed by a fact; but these modern wise-acres spared themselves such pain by the simple device of disregarding the fact. When Doctor Rhine of Duke University set patiently to work and by millions of experiments proved that some human minds could call a high percentage of cards that were going to be turned up in a well-shuffled pack, and could cause a high percentage of dice to fall the way they willed it, even when the dice were thrown by a machine—what did these rigid-minded ones do to get out of that trouble? They proceeded to cast doubt upon the laws of probability, which prior to that time had been supposed to be as fixed as all the rest of mathematical science!

VIII

Just a week before Christmas Lanny learned from the newspapers that the President had come back from Teheran, after having traveled nearly eighteen thousand miles. He had come on the battleship *Iowa,* and Lanny knew that he enjoyed sea travel and would feel refreshed. He would have a string of people a mile long waiting for engagements; but, even so, it was a P.A.'s duty to report, and Lanny did this. Baker called back, saying that the Boss would like Mr. Budd to have a merry Christmas and then report again.

An art expert permitted himself the luxury of spending several days in the Metropolitan Museum of Art inspecting the new treasures it had acquired. He took his wife to see *Life with Father*, a play that was to break all theatrical records. He drove her out to meet Mr. Winstead, his favorite client, who was in a state of excitement because Lanny had got him an option on a Correggio in Rome. When would the American Army get there, and what chance was there that the Germans would sack the city, as they had done with Naples?

Carrying Indian products from New Mexico, they motored up to Newcastle and spent another of those plethoric Christmases; too much of everything, and yet a great deal of kindness also, for most of the Budds were willing to put off their disputes for a period of ten days in honor of a Jewish baby born nearly two millenniums ago. Lanny counted back: it was twenty-six years since he had spent his first Christmas in this home; it was thirty years since he had spent his first Christmas in Kurt Meissner's home in Stubendorf—and what a whirlwind of events had swept over mankind in those years! For Lanny personally there had been successes, but for the human race mostly tragedies and failures. Lanny wondered, if he had known what was coming, would he have had the courage to go on with it? Would the human race have had that much courage? Lanny thought, If the scientists or the philosophers ever solve the problem of foreseeing the future, let them make sure that it is to be better than the past!

Early on Christmas morning Lanny sat by the very good short-wave radio set in his father's home and listened to a carol service from a village near the front. It was the British Army, and in the middle of it General Montgomery spoke a little piece to his troops. The English employed by the High Command is a something all by itself, and "Monty" was a character all by *him*self—extremely pious, and certain of the Lord's own personal guidance. The year's victories were the Lord's doing, and peace on earth and good will toward men were what the troops were all fighting for. The singing was hearty, and a sergeant said a short extempore prayer, exactly as it would have been on a normal Christmas Eve in an English chapel. To the listener in Connecticut it meant that nothing really made any difference to or in the English people, and that they would never be beaten except possibly by themselves.

Back in New York there came a telephone call from the President's man. Could Mr. Budd make it convenient to visit "Shangri-La" on the evening of the following day? Mr. Budd could, and made an appointment for eight in the evening at the little mountain town of Thurmont, Maryland. Lanny was now permitted to tell his wife a bit more about his doings, and she elected to go along for the ride. She could lie contentedly on a bed in a hotel room and work on her manuscript while her husband kept his appointment, and she would promise not to weep if he told her that he was going away on another mysterious errand.

They started early, so as to reduce the chance of being delayed by a storm. There being no trailer behind them they went by the Holland Tunnel and the Skyway to Newark, and on past Philadelphia on U.S. 1. They cut across a corner of Pennsylvania into Maryland, on a road that had been covered with snowdrifts but had been cleared. The President's summer hideaway, which he had come to like so well that he used it in winter too, was in a low range of mountains called the

Catoctins, and the little hotel in the near-by village was enjoying a tremendous war boom, because of the military and other VIP's who came for conferences. Baker had seen to it that the P.A. had a room, and there the couple rested, then enjoyed a walk, and after that a dinner. Winter in the country is delightful to city folk who have money and can enjoy modern conveniences wherever they go.

IX

The P.A. went out in the darkness and strolled, and a car came along and picked him up. They sped out of town and into the hills, on a winding road that had taken a lot of labor to build. But labor had been the cheapest thing in America at that time, for this had been one of the CCC camps, where idle young men were put to work during the great depression. Now labor was scarce in America, and so was everything else. As the car lights picked out the tree-clad slopes, Lanny asked, "How is the Boss?" The reply was, "They are working him hard." And the visitor could be sure that was an understatement.

The camp had a military guard under the direction of the Secret Service; but there were few formalities where Baker was concerned. There was a list, and Lanny's name was on it, and the car drove in. The main building of the camp was low, one-storied, and rustic in style. Lanny sat in the reception hall, with the burlesque map of Shangri-La on the wall. He had to wait only a minute or two, and then was taken to the President's room, which was small and plain, with half a dozen pieces of cheap white-painted furniture.

The crippled man was in bed, as always when Lanny saw him. He had on his blue crew-necked sweater that the moths had got into—but he still clung to it. The moths of sorrow had not been able to damage his smile that Lanny loved; no matter how many cares he had or how tired he was, he would summon up a smile for a friend, and some joshing remark or amusing story out of the political and social world of Washington. Now his face was lined and his bed was piled with documents that required attention; but he remembered Lanny's last visit and remarked, "I see you have got back your weight. Be careful you don't overdo it."

Lanny said, "You should have seen me, Governor, the day I came out of Italy. I had about an inch of brown beard. I'd have brought it home to show it, only I was afraid my wife would faint."

This time it was F.D.R. who had had the adventures, and it pleased him to tell them. He had been taken to Oran on the battleship, and a U-boat had been sunk trying to get him in the Strait of Gibraltar. He had been flown to Cairo, and before landing had been taken on a little side trip to see the Sphinx and the Pyramids. In Cairo he and Churchill had had their first consultation with Chiang Kai-shek—Stalin wouldn't meet him because there was no war between Russia and Japan. Madame Chiang had come to act as her husband's translator, and she had clapped her hands to summon the servants—in this case American GI's, who didn't like it the least bit. Lanny remarked, "She has lived in America long enough to know that that is not our custom." To which the President answered, "Don't quote me, but I suspect that she may be getting a little bit too big for her Chinese breeches."

Next had come the trip to Teheran; it was just a short flight over the Russian border, but was as far as the Red Marshal would come. F.D.R. told about the flight—over the Suez Canal, and circling both Jerusalem and Bagdad on the way. They had landed at a Russian airport on the outskirts of Teheran, and the President had gone to stay at the American Legation, in a walled area outside the city; but the Russians were disturbed about this, because thirty-eight German paratroopers had just been dropped in the neighborhood, and six of them were still at large. One sharpshooter would be enough for their purposes, so the President consented to move to the Russian Embassy, which was inside the city, and where the Big Three could meet without having to travel.

Lanny's Boss was as happy as a schoolboy telling the good story of how this transfer had been carried out. It was evident by now that the enemy knew everything that was going on; so a cavalcade of armed jeeps was got up, and the route was lined solid with soldiers, and a Secret Service man rigged up as the President rode solemnly through the main streets, acknowledging the applause of the populace. In the meantime the President was put into another car and, with only one jeep preceding, rode at high speed through the back streets of this aged and crowded city, and so to the Russian compound—without any German sharpshooter getting a crack at him.

At last the American Commander-in-Chief had had his heart's desire and met the Russian Commander-in-Chief face to face. "How did you find him?" Lanny asked, and the answer was, "As you described him. He is a small man, but wears a big uniform. I had come determined to make friends, but it was pretty hard at first, for he seemed suspicious, and in a dour mood. I knew how little he liked Winston, so I had the happy thought to kid a British Tory, telling him that *he* was in a bad mood, and was an agent of imperialism. The more cross Winston got, the better Stalin liked it, and finally he burst out laughing. After that we got along famously."

"How did you make out with the banquets?" inquired the P.A.

"I observed that Stalin went easy on the endless toasts that seem to be essential; so I did the same. Winston, of course, could have drunk all the vodka in the house and never shown the effects of it. The party lasted for four days, and Uncle Joe got most of what he wanted; enough to make sure of keeping him in the war. He absolutely demanded a Channel crossing next spring, and he helped us to bowl Winston over in that little matter. The Russians are to make the heaviest possible attack at the same time, and that is all we need. We agreed to be friends, and to meet again and work out details. If I can have my way it won't be in the capital of Iran, for that is surely one hellhole."

"From what I've been told," commented the P.A., "you were in more danger of typhoid and cholera than of German paratroopers."

"Imagine it, if you can. There are some modern business buildings in the city, but the only ones that have clean water are the legations, which have it piped down from the mountains. The rest of the town scoops up drinking water out of the running gutters, which are also the sewers—there are no others. And yet the Shah and his court derive an enormous income from the American and British oil companies! Something will have to be done to those birds before long!"

X

So far the Boss had done most of the talking; he wanted it that way—it was his form of relaxation. Good form suggested that Lanny should wait, and he did so. At last the other stopped and said, "Tell me what you have been doing."

"You told me to take a vacation, Governor, and I obeyed. We took a motor trip to the town of Budd, New Mexico." Lanny told about the horrors he had seen preparing there, and then about the different kinds of horrors he had come upon in Hollywood and San Simeon. "I met a number of pro-Fascist and Nazi sharpshooters," he said, "but I think they have given up their idea of getting you with steel bullets; they are preparing a battle of gold and silver bullets for next year. Take it from me, they are filling up their arsenal. The motion picture industry will raise more money to beat you than they did to beat the End Poverty in California movement ten years ago."

The other smiled. "By next year we should be in Germany, and we should manage to pick up quite a lot of campaign ammunition there."

Lanny's conscience troubled him when he kept this overworked man chatting. So he chose the moment to inquire, "What did you have in mind for me, Governor?"

"It may sound like another holiday to a man who has been in the Axis countries. Have you ever visited the Holy Land?"

"Never."

"I suppose you have a general idea of what is shaping up there. For the past twenty years the agents, first of Mussolini and then of Hitler, have been stirring up the Arabs against both Jews and British; there were five Arab revolts before this war began, and now the Arab lands have been getting together against the Jews in Palestine. The Arabs are fanatics and so are the Zionists, so it's a religious quarrel as well as economic. You know how nasty that can be."

"The nastiest in this world, Governor."

"It's Britain's problem; but we are discovering day by day that all Britain's problems are ours. A few days ago we learned that two of the most violent Arab agitators have escaped from British custody in Jerusalem, and that will mean more trouble. The Axis is spending money to bring about another revolt, and we surely don't want any during this war. I have promised that the next time I go abroad, which will be in a month or two, I will have a meeting with King Ibn Saud and other Arab rulers. I shall have to know what I'm talking about."

"You have to know about too many things," put in the P.A. with friendly sorrow.

"Harry Hopkins is worried about the situation and thinks that something will have to be done in the way of mediation. He suggested you as the man to go there and stay for a while and give us an impartial report."

"Well, Governor, I can surely promise impartiality. I'll be starting from scratch."

"What we want is to lick the Axis, and after that to settle disputes on a reasonable basis and get the nations together to protect the peace."

"Would I go as an official agent?"

"I think you should slip in unobtrusively and talk with all sides as a friend. If you went as my representative, everybody would stand on ceremony and insist on his maximum demands. Can you think of any art business that would take you to Palestine?"

"I can't think of any offhand, but no doubt I could learn of something in the libraries, and I could get one of my clients to write me a letter giving me a commission. I suppose that archeological research has been suspended for the duration, but I might be talking over plans for something to start up when the war is over."

"Good! If you wanted a museum to commission you, that could be arranged. Have you used up that money I gave you?"

"Only a small part of it, Governor."

"Well, use the rest on this."

"One thing more. My wife is a shrewd woman, and in California she served as an extra pair of eyes. She talks to the women—something a man can't do in Arab lands."

"Take her along, by all means. I want you to have a talk with Harry, he has a lot of ideas. Choose your route to get there, and Baker will fix you up. Good-by, and take care of yourself."

"The same to you, Governor. You are in more danger than I, because so many people are trying to kill you with overwork."

"Don't worry, I've got a rabbit's foot in my pocket! I am predestined to see this job through."

XI

"Harry the Hop" was in his room, sitting in front of a log fire, slumped down in a chair—he was never content until he had got onto the back of his neck. He was a tall gaunt man, in wretched health, but there was animation and friendship in his eyes. He offered Lanny a drink and a cigarette, and then put him through a grilling as to what he had learned in Germany and Italy.

Lanny found it a pleasure to answer the questions of a man who knew what he wanted and who got the meaning of every sentence before it was finished. "Hurry up!" his mind seemed to say. "We have to get on with this war!"

He told the P.A. a lot about Palestine, the factions he would find there and the problems that had to be solved. He pushed a writing pad across the table and dictated the names of books Lanny should read and people he should meet in New York before he started. Lanny made notes, and by the time that briefing was over he understood what his job was, believed that he could do it, and said so. This pleased the President's helper, who was that sort of man himself.

By way of reward he favored the son of Budd-Erling with many details of the world-shaping conference in Teheran. He confided the rather horrifying fact that the Soviet government had been carrying on secret negotiations with the Nazis practically all the time since the repulse of the Germans in their first rush at Moscow. The agents had been, first, a Russian emissary in Stockholm, then one in Bulgaria, then the Japanese Ambassadors in Moscow and Berlin. The object of the Russians was to get out of the war with the most territory they could; and when Lanny expressed his dismay, Harry the Hop smiled and said that a man who had lived most of his life in Europe ought not to be so naïve. European diplomacy had always been the same; each for himself and the devil take the hindmost.

"I thought the Soviets represented a revolutionary tradition," objected the P.A.; and to this the reply was, "That is true to a certain extent, but less so when you get behind the scenes. It appears to be a principle of revolutions that they degenerate, and I fear that Red Russia is no exception. All leaders think about themselves and their own power, and the longer they hold power, the more true that becomes. It is a fact that must be faced, that the aims of the Soviets are identical with those of Peter the Great: an ice-free port on the Baltic and one on the Pacific; access to the Persian Gulf and control of the Dardanelles. All those proposals came up at Teheran."

"And did we give in to them?"

Harry the Hop smiled his quiet, slow smile. "We gave enough to stop the negotiations with Hitler, at least we hope so. We shall keep track of developments and make sure."

"I hope you have better agents than I!" remarked the son of Budd-Erling apologetically.

"I wouldn't say that," chuckled the other. "We have many in different places, and the whole is always greater than any of its parts. We find amusement in fitting the pieces together; but that isn't saying that we like the picture when we get it!" A plain-speaking fellow was this former social worker, and he made many enemies that way.

XII

It was after midnight when Lanny was returned to the hotel. He had forewarned his wife, and found her sitting up in bed, reading. When he told her that she was a duly appointed presidential agent, she didn't want to sleep that night, but to ask questions, not merely about the Palestine job, but about all the last five or six years. The husband didn't mention Germany or Italy, but revealed that he had been working for Roosevelt, and how their meetings had been arranged and the secret kept. Laurel said, "I was fairly sure what it was; but I never hinted about it to anyone else."

She plied him with questions about that great man whom he was so fortunate as to know. She exclaimed, "He's so much better than we deserved!" That was her constant theme: the American people were so ill informed that they would never have elected Franklin Roosevelt if they had known what they were going to get. He had had to use his political arts, and his command of the radio, to keep them in line—and then only by a narrow margin! "What would have happened to us if he hadn't tricked us into getting ready! And inventing dodges like lend-lease to help our allies!" Lanny told her how "That Man" had put Robbie Budd "on relief," ordering him to build fighter planes and paying him out of WPA funds, intended for the unemployed. F.D.R.'s argument was unanswerable; were not unemployed airplane builders as deserving of jobs as any other sort?

Lanny and his wife were going to have another honeymoon, this time in the Holy Land. As a writer, Laurel began thinking about local color, and the sort of stories in which she could make use of it. "When the war is over, you must tell me many stories, Lanny!" And he promised her an "exclusive." Then he persuaded her to go to sleep, saying that he was tired from the long drive, and had another before him in the course of this new day.

But even after he had put his head on the pillow and closed his eyes she wanted to know, "How shall we fly, Lanny?" When he told her that they would have a choice of routes, she wanted to know on which one she would see the most. He realized how much this meant to her, this new status, this new vista opening before her. It was like being married all over again. "So far I have had less than half a husband. Your work is the most important part of you."

He chuckled and told her, "You're in the Army now!"

XIII

In New York they had much to do. Lanny ordered the books which Hopkins had recommended and packed them to be taken on the trip. More important at the moment was to find out what art there was in Jerusalem, and especially in private hands, so that it might be purchased, or at least negotiated for. For that the best authority was Zoltan Kertezsi, whose mind was a world catalogue of painting and sculpture. He must have observed long ago that his friend developed these sudden curiosities only as to parts of the world where the American armies were about to penetrate; but he never asked any questions. He was at once a wise and a kind man, and he disliked the unwise and unkind Nazis as much as Lanny did.

He informed his associate that there was under way a movement to establish a Jewish Museum of Art in New York; it would contain not only Jewish ritual instruments, Torah, candelabra, ancient coins, and so on, but mosaics and architectural fragments, and modern Jewish paintings as well. Lanny could be looking for such things, and Zoltan offered to take the burden of arrangements off his friend's shoulders. He went to the libraries and also to the dealers, and after two or three days he came back with a small dossier on the subject, enough to provide a P.A. with perfect camouflage in both Jerusalem and Tel-Aviv.

The next person Lanny wanted to talk to was Johannes Robin, wise man of the world, who knew the Jews in the only way it was possible really to know them—by being one. For the past few years he had managed the New York office of Budd-Erling, and had received a very good salary. That was far different from being the great financier that he had been in Germany; but Johannes said that he would rather work for a day laborer's wage in America than be the richest man in Naziland. He had bought a comfortable old house about halfway between New York and Newcastle, and there he had assembled his family: his devoted old wife, whom they all called Mama; the son of the murdered Freddi, who bore his father's name; the mother of that son, who had remarried and had a husband and three children; and, for the past two years, the two children of Hansi and Bess. They all stayed together, because they had learned so dreadful a lesson of the world's cruelty; they had been taught love by their fear of hatred.

Lanny and Laurel went out to spend a Sunday with this household. He had known them since his boyhood and had been a sort of Prince Charming to them, being so elegant and rich, whereas Johannes had then just begun to accumulate his fortune. Lanny, Hansi, and Freddi had made a musical trio, piano, violin, and clarinet, and they had been enraptured—each with the others. The part which the grandson of Budd Gunmakers had played in trying to get Freddi out of the clutches of the Nazis had made him forever the adored hero of the family and there was nothing they wouldn't have tried to do for him. When he came to visit, Mama prepared an elaborate Jewish meal and did her best to make him eat more than was good for him. The children had been taught to hang upon his every word, and sat gazing at him with their beautiful dark eyes.

Now Lanny was going to visit Palestine with his wife. He said it was to collect art works, and the children no doubt believed it. The grandfather, a hard man to fool, must have had his guesses, but he wouldn't say anything, even to Lanny when they were alone. However, he would talk about politics, and the dreadful problem of Arabs versus Jews, and what could be done about it. The Jewish race, or people, or whatever name you chose to give them, had been scattered over the earth, and it was their fate to be used as footballs, to be kicked here and there in other people's games or battles. The British had the job of defending Palestine, so the Nazi-Fascists incited the Arabs against the Jews as a means of making trouble for the British and interfering with the functioning of oil pipe-lines from Mesopotamia. Johannes said sadly, "Wherever we go we are in somebody's way." And he added, "There are several pure Anglo-Saxon country-club members who think they could manage the New York office better than I do."

Johannes himself was not seriously interested in Judaism as a religion; he took the ceremonials as grownup Christians take Santa Claus, as something that gives pleasure to the children. He had no interest in Zionism for himself, but thought it would be a good thing for those miserable millions of brethren whom he had left behind in the Polish ghetto. When the zealots came to him, he would write a check for them, at the same time explaining that he was no longer the rich man he had been and that he had a large family dependent upon him.

All the grown members of this family took part in the discussions with Lanny, and he was especially interested in the attitude of young Freddi, who had just had his sixteenth birthday, and was the living image of his father as Lanny remembered him when he had first visited Bienvenu and played the clarinet. Tall and slender, with beautiful dark eyes and wavy black hair, young Freddi was making a good record in high school, but all his ambitions were centered upon the day when he would be old enough to volunteer for the Army. He wanted so to be in time, and he hoped that the president of Budd-Erling Aircraft might somehow be able to pull wires and have him assigned to the invasion of Germany.

After that, everything would be simple. He would find a sympathetic officer to hear the tale of what the Nazis had done to his father, and would assign him to the unit which would march or perhaps parachute into Bavaria, so that Freddi might be one of those who would deliver the ten or twenty thousand captives of Dachau. It might be that there were men who had managed to survive ten years of that horror and would remember Freddi's father and tell about him. Freddi had cross-questioned Lanny Budd, and had studied the maps in the public library, and knew exactly how he would get to the small market town which lies some nine miles from Munich. He dreamed of rolling in a jeep up the well-paved highway, and he had figured out the strategy of taking a concentration camp which occupied more than a square mile and was surrounded by a high concrete wall with electrified wire on top.

Quite solemnly this shepherd boy out of ancient Judea discussed with Lanny his project of storming the castle on the height, and there setting up artillery with which to shatter the power plant and the entrance gates. No less solemnly the well-instructed Lanny explained, "The first military objective is always the enemy's armed forces. If you defeat and rout them, Dachau will be pretty sure to surrender. A concentration camp is not a fortress; it is built to keep prisoners in, not to keep an army out."

XIV

Johannes had a friend who was a Zionist and had lived in Palestine; so Lanny and Laurel paid a visit to another Jewish household. Here were people of considerable wealth and high culture—they were interested in Lanny not so much because he was the son of Budd-Erling, but because he was the half-brother of Bessie Budd Robin, whom they had heard in concerts. There were a father and mother, a grown son and three daughters, all people of modern ideas. The father had fallen under the spell of Jewish racialism and had decided that it was his duty to help rebuild the Zion of his ancestors; he had sold his home and taken his family, his furniture, and all his belongings to Palestine.

They had lived for a couple of years in the new city of Tel-Aviv; but the father had had to give up because of the discontent of the young people. All four thought of themselves as Americans before they were Jews, and none of them had the least interest in pioneering. They didn't want to learn Hebrew, and they had little sense of kinship with the pitiful oppressed people who were being brought from Central Europe, in great part with British and American money. They missed the crowds, the bright lights, and the cultural opportunities of New York, and they had banded themselves together to break down the resistance of their father and shatter his dream.

And yet—a curious thing—now that they were back, they chose to remember the good side of their Zion; they wouldn't have liked it if Lanny had agreed with them too heartily. It was a pleasant dream to look back on, and they chose to blame themselves rather than the New Jerusalem. They were not tough enough; they were too sophisticated; they had become worshipers of the golden calf. They had been seduced by the lures of New York—the limousines, the fashionable shops, the smart conversation. People who had never known these things could be happy building dams and irrigation ditches and planting orange groves in deserts. Let them do it, and in another generation the university and the libraries would have grown, and there would be more concert halls and theaters, and something to talk about besides the rights and wrongs of Israel.

Lanny was amused by a heart-to-heart remark made to him by the son of this family, a newly trained Air Force officer home on a brief leave. This young man took him aside and said, "I'll tell you the God's truth, Mr. Budd. I got tired of seeing so many Jews. I found that I liked a variety of faces!"

XV

Lanny might have met some Arabs in New York, but he figured that he would meet enough at his destination. He knew their religion, because he had met so many Moors, and his stepfather had become a sort of lay brother to the Mohammedan scholars and marabouts of Morocco. Lanny would stop in Marrakech to ask questions and get letters of introduction, and pose as being on the verge of becoming a convert to the seventh-century camel driver's creed.

Baker arranged matters, and the favored couple were flown to Key West, and then to Belém in Brazil and to Dakar in West Africa—a delightful journey in midwinter. In Marrakech they spent a couple of days with Beauty and Parsifal, and Lanny found that his mother was greatly worried over not having heard from Marceline; he, of course, said not a word. He told all the good news about Frances and the rest in Newcastle; also he improved his education by meeting an Arab propagandist who was stirring up his co-religionists in French Morocco on Nazi funds.

The next stage was Cairo, where they spent a night in the famed Shepheard's Hotel, favorite resort of British and American officers. Lanny didn't meet any Mohammedans there, for this would have attracted unfavorable attention. Next morning the couple were packed closely in an Army dispatch plane, and in a few minutes were being flown over that rugged Sinai Desert where Moses had caused the water to flow from the rock. It looked exactly like the desert of Tunis where Lanny had come so near to losing his life, and indeed it was a part of the same vast tract, extending from the Atlantic Ocean deep into Asia Minor.

The journey had taken the children of Israel forty years, and it took a fast airplane less than an hour. Below them were vineyards and orchards, and Lanny leaned to his wife and called above the roar of the engine, "The Holy Land!" Presently they were over a much-crowded old walled city on tumbled hills, and as they swung round to come down to the airport, they passed a hill with stunted trees and a temple with a round dome on top. Once more Lanny leaned over. "The Mount of Olives!" he said.

18

Promised Land

I

AS A CHILD, Lanny Budd had been taken all over Europe, and being the near-stepson of a painter he had gazed at innumerable stained-glass windows and paintings and statues of blessed virgins and saints. He had listened to technical discussions of these figures as art works, but it hadn't been until the age of fifteen that he became curious about them as historical characters. He had asked questions of an elderly Swiss diplomat, and so had been told about an ancient work of literature known as the Bible, pretty well forgotten by fashionable society on the French Riviera. Alone and without guidance he had read the story of Jesus, four times over in four varying accounts; tears had come into his eyes because of the mistreatment of that good and kind man, and the figure had lived in his imagination all through the years, making him more concerned to do good and more ashamed to do evil.

As for Laurel, she had been brought up in a proper Episcopalian family, and had learned all the Bible stories as a child. However her view might change as she grew older, they would continue to shine in her memory and to be a vital part of her culture. She had hundreds of names of persons and places in mind, each one connected with scenes and stories; she had sung hymns about them, she had seen pictures of them, and few had been the days when some of them were not brought into her thoughts. The Holy Land! And now here she was, actually treading its soil! The faces, the costumes, the animals, the landscapes—everything was here, and it was like having your childhood come back to life.

They put up at the King David Hotel in Jerusalem, for of course you had to have the physical comforts, no matter where you went in your mind. Poverty and primitive life were fascinating to imagine and to employ as art subjects, but you wanted your orange juice cold and your toast hot in the morning and must not forget your waterproof coat when it rained. They engaged a dragoman, or guide, to show them the sights—it wouldn't do to go out on their own, for there was such a tangle of civilizations here, so many etiquettes and taboos, that they might have made a host of enemies without having the least idea of offending. They wanted to see the country as a preliminary to meeting anybody; and there were dangers, even as there had been nineteen centuries ago.

The guide was an Arab, his name Hafiz. He was elderly and lean, and wore a red tarboosh and a not very clean white robe; also a smile which was meant to be ingratiating, but unfortunately his teeth were bad. Lanny wondered if there was a school for dragomans, where they learned their elaborate discourses; there wasn't a village, a ruin, a hill, or object of other sort about which he did not know everything and have a prepared spiel, with names, places, and dates—and this regardless of whether it was a Mohammedan, Hebrew, or Christian object. The tourists learned that it was best to let him reel it off, for if he was interrupted he would become disconcerted and unhappy. There was an etiquette for dragomans!

II

"Jerusalem the golden, with milk and honey blest!" So ran the hymn which little Laurel had been taught to sing. Perhaps it was a heavenly Jerusalem, a transported and transmogrified Jerusalem which the poet had had in mind; surely it could not have been this walled slum through which the American pair groped their way. They had traveled through China together, so the shock was reduced; this was the mess out of which human civilization had climbed, and it was the same on all the continents of the Old World: narrow, crooked streets, many of them roofed, swarming with dirty, ragged people with many signs of disease; camels, goats, and donkeys threading their way through the crowds and leaving their dung behind them; children playing underfoot, the older ones following the foreign visitors and begging for baksheesh. Such was every "old town," all the way around the Mediterranean littoral.

They found it the same in the Arab quarters and the Jewish; the costumes and the language differed, but the poverty and the smells were alike. All the trades of primitive times were carried on in full view of the throngs. Workmen with their trousers rolled up trod the oil from sesame seed in vats, and in the next dark place a camel harnessed to a pole went round and round, working a press which squeezed olive oil from loads of the fruit; the camel had a hood over his face, so that he wouldn't see what he was doing, and might dream that he was out on the desert trails where he had been born. Next came an underground forge, where iron was heated and pounded out by hand—the method by which swords had been shaped and this land kept drenched with human blood for centuries beyond reckoning.

The bazaars were most of them mere booths, hung with sackcloth, offering bread and meat and fish and produce from the country. Nothing was ever sold without arguing; everything was pawed over, and the heavenly powers invoked against extortionate prices. Presumably the different tribes came to the shops where their words were understood; or perhaps they relied upon gestures, facial expressions, and the counting of fingers. So many human kinds were here, so many languages, faiths, customs, and costumes. The Jews wore round black hats and beards as long as nature made them; the dervishes wore tall felt caps; the Druses wrapped their heads in white cloths; the Turks wore red fezzes and the Arabs their embroidered headgear. There were Syrians and Armenians; desert people in nondescript rags; peasants straight out of the Bible; and all the various religious orders—Coptic priests, Greek priests with black beards cut flat across the bottom, white-robed Dominicans, and brown-robed Franciscan friars. In the better streets one saw British troops in varied uniforms and a variety of people in European costumes.

Jerusalem has been destroyed and rebuilt many times. The dust of the centuries has settled over it, and new buildings have been erected on the ruins of the old, often with the old materials. Egyptians and Jebusites, Hebrews and Babylonians, Assyrians, Romans, Persians, Saracens, Crusaders—and now it was the British, holding power under a mandate of the League of Nations. Somebody had to keep order and forbid these fanatical tribes to squabble and tear one another to pieces. Also, in modern times, somebody had to guard oil pipe-lines for a great fleet.

There is a high wall which belongs to the Moslems; it is supposed to have been a part of the Temple of Solomon, so the Jews have chosen it as a place to come and mourn for the departed glories of their nation. They come, mostly bearded old men, many having traveled from far places to this sacred spot; they are so moved that the tears run down their cheeks as they kiss the stones. They sit before it and murmur, or they stand with open ritual books in hand and chant or recite or pray. Sometimes there will be hundreds of them, shouting in chorus, always, of course, in the sacred ancient Hebrew. Lanny read a translation of some of their liturgies: "For the palace that lies desolate, We sit in solitude and mourn. For the temple that is destroyed, We sit in solitude and mourn. For the walls that are overthrown," and so on and on. Laurel had heard such litanies recited in the Episcopal churches as a child and had joined in the responses. The only difference was that she had been praying for her own soul and its welfare, whereas these cries were for a nation. "We pray Thee, have mercy on Zion! Gather the children of Jerusalem. Haste, haste, Redeemer of Zion! Speak to the heart of Jerusalem."

Here at this Wailing Wall Lanny and Laurel got their first glimpse of the problem they had come to solve. Hafiz told them of the dispute which had arisen here only a few years ago. For some reason the Jews had taken up the idea of fastening pieces of matting to this holy wall. Why they wanted to do it Hafiz didn't know—he was too contemptuous of their nonsense ever to have asked. The wall was claimed by the Arabs, and they didn't want it defaced by hanging rags, so they had forbidden the practice. The Jews had persisted, so a wave of fanaticism had run through the two quarters and had been fanned to fury by agitators. There had been riots, and a number of people killed, and British troops had intervened. The dispute was carried to the League of Nations in Geneva, where bewildered elder statesmen, laboring unsuccessfully to stave off World War II, had to stop and listen to harangues in strange tongues on the subject of pieces of matting being hung on an ancient weed-grown wall.

It was necessary that the visitors should make a tour of the old city and inspect the various shrines which the dragoman had to show them. Each had its sacred associations, and Hafiz had a spiel which he reeled off. He was positive in every statement that he made: here was the portal through which Jesus had passed in entering the Temple, here was where He had sat in front of the Temple, here was where He had healed a leper, here was one of His footprints, miraculously preserved in stone. But Lanny could read in his Baedeker how, a hundred years after the death of Christ, the Romans had completely destroyed Jerusalem, plowed its site over, and erected a new city with a new name and no Jews admitted. So he was skeptical about these venerated spots; but there was no use hurting the feelings of their guide, and they let themselves be led down into ancient crypts and through tunnels which had been excavated by modern archeologists. The Bible events might not have happened in this or that particular chamber, but they had surely happened somewhere in the neighborhood. To a modern political investigator what mattered was not where they had happened, but where living people believed they had happened, and were ready to fly at one another's throats to defend their beliefs.

III

The tourists also wished to see the country. This required a car, and the dragoman said it would be easy to hire one, but difficult indeed to get gasoline in wartime. Lanny had a secret to which he would not refer even by a smile; he went to the address the OSS had given him and presented the engraved visiting card reading "Mr. Franklin Delano Roosevelt" and commending the bearer to favor. Matters were quickly arranged with the British so that the President's friend could buy what he needed. Incidentally, he was warned that native drivers were apt to be reckless of their own lives as well as of their passengers', so he rented a car to drive himself. To arrange that he had to deposit cash in a bank. It appeared that in this Holy Land men did not trust one another so readily as in more secular places.

They set out, with Hafiz riding in the back and delivering his speeches as if addressing a large audience. The highways were few but good, having been built by the British for war purposes. Eastward was the Dead Sea, only fifteen miles distant; the route was downhill all the way, that sea being the lowest place on the globe, the deepest depression in the earth's crust. It has no outlet—the rivers flow into it from all sides and the water sinks into the sand. It is a kettle of salt some fifty miles long and ten miles across, and a commercial concern was engaged in extracting potash on a great scale.

Palestine is a tiny country, not much bigger than the state of Vermont, and all its history has been crowded together. At the northern end of the Dead Sea the River Jordan flows in, and they drove northward along its bank. On the way the dragoman told them that tourists, coming in great numbers before the war, had been accustomed to collect water of the river in bottles and take it home to be used in baptizing their posterity. Just now the river was yellow with mud, it being the rainy season, and Lanny did not collect his share. He and his wife had heard the singing of spirituals about crossing over Jordan, but they could look across and see that the same tamarisks and poplars grew on the east side as on the west. There were bridges by which they might have crossed, but beyond were only the Moabite hills of Transjordan, and no cities with streets paved with gold.

A couple of hours' drive up the river brought them to the Sea of Galilee, where they watched fishermen hauling their nets. This really moved them both, because their interest was in human beings, and these were without doubt the authentic types which had been doing that same work nineteen centuries ago. Lanny could not talk to them, except through a bad interpreter; but he wondered, if he had known their Syrian Arabic dialect, and had told them to leave their work and follow him, would they have obeyed? A well-dressed European in a motorcar, he could no doubt have offered money and obtained their services; but could he have won them without pay, and for a doctrine, a cause? He might have said, "I know a way to end poverty and war upon this earth, and it is only a question of persuading people to understand and follow." But could he have got them to believe him?

The difference was that Jesus had spoken in the name of God, and modern men had lost that habit. Lanny had prayed only when he was in deep distress; but now, standing on this historic shore, and recalling his deep emotions when he had first read the story of Simon and Andrew, and of James and John, the sons of Zebedee, he found himself aware that the men of his time had lost something important from their lives.

The tourist couple did not stop to make any Socialist converts. They drove a few miles to the town of Nazareth, and enjoyed a good lunch at an inn kept by an English woman. Then they drove about this collection of white stone buildings spread out on a hill slope, and looked at places with legends and traditions which you were free to accept if it gave you pleasure. There was the church where the Annunciation had taken place, the cave in which Joseph had worked, the table at which Jesus had eaten, the well to which Mary had gone. The only one of these which seemed plausible was the well, for these do not change through the ages, and if filled up with debris can be cleaned out again. This will be done whether it be Crusaders or Saracens, Beibars or Allenbys who have conquered the district.

What struck the tourists about this tiny land was its resemblance to the much more extensive land which they had visited only recently. Except for the buildings, and the costumes and speech of the people, they would have thought they were in Southern California. The climate was the same—rainy in winter and entirely dry in summer, blazing hot when the sun shone and nearly always cool at night. There is a joke about Los Angeles weather being always "unusual," and it was the same here, for the combination of sea, desert, and mountains frequently caused the winds to box the compass in the course of twenty-four hours. Most of the hills were bare; the fig, the orange, and the olive grew only where they were planted and irrigated. The mountains were not high, and when you came down from them toward the Mediterranean it was like the San Gabriel plain.

This was the promised land, the land of Canaan, the land flowing with milk and honey. "In the same day the Lord made a covenant with Abram, saying, Unto thy seed have I given this land, from the river of Egypt unto the great river, and river Euphrates: The Kenites, and the Kenizzites, and the Kadmonites, And the Hittites and the Perizzites, and the Rephaims, and the Amorites, and the Canaanites, and the Girgashites, and the Jebusites." The Lord had kept His promise as regards these tribes; they were no more. But there were Arabs and British; the Jews were still wailing at an Arab-owned wall and being kept in order by the Transjordan Frontier Force, under the command of Brigadier John Bagot Glubb, graduate of the Woolwich Military Academy and friend of the Arab world.

IV

Next morning the tourists set out for the coast, downhill again, an hour's drive over a first-class road. Here were two cities, the ancient port of Jaffa and, just to the north of it, the modern Jewish city of Tel-Aviv. Jaffa had a long breakwater and a concrete dock on which railroad cars could be loaded for Cairo or Damascus. Between the two world wars much capital had come in, mostly Jewish, motivated by a convenient blend of religion and business, God and Mammon reconciled after long efforts. There was a cement mill and a great flour mill, and plants for making oil and soap; on Jaffa Street were hotels and office buildings, up-to-date and shiny as if it had been Seattle or San Diego. Near by was a new Jewish suburb called Bat Catlim, meaning "Daughter of the Wave," with a large hotel built for the Jewish immigrants who were being smuggled in from all over the world.

From there the travelers stepped gingerly through the Arab Old Town, another miserable slum, swarming with animals and humans, bleary-eyed children and adults who wore flowing black robes and stank like their goats. A terrible contrast, and no one seeing it could fail to understand that the underground war going on in this Holy Land was between the Old and the New. The Jews brought in modern techniques and taught these techniques in their schools; they produced goods and made money, and then bought land from the natives. Hafiz complained bitterly of this; he didn't say, but Lanny could guess, that the natives, ignorant and improvident, spent their money soon and then discovered that they had been robbed and ousted by hated infidel dogs.

All this became crystal-clear when the visitors came to Tel-Aviv, the new city, the all-Jewish city, where the moderns had been free to have their own way, unblocked by ancient shrines or taboos, Hebrew, Christian, or Moslem. They had gone out of their way to break completely with the past. Here were whole streets of apartment buildings of those fancy designs which have no corners and have little balconies outside of each apartment; "functional," the architects call them, and vie with one another to produce something that nobody ever saw the like of. It is all new and white and shiny, fronting on a clean yellow beach.

And when the travelers had got enough of modernism they drove northward up the coast until they came to a mountain—a long wedge-shaped, tree-covered mountain, which is none other than that Carmel from which the prophet Elijah ascended into heaven in a chariot of fire. They drove up that mountain, and saw an ancient monastery, and a statue of the Virgin which would heal their sickness if they had any, and numerous caves in which hermits and saints had dwelt, also robbers and fugitives from the tax collector and the impressment officer through centuries beyond counting. Here the gazelles and wild jackals still roamed; but the modern subdivider had his eye on it, and once peace had returned, the slopes of the mountain would be covered with villas and summer hotels with all modern conveniences. The rich Jews would put up the money and the poor Jews would do the work—and the Arabs too could have jobs if they were willing.

There were even large groups of Socialist Jews, who were building co-operative stores and setting up land colonies all over Palestine. Even in the midst of war and civil strife people were planning the New Jerusalem and striving to reconcile ancient texts with modern techniques. It wasn't at all difficult, for most of those old prophets had been red-hot radicals; Amos on the rich sounded exactly like any modern soap-boxer, and Isaiah like a single-taxer or English land reformer. "And they shall build houses, and inhabit them; and they shall plant vineyards, and eat the fruit of them. They shall not build, and another inhabit; they shall not plant, and another eat: for as the days of a tree are the days of my people, and mine elect shall long enjoy the work of their hands."

V

The travelers went back to Jerusalem, paid off their guide, and settled down to their secret task. The first step was to establish themselves as art experts, and to this end they presented letters they had brought and began inquiries as to what there was in the ancient city which might be purchasable and worth purchasing. Mostly it was the Jews with whom they would deal, for the Prophet of Islam had forbidden his followers to make images—this in order to save them from idol worship. Apparently he had been right—if you had art you would have idols. The innumerable statues and paintings of madonnas and saints which the Catholics had in their shrines were idols in every sense except a quibble. The Mohammedans, forbidden to have paintings and statues, worshiped shrines and tombs and two hairs from the beard of their Prophet—they were here in the Mosque of Omar, kept in a golden box and exhibited to true-believers on special occasions. Here, also, was the stone from which Mohammed had ascended into heaven.

The dealers had things to sell and were prepared, in oriental fashion, to spend a long time bargaining. Lanny, who had purchased carved doorways and fountains for ablutions in Algeria and Morocco, understood this game. He knew that as soon as he made his wants known, the word would spread all the way from Dan to Beersheba, and his door would be besieged by those who possessed treasures, ancient or modern. He would be polite to them all, inspect what they had and hear their stories—mostly untrue. He would ask the price and hint that it was somewhat high; he would promise to think the matter over, and then in the most tactful way would lead the conversation to what they had observed of conditions in this historic land. The time was so tense, the feeling so high, that no man, regardless of his race, religion, and occupation, could help having ideas and explaining them to an important lady and gentleman from the richest and most powerful of nations. Lanny and his wife would listen, and after the visitor had gone they would compare impressions and make notes.

That was the way to work, quietly and unobtrusively, without giving offense to anyone. It appeared that there were not merely dealers, but persons of wealth who had fine homes with *objets d'art* which they were happy to show to an American expert. In this polyglot city were Jews and Gentiles from all parts of the world; there were innumerable social sets, military, official, commercial, religious, and just plain idle rich who liked the climate and had fled here to get away from the war. Once you had drunk coffee with them, or visited their homes, they would pour out stories of the mess the world was in—and particularly this small corner which had been "promised" to too many different people.

It wasn't as easy to meet the Arabs as the Jews. The Arabs kept to themselves, and few of them aspired to be thought of as cosmopolitan or sophisticated; they had peculiar notions and customs, which called for special tact. But Lanny's stepfather in Marrakech had obtained for him a letter of introduction to a Moorish rug merchant who had established himself in Jerusalem and become a financial supporter of the Pan-

Islam movement. Lanny called upon him in his fine shop—Laurel staying at home, since in the Muslim world the ladies do not take part in business or political discussions. Lanny managed to down a cup of what in that world is called coffee, a very sweet and thick brown paste, and told this gentleman about his researches into Moorish architecture and archeology, his father's former activities in the New England-Arabian Oil Company, and, more especially, his stepfather's researches into Mohammedan literature and practices bearing upon religious healing.

This black-bearded merchant, who wore a red fez and a white linen robe in his shop, was immensely interested to meet a Nazrany—a follower of the Prophet of Nazareth—who had actually read the words of Allah's greatest prophet and understood them. Lanny told how he had met Adolf Hitler, whose propagandists had succeeded in making him something of a hero to the Mohammedan world; and how the Führer had taken him to his secret retreat on the top of the Kehlstein, near Berchtesgaden, and there had revealed his great admiration for the Arab camel driver who had known how to found a religion and make it stick for a dozen centuries. Lanny, of course, said that he was not a political person of any sort, but a lover of peace and a student of mankind's great teachers and prophets through the ages. He knew that Mohammed had recognized both Moses and Jesus as God-inspired, and had advocated a union of the entire Semitic world, including the Jews. Why could it not even now be brought about, the swords beaten into plowshares and the tanks converted into tractors?

The rug merchant opened up and told the grievances of his race against both Jews and Christians. Afterward he told his friends about this just and considerate Frankish person—this name meaning not that Lanny had lived most of his life in France, but that the Muslims still remembered the Crusaders; through a freak of language, Frankish and frank meant the opposite. But the son of Budd-Erling was both, and the merchant invited him to his home to meet his friends—all men, of course. Later, when the friendship had become established, Laurel was invited to meet the ladies, and so had an interesting story about women under a religious system which allowed four wives to every man who could afford such a luxury. What did these women think about the world that was forever at war and forever demanding that their sons be thrown into the slaughter pit? Like all the other women whom Laurel had met—in America, England, France, Germany, China, and the Soviet Union—she found them convinced that it was the evil nature and intention of other peoples and governments which made it necessary for the sons of women to be armed and drilled.

VI

After a couple of weeks the travelers moved down to Tel-Aviv. This was an even more interesting city, for here were the intellectuals, the specialists, and professional men who were providing plans for the building of a new-old nation. Architects and engineers, scientists, agriculturists, teachers—trained mostly in America—they were alert, full of enthusiasm, and all had political and social ideas to impart to friendly guests. They were too polite to ask how it came about that an art expert could bring his wife on a holiday jaunt through or into a war zone. No doubt they knew enough about America to take it for granted that the son of a great airplane manufacturer would enjoy special privileges. Anyhow, here the couple were, and they wanted to see everything and listen to everybody's ideas, and nothing gives more pleasure to the propagandist type of mind.

To Lanny this was a holiday, to be compared only with his visit to Yenan in Red China. For the past decade, with that single exception, he had been obliged to conceal his real beliefs and feelings, to avoid the people he liked and associate with those whom he despised. But here he was in the company of young Socialists, men and women who were working all day and studying or discussing modern ideas most of the night. They were building the New Jerusalem—not in England's green and pleasant land as William Blake had called for, but in their own racial heritage, the Promised Land of their history and their religion. They were combining the very oldest and the very newest in culture, the messages of their ancient prophets with the tools and techniques of modern science. They had a nation in their hands, and were shaping it and seeing it grow day by day.

Co-operation was their keynote. One young couple got into the car with the Americans and shepherded them on another drive to the Dead Sea. Their goal was one of the *Kibbutzim*, the collective farms, which had been established in that most unpromising region, twelve hundred feet below sea level and with a climate hotter in summer than Arizona. More than a hundred persons had come here, pledged to carry out their biblical formula of making the desert blossom like the rose. The soil was saturated with alkalis and had to be washed before anything would grow in it; by prodigious labor they had diverted the waters of the Jordan to this purpose, and now were planting bananas, and also growing carp in ponds which the river filled for them. The members of the co-operative got no wages, but lived like the early Christians, having all things save women in common. Half their members worked in the potash plant near by and brought their wages to pay the interest on the debt incurred for building materials and tools.

The co-operatives had ancient Hebrew names, and this one was Bet Haarava, which means "House of the Wilderness." Lanny and Laurel sat at one of the long wooden tables in the communal dining hall and partook of a lunch consisting of buttermilk, whole wheat bread, and the young onions and radishes which are the first fruits of any agricultural enterprise. He pleased his hosts by quoting those immortal words of the Prophet Isaiah, which have long had their place in Socialist textbooks. He and Laurel told about what they had seen in Yenan, where the same kind of young people were trying the same communal life; only it was a cold climate, and the Chinese were living in caves, and did not have plentiful water. The texts they quoted were not from Amos and Isaiah, but from their founder, Sun Yat-sen, and their ancient philosopher, Wang An-shih. There had been some twenty thousand workers in Yenan, and Lanny was told that there were already thirty thousand in the agricultural co-operatives of Palestine.

VII

Wherever you talked with these people, in the meeting places of the workers or the drawing-rooms of the well-to-do, there was never any difficulty in guiding the conversation to international and interracial affairs. The world was being rent by the most dreadful of all wars, and the task of keeping this nascent nation alive through the storm was one which engaged the attention of every man and woman in it. The Jews were in a state of agony over what was happening to their brethren in Central Europe; fugitives were continuing to put in appearance, telling ever more frightful tales—the most merciless slaughter of a race in recent times and perhaps in all history. To save as many as possible was the desire of every Jew, and it was hard indeed for them to face the fact that the British government and military would not permit them to admit and care for the refugees.

According to the so-called Balfour Declaration, issued before World War I, the Jews were to be permitted to establish their homeland in Palestine. Why had the British backed down and violated this pledge? The answer was written plain for all the world to read—written in a substance that was thick and black and greasy, and very difficult to erase. Every Jew, and also every Arab, knew that the oil from the great Mosul field, British-owned, was pumped through a pipe-line across the deserts of Transjordan to the port of Haifa, on the Mediterranean near the top of Palestine. To that port came a constant stream of tankers, and the oil was essential to the operation of the British Navy, the British Merchant Marine, and even British industry at home.

Jewish immigration had stirred up the Arabs and led to the forming of the Arab League and the financing of a swarm of agitators, calling for united action by the seven states which made up the Arab world. First Mussolini and then Hitler had taken up this cause, proclaiming themselves near-Muslims and friends of all followers of the Prophet. That, no doubt, was why Adi Schicklgruber had taken the son of Budd-Erling up to his mountain hideout and there informed him that he considered the onetime camel driver the greatest man who had lived, prior to Adi himself. Anything whatever that would cripple the British Empire and enable Adi to get down to the Mediterranean and the Dardanelles ahead of Stalin!

Now the issue was being decided by war, and all the Jews with whom Lanny talked wanted the Allies to win; but there were a few who could not see very far and hated the enemy who was nearest to them. The British were here, governing in their rather cold impersonal way. In order to keep from driving the Arabs to frenzy and causing them to destroy the pipe-lines, British officials had to keep Jewish refugees from pouring into Palestine. These refugees came in wretched tubs, likely to fall to pieces in the first storm; the passengers would try to get ashore, even by swimming; and what a hideous thing to send them back to sea with no destination—and after having caught a glimpse of the land which the Lord their God had given them!

So a wartime truce was being broken, and there was an underground war between the British troops and a Zionist organization called the Irgun. Some refugees were always getting in, and the Arabs took note of that, and their agitators fanned the flames of hatred. A complicated situation indeed! Lanny Budd talked to these different kinds of people and heard their arguments; he did not try to answer, but said that it was all very complicated and troubling to a foreigner. A young Jewish engineer, no fanatic but a man of science, compared it to the situation between the Indians and the white settlers on the American continent. The Arabs were a primitive people, ignorant and helpless, with a culture many centuries out of date; the Jews brought machinery and machine techniques, and modern knowledge of a thousand sorts. Was it not in the interest of progress that they should replace the inferior culture?

Lanny assented, but pointed out that the Americans had come to be troubled in conscience over the way they had treated the Indians, and that you could not do in the twentieth century what your forefathers had done in the sixteenth and seventeenth. To this the Jew answered that his people were prepared to grant the Arabs full political rights and all the benefits of education. The trouble was, the Arabs didn't want to be educated, at least not in modern ideas; they were content to have their children sit on a dirt floor and scratch fleas and learn to recite texts out of the Koran which had no remotest relationship to modern life.

Lanny, trying to draw the man out, said that he had seen Jewish boys at school in Poland under precisely the same conditions, only the book from which they were learning was the Talmud instead of the Koran. Yes, that was true, the other admitted; but modern Jews had a different sort of education and the Palestine they built would be different from the old.

There were at the time about a million Arabs in Palestine, as against a half-million Jews; therefore, in a democratic state, the Arabs should have been able to keep control. But when you talked to the Arabs you found they were afraid of the superior ability and aggressiveness of their rivals; the Jews could talk faster, think faster, act faster. Moreover, they had money coming in from the outside world, and money was power; just as it was buying up the land, so it could buy up elections, and the control of public opinion. The Arabs felt that the immigration that was going on was an artificial thing, and was unfair; a few more years of it, and the Arabs would be a minority, reduced to the status of laborers and serfs.

VIII

So ran the arguments, pro and con. Most of the young Jews Lanny met were Socialists where they were not Communists, and one and all they pointed out that political affairs did not work out in modern states as they had formerly. Give Palestine self-government, and wait a few years for the issues to be clarified, and you would not find Jews voting against Arabs, you would find propertyless Jews and Arabs voting against well-to-do Jews and Arabs. That was true everywhere, as soon as the people began to realize their true interests. In New York you didn't find Jews voting against Gentiles; in Detroit and Chicago you didn't find Negroes voting against whites; all over the North you found New Deal Jews and Negroes and whites voting against reactionaries of the same races.

But the trouble was, you couldn't tell that to the Arabs: few of them had ever heard of either Socialism or the New Deal. The Arabs held it as their creed that everything was predetermined by Allah, and that there was no use trying to change anything. They lived under a primitive tribal regime, in which the sheiks and their relatives and friends absorbed all the surplus value and left the masses hungry, ragged, and sunk in superstition. All that immense wealth which the British and American oil companies paid for drilling and pipe-line concessions went to kings and shahs and regents, and was spent for palaces and motorcars, jewels and banquets; the toiling masses got little or no benefit from it. Here in Palestine the British were just, but entirely capitalist-minded, and they left the rich to go on exploiting the poor as they had done from ancient times in spite of all the scolding of their prophets.

Such was the East, which Rudyard Kipling had said would never meet the West, but he was turning out to be a poor prognosticator. Right here in the land of Canaan East and West were meeting every hour, and the whole community was in turmoil caused thereby. They were meeting in China, and in India, and even in the far Pacific islands, where black men and brown were getting to know GI's, and riding in tractors and jeeps, and having their thoughts turned upside-down by radios and phonographs and motion pictures. The new was replacing the old because it had more intelligence, because it could understand the old, whereas the old could not understand the new—or if it did it became the new. That was a world process, and the only problem was to keep the old from destroying the new by sheer physical force and animal cunning—something which had happened in Italy, Germany, and Spain.

Lanny and Laurel could observe the fires of fanaticism smoldering in this tiny stretch of land and ready to burst into flame at the slightest breath. Wandering about in the Mosque of Omar, supposedly built on the site of Solomon's Temple, they had observed the Moslems at their prayers and had stopped to watch; they had observed that the worshipers were becoming restless, casting side glances at the strangers and muttering to one another. The dragoman had nudged the couple and whispered that they should move on. Under the British law they had a right to be there—with big canvas overshoes on their feet, so as not to pollute the sanctuary; but the Moslems believed that their prayers were rendered ineffective by the presence of unbelieving dogs, and if the dogs had insisted upon staying, they might have started a *jehad*, a holy war, that January afternoon.

It was the same when you went out into the country and met the desert Arabs—black, filthy, and covered with gunnysacking almost falling off them in rags. Lanny and Laurel met a band of them, a wedding procession escorting a thirteen-year-old girl; they were dancing, singing, shouting in excitement. The tourists thought it would be safe to stop and watch this scene; but instantly the band forsook their child bride and surrounded the motorcar, screaming for baksheesh. Hafiz had warned them never to give anything, for the crowd would only clamor for more. They must reply sternly, "*Imshi!*"—which means literally, "It is nothing," and is presumably the Arabic equivalent of the American "Nothing doing." Laurel was frightened, and both of them did their best to appear fierce; but Lanny had to start the car and pretend that he meant to run over these wild people before they would give way. Again it was the East; to the nomads another form of bargaining, in which generosity is taken for weakness and regarded with contempt.

IX

The two explorers had been sent not merely to observe these phenomena, but to advise what should or could be done about them; and so, each night before they slept, they spent an hour discussing what they had seen and what they made of it. The longer they stayed, the more clearly they realized the complexities of this problem. It would be hard indeed to persuade the Arabs to dwell in amity with the Jews in a democratically controlled state; also, there were many Christians, Roman Catholics, Eastern or Byzantine Catholic, Armenian, Coptic, and even some Protestant sects who were scarcely less unwilling. Jerusalem was the Holy City of all these groups; they had their shrines here, and the trouble was, so many of them wanted the same shrines, and to decorate them with their own kind of tinsel and jewels, and perform their own kind of exclusive rites in front of them.

The founders of all these groups had been men of peace and worshipers of one God, whatever name they gave him. Lanny never failed to remind the Mohammedans that their Prophet had recognized both Moses and Jesus, and he reminded the Christians that Jesus had told his disciples that the Gospel must be published to all nations; He had taught love and forbearance, and His commands were read in all the churches. But, alas, it is far more difficult to hunger and thirst after righteousness than it is to repeat a formula or to wear a charm or to make a magical sign on your chest or forehead. He had said that when you prayed you should enter into your closet and shut the door and pray to your Father in secret; but, again, it is so much easier to let some priest do it for you, and to drop a coin in a collection box for his hire. St. Paul had warned that the letter killeth, and the spirit giveth life; but it is so hard to be kind and just, and so easy to bury yourself in the study of ancient texts, and to become learned in the interpretations of this or that church father, or pope, or learned doctor of the law.

So all these groups, the three great monotheistic religions which had become the bases of Western civilization, had hardened and become dogma-ridden; they had forgotten mercy and brotherhood, and had become the means of livelihood for ecclesiastical establishments, and, worse yet, a means whereby the propertied classes kept the poor contented with their lot. Every Church organization fought for its own, and made a virtue out of excluding the others; so Jerusalem, the Holy City of God, had become a caldron of seething hatreds, a nest of vipers—even worse, for vipers do not sting one another. Here as elsewhere Lanny observed that it was the young Socialists, many of whom called themselves materialists, who were preaching peace and reconciliation, and it was the Grand Mufti of Jerusalem who was proclaiming a holy war throughout all the Arab world. The rabbis and the priests passed one another on the streets and glared with hatred hardly to be restrained.

Lanny spent an evening with Rabbi Judah Magnes, who had been head of the richest congregation in New York City, and was now President of the Hebrew University in Jerusalem. A rare spirit and an independent thinker, he pointed out that there was a precedent for a multilingual free nation in the case of Switzerland, where people of German, French, and Italian descent had managed to live together in peace for six or seven centuries. He maintained that the partition plan so widely recommended would be ruinous, because every section of the chopped-up land would have its discontented minorities. First of all, there must be education in tolerance. Said he, "The very idea of compromise—the word itself—has been made abhorrent to too many of the inhabitants of this little land. Their political education has not yet taught them that political compromise is the very breath of life of the Western democracies."

Lanny wrote a report once a week, telling what he had observed, and making it short for the busiest man in the world to read. According to orders, he sealed these reports and turned them over to the American Consul, to go in a diplomatic pouch by air mail. He gave his conclusions as he arrived at them: that after the war there would have to be some sort of international government to control the hostile forces throughout Palestine and the district immediately surrounding it. Either that, or there would surely be a civil war. The same thing was true of many strategic points on the globe—Trieste, for example, and the Dardanelles, not to mention China and India and the East

Indies. There would have to be some international organization, a revived League of Nations, with real powers to prevent civil wars and to keep the peace in areas where rival claims were not especially hot. "Either that," wrote the P.A., "or we have got nothing out of the war."

X

All this time Laurel was making notes, of a different sort and for a different purpose; some day she would write stories about Palestine, fact stories and fiction based on the facts. Landscapes and buildings, costumes, faces, and the tragic and touching episodes which people told her, all were being stored away for future use. The impressions of a mature woman were being mingled with those of a child—for before she was old enough to read there had been read to her a book called "The Story of the Bible," profusely illustrated with drawings of this Holy Land and its people, their flocks and herds and tents and temples. Such impressions are indelible, and now, day after day, Laurel's own childhood and that of the Jewish people were mingled with the present and the guessed-at future.

Manifestly, her subconscious mind would be deeply involved in all this; and Lanny had suggested that they try a séance. They tried two or three, but nothing of interest came. Then, just as they were getting ready to leave—the early springtime was spreading over this storied land—they had a strange experience. It developed that Madame Zyszynski had traveled with them to Palestine, by whatever means of transportation these psychic entities use, and here she declared that she was sitting on a hillside in bright sunshine, and on the top of the ridge, outlined against the sky, was a small flock of sheep, tended by a half-grown boy. As it happened, that was exactly the view which Lanny and Laurel had commented upon that morning, standing at the window of a little inn on the outskirts of the Galilean village of Capernaum; so Lanny was not greatly impressed. He said politely, "Could you speak to the boy, Madame, and ask who he is?"

The boy was too far away, the old woman answered; but perhaps he could come to her. Presently she said that he was standing by her side; he was rather tall and thin, had a staff in his hand, and black hair which hung to his shoulders. That was the way Lanny had pictured the Robin boys in his fancy, and he wondered if he had ever told that to Madame. He said, "Ask him his name," and she replied, "He speaks, but it is a strange language and I cannot understand a word."

Very baffling; after a few tries Lanny suggested, "Try pointing to him repeatedly and perhaps he will give his name." Madame tried that and reported, "He says 'Peretz.'" Lanny said, "I don't know what language that name belongs to. Speak to him one word at a time, and perhaps he will do the same, and I will write it down."

Laurel was lying on the bed in her trance, and Lanny was sitting by the bedside with a dim light, making notes with a pad and pencil as he always did. The voice which came from Laurel's lips began to speak strange syllables one by one, and Lanny wrote the way they sounded, hurriedly, and without any idea what the language might be. "*Ani Peretz ben Jehuda*," he wrote; and then, "*M'shephet Jehuda*." This went on for several minutes and Lanny recorded every sound he heard. He couldn't ask any questions—at least not until Madame stopped speaking. Finally she said, "The boy waved his hand and called his dog and now he has faded away."

"Have you any idea where you are, Madame?" inquired the observer.

"No," she replied, "but it's a different land and it's warm. I feel that I know it very well, but I don't know how."

"Could it be the Bible land, where Christ lived?"

"It might be that; I cannot tell."

"You don't know how you came to be here?"

"I came because I wanted to be with you. You know that I promised to come whenever I could."

"Can you stay a while now?"

"No, because your wife is tired; she is complaining that she has no more power."

Sure enough, Laurel had begun to moan, and that was always the end She came out of her trance; and this time Lanny could tell her everything that had happened. He read over the strange syllables to her, and she exclaimed, "Did I really speak all that? And can it be a language?"

XI

Lanny had read of numerous cases of persons in a trance who had spoken languages which they had never known or heard; it was a common phenomenon—but no matter how much you may have read, it gave you a thrill when you came upon it in the flesh, or, to be more accurate, in the atmosphere activated by flesh. They went to the Hebrew University in Jerusalem, and Lanny introduced himself to a scholar connected with the library, an elderly gentleman with a black beard turning gray. Lanny didn't say, "My wife is a psychic medium and spoke these words in a trance." No, for he didn't want to attract attention to himself, and possibly get his name in the newspapers; he was still a secret agent, and the first word in his code was silence. He said, "I wrote down these syllables at the dictation of a little shepherd boy out in the country. I wonder if you can tell me what they mean."

The grave old gentleman took the paper and glanced at it. A look of great surprise came upon his face. "But this is ancient Hebrew!" he exclaimed.

"Indeed!" said Lanny, and did not have to pretend his own emotion.

"This phrasing has not been used by our people for many centuries, Mr. Budd. Where was this boy?"

"He was on the road to Capernaum. I did not make any special note of the place. What do the words mean?"

" 'I am Peretz, son of Jehuda. We are of the tribe of Jehuda. We are descendants of Abraham. We have seven sheep and eleven goats. I have a twin brother.' " And so on. "That is really a very strange thing, Mr. Budd."

"Perhaps the boy heard the words in a school, sir."

"They are not words that would be taught in any school. They sound like a boy's conversation. In English it would be Phares, son of Judas, and we have such a person in our Book of Genesis; there is a story about him—that he was the first-born of a pair of twins, and the midwife tied a red string upon his wrist when he was the first to emerge from the womb. The name means 'the breach.' That was well over three thousand years ago, according to our reckoning."

"Very curious," remarked this unimpressionable American. "We must suppose that the lad was told the story in his Sabbath school, and perhaps had been required to compose a dialogue as an exercise in Hebrew."

"It must be," said the learned gentleman. "But it is not what we do in our schools and it seems hard to believe."

Lanny wrote the translation in his notebook. He wanted to learn all he could about this Peretz, alias Phares, and in the library he obtained an English Bible and a Concordance. It took but a moment to learn that the ancient one was named in the New Testament as well as in the Old. As Pharez, son of Judas, he was in that long line of ancestors who had been listed for Jesus by both Matthew and Luke, and listed differently—thus providing ammunition for the scoffers. It had seemed strange indeed to Tom Paine and Robert Ingersoll that a man who had been miraculously conceived should have had his paternal ancestry traced back through an earthly father to Jacob and Abraham.

But Lanny was on the trail of a different mystery from that. They tried one more séance before leaving Palestine, but this time it was the oversophisticated international banker who came upon the scene, demanding to know what the devil they were doing in this unlikely place. He didn't know anything about the shepherd boy out of ancient Judea, and when Lanny told him the story he exclaimed, "Really, I don't see how you can believe such foolishness! It is unworthy of an educated man."

BOOK SEVEN

Humanity with All Its Fears

19

Lull before Storm

I

FROM Palestine Lanny had written a letter to Captain Denis de Bruyne, who had been fighting at the front in Italy. He had received a reply, telling him that Denis was in Algiers, wounded again, this time severely. Lanny and Laurel planned their return trip by way of that city, so that Lanny might visit the *capitaine*, also Robert Murphy, and other friends he had made there. He was in no hurry, for his report had gone in and he had nothing to add to it except anecdotes and sociability.

First Cairo. They took a trip up the Nile to see the Pyramids and the Sphinx; they were driven along the banks of the river and permitted the driver to show them the precise clump of bulrushes in which the infant Moses had been found by the Egyptian princess; they explored excavated tombs, and in the great museum in the city inspected the relics of the Pharoahs. They might have seen as interesting specimens in the Metropolitan Museum of Art, but they hadn't found time in busy New York. They rode on camels, and Lanny forbore to say that he had ever done this before; he kept all his misadventures to himself, for there was no use supplying his wife's imagination with fuel.

When friends meet in strange places, they always remark that it is a small world. They forget that they make it small by promoting more and more travel. This war had shrunk the world to the dimensions of an Air Force officers' club. The P.A. seldom stopped at an airport without meeting some man whom he had chatted with in some far place, Hollywood or Hongkong, Bermuda or Belém. This time it was the banks of the River Thames in Buckinghamshire; there came striding through the lobby of the picturesque Shepheard's Hotel a British officer in khaki shorts and shirt with wings on the sleeve and the desert tan on his arms and legs; an officer extremely young and what the British call "leggy," meaning that he hadn't had time to fill out his sudden growth. When Lanny had last seen him he had been a schoolboy, punting on the river while a girl read some modern poetry to him; she had read some to Lanny and he had wondered what the deuce it was about, but had been too polite to say so. Evidently words are wonderful things in themselves, and if you string enough of them together they exercise an intoxicating effect upon the young.

This was one of the grandsons of Sir Alfred Pomeroy-Nielson, Bart., and they called him "Scrubbie," for what reason Lanny hadn't inquired. Here he was, bubbling with delight to meet this old friend of the family. He was only nineteen, but what a story he had to tell! He had been wild to get into the "show," and already at his age had been all the way through and come out at the far end; they had grounded him, because he had been on the maximum number of missions permitted to anybody. Beastly stupid, because he was quite fit, but all he could do now was to train others. He had piloted a bomber on that mission to wipe out the Ploesti oil fields in Rumania; few had come back unscathed. Oil fields had proved unexpectedly tough targets; but they had cut the German production by at least half for the present.

This sprig of the aristocracy wasn't the typical Englishman, who is supposed to cultivate reticence as the greatest of dignities, and to discuss his military exploits only in monosyllables. At lunch Scrubbie told these Americans everything they wanted to hear; not merely what he himself had experienced, but what this wonderful Combined Air Force was achieving against the foe. They had got together under one command, and without rivalry or jealousy were giving everything they had. Now there were magnificent bases in Sicily and Italy; Egypt was becoming a training center, far behind the front. The driving back of Rommel had been an airmen's job, and they were going to do the same all over Europe; more and more were getting ready, all around the perimeter. The Budd-Erling was the world's wonder, and Lanny promised to pass that information on to his father.

Also, of course, talk about home. Lanny explained that he had taken his little daughter to America, and so didn't get to England as often as previously. The bomber pilot had been home for a couple of weeks' leave and reported that the Pater was working hard at his writing jobs. Alfy had got caught in a "tip and run" raid on an airfield in Hell's Corner, and had got laid up but was all right again. There was a lot of talk about the Germans having a new weapon, a flying bomb, and did Lanny know when it was coming? Lanny knew more than he was free to tell.

II

From Cairo to Tripoli, a city where Mussolini had built monuments to his glory, and which now the British were well pleased with. From there to Algiers, a city which the French had taken from the Moors and now called a part of *la France métropolitaine;* a city like all the others on the Mediterranean shore, with an Old Town of wretched slums crowded with the poor, and suburban streets with modern apartment houses for the middle class, and up on the slopes overlooking the sea magnificent estates with villas and palaces for the rich. They became rich because they owned the productive land and the natural resources and the means of manufacturing and transportation; they stayed rich because they had "inherited that good part." Lanny Budd, who moved freely among them, didn't point this out, because they wouldn't have liked it and he would no longer have been able to hear their conversation; instead he told them that they were elegant and gracious and possessed exceptionally good taste, and that he knew where there was a remarkably fine Ingres or Renoir or whatever would go well over their dining-room mantle.

Lanny's first duty was to see Denis *fils,* in one of the hotels which had been taken over as a war hospital. Lanny didn't take his wife, giving the excuse that Denis wouldn't feel free to talk about military affairs in her presence; the real reason was, he wanted to tell the *capitaine* about having met Denis *père*, in Paris, and also the news about his younger brother. Lanny found the Frenchman pale and wan, having got a severe thigh wound from an exploding shell; his life had been saved by blood transfusions. Now he would have to be a desk man, he remarked sadly; but he had done his little bit to redeem the honor of *la patrie.* Had Lanny heard about the fine record which General Giraud's men had been making all the way up the eastern coast of Italy? Yes, Lanny had heard it; they were all doing well, even the American Japanese, the Nisei, who had the special motive of proving themselves Americans and wiping out the shame of Pearl Harbor.

Lanny told about his meeting with the father, and the messages which the aged man had sent to his sons. There was nothing that either Lanny or the younger Denis could do about the situation. Lanny hadn't been able to see the *capitaine's* wife and children, and could only pass on the word of the *père* that they were alive and well. As to the younger brother, it was odd indeed that he was staying in Lanny's old home in Juan-les-Pins. "Taking care of it!" Denis said. "We all know how troops take care of things; but no doubt Charlot will do his best. He is a conscientious fellow, even though his ideas are so cruelly perverted."

Poor Denis! He couldn't get it out of his head that if only he could get a chance to talk with his beloved younger brother, he could bring that lost sheep back into the fold. The *capitaine* brooded over it all the time. He was so sure that he was right in co-operating with the Americans, and so unable to conceive of any reason why a Frenchman should co-operate with the Nazis! Lanny took the part of the devil's advocate for the nonce, explaining the younger man's idea that the only victors in this war would be the Russian Reds, and that the French people would find that they had laid themselves open to the march of revolutionary Communism. Charlot had explained this in detail to Lanny, and Denis now explained why it wouldn't necessarily be that way. But convincing Lanny was not the same thing as convincing Charlot.

Lanny said, "I'm not telling any secret, but just guessing that before this year is over we shall be landing somewhere on the Riveria. I could be useful to the Army in that locale which I know by heart, and I am hugging the idea that I may get an assignment to help prepare the way. If so, I may drop in on Charlot at Bienvenu and have another argument."

The elder's reply was, "Do for God's sake keep him out of the hands of the French, for they will certainly shoot him. There could be no other verdict!"

III

In his capacity as presidential agent Lanny Budd had made many acquaintances in Algiers. He had made them among groups both rich and poor; he had made them among those who had ardently desired the American landing and among those who had guessed that it was coming and had jumped to be on the winning side. Among the former was the Jewish physician, Dr. Aboulker, and his two sons, who had made their home the headquarters of the youth group, the Chantiers de la Jeunesse, which had seized the city government and held most of it until the Army had got ashore. They had risked their lives, and now they found that they were completely out of everything; no one paid any attention to them—unless it was the police spies. The elderly crippled doctor had been kept under detention for some time.

Those who were in power were the rich, the big business group which had been exploiting the colony, and were so close to Fascism that it would have required an expert to find the dividing line. Now they had all changed their color; they were all for General de Gaulle's formula of "liberation first and then liberty." "Big Charlie" had at last succeeded in his long struggle with General Giraud, and was now the head of both army and government. The French trusted him, but Lanny felt sure that in his heart he had no idea but to restore the old Catholic, military, autocratic France. His creed was very close to that of Marshal Pétain, except that surrender to the Germans was excluded from this picture.

This was the sort of government the American Army wanted in order to win the war quickly, and it was the sort they would want after the war, with no nonsense from reformers and crackpots. The big businessmen were those who got things done; they were the men the big brass dealt with in Washington, and whom they understood and liked. In Washington they had fine homes and gave elaborate parties, and in North Africa it had turned out to be no different. Lanny and his wife were invited to a soiree at the home of the French General Juin, who had married an Algerian heiress and lived up on the heights in an ancient Arab villa, large in size, square in shape, and yellow in color. The visitors bought proper clothes in order that they might appear at this and other functions; they met a wealthy provincial hostess, who had been so anti-American that Lanny had been warned against her. Americans in her eyes were democratic, they were enemies of property, Jew-lovers and even Freemasons!

But now all that was water over the dam; the lady was all smiles and charms, all pearls and diamonds; her drawing-room was full of French, British, and American uniforms, the tiptop of the armies in this main thoroughfare to the war in Italy. Lanny listened to groups of these men discussing their problems, and he did not hear of any plans to establish democratic government in these colonies, which included such large numbers of dark-skinned peoples—whom some of the officers referred to as "niggers" and others as "wogs."

General George Patton had come ashore at Casablanca, flourishing his two pearl-handled revolvers and roaring for action. He had swept all the way across North Africa, a couple of thousand miles; he had swept across Sicily and was now on his way up the Italian boot; he had boldly announced his intention of conducting the same sweeping operations in France and Germany. Georgie was the man for the times, loving his job, sharing Othello's delight in "the neighing steed, and the shrill trump, the spirit-stirring drum, the ear-piercing fife, the royal banner, and all quality, pride, pomp, and circumstance of glorious war." The P.A., desiring victory in this war but also victory in the peace, had heard with dismay how Georgie, in a company like this, had expounded his idea that war was the natural and inevitable condition of mankind. "Man IS war!" the commander of the Third Army had proclaimed. He was not content with the formula, "In time of peace prepare for war," but wanted it to read, "In time of war prepare for the next one."

So everything would go back and be what it had always been. The swarms of the poor whom Lanny and his wife had seen crowded into the slums of Jerusalem and Cairo, and whom Lanny in past times had seen in Barcelona and Marseille and Cannes and Nice and Genoa and Naples and Athens—all around the perimeter of this great midland sea—they were going to stay right where they were, sunk beyond hope in poverty and ignorance; meanwhile the capable intelligent gentlemen who exploited their labor would continue to live in palaces on the heights, deck their wives in pearls and diamonds, and give dinner parties to the fancy-dressed foreigners skilled in the use of instruments of killing. That was the program; the near-Fascists would rebuild Fascism with the label changed—probably to something religious, since "Big Charlie" was a devout Catholic and "Two-Gun Georgie" a devout Episcopalian.

IV

Ambassador Robert Murphy, genial and kindly Irish-American career man in the Department of State, had a juggler's job of balancing himself between the two factions in that faction-ridden organization. The old-liners, the permanent staff, were tight-lipped conservatives, most of them Republicans; on the other hand, some New Dealers had crept in, and these had the backing of the Chief, who might step in and upset anybody's applecart at any moment. The genial Bob must have guessed by now that the son of Budd-Erling was far from being a proper "striped-pants" man; but he was a friend of the Big Boss, and carried the most powerful visiting card in the world. Lanny would never know what Murphy really thought of him, but found him friendly and obliging, and that was enough.

What Lanny wanted was to get in touch with two of his old friends: one, Jerry Pendleton, who had been his tutor away back before World War I, and recently had helped to put through a job on the Germans prior to the Casablanca landing. Jerry was an OSS man, so one didn't ask what he was doing or anything of that sort. One said, "I have an important reason for seeing him," and when the answer was that he was probably still in Casablanca, Lanny said, "Can you get a note to him?" He wrote, saying that he was going to be in Marrakech in a few days. He didn't sign his name, because Jerry knew his handwriting.

The other person was Raoul Palma, Spanish-born Socialist, whom Lanny knew to be working with the underground in the Midi—that is, if he was still alive. Lanny explained to the Ambassador that he had lost contact with this old friend and wanted the OSS to get a message to him if it could be arranged. It wasn't proper to ask the name or address of the OSS head in Algiers; it was enough that Murphy would forward a note. Lanny wrote, asking Raoul—who was working under the name of Bruges—if he had found any worth-while paintings; he signed this letter "Neuchâtel," knowing that Bruges also knew his handwriting and would understand that he was to reply to Newcastle.

The Budds were flown to Marrakech, and there was Lanny's mother, enjoying the elegance of the Hotel Mamounia—she too had "inherited that good part," or at any rate had won it by her combination of endowments and efforts. She and her husband and grandchild and maid were costing a lot of money, but then Robbie was sending his regular thousand dollars a month, and Zoltan was selling Detaze paintings and putting the money in a New York bank. You couldn't live forever, and might as well have the good things of this world while you were in it. Impossible to find even a small cottage to rent, and you could thank your stars and your social talents that you had made yourself popular in a great hotel, so that you and yours were the last persons they would turn out on the demand of the brass.

One thing tormented Beauty's soul, and that was the continued silence of her daughter. She besieged Lanny on the subject, and all he could tell her was that he could think of no circumstance under which friends of Marceline in the Allied world could do anything but harm to her in the Axis world. If she was dead, or in a concentration camp, she was equally beyond help for the present. If she had gone into hiding—as many people in Germany had done—the last thing she would want was any effort to find her. If she got out, she would surely let them know; meantime she was one of many millions lost, missing, displaced, or whatever the word might be, on the tormented Continent. Lanny pointed out to his mother that Marceline had a powerful friend in her Junker lover; she had made many other friends by her art. It might well be that the friend in Switzerland who had been relaying messages for her had died, or that some law had been passed forbidding the practice. Beauty's daughter was a capable young woman and would surely not be wanting help from enemies of the land where she had chosen to make her home.

The voyaging couple were free to tell what they had seen in Palestine, and Lanny was free to tell his stepfather about the various religions which were supposed to be agencies of love, but which somehow had been taken over by Satan and his minions. How else could a religious man account for what was happening in the world? Your adversary the devil, as a roaring lion, walketh about, seeking whom he may devour! So Peter had warned, and he was the Rock on whom the Church was built. Parsifal was deeply grieved by what Lanny told him of the sectarian wars over the tomb of Christ; Beauty took her son aside and asked him not to talk too much about this subject, for fear that Parsifal might take up the notion that he had a call to go there and preach love and brotherhood to the warring factions. Let a white-haired old gentleman stay in a luxury hotel and love his wife, and surely that would be sufficient in the sight of God.

V

Jerry Pendleton came to Marrakech on the crowded, dusty, and rather dilapidated train. To Lanny he was the same young companion, and it was hard to realize that he had passed fifty and that his hair was turning gray. They had played tennis together, swam and fished and sailed together, and Jerry had risked his life for Lanny in their secret war upon the Nazis. Now the ex-tutor, ex-lieutenant was a full-fledged OSS man, and wasn't permitted to talk about what he was doing, even to Lanny who had got him the job. They had to deal in generalities; Lanny could say that he and Laurel had been to Palestine, and what they had seen there, but not who had sent them.

Good old Jerry was much worried about the war and how it was going. The month was March, and the armies in Italy had been making no gains worth mentioning; they were stuck in front of Monte Cassino and had been pouring out blood there for weeks; they had made a landing at Anzio, a beach below Rome, and had barely been holding on by fingernails and toenails. The censorship was keeping the facts from the public, but all the world was coming to realize that we weren't winning this war.

Lanny answered, "We knew that campaign was going to be tough, Jerry; up one mountain and down to another."

"Yes, but if we can't take Italy, how can we expect to take France?"

The P.A. was far from contented himself, but he knew it was a test of endurance, and every man had to attend to his own spirit. "You know where the real war will be," he said, "and it's not in Italy. We're keeping a dozen or a score of German divisions occupied there, and keeping them away from the Russian front. That's our winter contribution, and you see the result—the Russians are in Poland and also in Bessarabia."

"I wish I could share your contentment," replied the other. "Hasn't it occurred to you that the Germans may be going easy on the Russians, and that when the Russians have got back everything that belongs to them, they may make a deal and quit on us?"

"I've heard talk about that, Jerry; but I put myself in Stalin's place and invite myself to trust Hitler and I can't see it. My guess is, the Russians will put the Germans to work for a generation to repair the damage they have done."

"Maybe so; but they may prefer to make Commies out of them, and we won't like that either." It was a complicated situation, all over the world, and every time you talked with a new person you got a new angle.

Lanny was free to tell his friend what Denis had reported about the fighting in Italy: the men were lying out in foxholes in the cold rain and snow, facing the fearsome new weapons which the enemy had contrived to make misery for them. There was a thing which the GI's called a Beetle; a crewless tank, guided by radio, low and flat, and carrying a heavy charge of explosives; it came hurtling along and crashed into an ammunition dump or other objective. There was a device for destroying railroad track, which ran on the track it destroyed; it had an immense hook in back which ripped up the sleepers; also, on each side a sort of trough, in which bombs slid down every few seconds and exploded after the hook had passed on. And whatever door the GI opened, or whatever obstacle he removed, there was sure to be a booby-trap designed to blow him out of this world. There were devilish little devices not much bigger than a fountain pen that shot up a bullet between a man's legs, just enough to ruin him for life.

Such were the things to which the German scientific brain had been devoting itself; and the American brain had been forced to follow suit. That appeared to be the way of all evil, it compelled the good to cease being good and to meet evil on its own evil ground. "Don't worry," Lanny said, "we have some surprises prepared for the Jerries, and it won't be long before they find it out."

The American Jerry's answer was, "I'm sick of waiting. All the Moors here are beginning to turn up their noses at me; and some of the French too—the high-toned ones who didn't want us in here and are glad to see us in trouble."

VI

Lanny had wanted to meet this old friend because he had an idea in his mind, important enough to justify him in breaking the rule of secrecy. "I'm going back to Washington," he explained, "and they will ask me what I want to do next. I'm not allowed to go into Axis territory any more, for reasons I can't go into. I have the idea that I might be able to be of use in Spain, and I wondered what you would think about it." Lanny was fairly sure that Jerry's duty was keeping track of Spanish agents working in French Morocco, and perhaps keeping contact with American agents in Spanish Morocco. The border was long and mountainous, impossible to keep closed.

The old friend replied, "No doubt you could be useful, but don't imagine that it would be safe. If the Nazis have got onto you, they could have you kidnapped and carried into France."

"I think that would be what we call a calculated risk, Jerry. Strictly between you and me, I don't know how much the Nazis have found out about me, or what their attitude may be. I have old friends in Spain, some of them important persons—General Aguilar, for example. It might be I could convince him that I had been lied about and misunderstood. Anyhow, it would be worth trying."

"If you're asking about my end of it, Lanny, of course I'd be delighted to co-operate with you and I've no doubt you could get your stuff out. Washington would have to give me the orders."

"The point is, I want to be somewhere near France—I'm sure it's no secret to you that the big push is coming there. The enemy knows that we are getting ready the biggest smash in all history. I don't know where it will be—I have carefully kept from asking—but I'd bet all I own in this world that we haven't been loading up the British Isles with troops for the purpose of holding parades. It happens that I know France better than any other part of the world, and I try to figure out what I can do that will count for most, this spring and summer and afterward. I'll consult the people in Washington, of course, and hear what they have to advise; but I'm pretty sure that at the end they'll say, 'Well, what do you think?' You see, I've been at this game for ten years, and most of the others have only had a year or two of it."

"You ought to be bossing the whole show!" exclaimed the ex-tutor.

"God forbid!" replied his friend. "I've learned to work on my own, but I don't know how to boss other people. If I had all those files on my mind, and the fate of all those thousands of men and women on my conscience, I'd never get to sleep at night!"

VII

That was the end of Lanny's duties in North Africa, and of the interest of both husband and wife in the region. He wanted to get back to F.D.R., and she thought more about the baby than about the blue skies and snow-white mountains and dark green date orchards of Marrakech. They consulted the Air Force officer who had charge of their flight, and he told them that the quickest way would be on one of the big transports which flew from Marrakech to New York. These had no bunks and carried wounded men, and it was no trip for a lady. Laurel asked, "Do they sometimes have women nurses?" and when the man said, "Yes," she answered, "I'll help." The officer could understand that attitude, and she didn't have to add that she was a writer and that everything was copy to her. She was even willing to suffer so as to make sure how it felt. Everything but getting killed, because then she couldn't write it!

So a delicately reared lady from the Eastern Shore of Maryland sat on a camp chair and talked with wounded men and heard their stories, and when she was tired out she slept for an hour or two on a cotton pad that was not much better than a floor. Meantime the four engines roared steadily, and the winds, blowing westward, helped them on their way. It was a routine flight, the navigator assured her; but many more flew eastward than came back. The pilot set them down, feather-lightly, on the runway of the great airfield on Long Island. A couple of hours later the tired mother had her baby in her arms—and the baby hadn't forgotten her, as she had feared.

Lanny phoned at once to the President's man. He learned that the President had gone south, and that there would be a delay. That was agreeable to Lanny, who had a lot of mail waiting, and business to attend to. He had found in Tel-Aviv a young painter of talent, and now he sent photographs to several of his clients. He told Zoltan about his adventures, and learned how many Americans had chosen Detazes as an investment for some of their war profits. An ancient but ever-strange state of affairs—where some men bled and died for their country, and others made huge fortunes out of it, and it was perfectly all right. Lanny drove his wife to Newcastle, and there were Robbie and all his friends and associates who had invested in Budd-Erling stocks; they were all making fortunes, and surely thought it was all right. If you had asked Robbie he would have replied, "What the heck! We couldn't help it if we wanted to."

Frances was well, going to school with the other children, and entirely happy. Nobody had tried to kidnap her, and the town had got over its excitement at having an heiress come to stay. She had kept her promise to write every week to her mother, and after long delays there came replies; Frances read the latest to her father, and it contained a sentence: "No bombs have fallen anywhere near us, and there are fewer of them every day." That implied, possibly, a hint of rebuke for the father, the idea that he had taken the child away under false pretenses. The flying bombs, the V-1's, were still only a rumor among the insiders, and Lanny said nothing. It could be that the British and American flyers had found the launching sites and destroyed the hellish things. Only time could tell.

Irma Barnes, Lady Wickthorpe, was another Budd-Erling investor, and her fortune was surely increasing in wartime. Somewhere in the Wall Street district was the office of the J. Paramount Barnes Estate, where an aging brother of that long-deceased traction king still guarded the securities in a vault underground, kept the books, paid the various taxes, and invested the surplus in "blue chip" stocks. Lanny no longer had anything to do with it and never mentioned the subject to his daughter. Let the Barnes half of her deal with those matters!

VIII

There came a telephone call; Harry Hopkins was at a New York hotel, and when Lanny went there he found Professor Alston in the room. So he could make two reports in one. As always they pumped him dry about the subject he had been studying. In the main they agreed with his conclusions. He said, "If we divide Palestine, somebody will surely have to keep the Arabs off the necks of the Jews." Hopkins smiled one of his dry smiles and responded, "I can see our Congress voting funds for military establishment over there!"

Alston, diplomatic adviser from the days of the Paris Peace Conference, recalled how the British and the French had there tried to put off on the United States a mandate over Armenia; but Woodrow Wilson had been wise enough to duck that one. Nations wanted mandates only where there was oil or gold or coal. The three in this room were at one on the proposition of an international authority having an armed force, and a big one. They all looked forward to a long struggle over the issue. Harry the Hop remarked, "This has to be the last war, or there won't be anybody left to fight."

Lanny had dinner with the white-bearded old gentleman who had been his first employer—his only one, in fact, since Lanny was a volunteer so far as F.D.R. was concerned. They spent an evening talking over old times and new problems. Lanny wanted Alston's advice as to his new project, but didn't feel comfortable talking in a hotel room to a person so well known as this presidential "fixer." It happened to be a mild evening, so he suggested that they take a stroll. They went up Park Avenue, and the P.A. made sure no one was following them.

"You know, Professor," he explained, "Jerry Pendleton and I fixed up a scheme to persuade the German agents in Morocco that the American Army was planning to land at Dakar. I really believe we succeeded, and had something to do with the fact that there were so few U-boats off Casablanca—only a couple of them, I've been told. Now I have the idea of going to Madrid and trying the same stunt, or something like it. I haven't been able to formulate a plan that satisfies me; but at the least I should be able to collect some information as to what the enemy is thinking, and as to conditions in the Axis lands."

"You would go as yourself?" inquired the old gentleman.

"I couldn't go any other way; too many prominent people know me there."

"It would be a pretty dangerous assignment, Lanny. Spain is for all practical purposes an Axis country. And if the Nazis have found out about you—"

"I'm not sure how much they have found out, Professor. It's quite possible they just wanted me for questioning. I have a spiel ready for them: I am hurt by their suspicions, and by the fact that Hitler has permitted some jealous person to tell him lies about me. I wouldn't want to try that in Berlin, but it might be good for Madrid. I'll be careful about going out on the street alone at night."

Alston agreed that something might come of such a mission. He would recommend it to the Boss, and Lanny of course would go to the OSS and be introduced to their Spanish section and get all the information and advice they had to offer. Said the "fixer," "I will tell you something. The invasion is set for this spring, probably May, and it will be across the Channel. I don't know the exact area—that is the General Staff's secret."

Lanny replied, "I had already guessed as much as you have told me. It seems inevitable."

"I doubt if it will be so to the enemy. I expect him to underestimate both our forces and our nerve. He certainly did so on the North Africa proposition, and that was why you could persuade him to send his submarines to Dakar."

IX

A quarter of a century had passed since these two men had begun working together, and seven years since they had been co-operating in the service of the man they referred to as "the Governor." In that time Lanny had never asked a question about secret matters, or passed on to others anything that had been confided to him. So Alston knew him as a man to be trusted. He had lived most of his life in Europe, and had been there, and all around the world, while Alston was tied down to exhausting conferences with politicians and industrial magnates and brass hats and miscellaneous persons who held power or craved it. So now the ex-geographer plied Lanny with questions, not merely about Palestine and North Africa, but about the whole Mediterranean area. Would the British-trained Arab Desert Force be loyal to Britain or to their compatriots? Had Franco learned his lesson and would we be safe in reducing our garrison in French Morocco? What was the present attitude of labor in the various lands? How strong were the Communists among the Partisans, and would they follow Russia or their own people in the end?

They had a long stroll; and before they got back to the hotel Alston asked suddenly, "Have you forgotten everything you learned in Princeton?"

It was a reference to atomic fission, without speaking those forbidden words. Lanny answered, "I've forgotten a lot, but not the essentials. The Governor saw fit to trust me with a tip a little over a year ago—that the first chain reaction had been achieved. I didn't ask where or how."

"I think you ought to know a little more because your course of action may someday depend upon it. You understand, this is the most closely guarded secret in the country. We are rushing to completion three enormous plants in widely scattered districts. The cost will go to a billion or two, and I think it's the first time in the history of industry that full-scale operational plants have been erected without even a pilot plant to test the procedure. We have plunged into it with top priority, solely on the word of the scientists that their formulas are correct."

"That comes from having a Boss who believes in science," remarked the P.A.

"Partly it's belief in science and partly it's a gambler's temperament; he's a man who loves to take a chance. It will be the biggest bust in all history—one sort of bust or the other." The onetime geographer didn't smile.

"I hope it happens where it's supposed to happen," said Lanny, "and not over here." He knew enough about the subject to appreciate what he had been told. We were hoping to make an atomic bomb and end the war with one bang!

They walked on, and just before reaching the hotel Lanny ventured, "While you're trusting me with secrets, Professor, there's one thing I've worked on and that I wonder about a lot. I brought my young daughter to this country because of what I had learned about the new weapon the enemy is getting ready. But nothing seems to happen."

"According to my information, you made no mistake. Our English friends are in for a tough time. We'll do what we can to help them, but I fear it won't be much."

"What I'm worrying about, Professor, is that the enemy may be saving up that thing for D-day."

"Nothing is more likely; but worrying won't help us. We have to do the best we can and take our losses. We have the fixed purpose to get ashore and invade Germany. The whole future of the world depends upon our carrying out that plan, and I don't think we can be stopped."

X

Lanny called up Major Jim Stotzlmann and invited him to lunch. "I have a story for you," he said, and when they met he explained, it might be a true story or not, but in wartime no clue was to be overlooked. The Major was one of those charged with the safety of the port of New York, and this came within his domain. In Haifa Lanny had got into conversation with a sailor who claimed to know the German agent who had set fire to the great French liner, the *Normandie*. That beautiful vessel now lay on her side by the pier, as big as a dozen dead whales, and it was too late to do anything for her; but according to the story the German agent was still in New York, and that was something to be looked into. Jim promised to report it to the right place.

Then he asked about Palestine. He knew some of the rich Jews who were financing that enterprise and could tell about their state of distress. They hadn't expected such a fury of reaction from the Arabs, and now they were accusing the British of perfidy, and F.D.R. of cowardice and vacillation. Only a small percentage of Jews were Zionists, but the horror in Germany had awakened their sense of solidarity. Surely it was right that there should be some corner of the world where a persecuted people could seek shelter, and bring in their relatives and friends! Surely the British government ought to stand by their pledged word, and the American government ought to make them do it!

What made the matter more urgent was the fact that a presidential election was coming this fall, and no party that wanted to carry the Empire State could forget the Bronx, which had more Jews in it than Palestine. Twice as many Jews in New York City as in the Jewish homeland, and now they were all buzzing like a swarm of angry bees. The Governor was worried about it; there wasn't any Arab vote to speak of, but there was Arab oil, and our fleet, as well as the British, was using all it could get. So it was a mess.

The scion of the Stotzlmanns had just been down to Washington. He was another man who entered the White House by the "social door"; he liked to tell his friends that F.D.R. had been present at his christening. They had both of them become what Jim called "mavericks," that is to say, unbranded cattle, individuals who had stepped out from the herd and taken the risk of being run down and devoured by the wolves. Jim adored Franklin, calling him the greatest man in the world. Franklin would have had to be more than human, or less, if he had not been touched by such devotion. They were both of them big fellows, both warmhearted and full of fun, and both heartily despised the majority of their own class—so blind with greed, so stiff with pride, so dull beyond believing! exclaimed Jim.

"Oh, why should the spirit of mortal be proud?" a poet had inquired, and no one had yet found an answer; but that didn't keep the spirit from continuing the practice. To hear Jim tell about that clan of his, famous throughout America and indeed throughout the world, was as good as a visit to a circus. Jim was fond of the clan's head, who was well over eighty, but he said she had no more comprehension of his New Dealish ideas than if he had come from the other side of the moon. She lived alone in a palace with seventeen servants, and could not give up the idea of being a social queen even in the midst of war; forty people for dinner was a normal event. She would scold the servants unmercifully, but when one of them wanted to quit and go into war work she would burst into tears and say they were abandoning her in her old age and that she would die without them; so they would stay.

Jim said that in 1940 he had labored hard to persuade the Governor to run for a third term; but this time the "old man" wasn't needing any persuasion. His dander was up, and he was determined to see the war through, and the peace. He thought he could do it without any campaign, but Jim said, "They'll smoke him out before it's over; and God knows how he's going to carry the load. He insists that he's all right, but he looks exhausted, and it's beyond imagining how a man can stand up under such pressure."

XI

After a winter of colds and influenza the doctors feared a break in the President's health and had persuaded him to take a month's vacation. He had gone to the plantation of his friend Bernard Baruch in the tidelands of South Carolina. Lanny was asked to visit him there; and since there was no hurry, and Laurel would enjoy the trip, he chose to motor. It was the familiar Highway One most of the way, and then off on a side road. They did not go to Georgetown, the nearest town to the plantation, for they knew that the hotel there would be full of reporters. Lanny left his wife at a hotel in Andrews, met Baker by appointment, and was driven to Hobcaw Barony, as F.D.R.'s hideaway was called.

It is a fish-and-game preserve some six miles square, in the tideland swamps of this subtropical coast. Lanny was surprised to see a very elegant two-story mansion of red brick, surrounded by immense live oaks draped with Spanish moss. He was taken in at night, directly to the President's room, which was on a ground floor corner. Baker had said that the Boss had been catching catfish from the dock, and Lanny knew that this must mean that he was far from well; he was a deep-sea fisherman, and proud of his prowess.

Even with this warning Lanny was shocked by his appearance; his face was drawn and without color. Every time the P.A. came, at intervals of two or three months, he could see a difference for the worse. The plain truth was, the presidency of the United States was a murderous job, and especially so in wartime. This President was waging three wars at once, one against the Nazis, one against the Japanese, and one against his political foes; a civil war, no less a strain because it was fought with political and propaganda weapons instead of arms.

He had been told about Lanny's Spanish proposal, so he was ready with one of his cheery greetings, "Hello, Don Quixote!" pronouncing it in the old English fashion, "Don Quicks-ut." He wanted to hear all about Palestine, the scenery and local color as well as the political problems. Many questions Lanny couldn't answer—nor any other man. How far would the Jewish fanatics go in their war on the British authorities? There had been an answer since Lanny had left—several British soldiers shot from ambush. How far were the Arab threats bluff, and where was the Grand Mufti hiding? Lanny answered questions for an hour, and had the belief that everything he said would be stored away in that extraordinary mind.

Then the problems of Spain. Lanny's proposal had come at a crucial moment, the Boss explained; trade relations had been broken off with the treacherous Franco, to pry him loose from his Axis pals. "We mean to penetrate even his dull brain with the fact that we're going to win this war."

"It's truly inconceivable to him," put in the other.

"I know; but he saw something in North Africa, and he'll see something in France before long. Meantime he gets no oil, and he won't be able to hold out. But it'll make matters hard for you—he and his gang don't love Americans."

"I don't need their love; it will be enough if I can make them think they can get some dollars out of me."

"My impression is that the Franco government doesn't permit the exporting of art treasures."

"Nevertheless, Governor, I managed to get some out, and I imagine it will be possible now. All Fascist governments are corrupt, and Franco's will be worse even than the Duce's. The country is poor, the officials are underpaid, and if their families are to eat they have to make something on the side."

"You plan to become a bootlegger of art works?"

"I'll have to be guided by circumstances. If I'm only going to stay a short while, it will suffice if I whisper about being a bootlegger. So long as I don't do anything, I can't get into trouble; I'll make friends, or pretended friends, and make alluring promises which I won't have to keep. According to what I hear, war profits in Spain are going to a very small group, Franco's big business friends who put him in power and keep him there. Many of the old families are poor and dissatisfied, and they are the ones who have the art works and might be willing to dispose of them. Also, they are in position to pick up gossip, and they usually talk freely among themselves."

"That sounds all right; but what will you do about the Nazi agents?"

"I just have to wait and see about them. It's inconceivable that they won't get reports about me, but what will be in those reports I can't guess. If I meet them, I'll never know whether they are telling me the truth; I'll just have to watch and wait. Tell me what you particularly would like me to get."

"There are so many things that it's hard to know where to begin. Anything that will help us in the invasion of France—which is coming. Anything that will enable us to undermine the Axis, or to starve them. We have been getting tungsten, or what they call wolfram, from Spain and Portugal under what is called 'preclusive buying'—paying hold-up prices, of course. I'm told we get about three-quarters of it, and one of the demands we are making of the little fat Caudillo is that he shall stop all shipment of wolfram concentrates to Germany. We demand some Italian ships that he is holding, and that he kick out certain Nazi agents we have named—the OSS will give you that list, and you will watch out for them. We demand that all German agents shall be put out of Tangier, where they keep tabs on our shipping through the Strait of Gibraltar and keep the U-boats informed. Quite a list, you see, and it's like pulling out Franco's teeth—but we're giving him the gas." The Boss chuckled.

"I've a wild idea in my head," declared Lanny. "I might cook up some way to make the Nazis believe we're going to invade through Holland instead of across the Channel. What would you give me if I could do that?"

"Golly! I'd make you majordomo of all the art museums in the U.S. I've recalled pretty nearly every spy story I ever read, trying to figure out how we could do it."

"I've done the same. But I fear I can never get the Nazis to trust me again. It might be that I could have some secret documents and let their agents steal them."

"Go on—you got that out of E. Phillips Oppenheim. Go and talk with Wild Bill; he knows the story and I'll OK anything he approves."

XII

Lanny drove his wife back to Washington, and put her up in a hotel while he paid a visit to the old brick building by the gasworks. First he met the genial stoutish Irish-American, who disarmed you by his friendly manner—but don't be fooled, for he had a shrewd lawyer's mind and didn't miss anything. He would call in two or three of his top people, also a stenographer, and they would put the visitor through a grilling—every question exactly to the point and nothing overlooked. Lanny spent a couple of hours with men who were experts on Palestine; and after that the Spanish section took the rest of the day, part of the night, and some of the next day.

The P.A. knew Spain fairly well; he could speak the language enough to get along—especially since educated Spaniards know English and French. He had motored through various parts of the country, inspecting paintings and buying several. During the civil war he had stayed for weeks in a town of Western Spain called Caceres, and hoped that nobody knew he had helped in the escape of an English flyer named Alfred Pomeroy-Nielson from a dungeon in that town. More important yet, he had been sent by the elder de Bruyne to interview Marshal Pétain at the time that quavering old gentleman had been the French Ambassador to Madrid—the period called *Sitzkrieg*, before the German invasion of France. All the Rightists had been clamoring for France to make terms with Hitler and get out of the war before it was too late. Lanny had had proper credentials, and had met all the "best" people, including General Aguilar, commander of the military district of the capital.

Wonderful, wonderful! the OSS people agreed; the only question was, had he spoiled it by getting exposed or suspected in Germany? If this had happened, the Spaniards would be sure to know about it; and what would they do? Let the Nazis kidnap the false friend and carry him into France? Or pretend to accept him, watch him, and find out what the Americans wanted to know, who their agents were, and where their "post office" was situated? Lanny would be in danger; he would have to use many precautions. They told him these, one after another, and it made a long list—a stenographer typed them out for him so that he could study them. But he wouldn't take them into Spain!

What was he going to find out? That was another list, of which such things as tungsten, alias wolfram, were only a small part. Franco, who owed his job to Hitler and Mussolini, was doing everything he dared to aid his benefactors: shipping critical materials to them; spying on the Allies in every land and turning over their secrets; giving fuel to U-boats, and information about Allied shipping; permitting Nazi sympathizers to attack Allied consulates—in short, everything except getting into the war. Recently he had gone too far, and the Allies had cut off his oil supplies, which would make it hard for Lanny or anybody else to get about in Spain.

What was this P.A. going to use for camouflage? He told about his acquaintances in Madrid and Seville and Barcelona who were art lovers; also about two of his clients at home who apparently suspected what he was doing, and obliged him with letters ordering *objets d'art* in any part of the world he desired to visit. He would renew old friendships in Spain and delicately hint to certain officials that they could earn generous fees by helping him get permission to take paintings out of the country. "I may take some," he said, "and you will have to fix it up so that I don't get jugged for trading with the enemy."

XIII

There remained the most important subject of all: the possibility that this art expert might be used to give the Germans the wrong idea as to the goal of that colossal expeditionary force which the Americans were preparing in most of the harbors of the Atlantic seaboard. The OSS experts on spy stories were called in for consultation: men who had spent their lives thinking up new wrinkles in "Whodunits" and now saw their imaginings turning into grim reality. Believe it or not, there was a man from Hollywood who claimed to have written a hundred and forty-seven such works of fiction, and to have turned more than half of them into screen treatments. There was an elderly lawyer who asserted that he had put himself to sleep every night for forty years by reading such stories. There was the head of a police department "crime bureau" who had spent a couple of decades probing the minds of criminals and finding out what they believed and what they tried to get other people to believe.

A strange place, and a strange assortment of occupations! At lunchtime, by way of recreation, the bespectacled young college professor who sat next to Lanny entertained him with accounts of some of the things they were doing. They had little pamphlets, top-secret, of course, on the details of committing most of the crimes known to man: how to open any ordinary lock with little strips of celluloid; how to open safes—they had men who in ten minutes could open a safe that had printed on it the manufacturer's statement that if you lost the combination there would be nothing you could do but have the safe blown. There were treatises on lifting seals and replacing them, on steaming letters open, or reading them without opening, by means of tiny lights inserted in the corner of the flap. There were teams of men working all over the country, trained in the details of entering an office at night, making photostats of thousands of documents, and leaving everything in perfect order, even to the dust on the desks and the floor. The owner of the place would never know it had been entered, not even if he had set traps, or if he made tests for fingerprints and so on.

In this case it was a question of how they were going to persuade the suspicious Nazis to believe the opposite of the truth. The professor of criminal psychology pointed out that when an American told something to a Nazi, the Nazi would naturally assume that it was false. But the Nazi might be capable of one degree of subtlety and figure that the American might be telling the truth, knowing that the Nazi would assume it to be false. Or the Nazi might be capable of two degrees of subtlety, and assume that the statement might be false, because the American would assume that the Nazi might assume it was the truth. This might go on without limit, like the girl pulling the petals off a daisy and reciting, "He loves me, he loves me not." The Nazis would always try to be one step ahead of their enemies in subtlety.

How could a supposedly innocent art expert convey information to the Nazis? If he had it in his suitcase for them to steal, they would assume that he had put it there to be stolen; and in that case, would it be better to put true information or false? It might be that Lanny could receive a letter from his father, a man who would have inside information; but would the father be indiscreet enough to write it to his son in Spain? Or could he write that he was sending important documents to some secret place where the son could get them? Pretty surely the Nazis would be reading the son's letters, and they would contrive to steal those documents—but even then, might they not suspect a "plant?" Just so, declared the Hollywood writer, did half a dozen men sit up all night in a story conference, thinking up complications to tickle the jaded palates of movie fans!

Lanny's guess was that the Nazis would know him for a secret agent, but would pretend not to; and what then? Obviously, they would assume that anything he had was false. But suppose he posed as an agent who had "turned," one who was serving both sides for the money there was in it? Suppose that a couple of known American agents, say at Cadiz, were to make an attempt to carry Lanny off and put him on board an American ship, and suppose Lanny were to appeal to the Spanish police and get rescued—surely that would cause the Franco crowd to think well of him, and the Nazis to come running to him with their hands full of gold! Lanny said, "Yes, but it would be pretty sure to get me into the newspapers, and that is the one thing I've always managed to avoid." The Budd family never got into the newspapers, and especially not as traitors to their native land!

After hours of pro and con this story conference agreed that the wisest course for a presidential agent would be to proceed to Madrid and feel out the situation. When he had made a choice of the best-seeming plan he would drop a note in code to the American "post office" in Madrid. The word would be radioed to Washington, which would provide all the props required for the most elaborate super-feature film. Code words were agreed upon and stowed away in Lanny's memory, and a copy sealed tightly and locked up in the super-secret files of the Office of Strategic Services. Let it be hoped there was no Hitler spy among those who kept the files!

20

Red Laugh of War

I

BAKER provided the P.A.'s passport, made out for Portugal, Spain, and North Africa. Lanny got a Portuguese visa in New York, but thought it best to wait and apply for the Spanish visa in Lisbon. He was flown comfortably on a Clipper by way of the Cape Verde Islands, and when he was set down in the harbor of Lisbon, he betook himself to the best hotel, put in his application for permission to enter Spain, and then telephoned to General Aguilar in Madrid. He had come, he said, because he had heard that Spain had excellent modern painters and he wanted to see their work; incidentally, he had interesting news about world affairs. The elderly commander was cordial and promised to see that the visa was granted at once. Lanny thought to himself, The Nazis haven't told him about me!

"At once" in the Spanish language meant almost a week, Lanny discovered; he called at the Consulate every day, but the clerks shook their heads. *Infelizmente, Señor*—but there was a routine which required time. Lanny revealed no impatience; he had all the company he wanted. Here in the greatest spy center of Europe there were people of all sorts, male and female, eager to talk to him in English, French, German, or Spanish. He was polite to them all, and happy to express his opinions of paintings, from those of the Aurignacian caves to Picasso and Dali. When it came to the present state of the world, he said it was very bad, and the only thing that a lover of art could do was to refuse to let the subject gain admission to his thoughts.

There were some of these persons who remembered him of old, for he had been coming through here since the days of the Spanish Civil War. He recalled well the Japanese, excessively polite little men, wearing the same black frock coats and pin-stripe trousers, bowing like automatons and wearing smiles that showed their large teeth to the gums, both upper and lower. Because of previous acquaintance, they presumed to speak to American gentleman in spite of unfortunate war so greatly regretted. American gentleman replied no less politely; he too greatly regretted, having nothing of personal ill will, most happy to learn concerning new Japanese painters in wartime, perhaps making use of new themes? So went this urbane conversation, Lanny knowing that he couldn't fool the Japs and guessing that they knew they were not fooling him. He could believe that there was real sincerity in their regrets about this war, for by now the American task forces had got under way among the Pacific islands, and planes from American carriers were shooting down flocks of the best-trained flyers the Japanese had been able to turn out. Their supply was not unlimited.

Official Portugal was carefully neutral in the whole conflict. The newspapers published the communiqués of both sides, and both were permitted to lease store windows and mount their propaganda for passers-by to read; the Nazis won out in this, because their propaganda included photographs of blond Aryan females exhibiting everything with which nature had endowed them. Big-business Portugal was likewise impartial, taking in dollars, marks, and pounds sterling in the process of preclusive buying. On the Avenida da Liberdade—which meant in practice Avenue de Laissez-Faire—you saw fine shops with jewels, furs, and every sort of luxury goods; you would also see barefooted peasant women carrying huge loads of farm produce on their heads.

Wages had gone up slightly—from fifty cents per day; this being another Catholic land, where birth control was banned or unknown, the population pressed inexorably upon the limits of subsistence. The well-to-do had the poor always with them and found it most convenient, because one could always get servants. Pleasure resorts were being developed, and all you had to do in order to enjoy them was to harden your heart to the starving refugees who sought you out and told you their tragic stories, imploring you for small loans or for help in getting passports to some part of the world where they might find conditions less difficult.

II

At last, a smile upon the face of the clerk in the Spanish Consulate; it took but a few hours to pay the fees and have all the various documents properly signed, sealed, and delivered. Customs papers, passport controls, money controls, ration card, hotel triptych—these and several other papers you must carry and be prepared to show at any time.

Lanny took the first plane on which he could get a seat, and a couple of hours later came down upon that Cuatro Vientos airfield, which he knew so well. Rick's oldest son, Alfy, had been flying a fighter plane from it in the days when Madrid had been the capital of Republican Spain. Now it was the capital of Falangist Spain, and it still had the marks of war upon its face; the ruins had been cleared out of the streets but not from the rest of the ground. Franco and his men were practiced killers but very poor builders; they had no idea how to proceed to restore the land they had seized.

Lanny put up at the Ritz Hotel, home of elegance, with a gleaming white front facing the great square of the Cibeles. Here everything was as if there had never been any trouble in Europe. The waiters all had long-tailed coats and the small busboys wore white spats. Lanny got a comfortable room and bath fronting on the court for only a hundred pesetas a day; the peseta was worth ten cents officially and five cents on the black market. You'd have no trouble in finding the latter; it would follow you down the street and give you for your American dollars large wads of Franco's paper money, very thin, black, and greasy, making you think of wilted lettuce out of a garbage can.

Prices were high, and many common things were unobtainable except on the black market; all you had to do was tip the porter, and he would show up with whatever you wanted. Spain had been under economic siege for a couple of months; the Allies were trying to break her will by depriving her of *la gasolina*. This meant the slowing up of traffic and, still worse, scarcity of goods, and the newspapers were filled with enraged protests, blaming Yankee imperialism for this insult to the dignity of a great nation. Lanny took refuge in a formula which had served him in past times: he had been born in Europe and had lived most of his life there; he was a Frenchman in his tastes and a Fascist in his sympathies, and he was humiliated to contemplate the role which the land of his forefathers was playing in world affairs.

He called up General Aguilar and invited the old martinet to dine at the hotel. This was the test. What, if anything, had the military commander of the Madrid district been told by his German friends concerning the son of Budd-Erling? Apparently he hadn't been told anything; or perhaps he couldn't resist the temptation of an elegant dinner, *vin compris*. Anyhow he showed up, in full regalia, with all his medals and decorations, and white whiskers flowing both sideways and down. He hadn't grown any younger since Lanny had seen him a year ago; his hands trembled and his memory was less keen. It didn't really matter, for he had competent subordinates, and he lived in glory upon his reputation as head of an army corps of Moors, Italians, and a few Spaniards, which had marched all the way from Cadiz, northward along the Portuguese border and then across to the east, through the Guadarrama Mountains to the rear of Madrid.

At the least sign of interest the old boy would tell you tales of those heroic days—and be sure that a visiting art expert did not fail to indicate such interest. The dinner cost him some six hundred pesetas—about fifty dollars—but was well worth that to him just to be seen in this dining-room in such eminent company. The wealthy and highly placed guests would notice it, the hotel staff would do the same, and all the hangers-on, the spies and agents of the Spanish government, the German, and the other interested lands.

Who was this good-looking and elegant stranger, and what was he after? He gave the General his carefully prepared story, that he had heard Spain had some important living painters. There was no law against the export of contemporary art works, and it was a part of the Franco propaganda that the new Spain had cultural activities of the very highest quality. Painters? Those of Spain had always been the greatest in the world, and never more so than now. General Aguilar didn't know their names, but Lanny did, and told them. He wanted to inspect their works and perhaps obtain examples for the National Gallery of Art in Washington and other great institutions. Had the General ever had his portrait painted? Had El Caudillo done so? And would it be possible for Lanny to inspect the work and perhaps arrange for the painter to make a copy for one of Lanny's clients?

The son of Budd-Erling went on to explain that it was his father's influence that had made possible this trip; and that, too, sounded plausible to an old soldier who knew all about the great firm and took it for granted that the president of such a firm would have influence and would use it on behalf of his son. Spain had always been a land of nepotism, and the old commander was busily collecting perquisites for the members of his large family. When he had got them jobs he was proud of it and would boast of the importance of the Aguilar clan. The name, accented on the second syllable, means eagle; the bird is predatory, and in Europe as well as in America has been taken by poets and statesmen as a symbol of worldly pride, pomp, and power. The word also means a gold coin—and that surely did not diminish its prestige in Spain.

III

There really were painters in Madrid, men who had managed to live through a revolution and a cruel civil war. Some of them painted portaits of the rich and great, the generals and the ecclesiastics, and these were able to live comfortably. Others painted landscapes, peasants at work or dancing in fiesta costumes, and these had managed to escape persecution, but not destitution. Picasso, who had painted a symbolical portrayal of bombed Guernica, had fled abroad, and so had others who had painted the people's army. Having met all sorts of artists from boyhood, Lanny knew exactly how to talk to them. Very soon he was a friend of the bohemian world, giving a few pesetas to some poor devil of talent, and purchasing several works which he thought had real merit.

Also there were dealers in art, and owners of paintings, from whom Lanny had purchased works in days before the war. He renewed these acquaintanceships and made himself agreeable wherever he went. In any sort of company, when the subject of world politics came up, he would smile and say humbly that the situation was beyond his capacity to form a judgment; his specialty was painting. Elegant, superior, and opulent, he spread his fame in the art world, and numbers of people came to call at his hotel. He took it for granted that every other one would be an agent of some sort, and he said exactly the right, careful things to them. He left his suitcases unlocked, and they contained letters on fashionable stationery, bearing the signatures of Americans whom any agent could look up in *Who's Who* and discover to be well-known collectors. From first to last there was nothing wrong about this *conocedor d'arte*, and no reason for the most suspicious of governments to interfere in his affairs.

All this took constant watchfulness, the guarding of every word, every facial expression, the very pulses of his blood. This ancient, proud land of Spain stood in Lanny's imagination as a symbol of the evil that ruled the modern world. "Truth forever on the scaffold, Wrong forever on the throne!" Spain was supposed to be a land at peace, but it was a land crushed and writhing in suffocation. Francisco Franco's crime of state had filled Lanny with fury, not merely because he had been here and witnessed it stage by stage, but because it was a crime against the future, against the faith by which Lanny lived.

Ever since his youth he had been telling the workers, and the friends of social justice wherever he met them, that the way to peace and freedom lay through the ballot box, that the democratic process would enable them to take power without bloodshed and chaos. The people of Spain had followed this course and had established a duly elected parliament pledged to long-needed reforms. Then had come the man of blood and terror, the assassin of the people's hopes; puppet of Nazi-Fascism, he had opened his country to the German and Italian bandits and had permitted them to use the people of Spain as practice targets for the new techniques of warfare—tanks and Panzer divisions, screaming divebombers and area bombing to wipe out the civilian population of whole towns.

The result had been to provide the Communists with an argument difficult indeed for a democratic Socialist to answer. "Look!" they would say. "You tried it in Spain and what did you get?" Lanny must have heard those words a hundred times in arguments with Jesse Blackless, his "Red" uncle; Laurel had heard it more recently in her discussions with Bess. "How many more people's governments do you have to see murdered in order to convince you that the capitalist class will never surrender power without a fight?"

Lanny was putting his hopes in Franklin Roosevelt—and what bitter laughter that brought from the Reds. What had Roosevelt done to help the people of Spain, except to deny them the right to purchase arms in the sweet land of liberty? The first time in history that a legitimate and duly elected government was denied the right to buy arms for its own defense! Franco could get all he needed from Hitler and Mussolini, but democratic Spain couldn't get anything, even when it came with gold in its hands! "*Conspuez Roosevelt!*" Lanny had heard the workers of Paris shouting at a mass meeting to demand airplanes for Spain. "*Des avions pour l'Espagne!*" But not even the Socialist Blum had dared to heed the cry.

On his return home Lanny had heard the President's defense. The country was without arms and in no position to take up the challenge of the three dictators. Britain was in an even worse position, with the menace at her very doorstep. Neither country was prepared militarily, neither was prepared ideologically. In America were the Southern senators, and the Catholic vote in the big cities, and the Church hierarchy cheering for their Spanish Defender of the Faith. Eight years ago this had been, and a presidential election coming on, even as now. "Politics!" Uncle Jesse had sneered; and Roosevelt's answer had been, "What is the democratic process but politics? And if I lose the election, what good will that do the people of Spain? Will they get what they want from the Republicans?"

So Lanny had to bite his tongue off, as the saying goes, and watch that wholesale murder for nearly three years. Now he had to bite every day, observing the crude luxury of Spain's wealthy classes, the great landowners and holders of state monopolies, and the higher clergy, who owned half the arable land of the country and made speeches denying the right of any other form of worship, thus inciting the Falangist rowdies to raid and destroy Protestant churches. Contrasted with their obesity was the sheer naked starvation of the masses in their rickety slum tenements, many of them still unrepaired after bombing. This was another Catholic land where the teaching of birth control was a crime, and the unwanted infants who came into the world with very little flesh on their soft bones went out again quickly, assured of eternal bliss because each one had had a cross marked on its forehead with consecrated water.

IV

Germans came to see Lanny, and others who said they were Swiss or Danes but who he felt sure were Germans. They were all lovers of art, and some of them really knew about the subject. They took an interest in Lanny's ideas, and he was friendly to them, inviting them to meals and talking "shop"—that is, painters, and the prices now being paid for their works in the various centers of culture. The visitors hinted at secret business to be done, and Lanny was politely interested but refrained from committing himself; they might be genuine black-marketeers, and again they might be agents of the Gestapo, trying to find out why he was here, and to get some pretext for having him expelled, either westward or—God forbid—eastward.

He was really interested in painting, and he was content to bide his time. Sooner or later he might pick one of these gentlemen as the one upon whom to try some device. Or perhaps it would be the lovely blond lady named Fridolin, who had twice invited him to her room, and hadn't taken offense at his refusal, but greeted him with unfailing smiles in the lobby. He would be friends with them all and try to make up his mind about each one. He agreed with them that Communism was a nightmare threatening the world, and that the Allies were making a frightful blunder in not helping Germany to overcome it; but he added that politics and world problems upset his mind and disturbed his esthetic sensibilities. It was his special task to help the peoples of both Europe and America to have beautiful paintings to contemplate. *Ars longa, vita brevis!*

This cat-and-mouse game went on until one morning a telephone call and a familiar voice. Lanny exclaimed in delight, "*Ist's möglich? Was machst du in Madrid?*" Heinrich answered that he would tell him about it. When could he come? Lanny said, "*Gleich!*" And, to himself, "Hitler has sent him!"

Yes, that was a pretty safe guess. Heinrich Jung was a desk man, and so far as Lanny could recall had never been outside his Fatherland. He was the logical man for the Führer to choose in order to solve the mystery of Lanny Budd's disappearance from Germany and his reappearance in Spain. Lanny's mind had been intrigued by the thought of both the *Nummer Eins* and the *Nummer Zwei*, and what they would be making of his escape. Heinrich wasn't the cleverest man that Adi could have found, but he was the most honest, and the one whom both he and Lanny would be most apt to trust.

The Jugend leader came, wearing civilian clothes, a gray tweed suit. This was the first time Lanny had seen him out of uniform in something like twenty years, and it was a mistake from the enemy's point of view, because it made him seem unnatural. But Lanny saw the same round, blue-eyed, rather dull countenance, and underneath the tweeds the round belly slowly but steadily expanding. After their cordial exchange of greetings Heinrich explained that he had been sent to consult with the Falangistas as to their educational techniques, which hadn't proved as successful with the youth of Spain as the methods of the Hitlerjugend in Germany. Heinrich had come as a civilian because —and he seemed a little embarrassed as he said it—the Spaniards were having trouble with the Allies just now and were trying to keep German officialdom a trifle less conspicuous. That might be true or it might be invented; no doubt Heinrich had been coached as to every word he was to say.

Of course Lanny wouldn't show the least trace of doubt. They were the same good companions they had been from boyhood; they carried on their conversation exactly as if the fates had not put their countries on opposite sides of a world war. "What on earth made you leave so suddenly?" demanded Heinrich. "I was planning a party for you at my home."

"Too bad," replied the other, and he became very solemn in voice and aspect. "Has nobody told you anything about me?"

"Nothing, Lanny. What do you mean?"

"Himmler came to see me and asked me a great many questions, which made it plain that somebody had been sowing distrust of me in his mind. Then one of my friends tipped me off that I was in danger. You know what an awkward position I was in—an enemy alien in the Fatherland. I was a foredoomed victim of any slanderer or intriguer."

"*Aber wie Schade!* What did they accuse you of?"

"How could I know? I suppose of not being a true friend to the Führer, of having abused his confidence."

"But why didn't you go to the Führer and have it out with him?"

"I had already seen him and realized what an overburdened man he was. I thought it would be a poor act of friendship to worry him with my problems. And how could I expect him to believe my word against that of his security chief, the man upon whom he depends for his very life? You know how it is, Heinrich—the Führer is surrounded by men who compete for his favor. I suppose I have made some of them jealous by enjoying too much of his trust and by being able to see him when they weren't able to."

"I am shocked, Lanny, and I'm sure the Führer must be shocked if he knows about it. He is always loyal to his old friends, and it must have hurt him that you deserted him."

"I haven't deserted him, Heinrich. I have been working just the same, doing what he asked me to do."

"How on earth did you get out of Germany?"

"I'm not free to tell you that. There are people near the Führer who distrust Himmler and consider him an evil influence. They provided me with transportation." The P.A. wasn't making this up on the spur of the moment; he had thought the matter out and decided that he might cause a little worry to both the Führer and the Gestapo head. Take their minds off the war for a while!

"Lanny, I think this is dreadful!" exclaimed the Jugend leader. "I'll finish my duties here quickly and go straight to the Führer. He has never refused to see me no matter how busy he has been. I'll tell him what you have said, and I can promise you he'll pledge you safe conduct and let you come back and confront your accusers."

"That's very fine of you, *mein alter Heinrich*, and what I would have expected. Of course I want to clear my good name; and I'll come if you can arrange it, provided that I can manage another trip. It grows more difficult every time. My father's influence can do a lot, but it can't do everything, and the American authorities are very suspicious of my traveling. You see how I am—between two fires!"

V

Such was the beginning of a duel of wits between two men who had begun as friends in boyhood and had been made into enemies by irresistible social forces. Lanny had been deceiving Heinrich for a matter of fifteen years, and all that time Heinrich had been sincere. What a shock it must have given him to learn that this adored friend had been an enemy of Heinrich's adored cause! Lanny was guessing that Heinrich had been told this, and that he had come here for the purpose of deceiving Lanny and paying him back. But there was always a chance that Lanny might be mistaken, that perhaps the Gestapo hadn't really had anything definite against him and had merely wanted to question him. Perhaps they had sent Heinrich just to try to get Lanny back into Germany, without telling him anything against his friend. Such complications lent piquancy to the duel of wits.

Heinrich attended to the urgent business which he said had brought him to Madrid: meeting the leaders of the Falange youth groups and tellings them the wonders which the Führer had been able to achieve with the bodies and minds of the children of Germany. As a concession to the Allies, Franco had recently abolished the Falangist militia; but that, of course, merely solidified his control of the country through the Army. El Caudillo had surely not given up his dream of "forging an empire," and all Spanish children were being taught that this heaven-sent leader was going to restore the country's ancient glory by retaking all the once-Spanish lands—South and Central America, the West Indies, Mexico, Texas, California. Then Spain would be really prosperous, and every Spaniard would be a lord. Heinrich mentioned this program to his friend, and Lanny wondered, was he really naïve, or was all this a subtle pose to make Lanny believe that he was exactly the same old comrade, having no idea that Lanny was in any way different from what he had always been? If Heinrich had been coached it would surely have been a good coaching.

Amid his pressing duties Heinrich managed to find time to dine with Lanny and spend the evening now and then. As usual, he let Lanny take the check, because he was a poor man. Was he really poor, or was he afraid it would look suspicious if he had an expense account for entertaining American spies? At every turn Lanny had to occupy his mind with speculations like this; yet he mustn't seem to be watching, he must be glad to see an old friend to hear the news from home. How was the family? A large and steadily growing unit—eight children, and they had all been given old Germanic names, Baldur and Horst-Michel, Ingomar and Chlodwig and Wilfried. Lanny had made it a point to remember these names, and every time he had left Germany he had given each of the little ones a present; that had made him into an American rich uncle, and Lanny wondered if the father had told them the shattering news that their benefactor was a spy and traitor to the Fatherland.

Baldur, the eldest, a tall lad, blue-eyed and yellow-haired, had just entered the Army, proudly and gloriously; in a few weeks he would be at the front. Naturally that led the talk to the war and its progress; Lanny, who knew what Heinrich believed, was careful to believe exactly the same. The Americans had taken a couple of months to capture Cassino, and at that rate it was obvious they weren't going to reach the Alps this year. As for the Eastern front, the German retreat was clearly strategic; they were leading the enemy into a trap, and as soon as the ground was dry this fact would become apparent to the world. Not since Hannibal's crossing of the Alps—successful at first but a failure in the end—had there been a madder military undertaking than the American proposal to invade and conquer the Axis lands. Lanny said it was well known in America that this program had been forced upon the Army by a Jew-dominated President.

Lanny had undertaken to find out about this Herr Rosenfeld for the benefit of Herr Schicklgruber, and he told how he had traveled across the American continent upon that errand, and what sentiments he had heard expressed by the powerful rich in New York, Washington, Chicago, Detroit, Hollywood, and Los Angeles. What he said didn't have to be true; he could follow Hitler's own formula about lying. Lanny had given thought to getting just the right sort of stories, stories which Heinrich would accept and which might cause even Heinrich's great Leader to wonder if he had not made a mistake in doubting the good faith of this scion of American big business. It was so utterly impossible for Hitler to conceive how a man like the president of Budd-Erling could be giving aid to the Russians and not realize what a trap he had fallen into. And the fact was, Robbie was almost as puzzled about the matter as Hitler thought he should be.

Heinrich promised to report this news to his Führer at the first opportunity, and Lanny was pretty sure he would do so. Air mail went to Berlin at least twice a day, and no doubt Heinrich could send a letter by diplomatic pouch. Adi might be at his headquarters in the Ukraine, or in the Hürtgen Forest, but he would get such a letter quickly. And sure enough, three days later the Jugend official came, rosy with pride and delight, bearing a note on the private stationery of the greatest man in the world. "I have read with attention what you tell me about Herr Budd, and you may assure him that I shall be, as I have always been, pleased to receive a visit from him. Of course I will grant him safe conduct, both from and to Madrid, and I hereby authorize you to escort him to me and bring him back to Madrid whenever he is ready to come."

To the humble and adoring Heinrich Jung, that was the greatest achievement of his lifetime. He bubbled with German adjectives: "*Prachtvoll! Herrlich! Beispiellos!*" He was chagrined when Lanny began explaining that he could not leave that very day. *Unglücklicherweise!* Lanny had incurred obligations, he had promised one of his clients to make a thorough investigation of contemporary Spanish painting, and he could not break his word to any client—no, not even to clear his good name in Naziland, not even to help eliminate Herr Rosenfeld from World War II! Lanny promised to come soon; and meantime he prepared a formal report for Heinrich to transmit to the Führer. Also, he started another report, signed "Traveler," which he would turn in at the American Embassy; but he thought the idea over and burned the document, deciding that it was too risky and there was not enough to be gained. Herr Rosenfeld would have to wait for this item!

VI

April had come, and was going. The Germans in the course of their strategic retreat had abandoned Odessa and been surrounded in Sebastopol. The Americans were slogging their way from one mountain to the next on the Italian peninsula, and the people at home read stories of rain and mud and blood, and waited, doubting and despairing, for the Army or somebody to carry out some of the wonderful promises which had been made to the world. Hope deferred maketh the heart sick!

Lanny had managed to get himself pretty completely surrounded by Nazis and Nazi agents in El Caudillo's capital. This had come about gradually and naturally; they had sought him out, and he had to like them; he spoke their language more fluently than Spanish, and all his life he had admired German culture, played German music, sung German songs. He introduced the others one by one to Heinrich, smiling inwardly as he did so, for he guessed that the Jugend leader knew them. In all probability they had come first and, finding that Herr

Budd would talk only about paintings, they had picked out an old friend to come and break the ice.

Anyhow, it was broken, and Lanny was, as of old, the Nazi-admirer and collaborator. He talked about his many friends in the Fatherland, and about conditions in America, and the prospects of the war. Occasionally he dropped items of information, nearly always things which he could be sure the Nazis already knew—though perhaps not these particular agents. F.D.R. had told him more than once that it was permissible to give the enemy small items which it didn't possess, provided that one was getting things of greater importance in return. Money was to be spent without limit; so Lanny entertained as became an open-handed playboy. He was amused to observe that the blond Fräulein Fridolin was willing to accept Heinrich as a substitute for Herr Budd; this was in accord with Nazi ethics, but, all the same, Heinrich mentioned to Lanny that it was a subject not to be referred to in Berlin-Grunewald where his family resided.

Everything was just lovely in this Axis *Liederkranz.* Lanny had a piano in his apartment, and they sang every time they met. They ate hearty meals in the dining-room—and perhaps none of them ever noticed that all this hospitality took place in Madrid's swankiest hotel, and that Lanny never came to their places, never went out alone with them, and never got into a motorcar, not even a taxi, with them. He wouldn't even visit the Velasquez Club where all the diplomatic set played tennis and swam in the pool. The Germans used one end and the Allies the other; the Spaniards circulated in between. Now and then the Japs came, and then all the others got out and left.

A shy, solitary man, not fond of outdoor life, he seemed content to have paintings brought to his apartment and to spend hours studying them and talking about them. No doubt the Nazis observed all his habits; if so, they discovered that he read newspapers from half a dozen countries and marked and clipped only passages having to do with art matters. They discovered that he was entirely without sex—they proved it by making several tries, with both women and boys, and of course they would not fail to question the porter and the bellboys, who always know what is going on in hotels.

A strange man indeed! Could he possibly be what he pretended to be, an ivory-tower art lover, wrapped up in his specialty and indifferent to the outcome of the greatest war in history? He seemed determined to know everything about Spanish painting; next to that came the Dutch—he read papers from Holland, all that he could get in

Madrid, and others that he had ordered by mail. He persisted in inquiring about living Dutch painters when everybody knew the Dutch weren't doing anything worth while in any of the arts—how could they, when the efficient Nazis had taken them all and put them at war work? This Budd fellow spent days in the National Library in Madrid, reading about Dutch painters and trying to find out which were still alive. Of course the efficient Nazis wouldn't fail to track him, and to find out what books he had consulted and what questions he had asked. Imagine thinking he could keep any secrets in this Fascist city, with the Gestapo and the Spanish police working hand-in-glove on security problems!

VII

The secret came out when the American revealed to his dear German friend that he had in mind to get in touch with an odd character of the Dutch art world, Hans van Meegeren by name. This unsuccessful painter had discovered several remarkable works by the old master Vermeer. They were said to be of extraordinary merit; Reichsminister Göring had paid an enormous sum for one of them called "Christ and the Adulteress." So that was it! This *Bursche* Budd wanted to get van Meegeren to find him a Vermeer, so that he could smuggle it out to America and sell it to some of his father's rich friends for a million dollars! From the German point of view that mightn't be so bad, because any money that van Meegeren or any other Dutchman got the Nazis would take away from him, and it would show up as *valuta* to buy wolfram in Spain or steel in Sweden.

Lanny talked frequently about this Dutchman, who seemed to fascinate him; he wondered where he could find the man's address, and whether the German government permitted the mails to go freely from Spain to Holland. Heinrich undertook to find out and reported that a letter could be sent, subject, of course, to German censorship; it seemed unlikely that there could be objection to an inquiry about an old master. Lanny talked about the extraordinary "Christ and the Adulteress" and another he had heard about, called "Visit at Emmaus," which showed Christ appearing to two of his disciples after the crucifixion. Heinrich thought that was rather silly, but Lanny replied that it was a favorite art subject and, besides, had cost a million marks. "Don't be a Hottentot," he said.

The Jugend official worshiped power and station, and surely didn't want to be that inferior thing; so he talked with other Germans and came back to report that some experts believed the alleged Vermeers to be frauds. To this Lanny replied, "The Reichsmarschall asked my opinion. I told him I believed the painting to be a Vermeer, but even if it weren't, it was so good that it was worth the money. Indeed, it might be worth more, for a man who could fool so good a judge as Göring would be an historical figure, and collectors would want his work as a curiosity."

"Is that why you're anxious to get one?" inquired Heinrich with unexpected shrewdness.

"It's part of the reason," was the reply. "The main thing is that I liked the painting, and so did one of my clients."

"Then," said the German, "I can't understand why you don't go and see the Führer and clear matters up, and then, on the way back, meet this van Meegeren and see what you make of him." Heinrich kept steadily insisting, and Lanny kept steadily refusing.

VIII

Across the foot of a mountain canyon a great dam is erected, by the labor of thousands of men and at a cost of millions of dollars. The waters of a river are pent up and form an artificial lake. A powerhouse is built, dynamos are installed, and transmission lines are run over mountaintops and down into valleys. All is made ready, and then one day an engineer in a control room pulls a small lever, and the waters of the lake rush down through the penstocks; giant turbines begin to turn, electric current leaps in a fraction of a second, and in cities hundreds of miles away an infinitude of factory wheels begin to turn and machines to roar and pound.

So now it was with the son of Budd-Erling: everything had been prepared, and the time for action had come. He had no lever, only a fountain pen with ink in it, and a scrap of paper on which to write words. He wrote only five, all of them short and none especially impressive: "My roses are in bloom." He sealed the paper in a plain envelope, stamped it, and addressed it to a so-called "post office" in Madrid. He hadn't been told the details of what would happen, but he knew the game well enough to imagine every step. The message would be radioed to Washington, and within an hour after it arrived, an OSS agent would take off by plane for New York and from there to Newcastle; he would interview Robbie Budd, even if he had to wake him in the middle of the night, and would present a letter which Lanny had composed and left in the keeping of General Donovan's office. Robbie would summon his trusted private secretary and dictate the text of that letter, have it typed on his impressive stationery—"Office of the President"—and then sign it himself. The OSS man would take the document, and it would be flown in a diplomatic pouch to Casablanca and delivered to Jerry Pendleton. Jerry would pack his suitcase, provide himself with an American passport and a forged Spanish visa, and be flown by way of Tangier to Madrid.

Lanny waited three days, according to instructions, and early one evening he slipped out of his hotel, taking every precaution to make sure he wasn't being followed. After circling several blocks he walked to the Salon del Prado, a natural place for an art expert to be strolling. Out of the shadows a man stepped forth and whispered, "Jerry." Lanny replied with his own name, and that was enough; an envelope was placed in his hands and he slipped it into the breast pocket of his overcoat. He did not stop walking, but whispered, "Wish I could have a talk with you, but it's too risky."

"Sure thing," replied the other, and gave him a pat on the shoulder. Ordinarily he would have said, "So long," but since Lanny had been in Palestine his former tutor thought it was fun to say, "*Sholem.*" He turned and disappeared in the darkness.

Lanny got safely back to his hotel, hugging that precious missive which had cost so much in time, thought, and money, and the services of so many persons. When he got into his room he locked the door and then opened the envelope. He knew the contents pretty nearly by heart, but he had to read it to make sure it was correct.

> Dear Lanny:
>
> Information has come to me from one of your clients that you are contemplating going into Holland to inspect paintings. I am deeply concerned, and am going to the expense of sending this letter to you by special messenger. You have many times told me that you are a grown man and have to have control of your own destiny; but for this once I am hoping you will respect your father's judgment and grant my request to drop this most dangerous project. I do not need to tell you that I have special information, which I dare not put on paper. I simply say to you, with all the urgency at my command: DO NOT GO INTO THE LOW COUNTRIES.
>
> Surely there is no art matter important enough to justify you in disregarding this warning from your father. The fact that I am paying more than a thousand dollars to get this message to you without censorship ought surely to convince you that I have reasons for what I am saying. Stay where you are until summer: or if you must meet your friends, meet them in France. The climate in Holland is damp and unpleasant in spring, and I understand it is a time of bright sun-

shine in Spain. If it is money you need, for heaven's sake draw on me.

I rely upon you to destroy this letter as soon as you have read it.

Your loving father,

Robert Budd

P.S. I am telling your client that I have written this, so you need not worry about failing to keep your promise to him.

IX

Lanny didn't destroy that letter. What he did was to put it back in the envelope, and then take his nail scissors and carefully cut some threads in the lining of his suitcase, and slide the letter down between the lining and the suitcase frame. He figured that the enemy would not fail to find it there, and he took the trouble to set a careful trap to make sure. The OSS men had told him about the minute precautions they took to conceal their photostating of documents, and Lanny had no doubt that the Gestapo men would know all the tricks. Lanny didn't do anything crude like sprinkling powder, or leaving a piece of paper with an edge sticking out of the suitcase. This had to be a really fancy job. He carefully removed one thread from the lining, a brown silk thread two or three inches long; being the color of the lining, it was inconspicuous, and he didn't lay it over the envelope, where it might be noticed, but carefully laid it between the lining and the envelope, held by the pressure between the two.

When the envelope was pulled out, the thread would drop to the bottom of the narrow space, Lanny tried this several times, making sure that its smoothness would keep it from sticking. It would fall into the narrow space, where there was no chance of its being seen; when the envelope was shoved back into place, the thread would be at the bottom, and not where Lanny had delicately hung it. So he would know that the envelope had been removed.

The suitcase was on a chair, and Lanny locked it. He locked his hotel room, being sure that the enemy would be equal to opening these. He went to the telephone and called the Jugend man; the evening was still young, and Lanny had some important news. "Come on over!"

Heinrich came and heard the extraordinary story that an American millionaire had sent a special messenger from Connecticut to Spain in order to carry a letter to his son. What Robbie Budd had said was—so

Lanny told Heinrich—Lanny must under no circumstances go into Germany or any Axis land again; the United States government had become suspicious of him, and he would almost certainly be arrested for treason, and his family would be blackened and shamed. Lanny was terribly depressed over this, it knocked all his plans into kingdom come. So he declared, and Heinrich quite certainly believed him.

"Lanny!" he exclaimed. "This is your great opportunity! Why don't you make a clean break?"

"Just what should I do, Heinrich?"

"Come over to us! Come with me to the Führer and explain everything. Give out a statement that you are with the German people in their struggle against Russian barbarism, and that you know they are going to win this war."

Lanny, playing his carefully thought-out role, looked taken aback. "What good would that do, Heinrich? My statement would be suppressed by the censors in America and it would end my usefulness to the Führer."

"You could talk over our radio and reach the entire world, Lanny."

"I am nothing of a speaker. There would be some curiosity about me, but it wouldn't last more than a few days; the newspapers would set me down as a crackpot, and that would be the end of my influence. You see, I have never been at liberty to tell you what I have been doing for the Führer; I have brought him much information, and he has acknowledged its importance. I have done the same for Reichsmarschall Göring; I have told him not merely about the Budd-Erling plane, but about other war weapons. The Führer sent me to Professor Salzmann of the Kaiser Wilhelm Institute to tell him what I had found out about American work on jet propulsion, and to Professor Plötzen to tell about experiments in atomic fission."

"*Aber*, Lanny, you won't be able to do anything like that now!"

"I expect to go right on doing my best. I can come here to Madrid, and perhaps the Führer will let you come and meet me. You know, I am fortunate in having independent means. Both the Führer and the Reichsmarschall many times offered to pay me for what I was doing, but I have never taken a pfennig from them. So I don't need their consent to go on with my work."

"What a shame, Lanny, that there is a misunderstanding between you!"

"It is something that was bound to happen sooner or later. They have honored me with their friendship, and it was inevitable that I should excite the jealousy of persons around them. I am an enemy alien, and how could I expect to come and go without awakening suspicion? I'm not going to let it get me down; I'm going on working for what I believe, and when the victory has been won I'll take chances on being able to clear my name."

Would Heinrich believe all this? Lanny had no means of guessing, because he didn't know how much Heinrich had been told; he didn't know how much Hitler was able to tell. He knew that Heinrich wasn't very bright; he was fond of Lanny and would want to believe the best. So now Lanny looked mournful, yet courageous, as heroic as any movie actor in Hollywood.

He had the movies in mind, for a special reason. Suddenly he said, "Let's take our minds off our troubles for a while, Heinrich, and perhaps one of us will get a hunch as to the wisest course. I was passing a cinema today and noticed that they have a German film, *Friedrich Barbarossa.* Have you seen it?"

"I don't have any time for shows, Lanny."

"How would you like to go with me now?"

The Jugend leader thought for a moment. "I have an engagement, but I could call it off."

"Fine. There's the telephone."

Heinrich hesitated. "Let's go downstairs. I have to look up the number." Lanny smiled to himself, it was exactly as he had guessed. Heinrich had something to say over the phone that he didn't want Lanny to hear. And Lanny thought that he could guess what it was.

X

In the sumptuous lobby of the Hotel Ritz the P.A. waited, well away from the phone booth. He didn't sit down, but strolled about, looking at faces—it was the fashionable hour, and there were many elegantly dressed people. Lanny was hoping to meet somebody he knew; and here sat a young Army officer whom he had met in General Aguilar's home, El Capitán Gonzaga, all dolled up, his last button polished, his boots shiny and immaculate, his little black mustache waxed and twisted to points. Lanny stopped before him and said, "*Bien venido,*" and then, with his best smile, "Waiting for a lady?" It took no clairvoyance or other occult art.

The officer, arising to return the greeting, spoke with unexpected frankness. "Damn her soul! She is late, as women always are."

"Too bad, too bad, Capitán. Why don't you teach her a lesson? Let her bad fortune be my good."

"What have you in mind, Señor Budd?"

"I am on my way to a cinema and it would delight me to have your company. A German film, very high class, I believe."

"*Carramba!* I don't like their barbarous language. They have forced me to learn to read it, but when I listen to it I am not so good."

"Fortunately I have a German friend who is going along. He can sit next to you and answer questions. It is an historical picture and will improve your education, to say nothing of that young lady's." So one plays with life in the smart world.

A great discomfort was removed from Lanny's mind. He had been smitten by the thought that his Jugend friend, instead of telling the Gestapo to come and get a photostat of a letter in Lanny Budd's room, might tell them to come and pick up this double-crossing spy and whisk him into France from one of the airports which they controlled. But now there would be three in the party, one of them a staff officer of the military commandant of this district, with his sword on his left side and his automatic on his right. It might seem strange that a gentleman should appear thus accoutered to take a lady out for an evening, but it was not strange in Spain. The country was supposed to have been at peace for five years, but it was really in a state of suppressed civil war. Up in the Guadarramas, not more than an hour's drive from Madrid, the desperate guerrillas still hid, and raiding parties came down during the night and held up motorcars on the highway; not infrequently the rebels stole into the capital, hid in the aged five-story tenements, and conducted bold raids from there. No well-dressed person would dream of going into the slums at night, and few ventured there even by day.

Heinrich came from the telephone, and he betrayed no displeasure when he was introduced to a Spanish officer. The three of them strolled down the brightly lighted boulevard and into the darkened theater. Lanny kept his promise and put Heinrich next to the *capitán*, and they watched the career of the red-bearded king of the Germans, here presented not as a Christian crusader, but as a champion and prophet of German racialism, making speeches that might have come out of *Mein Kampf*. Lanny soon forgot the dull show, thinking about the far more exciting one which he believed to be going on in the hotel. He felt pretty sure that Heinrich and his Gestapo masters were not overlooking the opportunity which he had so carefully provided.

XI

Back in his room Lanny turned on the light and locked the door behind him. First, like any timid old lady, he looked under the bed and into the closets; then he went to the suitcase on the chair. He surveyed it, and the carpet around it; there was no change that he could note. He had no doubt that any fingerprints would have been wiped away, and anyhow he had no fingerprint apparatus. With care he held the suitcase steady, turned the lock, and raised the cover. Again there was no sign that anything had been touched; he didn't expect it, being sure that this important job would be done by experts.

There was just one point—the tiny silk thread. Where was it? The least touch or jar might cause it to drop; so Lanny pressed his left hand firmly against the side of the lining to hold the thread in whatever position it happened to be. The envelope was there, he could feel it through the lining, and he began pulling the lining back, a quarter of an inch at a time, looking for the thread. It wasn't there.

Still holding firmly with his left hand, Lanny worked the lining loose with his right, all around the envelope; but there was no thread —until he got to the bottom of the cavity after taking out the envelope. He could feel sure that someone had come and opened that suitcase and taken the letter out, no doubt to photograph it, something which a skilled operator could do in a few seconds. The whole operation, what the OSS called "surreptitious entry," would not have taken the American outfit more than a few minutes. Lanny had given the Gestapo more than two hours.

He had lied to Heinrich Jung about Robbie's letter, and Heinrich would find that out. Lanny had planned it that way, for he wasn't trying to win back Heinrich's trust, nor Hitler's; he had the idea that both of them would find it easier to believe that he would lie to them than that he would tell them the truth. Now, when he got into bed, he could speculate for hours as to whether or not he had guessed their psychology correctly. The Gestapo had in their possession a photostat of a letter which the president of Budd-Erling Aircraft had taken the trouble to send to his son by special messenger, and which that careless son had failed to destroy. The envelope itself was evidence, since it bore no stamp and no postmark. It wouldn't take the Nazis, with the help of the Spanish secret police, very long to find out that an American had been flown from Casablanca to Madrid on that day—and that he had been flown out again that night.

The letter implored the son of Budd-Erling not to go into Holland, but to stay in Spain or in France. The meaning of that was obvious, and the only question was whether the letter was a genuine warning or a "plant." Here was something to make the chiefs of the Gestapo lie awake at night! Lanny could be sure that copies of the letter were already on their way by airplane to Berlin. They would be widely distributed; Himmler would have one, and Göring, and all those who knew Lanny Budd would be called in to discuss his psychology. Experts of many sorts would wrinkle their brows over the problem. *Der Dicke* would take many more benzedrine pills because of it. Adi Schicklgruber, who slept badly and took a variety of drugs on that account, would be another who would torment his brain. "He loves me, he loves me not!"

The verdict would depend in part upon how much and exactly what the Führer and his advisers had found out about this son of Budd-Erling. If they had found very little and had merely wanted to question him, they might still believe that he was something of a boob, a *Tunichtsgut* who wanted to come blundering into a war zone, trying to buy what might be a Vermeer and might be a van Meegeren. On the other hand, if they had discovered him to be a viper who had crept into the Führer's bosom, then they would be apt to judge the letter a clever device.

But they could never be entirely sure; the doubt would stay in everybody's mind and come up at every *Generalstab* council on strategy. It would affect military minds and alter the balance in every decision. If it should have the effect of causing a single division, intended for the Channel Coast, to be held back in Holland, if it caused a single battery of high-powered cannon intended for Cherbourg or Dieppe or Le Havre to be mounted instead at the mouth of the Scheldt or the Rhine, then thousands of American lives would be saved, and the labors of Lanny Budd and the Oh-So-Secret gentlemen in Washington would be justified many times over.

21

Into the Cannon's Mouth

I

LANNY BUDD stayed on in Madrid although he hated it. He was afraid that if he left suddenly he might convey to the Nazis the idea that he had come in order to plant a letter with them. Also, he had made the acquaintance of an official who knew about wolfram concentrates and talked freely. Moving in fashionable society, one heard much conversation about the war, and now and then somebody would drink too much good wine and blurt out a secret. Man is by nature a gregarious animal, and the impulse to share knowledge with other members of the horde is difficult to resist. There was talk about the "Blue Division" fighting on the eastern front and getting severe punishment; about sabotage being practiced in Spanish industries; and even about the plans for a revolution against Franco, whom the old families despised.

The industry of the country, deprived of oil, was grinding slowly to a halt, and the fat little Caudillo was forced to humble his pride; in the month of May he gave way and accepted the Allies' terms. He would expel the German agents whom the Allies had listed; he would stop the attacks of Falangist rowdies on Allied consulates; he would release to the Allies the Italian ships; and he would limit the sale of wolfram concentrates to Germany to ten per cent of his total production. Would he keep that last promise? Franco's officers joked about it in the presence of a genial art expert; there was a black market, and it was notorious that there had always been smugglers in Spain. These jokes were reported in the weekly letter which, with infinite precautions, the art expert managed to deliver to the American "post office."

One result of this settlement was that Lanny lost some of his Nazi friends. Heinrich had already gone; and now others took their departure, including the lady Fridolin. But the Allied list had apparently not been complete, and Lanny turned in the names of Germans who were still active; also of Spaniards and alleged Danes and Swiss and what-nots who had taken the places of the departed. The new arrivals cultivated the acquaintance of the charming art expert who had so much more money than they did. Now and then one of them offered to sell him secrets, but he did not take this bait. They favored him with gossip about El Caudillo's succession of mistresses, and he listened but refrained from comment. When they brought him bad paintings, he politely feared they wouldn't appeal to his clients. Once they brought him a good painting, and for this he paid a little more than it was worth.

II

May is a lovely month in the land of Castile. The sun shines, and the sky is clear; showers fall, and tiny jewels gleam on every leaf and blade of grass. There are delightful gardens, where every sort of flower blooms and the bees and the birds are busy from dawn to dark. Lanny had loved such sights in boyhood; and now a wealthy landowner gave him the use of extensive grounds, with smooth green lawns, a summer house covered with a trumpet vine, a pool with water lilies and gold and silver fish, a sun dial, and many mischievous little statues—cupids, fauns, and satyrs. Best of all, there was a library, and Lanny would take into the garden an old volume of Lope de Vega, full of a wild kind of melodrama which had thrilled Spanish audiences for more than three centuries.

Yes, the world was full of delightful things, and always had been for the grandson of Budd Gunmakers and son of Budd-Erling. There were times when he enjoyed them wholeheartedly; but now he was restless, anxious, and troubled in conscience. What right had any man to be happy in such a critical moment of history? The month of May was the time when all the military experts agreed that the second front must be opened, if ever. The English Channel and the North Sea were unquiet bodies of water at best, and their south shores were those upon which the winds beat hardest. There was no use putting an army ashore unless you meant to keep it supplied, and the days in which you could do that were passing. The newspapers of the whole world explained this and speculated about the date which the Americans called D-day and why it was delayed.

Lanny watched the papers and listened to a radio when he got a chance, expecting news every hour—but none came. The Allied armies in Italy were now fighting their way toward Rome, and that was something, but very little. Where was the big army, the big push? Day after day passed and nothing happened, and there wasn't a soul of whom he could ask a question or with whom he could have a frank discussion. He had to listen to the jeers of his Axis friends and admit sorrowfully that they were right; the Yankees had given new meaning to the word bluff, also the game of poker in which you succeeded by means of it.

Once a week Lanny wrote to his wife, and now and then to his father and his clients. There wasn't supposed to be a censorship of mail between Franco's land and Roosevelt's, but Lanny was sure that letters to him had been opened, and he took no chance with letters going the other way. Those to Laurel were addressed to Agnes Drury and dealt with his art activities, his health, the pleasantness of the climate, the courtesy of the Spaniards, and similar innocuous subjects. Letters that came from Laurel were equally noncommittal: the baby was thriving, her work was progressing satisfactorily, and New York was another place where the month of May was delightful.

But at the end of the month came a different kind of letter, brief and businesslike: "This is to tell you that I have sold three paintings dealing with the life of Moses and am sailing for England in a few days. I have information concerning a fine portrait of the Duke of Marlborough, and the owner has arranged for me to come and view it. If it is possible for you to join me and give me your advice, I should be pleased. I am sure you will be able to interest one of your clients in this unique work of art. My address will be the Savoy Hotel. Affectionately, Agnes."

That surely gave Lanny a jolt. He had married a feminist, and once more she was letting him know that she meant it. She had borne him a baby, but she wasn't going to settle down and take care of it; a baby would keep, but this war wouldn't, and an aspiring writer was going to see some of it for herself.

He had no trouble reading her code. "Three paintings dealing with the life of Moses" meant magazine articles which she had written about Palestine; and as for the Duke of Marlborough, he had successfully invaded the Continent, and now his lineal descendant was planning to give a repeat performance. The "owner" of this "painting" doubtless meant some magazine which had commissioned her to write about the war. Lanny was left to guess whether it was the magazine's idea or whether Laurel's own lively brain had hatched it. Also, whether she would be going as Mary Morrow, Laurel Creston, or Mrs. Lanning Prescott Budd. Surely it couldn't be as Agnes Drury!

III

The P.A. had been thinking for some days that his work in Spain was about done. He had looked at all the paintings he could find and had tried in vain to think of some other device to persuade the Germans that the Allied armada was going to Holland. Now he found himself thinking about London; it had been so long since he had been there, and he really had a lot of information which he could turn over to Rick, a capable journalist who would use it in ways that would not point to an art expert as its source. In England he could surely find out what was going on and break the suspense that had become all but unbearable.

He sent the customary cablegram to his father, saying that he had some art business in London, and was on his way to the Avenida Palace Hotel in Lisbon. He packed his suitcase and his paintings and betook himself to Salazar's capital, certain that Robbie would pass on his message to the mysterious telephone number in Washington and that results would come. He waited two impatient days before a message was brought to him that he had a seat in the plane the next day. How those miracles were performed he never knew; he was in the hands of higher powers, such as mankind had dreamed of all through the ages—the flaming chariot which had come down for the prophet Elijah, the flying carpet which had borne Sinbad the sailor, the *deus ex machina* who had solved all problems for the Greek dramatists.

It was a land plane this time, English, and very comfortable, meant for distinguished passengers: officers in uniform, couriers with dispatch cases which they never let out of their hands, and preoccupied-looking businessmen. Nobody talked about his affairs, and few wanted to talk at all. Lanny had newspapers and magazines for which he had paid multiple prices, so he was content to be quiet. Most of the way he had to read by artificial light, for one of the crewmen came through the saloon and fastened black covers over the windows. Nobody was going to look down upon that sea! Lanny occupied his imagination with what might be there. Once he had seen a convoy, hundreds of vessels, spread out in long lines and leaving a trail of black smoke a hundred miles behind them. This time, he knew, there would be thousands—three thousand, four, five—surely the greatest congregation of ships since men had gone down to the sea.

The P.A. hadn't been told where this plane was going to land, and he doubted if anyone else had. They were ordered to buckle their safety belts, and soon they began to feel the crackling in the ears which told them they were coming down. There was a high wind blowing, and everybody was a bit nervous, but nobody would show it. They felt the wheels touch the ground and discovered that they were at Bovingdon, an airport the P.A. had not seen before. He didn't see much of it now, for there was a bus waiting and they were put aboard and driven at top speed to London.

A funny thing to have a wife and not know her name! Lanny decided that he wouldn't go into a swank hotel and ask for several ladies; he found a vacant telephone booth—something not so easy in this crowded time—and called the hotel. No, there was no Mary Morrow registered. When he asked for Laurel Creston, yes, a lady from New York, but her room did not answer. He left word that Mr. Budd would call and then checked his bags and went for a walk around this unconquered city, the greatest in the world, built on the "unsinkable aircraft carrier." Lanny recalled the joke to the effect that there were so many American soldiers on the island that it would have sunk if it had not been for the barrage balloons holding it up. The Americans were swarming on the streets in many different uniforms; the balloons were visible also, huge fat silvery sausages bobbing about in a heavily clouded sky.

There were almost as many people in uniform as in civvies, the P.A. decided; and more than half the uniforms were from overseas. Some of the GI's hurried, others strolled and gazed, getting their last look at this storied town, noting differences rather than resemblances to home. Two years and a half had passed since these tall lads had begun pouring onto the island, marching and drilling, rehearsing maneuvers on the beaches and the downs, in the forests, wherever there was uncultivated land. The islanders had got used to their unfamiliar words and nasal tones, and made a duty out of taking them into their homes and making them feel comfortable. It had been discovered that some were good and some not so good, just as was the case among the natives.

IV

Lanny went back to the hotel, and this time Laurel Creston was reported in. He went up to her room, and oh, what a sight! Could any husband have imagined it? A wife in uniform, a natty khaki blouse with pockets all over, a short skirt, a saucy cap, and insignia—a captain, no less. On the sleeve was a white brassard with a large letter "C"! That wasn't for captain, but for correspondent. She had up and done this all by herself, and now she was amused by her husband's consternation. It was a feminist's holiday, and he pretended that he didn't dare to touch her until she commanded, "Kiss me, sir!" Only after he had done so did she tell him that hers was only what the Army called a "simulated" rank.

She was only a woman after all and burning with eagerness to tell him this exciting story. It had occurred to her that she was missing a lot of history, and she had gone to the editor who had accepted her Palestine report and inquired, "Why don't you send me over to do the invasion of France?" He had been interested, and there had been an editorial conference in which they had put her through a grilling. The upshot was that they had made application to Washington and the request had been granted. She was not to get near the front—no woman was to have that high privilege—but she would follow behind the armies and write what she saw, subject, of course, to the censors. She had had to fill out half a dozen documents in quintuplicate, and to take half a dozen medical shots, and then they had shipped her across.

It was going to be not merely the greatest invasion in history, but also the most completely reported. Its Commander-in-Chief was a man who believed in publicity—loved it, swam in it like a fish in water—and he had sent that impulse all the way down the line. This was a people's war, and the people were going to know everything about it that would not give help to the enemy. Army, Navy, and Air Force, all were going to have their historians, working in teams and equipped with filing clerks and secretaries, photographing outfits, messengers and chauffeurs and jeeps. All the important newspapers and magazines would have their correspondents, and these would wear uniforms and enjoy military privileges. The women would be "simulated" WAC's—Women's Army Corps, and one of them would be "Captain" Laurel Creston!

"When is it coming?" Lanny asked. It was the question in everybody's mind, if not on his or her tongue. Laurel said, "No one is told, but there are many signs. Our men have been pouring through London, and all going south. Today I noticed what I believe is the crucial sign—the correspondents are disappearing. I wanted an item of information this morning and I phoned a colleague and was told that he was out. I tried another and it was the same. My curiosity was aroused and I tried half a dozen and got the same result. They have been told to disappear, without saying a word to anybody."

Lanny answered, "I was struck by the number of uniforms on the streets. I've never seen anything like it before. The day I left Madrid the newspaper *Arriba* reported there were fifty American divisions in Britain and the same number of British troops equipped for combat. That means something over a million and a half. Of course it comes from German sources and represents what the Germans believe."

"Or what they want the world to think they believe," remarked the wife sagely. "Both sides are doing their best to keep the other in the dark."

Lanny smiled and didn't say what part he had been playing in that effort. He thought he would try out this observant lady. "There seems to be an impression in Madrid that the invasion will be by way of Holland," he commented.

The answer was, "It could be." He was amused to see her doing to him what he had done to her for so many years—keeping secrets!

V

Laurel's first article was to deal with Britain on the eve of invasion. She had been here about a week and had been going about incessantly, interviewing all sorts of people and taking notes. A wonderful people, at a great moment in their lives; they had fought for survival and endured terrific punishment; now their rations were low but their spirits were high. From top to bottom in the social scale everyone knew what was coming, and Laurel hadn't met one who doubted the outcome. The common people expressed their feelings with exuberance, for they were the most sociable of humans and full of what they called ginger. Even the upper classes unbent in the presence of a woman soldier, but never any heroics! Laurel told with amusement of an elderly dowager who had inquired, "My dear, have you seen the tulips in Birdcage Walk?"

Lanny's reply was, "Let's see them!" That was after they had had lunch and had decided to treat themselves to a holiday. No use hovering over the radio, for D-day couldn't begin until the small hours of any morning, and there wouldn't be a whisper about it meantime.

They strolled through streets crowded with traffic and looked at landmarks which Lanny could tell about, for he had been visiting here since childhood, off and on. Many of the landmarks were gone, alas; there were whole blocks that had been laid flat, and few streets that did not have gaps in them. Lanny compared them to the mouths of the Cockneys, who couldn't afford dentistry, and when a tooth ached, out it came and that was the end of it.

Bombing was infrequent by now; but people had heard about new weapons on the way—the Nazis had been boasting about them over the radio for a year or more. By now most people had stopped taking them seriously. Lanny said this was a great mistake. His wife repeated what she had been told, that the reason for the delay was the successful bombing of Peenemünde, where the devilish things were being contrived. Lanny could have said, "I know quite a story about that," but he didn't. He expressed fear that the new weapon might be ready now, to be launched against ships and beaches. All conversational roads led to D-day.

They strolled in Hyde Park and admired the lovely flowerbeds, a source of delight which war had not taken from the people. There was a long path with lawns on each side, and this was the famed place where the Britons who never would be slaves came even in the midst of war to exercise their right of free speech. On a Sunday afternoon they would bring soap-boxes or light platforms and take their stand and begin to orate, and you could stroll along and take your choice of half a dozen different social doctrines and as many religious ones, not to mention astrology and numerology, the evils of tobacco, vivisection, meat-eating, and divorce. You might laugh and jeer, or ask questions, but never enough to keep the speaker from getting his proper hearing. Here and there a bobby strolled, keeping watch, but he seldom had anything to do; he never interfered with the speakers, not even if they called for somebody to murder the King. It was the British idea that the reason they never had assassinations was that they let everybody come here and blow off steam.

There was Rotten Row, a wide bridle path, with a walk for people, and a wooden railing between. Now there were few riders, for most had gone to war, and so had the horses. "What an odd name for a bridle path!" Laurel remarked, and her husband explained that it had once been the "Route du Roi." He took the corruption as an expression of the old-time Englishman's contempt for foreign lingo, and indeed for everything that wasn't on his tight little island.

And then Birdcage Walk, a rather dull parkside walk, but made lively by the beds of tulips. They were of every color and pattern, and nature offered few brighter spectacles. Lanny recalled the days before World War I when his father had been doing business with Zaharoff, the munitions king, and they had called at the Greek gentleman's Paris mansion. He had a Spanish noble lady whom he adored but couldn't marry because she had an insane husband; the lady had loved tulips, and she had told a little American boy about them. "I remember bizarres and bybloemens," the grown-up boy remarked, "but I have forgotten what is which."

The flowers bowed gently in the wind—not a gale, but what the sailors would call a stiff breeze—and that brought their thoughts back to D-day. It was from the north, and Lanny said, "That will be bad on the beaches. They'll hardly try it tonight." It wasn't until later that he heard the story, that the sailing had been set for the previous night but had had to be called off on account of bad weather. Now General Ike and his staff were in a dreadful state of anxiety. Their meteorologists expected the wind to die down, but they might be mistaken, and in any case there would be swells on the beaches. On the other hand, if the landing were postponed, it would have to be for another month, on account of the tides; and here were the ships in the harbor, many with troops already on board, and all exposed to enemy bombers; here was a vast armada approaching from the Atlantic, four thousand vessels in all, and no man could guess how many U-boats lurking in wait for them. To go or not to go, that was the question.

VI

Husband and wife strolled back to their hotel. He had been accustomed all his life to have what he wanted when he wanted it, and now he wanted a radio set. The hotel had none it could spare, so he went on the hunt and found a dealer who could not resist a double price for a week's rental. It had to be brought right away, and it came to the "goods" entrance of the hotel in a wheelbarrow. After that the couple could sit and listen to news from all over the world: the Americans were swarming northward out of Rome, and it was not believed that the Germans could hold anything below what they called their Gothic Line, defending the River Po. The Japanese were being driven back in New Guinea, and oil plants were being bombed all over Germany. About that too there was a story that Lanny could have told, but his lips were sealed.

Concerning D-day you heard, from the Axis radio, speculation, skepticism, and ridicule, and from the British and American radio complete silence. Every day the BBC warned the French Partisans to make no move until they received instructions in the French voices which they had been taught to recognize. Every day the Axis threatened the conquered peoples with dire penalties and reassured their own people by quoting the victory promises of *Unser Hermann*, the fat man whom they adored, though not so ardently as formerly. "The invasion must be beaten off, even if the Luftwaffe perishes," he had declared; it was that kind of war, and both sides were girded for a life-or-death struggle.

The couple talked about Göring, whom Laurel had never seen except in photographs without number. Lanny had told much about him, but nothing in recent years. He was amused to discover that he was slightly embarrassed by the thought of this old-time robber baron. *Der Dicke* had been his host, and Lanny hadn't been able to help liking him in some aspects. Now, how much did Göring know, and what was he thinking about this false friend, this snake in the grass, this double-dyed deceiver? It might be that Hermann's sense of humor would dominate, and he would burst into a loud guffaw over the idea of having been fooled. Lanny had made up his mind that that was how he himself would take it if ever he should meet the *Nummer Zwei*, in this world or the next.

With Hitler, of course, it would be different. Adi was a man with no trace of humor, a man who identified himself with God and took an offense not merely as *lèse-majesté* but as sacrilege. He was a man without mercy and, strange as it might sound, without guile. He thought of himself as a man of infinite guile, but he had gone and put it all into a book and had circulated seven million copies. To be sure, he could figure that nobody but Germans would read the book, and that if others read it, they would be unable to believe it. But in the end all the salient passages had been dug out and quoted, and all the world had caught up with this man of maniacial ego. Lanny could look forward with no pleasure to meeting him, in this or any other world. As for Laurel, she loathed him with a special and peculiar kind of horror. If Adi Schicklgruber were ever taken captive he need look for no mercy from "Captain" Laurel Creston of the Women's Army Corps!

VII

The happy couple slept soundly, and no spirits or psychic entities came to warn them that this would be the great day. During that night a hundred thousand men boarded ships and landing craft in Southampton and other harbors on the English south coast. During that night another enormous convoy came stealing in from the Atlantic Ocean, a couple of thousand vessels, transports, freight ships, tankers, repair ships, hospital ships. Leading the way and bringing up the rear were hundreds of war vessels of every kind and size, battleships, cruisers, destroyers, and small escort vessels darting here and there at speeds up to forty miles an hour. All were equipped with marvelous new devices which enabled them to detect vessels under the sea or on the surface, and planes of any sort in the air. Radio Detection and Ranging was its full name, and the ships had automatic guns of a hundred sizes which could be turned, some of them in the fraction of a second, upon an enemy object thus reported. Their anti-aircraft shells were provided with proximity fuses, incredible little radio devices which drew the shell close to the target and caused it to explode when it was near. Keep out of the way of this new scientific armada!

Sunrise had come early, and the landings had begun a few minutes later. Transocean, the German radio, began telling the news at once; the Germans had nothing to lose by telling—they could be sure the enemy knew what it was doing. The Allies, on the other hand, couldn't be sure how much the Germans knew, so they kept silent. Lanny and Laurel listened to German accounts, in the English language. They told of forces coming ashore on the beaches, all the way between Le Havre and Cherbourg, a distance of about a hundred miles, and of swarms of parachutists being dropped upon the countryside, as far back as Rouen, forty miles from the sea. They were seeking to seize strategic points, destroy bridges, mine roads; the Germans said they were being mopped up, and that, of course, was according to formula.

Three hours passed before the BBC made itself heard, and then it was only one sentence. General Ike's press aide, who had a good voice, interrupted a program with the statement, "In ten seconds I shall make an important announcement." He solemnly counted, "One–two–three–four–five–six–seven–eight–nine–ten." Then, "The invasion has begun on the northern coast of France." Exactly ten words, like a telegram; the Americans were learning reticence from the British. Nobody was going to accuse them of boasting, of making claims, or in any way resembling Hitler and Göring and Goebbels.

Later in the day the correspondents were turned loose to tell what they saw with their own eyes; all carefully censored, but no less thrilling for that. Lanny, who had been over all the war zones, talking with all sorts of men, knew the details and could supply them to his wife. He had watched the landing at Algiers and had seen the paratroopers with their faces and hands blackened for night operations—the Moors had thought them a new race of dark-skinned people, amazing to behold. He had had to bail out from a plane, but he didn't tell Laurel that; he described it as something he had been told about. Besides the parachutists there were airborne troops, whole divisions of them, packed into glider planes, towed by elastic ropes, and turned loose to glide to the ground. During the night preceding the landing the British and Americans had dropped four such airborne divisions and two parachute divisions, somewhere between sixty and ninety thousand men. The planes which had dropped them would return for more, and for loads of supplies. The men had ground-to-air radio equipment and could tell in code where they were and what they needed; within the hour it would be dropped to them.

Such a coming and going of planes had never been in the world before. During the entire time, a couple of weeks, that Lanny spent in London, the roar of planes was never once out of his ears. It was a sound like nothing else on earth, a multiple drone made up of hundreds of individual ones, no one of which could be distinguished. The sound never died for an instant, because as some planes passed, others came on, and all going north or south, pointing the way to the war.

The correspondents told of scenes near the beaches: the transports and large landing craft trailing barrage balloons, to keep divebombers away; the PT-boats darting in every direction, searching for U-boats; the great battlewagons parading slowly, several miles offshore, their spotter planes picking out the targets and radioing the data. There were a dozen American battleships here, more than there had been at Pearl Harbor; some had been sunk there, and had been lifted and made over, better than ever. Some of the old fellows were no longer fast enough for sea fighting, but here, protected by cruisers and a swarm of destroyers, they were moving fortresses, hurling a tremendous weight of metal against the smoke-blanketed shore line.

The Germans had had three years to fortify this coast. They had surveyed and plotted every beach and knew the exact angles and distances. They had mined the entire shore and all the paths, and had blocked every approach with ingeniously constructed obstacles. But on that fateful night midget submarines had crept in and laid beach markers, and a hundred or two minesweepers had worked all night, protected by airplane bombing. Channels had been cleared to the beaches, and up on the bluffs the paratroopers were raiding the pillboxes and dropping grenades into the firing slots.

In some places all this succeeded, and the swarms of landing craft came through the surf and let down their ramps; the combat men poured out and raced over the sand and up the pathways to the top. In other places there was less success, and men were trapped on the beaches and had to dig themselves in under a hail of machine-gun fire.

Many died in the surf and in the soft sand; tanks were wrecked and landing craft sunk; but more came, and all day long the guns of six hundred war vessels and the bombs from several thousand planes found out the enemy's hiding places and wore down his fire power.

VIII

Lanny wanted to do nothing but sit by the radio, and his wife stayed with him. Once he saw tears running down her cheeks; he knew that she was thinking about those pitiful boys, some of them no more than eighteen, trapped in the midst of that concentrated horror, pouring out their life's blood and enduring agonies of pain and fear. He said, "You're going over there, darling. You asked for it, and you'll have to keep your nerve."

"I know, I know," she said, "and I will." But the tears continued to flow, and he shut off the radio and put his arms about her and let her sob on his shoulder. There was something about women which made this necessary; in some mysterious way, physiological or psychological, it did them good. When Laurel dried her eyes she said, "I'm all right now; I'll see it through."

"We have to see this war through," he told her. "Then we have to prevent the next one."

"I keep wondering, Lanny—will any war ever prevent the next one? I hate the whole thing, and in the depths of my heart I'm just as sorry for the German boys as for the American."

"You'll have to keep that out of your articles," he said, smiling, "or your editors will drop you."

IX

Lanny phoned Rick, who came over to the hotel. Nina came into town—impossible to stay quiet on such a day. Now there were two military experts, and two respectful wives to absorb their wisdom. Lanny hadn't seen Nina for several years; she was thinner and her hair was beginning to show gray; she brooded over her boys, but did not let it interfere with her household duties or her support of her husband's cause. Lanny was pleased to tell her good news about her youngest son, her baby; he was in a safe place, for the Germans rarely got a chance to bomb Egypt. Nina exclaimed, "I wish the airplane had never been invented!" Lanny thought, but did not say, "Wait until you see the flying bomb!"

The two men listening to the news agreed that its most surprising aspect was the almost complete absence of the Luftwaffe from the scene. Göring had said that it must stop the invasion even if it perished; but up to noon of that crucial day no more than fifty of its planes had showed up. The conclusion was irresistible—*Der Dicke* simply didn't have the planes to defy the eleven thousand which the Allies had at work. What Göring had he was saving for the counterattack by which the Reichswehr was promising to drive the invaders back into the sea. Another Dunkerque, which Radio Transocean was incessantly predicting, and which Winston Churchill had been dreading for four long years.

This much was certain by the end of that day: the landing had been achieved. The invaders had taken beach after beach, including the fashionable *plages* of Trouville and Deauville, which both Lanny and Rick had visited in happier days. The invaders had climbed the bluffs and were spreading out, joining their paratroopers and glider men, over a front of some sixty miles. The people who were praying in all the churches wouldn't have dared ask for more, and might easily have got far less. The radio reported that in Brooklyn the bearded old men of a Jewish home for the aged had put on their prayer shawls and skullcaps and marched through the streets, blowing the *shofar*, the ram's horn.

Another question—what were the Partisans doing, the French? That was news for which the public would have to wait for some time. General Ike had said over the radio, "The hour of your liberation is approaching." He had told the Partisans to perform those duties which had been assigned to them, and he had told the rest of the population to keep out of the way and do nothing to provoke enemy reprisals. Both Lanny and Rick knew that an elaborate underground organization had been built up; planes had been flown in at night, supplies had been dropped, and a secret army had been equipped. Now, all over France, that army would go into action, blowing up bridges, wrecking rail lines, chopping down trees to block highways, raiding enemy munitions dumps and oil storage depots. These Free French knew the country they lived in, and nothing could be hidden from them; what they couldn't destroy they would let the Allies know about, and the Air Force would come and do the job.

The result of this uprising would show gradually and in negative ways—there just wouldn't be any German counterattack. Plenty of resistance, desperate, hard fighting, step by step backward, but no mass advance, no driving the Allies into the sea. The Germans couldn't get the forces up. They couldn't run trains and they couldn't travel the highways except at night because of the incessant bombing. They would learn the bitter lesson, which they had been teaching the rest of the world, that it is impossible to win a modern war without command of the air; also, that it is impossible to win when the Commander-in-Chief is six hundred miles away from the battlefield, and when he does not trust his commanders, and will not let them move troops without permission.

Oskar had told Lanny about this preposterous situation, and Göring had told him about the helplessness of the Luftwaffe; so Lanny could speak as one having authority, even though he did not name the authority. Eric Vivian Pomeroy-Nielson, an authority on air forces, reminded him of the occasion, in the spring of 1914, when Robbie Budd had taken the two boys to visit Salisbury Plain, where the English Army had been making its first feeble efforts at military flying with a few old biplane "crates" held together with piano wire. The pilots were hoping to shoot at the enemy with automatic pistols, and one bold man had the idea that he might carry a machine gun, lift it with his two hands, and fire it before the plane started into a dive. There had been no augur or diviner to tell the boy Rick that within a couple of years he would crash while flying one of those planes, a crash that would cripple him for the rest of his days.

X

All over the world people sat glued to their radios; uncounted millions in their homes or in public places, hotel lobbies, cafés, cigar stores, wherever they could find a radio set. It was a new way of life, a new kind of adult education that had been developing for the past quarter century and met this great occasion well prepared. The men in the studios read the news bulletins, they commented and explained, they introduced experts, they shifted back and forth between New York and London and the actual war scenes. With the help of those in power who had learned to love publicity, they would set up their apparatus on a battleship and let the public at home hear the great guns going off; then it would be a tank rumbling out of an LST, or an airman just returned from a flight over the battlefield.

By the end of the second day it was clear that the invasion had succeeded; the troops were ashore along a sixty-mile front; they were from five to ten miles inland and were holding while reinforcements and supplies continued to pour in behind them. The bombardment went on, for the big guns of the ships had a range of twenty miles or more and were hurling their shells into enemy entrenchments far inland. The weather was making trouble, but not too much, and the airmen maintained cover over the whole scene, keeping the enemy miserable and blocking the roads behind him.

The four friends stayed together, listening and discussing, arguing and exulting; for each it was a personal triumph, something for which they had waited long years. Eleven years and a half, to be exact, for Lanny and Rick had agreed from the day Hitler took power that sooner or later the democratic world would have to put him down. In the early years it would have been easy, but now it necessitated this colossal battle, which was just beginning and might go on for a year, two years—who could guess? Surely not anyone who was talking over the radio.

Laurel's first article was to deal with the English people in these exciting days: what they thought, how they felt and behaved. Nina and Rick were English people, among the most intelligent, and their minds were laid bare in this crisis. The four would go out and get a meal, and then come back to their vigil. They would telephone to friends, and these were more English people. The chambermaids in the hotel, the bellhops, the porter, the clerk at the desk—all had something to say, something lively and odd to American ears. The people on the streets were bursting with delight, hardly able to keep their feet from skipping, their lips from breaking into song. "Ow, that ole 'Itler! 'E's gettin' 'is!" The old women who sold flowers—the young ones were all in the factories these days—would pat the soldiers on the back, Americans as well as British, and cry, "God bless yer, laddie!" Laurel would come in and scribble in her notebook. 'Ere the fleeting hour go by, Quick, thy tablets, memory!

XI

The Cotentin Peninsula thrusts up from France into the Channel, and at its head is the great port of Cherbourg. Now it was becoming plain that this port was the first goal of the American Army. They held the western part of the beachhead and the British had the eastern; the British goal was the railroad town of Caen, and it was a harder assignment, because Germany lay in that direction, and also the great network of railroads through Holland and Belgium and the industrial part of France. The bulk of the German armies along the Channel were east of the invasion zone, so the British would have their hands full holding on, while the Americans were able to advance. That might be hard on British feelings, but there was no helping it; they had been holding on for nearly five years, all over the world, and it had become their specialty.

The American plan was to cut across the base of the Cotentin, thus isolating Cherbourg, and then taking it. Normandy is the name of the province, and it was from here that William the Conqueror had launched his invasion of England, not quite nine hundred years before. It is a land of granite rocks, and the houses are built of them, and each house makes an excellent fortress—from the point of view of those who hold it. Even when it has been shelled and bombed to ruins, it will be discovered that some of the enemy have stuck it out in the cellars and then come up with machine guns.

The rest of the rocks have been patiently dragged off the fields on sledges and built into fences, or more properly, continuous stoneheaps; the underbrush has grown up through them and covered them, and so the enemy had a series of ready-made fortifications, mile after weary mile. The *bocage* country, it is called, the French word meaning copse. Some of the fields were pasture; others were apple orchards, and in June they were in full foliage, making a cover which could never be entirely destroyed. No matter how much the hedgerows were bombed, there would always be Jerries left in the trenches, with weapons and ammunition in abundance; it meant that thousands of American boys had to die among the poppies, or be wounded and carried back to hospitals in the English coast towns.

Such was the Army's job. Tanks and guns had to be unloaded on the beaches and carried up to the roads. Trucks had to follow, bringing fuel and ammunition. Divebombers and artillery had to blast holes in the *bocage* so that tanks could force their way through, while planes were bombing the next *bocage* to keep the enemy there from interfering. How many *bocages* to the mile depended upon the size of the farms; there might be a dozen or there might be two dozen; each had to be taken, and there was no such thing as outflanking them, because the whole country was the same.

Lanny knew this land, having motored through it on his sort of honeymoon with Marie de Bruyne, when he had had only half as many years as he had now. That too had been summertime, and they had thought it marvelously beautiful; they hadn't happened to think of it from the military point of view. Lanny had just missed World War I, being too young, and while he predicted direfully that another was on the way, he didn't let it keep him from being happy with music and art and poetry and love. Now he described the country to the others, its farmhouses of granite, its chests of ancient oak, its sturdy horses, its sweet cider, and another kind of cider that was sour, with a powerful kick. There were aspects not so pleasant to contemplate—bedbugs, for example. A pious land, with a shrine at every crossroad, it had been a center of reaction through all French history. Now, alas, its crowded little towns would be blown to rubble.

Thus the map of the great adventure was unrolled and spread before them. The British were expecting to take Caen, and then the great harbor of Le Havre; the Americans would block off Cherbourg, and then turn southward and block off the peninsula of Brittany and take the harbors there. Harbors were what the forces had to have, and quickly, if the expected counterattacks were to be repelled. It was only after Lanny got back to America that he learned from Alston of the devices which had been prepared to meet this situation; they were the most elaborate devices ever used in war: two artificial harbors, each as big as the port of Dover, built in movable sections and towed across the Channel.

A job for the Royal Engineers: at twenty-seven different sites in muddy coves scattered around the shores of the British Isles they had dredged out great basins, and in them had built a total of a hundred and fifty caissons made of concrete, each as big as a house. They weighed up to thousands of tons, but they would float because they were hollow; when they were completed, the water was let into the basins, and they were floated out and towed by tugs. Anti-aircraft guns were mounted on top, little PT-boats darted around them to keep off subs, and they dragged barrage balloons against divebombers. Thus guarded, they moved at three miles an hour until they reached the invasion shore. Each caisson had its appointed spot, marked by a buoy, and it had stopcocks so that water could be let in to sink it in an hour. There was a mile-long line of them, behind which great fleets of ships could lie safely.

The sides of this artificial harbor were made by bringing in old ships, assembled from far and near, and blowing out their bottoms with dynamite. Outside, beyond the line of caissons, was a breakwater made of large watertight steel boxes, the shape of cigar boxes; they were securely anchored and served to break the force of the immense waves which beat upon this coast during storms. Inside the artificial harbors were piers made of floating steel boxes ingeniously contrived to rise and fall with the tides—tremendous tides in this Channel, as high as twenty-two feet. As many as seven Liberty ships could unload against these piers at one time. The artificial harbors were known as Mulberry and Gooseberry, and all their various parts had code names, Phoenixes and Bombardons and Whales; the old ships were Corncobs, and the invasion itself was Overlord. In his youth Lanny had wondered who gave all the names to the Pullman cars, and now he wondered who had the job of thinking up these odd military appellations.

XII

The colossal meatgrinder was now working at full speed, grinding up German bodies, and German tanks and planes and guns and transportation. It would grind British and American and Canadian, also—the difference was that the Allies had more of everything than their foes and could bring in replacements. It was a war of attrition, and the side that had something left at the end would be the victor. No use shedding tears over it, that was what the world was like, and you had no other world to live in. The Allied chiefs had said unconditional surrender, and that meant no talking, only fighting.

Laurel tore herself away from the radio and wrote bits of her article. She would bring each one to Lanny and wait eagerly while he read it. He was glad they were good—for what would he have done otherwise? She would write, and then become dissatisfied, and put in something else, and then change her mind, back and forth. John Burroughs, the naturalist, had once declared, "This writing is an uncomfortable business; it makes your head hot and your feet cold and it stops the digestion of your food." Lanny, who had been married to a writer for two years and a half now, decided that it was worse than having babies.

At last he persuaded her that the manuscript was good enough, and then she had to submit it to the censor, another ordeal. While awaiting his verdict, she went to see her commanding officer, a much harassed lady, for this was the first time women had ever been taken into the Army, and it was still a man's world. Laurel wanted to get across that Channel; she would never feel happy until she was sharing the danger and the pain. But they wouldn't let her across; it was no place for a woman. After arguing and pleading and cabling her editors, all she could get was a promise to send her down to one of the Channel ports—on the English side—and there let her talk to the men going across and those who had come back to the hospitals. Surely there was story material in that.

Laurel's husband was having trouble with his conscience, too. He was too comfortable in a de luxe hotel. There ought to be something more he could do to help fool Hitler. He wondered, had he accomplished anything in Spain? Days passed, and the great counterattack did not come; and had Lanny had anything to do with that? Were the Germans worrying about the possibility that this Normandy landing might be a feint, and that the Allies were planning a still heavier stroke in front of Calais, or farther east, in Belgium or Holland?

A picturesque situation over in Normandy: the German commander, Rommel, was facing his old enemy from North Africa, Montgomery. Rommel was the violent man, and it would be his temperament to hit the invaders with everything he had or could get hold of. But the over-all commander was General von Rundstedt, whom Lanny knew from the old days at Berchtesgaden, and also through Emil Meissner, whose friend he was. Rundstedt was a cautious man, who would weigh the consequences and not stake his everything on one throw. Among the factors he was weighing, would there be a letter from the president of Budd-Erling Aircraft, warning his son under no circumstances to go into Holland?

XIII

Lanny cabled Robbie in the usual way and waited for his airplane ticket to show up. Laurel was to leave on Saturday morning; and on the evening of Thursday, the 15th of June, they went to a show, and afterward had a bite to eat. You were always hungry, because meals were so strictly limited; if you had bread you couldn't have dessert. They came in about midnight, and just as they entered the lobby an air alert sounded. They went down into the shelter, the fashionable guests and hotel staff mixed together, something which would never have happened in Old England.

Here was one more chance to observe the English people, and Laurel learned that their reaction was one of boredom; they had thought they were through with this sort of nuisance, and that it was the Germans' turn. Everybody was tired and sleepy and nobody talked. They waited, and listened to the rattle of ack-ack, and felt the ground shake with heavy explosions. Usually these ceased quickly, for there were only a few German planes and they passed on or got shot down. But this time the sirens went on sounding, and the shaking of the earth continued, sometimes heavy, more often light. Disgusted rich people sitting on benches leaned back against hard walls and used bad language under their breath. They had to stay all night, and all day too, unless they got sick of it and decided that they would just as soon be dead.

The P.A. leaned over to his wife and whispered, "This must be it—the V-1's." He had told her about them at the time he had brought Frances to Newcastle; but so much time had elapsed that she had decided he must be mistaken. Most English people had decided that it was just another of Dr. Goebbels' bluffs, an effort to keep his people hoping and working. The German people had decided the same. In Spain Lanny had read that their question had become, "*Wo ist die Wuwa?*" Where is the Wonder Weapon! Even B4, the British Intelligence, was divided on the question; some reports said yes and some no.

But here the damned things were at last! In spite of all the bombing of launching sites, the enemy had got enough of them ready so that some three hundred could be sent over in the first twenty-four hours. A period of stormy weather had been chosen, so that British flyers would have trouble in finding the objects in the sky and couldn't see the sites on the ground. But the people on English ground could see them, and hear them too. They made a loud hissing noise, and a sort of put-put-put like an old Ford engine, but much bigger. So long as you heard the sound you were all right, for the thing was going overhead; but when the sound ceased, as it did suddenly, then look out for yourself! It meant that the power was shut off and the thing was coasting down; you had about two seconds in which to dive into a ditch or a foxhole before it hit the ground and exploded.

What you saw in the air was a plane fifteen or twenty feet across and twenty-five feet long. It had no propeller, but shot out a streak of flame behind. Its speed was about three hundred miles per hour, and only the fastest pursuit planes could catch it; often the thing was over London before they shot it down, and what good did that do—since it exploded just the same? It had the force of a one-ton bomb, and Londoners knew what that meant: houses blasted, fires blazing, people having to be dug out of ruins, dead or dying. It meant women cowering all night in damp and chilly shelters, and children having to be sent out into the country again—all the miseries that Londoners had been enduring for four years and a half.

Laurel said, "You were right about Frances"—and that was some satisfaction, but not enough. Lanny had called Irma on the telephone and told her about the child. He hadn't offered to see her, and she hadn't asked him to come. When his daughter was there he had a right to visit the Castle, but when she was not there it would have been bad taste—besides being a bore. Apparently the new weapons were all aimed at London, but many of them went astray, just as Lanny had predicted, and nobody in the southern half of England could feel safe for a moment.

Rocket planes, robot planes, flying bombs, buzz bombs, doodlebugs, junebugs—the British people had many names for their new tormentors. It didn't take the authorities long to gather up fragments and learn just what was hitting them: steel-bodied, pilotless planes, jet-powered and not radio-controlled. Search planes and bombers would have to be sent after the launching sites, and pursuit planes would have to patrol the coast day and night, find the objects by radar, and get on their tails in the few seconds their speed allowed. In that way more than half of them would be stopped; but London and its environs would never again be free of terror until their armies had fought their way eastward along the coast and captured the nests from which these stinging hornets flew.

Laurel was going to Southampton, and Lanny would have had to get a pass to accompany her; he couldn't because his own ticket might arrive at any hour. Business as usual, in spite of all the instruments in the devil's armory! Lanny saw her to the station, and there they parted, as people do in wartime, knowing that they may never see each other again. "If anything happens to me, take care of Baby," she said, and of course he promised, but added that she would be all right, not so many of the *Wuwas* were hitting that far south. He didn't make a similar request of her, but left her to think that he was going to be safe in the land of his fathers, at least for some time. He didn't suggest the possibility of her giving up this assignment; she had put her hand to the plow and he knew she would go to the end of the furrow. Standing in Waterloo Station, he let her have a little cry on his shoulder; he had tears running down his own cheeks, and didn't have to be embarrassed, for it was one of the commonest sights all over this realm, this England.

BOOK EIGHT

Action in the Tented Field

22

Thou Hast Great Allies

I

LANNY was flown by the familiar northern route, Prestwick to Newfoundland. The earth was at its summer solstice, and afforded an all-daylight trip. When he was set down on Long Island, the first thing he did was to phone Baker and tell him to call back at the New York apartment; then he made haste to inspect that wonderful baby, now twenty months old, who toddled about and gazed with wonder at this big tall man who came in so suddenly, smiled at you so agreeably, tossed you into the air, and taught you new fascinating sounds. The big man went to the telephone and kept his promise to his wife, sending her a cablegram saying that everything in the world was perfect. Then he called his father to report on his own family and ask about the father's. Having performed these duties, he sat down in front of the radio to hear what Raymond Swing and H. V. Kaltenborn and the rest had to report about progress on the Cotentin.

Lanny's appointment gave him several days, time enough to get a car from his father and to call on some of his clients and report on the state of the arts in Spain; time to write a lot of letters and have a talk with Zoltan and consent to another raise in the price of Detazes. Shameless profiteering, but then, what is the value of a painting except what people are willing to pay? The supply was getting lower, and Beauty Budd had to live, and Marceline would need money if ever she got out of Germany alive. Art was art, but it was also business, and objects of beauty were surrounded by hordes of speculators, talking eagerly about prices, and the changes in taste which unaccountably swept over the world and made some things "the rage" and others "old hat." You had to guess; if you had guessed Cézanne and van Gogh you rode on a wave of prosperity, and if you had guessed the Barbizon school you were sunk.

Alston was passing through New York, and somehow he always knew where Lanny was. They spent an evening together, driving up the Hudson on a lovely moonlit night, talking secrets for which the Nazis would have paid many millions of dollars. The old gentleman was beginning to feel his years; he looked tired, as everybody did who was carrying the burdens of this war. Lanny's heart was sad and he wished he could do more. Alston said he helped by being cheerful and keeping a clear view of the ultimate goals. Perhaps also he had been the means of persuading Rundstedt to hold an extra division or two in Holland—who could say?

The slugging match was continuing, and, as always, it wasn't going as fast as you wanted it, as you had dreamed it. They were having the worst June weather in some forty years, high winds and heavy overcast making co-operation between land and air forces almost impossible; the Phoenixes were shifting their positions and the Corncobs were breaking up; the American artificial harbor was about half ruined. Cherbourg, although surrounded, was still holding out, and Monty had been beaten back from Caen. More than a million men had been put on shore, and the efforts to get them what they needed was breaking the back of SOS—Services of Supply. It was by accident that the designation of this Army branch happened to be identical with the emergency call of ships at sea, but the ex-geographer said it fitted exactly in this crisis.

II

Lanny motored to Washington, with the memory of Laurel in the seat beside him; he missed her, but kept himself happy thinking of the service she was rendering. He had brought a carbon copy of her manuscript in his bag, by way of precaution; he called up her editor—not saying that he was husband but just friend—and learned that her copy had arrived and was thought well of. He imagined her under the buzzbombs, talking to wounded men in improvised hospitals—schools, theaters, any sort of place that would give shelter. She would suffer poignant grief, but then she had to suffer in order to write. He recalled the remark of Liszt concerning some woman with a voice lacking in temperament. He had said he would like to marry her and break her heart in order that she might be able to sing.

Highway 1 was crowded with trucks, never so many. They went loaded to the ports, to Philadelphia and Baltimore; they were emptied in record time and came back with raw materials for the factories. Great clouds of smoke poured out from tall stacks all along this route; America was maintaining this greatest war on a hundred fronts all over the earth. Americans were proud of it, and few stopped to reflect that we were exhausting the resources of a continent, sinking the products in the sea or scattering them over the earth—wrecked planes, trucks, tanks, guns, not to mention countless billions of shell fragments that would never be collected.

He put these melancholy thoughts behind him; he bathed, shaved, dressed, and ate a delicious dinner of soft-shell crabs fresh out of the Chesapeake, and lettuce, tomatoes, and strawberries from Maryland—"Anne Arundel strawberries!" he had heard a hawker call as he passed through Baltimore. He sat and read the evening papers; Cherbourg had fallen. The port had been badly smashed by the Germans, but the American engineers wouldn't take long to clear the entrance and rig up some makeshift docks. The American armies were turning south, to keep the Germans from sealing them in the Cotentin. "Keep them moving!" was General Ike's formula.

So the P.A. wore his most cheerful smile when he was escorted to the upstairs bedroom in the White House; he found his Boss grinning like the Cheshire cat. "We did it, Lanny! We did it, and it can't be undone!" They exchanged a strong handclasp on that, and Roosevelt went on, "I can't tell you what a struggle I had over it—more than two years. Winston is the British bulldog, he never lets go."

"But now it's Rommel he's got by the nose," chuckled Lanny. Then he added, "And Rommel is throwing pepper into his eyes." He meant the buzzbombs, and of course the President wanted to know what his agent had seen and heard in London. He had before him a report on a launching ramp which had been captured near Brix, on the way to Cherbourg; it was covered by from sixteen to twenty feet of reinforced concrete, and the engineers declared that a twelve-thousand-pound bomb wouldn't penetrate it, even by direct hit. "The infantry will have to take them all," said F.D.R.

It was a long session, because there was the whole story of Spain to be told: the attitude of the Franco regime, and the extent to which they would keep their word, if at all. "Portugal has just signed up to send no more wolfram concentrates to Germany," the Boss revealed. "We are convincing them, step by step." Lanny said that the taking of Cherbourg would help, but a better persuader would be the taking of Paris. He described the state of shellshock in which the Spanish people lived; one businessman had remarked that he would rather have another hundred years of Franco than another hundred hours of civil war.

The best story was of Robbie's letter, which Lanny hadn't risked mentioning in his reports. He had no copy of it, but he could recite it pretty nearly by heart, and the President slapped the bedcover and gave his favorite exclamation, which was "Golly!" When Lanny said he would never know whether his trick had worked, the other said it was very significant that Rommel had held off and made no real counterattack. Lanny was pleased, but at the same time wasn't sure how much of this Roosevelt really meant; he was such a kindhearted Boss and so liked to make people feel good!

III

"What do you want me to do next, Governor?" Lanny took it as part of his duty not to take up the time of this busiest man in the world.

"Something has turned up that is right up your alley," was the busiest man's reply. "We are organizing a team to handle the works of art that we recover from the Germans. I don't need to tell you what a tremendous job that is going to be; they've been plundering the Continent, and we shall have tens of thousands of priceless objects to dig out of hiding places, and protect, and restore to their rightful owners. I've appointed a commission, and it occurs to me that you might be the man to take charge of the field work."

"Governor, you're paying me a great compliment, but I'm surely not the man. I've never had any experience in managing other people—I've had all I could do to manage myself. That job calls for an executive, a fellow who knows how to open an office and pick a staff and assign duties and see that people do them. I don't know anything about giving orders. I'd hate it so much I couldn't be a success."

"I hate it too," confessed the head of the United States government. "It hurts me to find fault with people, and when I find that a man I like isn't equal to his job, I lie awake nights agonizing over how I can tell him. Generally I wiggle out of it by writing him a letter."

"Or by kicking him upstairs," suggested the P.A. "Giving him a job with a bigger title and fewer duties." This brought a chuckle, and the P.A. went on, "You know, I'd do anything on this earth for you, but it's no good starting on a job that I know I'm not fit for. You find a big, strong-jawed, hard-fisted businessman to run the team, and let me go along and whisper into his ear. I can be a good adviser. I know the languages and the people. I know the salt mines and the castles where the pictures will be hidden, and I know the Germans who have the secrets. I know the threats that will scare them and the bribes that will tempt them. All that might be a lot of fun; but running an office and keeping records and signing checks would worry me to death."

"All right, Lanny. I've already asked the advice of some of the people at the Fogg Museum, and no doubt they'll suggest the right director.

I'll give you a card to them, and you can get their ideas and give them yours. But don't say anything about the secret work you've been doing."

"Of course not, Governor. But, may I take a minute or two more of your time? I've an idea of my own that I think might be important."

"By all means. Shoot!"

"I'm not asking any secrets, but I take it for granted that we'll be landing in southern France sooner or later and going up the Rhône valley. That's the country I know best in all the world; I lived most of my life on the Riviera, and I am certain I could be of use and help prepare the way for the Army."

"You mean to go in ahead of the landing?"

"It wouldn't be as risky as it sounds. I have so many friends there, and some would shelter me. There is one special situation that has fascinated my mind: I think I have told you about the de Bruyne family, whom I have known intimately. The old man is in Paris and I saw him there the last time I came through. There are two sons, who are practically my godchildren—their mother commended them to my care on her deathbed. The elder, Denis *fils*, is on our side, and is now in hospital in Algiers; the younger, Charlot, went with the Vichy crowd and is now a captain in the French auxiliary force which helps the Germans to keep order. The last I heard he was quartered in my mother's old home at Juan-les-Pins, and sent me word that he was keeping it safe. I want to get to him and persuade him to do a Darlan."

That was a phrase which had come to be current in the war; it meant coming over to the Allied side, in the nick of time, just fast enough to keep out of jail or away from a firing squad. "But suppose he won't do it, Lanny?" asked the Boss.

"I think I know how to fix it so that he will. It is my idea to get a letter from his father, ordering him to come across. You know how it is with these St. Germain French, the family and the Church rule their lives. The old man made the boy's marriage for him, and he'll make his Darlan for him."

"What is the old man's attitude?"

"Denis *père* is a businessman, and the last time I visited him I could see that he was ready to come over; he's a heavy investor in Budd-Erling stock and can't possibly want to be on the losing side. By now he must know that National Socialism is *fini*."

"But how can you get to him, Lanny?"

"The Air Force is putting little planes down in cow pastures all over France now, and I can draw them a map of a field not more than a mile from the Château de Bruyne, which is in Seine-et-Oise close to Paris. I was a member of the family, to all intents, and I know the country so well that I could get to the château on the darkest night. The old servants know me and would never give me away. If Denis is in Paris, they can call him home. I'll get the letter to Charlot, and incidentally a lot of information, and the OSS can pick me up and fly me out. It sounds like a dangerous stunt, but it's routine for them and easy compared to some that they do. The point is, Governor, I might not merely bring over Charlot, but all the officers in his group. If he throws his lot in with us, he won't stop there, for he's a bold man, and something of a fanatic. It's my guess he's been in the Nazi service long enough to hate their guts; and even if he won't take my advice, he surely won't betray me. His mother's ghost would rise up before him."

"Well, you know, Lanny, I hate to risk losing you—"

"You won't lose me, Governor. I promise. And anyhow, I'll meet your Fogg Museum people first and unload everything I have, so nothing will be lost. After that, I'll be expendable."

"All right, old man, if that's what you want, I can't say no. When would you want to go?"

"I figure that I ought to be in Juan about a week before the landing. No use going too early, because any plot is bound to leak in course of time. I learned in Algiers that it's a mistake to strike too early."

"I would tell you the date of the landing, but I don't know it. Everything depends upon landing craft—how soon we shall be able to spare them from the Channel. We've lost a number of them, and there's a continuing clamor for them from the Pacific. All I can tell you is, we shall invade France from the south on the day we can get the ships and the planes there. I'm having my continuous fight with Winston—he wants to take us over to the Balkans, but I'm just not picking any quarrels with the Russians in the present state of world affairs. We shall go into France by the Mediterranean if we have to do it alone."

Said the erudite Lanny, "The Rhône valley has been the gateway of all conquerors of Western Europe ever since the beginning of history."

"Exactly so; and when we get to the top we'll just walk around Switzerland and into Bavaria, and block the Nazis' little plan to hole up in the mountains there and make them into a fortress."

"OK, Governor, it's a date!"

"What you do is to talk the whole thing out with OSS, make your plans, and let them call you when the time for action comes. I won't be here, because I'm going to take a long trip." (It was to the Pacific, as Lanny learned later.) "Meantime you can be helping the art people. Also, maybe you can give some tips to another outfit we're getting together—

a bunch of young scientists who are going to dig out everything about the German secret weapons, atomic fission and jet propulsion and the rest that you know about. OSS will put you in touch with them too."

The P.A. said, "You make my heart jump up and hit me under the throat!" He jumped up himself and held out his hand. "I've no right to take any more of your time, Governor. I've got my career laid out for the rest of the war!"

IV

In the old brick building by the gasworks Lanny went through the usual routine: he told his story to General Donovan and his top people, and was plied with questions about the Nazi-Fascists in Spain and about London under the buzzbombs. Everything he said was taken down—they had a marvelous new instrument which recorded what you said on a tiny aluminum wire, and it lasted forever, unless you wiped it off with a magnet. Later they turned him over to the Spanish section, and then to the section which had to do with Operation Anvil, the invasion of the French Riviera.

An interesting experience to the grown-up playboy of Bienvenu! They had detailed air photographs of every foot of the French coast from Mentone on the east to Port Bou on the west; all were numbered and indexed, and you could get any one in a fraction of a minute. Lanny could look down on his mother's home, and the beach where he had played with the fisherboys, and the rocks from which he had dived; he spent hours with a young Air Force lieutenant, marking these maps and answering questions about winds and waves, the temperature of the water, the depths and visibility, the character of the bottom. Maybe the Commander-in-Chief of Army, Navy, and Air Force didn't know when this invasion was coming, but it looked as if this young lieutenant did, for he confined his questions to conditions in midsummer—and summer was already here!

Also, the shore: how high were the rocks and how solid, and what were the buildings made of? Especially important, the photographs showed structures which hadn't existed when Lanny had last visited Bienvenu, two years ago. They might be camouflaged blockhouses, radar stations, anything military. They were studied through a microscope; then an extra set of the photographs was brought and two were placed in a stereoscope. Amazing—the houses, the trees, the rocks rose right up before your eyes!

And then questions about the population: what sorts of people could be trusted and what not? Lanny explained that it was a miscellaneous population, mostly parasitic, and its industries were parasitic. This puzzled the young officer, who had specialized in photography, not sociology. Lanny explained that what they produced on the Riviera was pleasures for the idle rich. He added, "A sort of very old Miami." That was a satisfactory translation.

He couldn't say how many of his old friends were still there. The Americans would have been interned. He named some of the French, including Jerry Pendleton's wife, who was presumably still running the *pension*, perhaps for the Germans—who could guess? Jerry would, no doubt, welcome an assignment to go in there and help prepare the invasion. Lanny desired especially the collaboration of Raoul Palma, Spanish-born Socialist who had conducted a workers' school in Cannes for some years and recently had given the OSS important help in Toulon. They told Lanny that Raoul, alias Bruges, was now the head of an active group of Partisans in the Midi, and they would arrange to have him on hand when the time came to put the P.A. ashore at Juan.

And then the affairs of the elder Denis de Bruyne. The OSS couldn't or wouldn't say whether or not the Army meant to take Paris, and certainly nobody could say when they would be able to; progress was discouragingly slow at present. But to set a man down among the estates and farms of Seine-et-Oise, and to pick him up one or two nights later would be easy enough. Cub planes were going out every night from England, and now from the Cotentin, carrying arms and supplies and money and instructions to the Partisans; since the invasion it had become a big business. No movie writer could imagine anything more exciting, and it was hard for the young people in this organization to keep from telling about their triumphs. But they were all under oath, and they just grinned and said, "We're doing it, all right—and we'll do it for you."

Everything was planned, and code words agreed upon, and the whole project, with a name of its own, Operation Bienvenu, was sealed up and put on file. Lanny was to call a certain man once a week to find out about the prospects. That ended that; and he was turned over, first to the art section, and then to the most secret of all sections, which had to do with German weapons and scientific discoveries. It bore the odd name of Alsos, which nobody could explain. It was so hush-hush that men in the same department had no idea what the others were doing, and a P.A. was warned that when he talked to a jet-propulsion man he mustn't mention atomic fission, and vice versa.

The German section, too, in which he had made many friends, wanted some of a P.A.'s time. All the Germans he had met in Spain had to be indexed, with everything he could tell about their activities and characters. Sometimes the smallest detail might lead to some important conclusion. What was their mood as to the war's events? Was the bombing of civilians breaking their nerve or stiffening it? Was the formula of "unconditional surrender" a help or a handicap to the Allied cause? What had the Nazis tried to find out from a well-informed American? Were they still in love with their Führer, and what would be the effect upon them if the effort to kill him were to succeed?

Lanny never asked questions; but he too could learn things from the questions asked of him. Obviously, those Germans who sought peace by the method of eliminating Hitler would be stirred to fresh activity by the Allied landing in France. OSS men revealed that they were keyed up over this subject and were expecting something to happen. They had a code name for it, Operation Breakers; they asked questions about this prominent Reichswehr general and that, and Lanny was astounded, for it seemed to indicate that this one and that were involved in the plot, and he could hardly believe his ears. But no one had heard anything about either Oskar von Herzenberg or Marceline Detaze.

V

The P.A. drove back to New York and from there to Boston, where, just across the Charles River, the famed Fogg Museum is situated. An old Puritan city, very proud of its culture, calling itself the Hub of the Universe, and not much interested in the spokes. Politically speaking, it had been taken over by the Irish; but its wealthy old families didn't speak politically, they withdrew themselves in cold reserve, and sent their sons to Harvard and their daughters to Radcliffe. When these young people came out, they felt desperately adventurous when they made contacts outside their narrow circle. There were stories such as the one about the New York banker who wanted an employee and made inquiry of a friend in Boston. The Bostonian recommended a young man and gave full details as to his ancestry: to which the crude New Yorker replied, "I want a man for business, not for breeding purposes." The New York wits also delighted to tell about President Lowell of Harvard in the days when William Howard Taft was President of the United States. A visitor came to Lowell's office, and the prim secretary informed him, "The President has gone to Washington to see Mr. Taft."

Franklin Roosevelt was a Harvard man; Robbie Budd had got his more hard-boiled education at Yale, which was perhaps one more reason for disliking the New Deal. As it happened, Esther Budd's family were Harvard, and she had a niece who was a graduate of the School of Art, connected with Harvard and the Fogg Museum. This well-brought-up and delightfully rich young lady had been put on the carpet before Lanny some three years before, when his stepmother had been hoping to find him the right sort of wife. Lanny had dutifully taken her to dinner and a show, but then he had disappeared on his business of trying to save the world from Nazi-Fascism, and Peggy Remsen had become a memory.

He knew that she had completed her course and was a perfectly educated museum director, looking for a museum to direct. In spite of being rich, she must have a job, that being the correct thing for a modern young lady in wartime. That she would get one was certain, for all museums have to raise funds, and none in New England would overlook a chance to gain the favor of two families such as the Remsens and the Budds. Lanny had thought of her the moment that F.D.R. had mentioned the Fogg; it was natural for Roosevelt to turn to Harvard, and it was natural for Lanny to wonder if Peggy Remsen would be one of the experts selected to take temporary control of the museum industry in the Axis lands.

There was nothing especially secret about the Monuments, Fine Arts and Archives Section of the Office of Military Government, United States Army; so when Lanny stopped off to visit his father's family in Newcastle, he mentioned where he was bound and what he had been asked to do. Sure enough, Esther remarked, "Peggy is working with that and expects to go overseas. She is greatly excited and considers it as the opportunity of her life." A curious thing about war, Lanny had observed, it provides opportunities for everybody, even more than there are people to take them. His mind was led to wonder, why couldn't this be arranged in peacetime also? But he didn't say that to his very serious and conservative stepmother, for it might have been taken for a Red remark, or at any rate Pinkish. He said, "I'll look her up and give her any help I can. I've managed to pick up quite a lot of information." He had never given his family a hint of having been in the Axis lands, but it could be that Robbie had guessed, and if so, he might have told his wife.

VI

Lanny found these people in Boston very nice indeed; they were intelligent, conscientious, and completely absorbed in their jobs. They were all in the Army, and wore uniforms, but that was more or less a formality; the Army had recognized them as specialists of a special kind and had put them off in a corner by themselves, so to speak. Family influence might have had something to do with this, but mostly it was the Army's awe of a subject as remote as the other side of the moon. What would a West Pointer know about telling a Titian from a Tintoretto, or how to repair a torn canvas, or how to prevent mildew in an old tapestry, or even how to pack an Aphrodite Anadyomene for shipment in a truck? Obviously, if a young man or woman had spent years acquiring such knowledge and had a diploma to prove it, you wouldn't send him to basic training camp or set her to pounding the keys of a typewriter.

Not when you had to discover, rescue, and protect property which had a money value of hundreds of millions of dollars, possibly of billions! There were single old masters which had been sold for half a million dollars, and others which were literally priceless, because the owners wouldn't have thought of parting with them. No one could guess how many tens of thousands of art treasures there might be, or what condition they might be in, or what difficulties might arise in locating and possessing them. People of the utmost integrity were needed for this job, and President Roosevelt had appointed Justice Roberts of the United States Supreme Court as the head of a commission, and he had turned to the leading museums of the country for the people who were equipped and whose character was such that when they found the crown jewels of the Holy Roman Empire they wouldn't steal them.

Lanny discovered that these young people had a great respect for him. They knew that he came from an old New England family, and that he had made purchases for the Winstead collection, the Taft collection, and others. He had lived abroad, whereas they had merely paid visits; he spoke the languages freely, whereas they were self-conscious and classroomy. Most impressive of all was his acquaintance with the top people in the various countries. He actually knew the Nazis; he was reticent about it, but evidently he had done business with them prior to the war. It was a bit suspicious, but he showed them a card from the President, and after that they guessed he must have been a secret agent—which put them still more in awe of him.

He was there to answer questions, and they gathered round in long sessions. For the first time they met a man who knew at first hand their opposite number, the German organization which they were to check and outwit. The ERR, the Einsatzstab Reichsminister Rosenberg, was named for the Baltic-born racial fanatic who was one of the chief Nazi propagandists. The word *Einsatz* means an enterprise or undertaking, and the whole word is equivalent to our naval phrase "task force." Theirs was a task force for looting, very certainly the most colossal of its sort ever known in the world. The young Americans had read about it, and now listened to the details which Lanny had observed in Paris and Berlin and especially Karinhall.

The looters had taken the Musée du Jeu de Paume, the former handball court of the Bourbon kings, as a sort of clearing house for French art. Everything was brought here, and the best was exhibited to the insiders, and they took their pick. Hitler, of course, had first choice, but of late he had been too busy to exercise it. Göring had second choice, and he was the world's greatest exerciser; he had his men on hand all the time. In various storage places which Lanny could tell about he had more than ten thousand of the greatest paintings of all schools. The best examples decorated the great rooms of Karinhall, which was intended to become a museum, and really was that now, only the public was not invited.

The son of Budd-Erling, who had been invited many times, told about the old-time robber baron's henchmen. The head of the Einsatzstab in Paris was Baron Kurt von Behr, an elderly aristocrat who had once lost his diplomatic post because of swindling. But that didn't matter in these days; he was now head of the German Red Cross, which gave him a pretext for being in Paris, and for having a permanently reserved table at Maxim's for the entertainment of his friends. He was as vain as his chief, and designed himself as many uniforms. He had the most elegant manners, and Lanny told these young people that if they captured him he would chat with them most charmingly and do his best to pull the wool over their eyes—and he would probably succeed, because it would be impossible for anyone who had been born and raised on Beacon Street to imagine such age-old corruption as this Baron represented.

Also there was Dr. Bunjes, head of the Franco-German Art Historical Society, Göring's own special looting group. He had published a pamphlet defending the procedure on the ground that the French might exchange the art works for planes and tanks. And there was Hofer, Göring's "curator," who was doing a good business on the side and might be a good person for the Army to catch. Even better might be Dr. Friedländer, who had been the director of the Kaiser Friedrich Museum in Berlin. He had been arrested and brought before Göring, and *Der Dicke* had given him a choice of destinies, either to go into a concentration camp or to become one of Göring's art experts. The director exclaimed, "But I am a Jew!" To that the reply was, "*Wer Jude ist bestimme ich.*" Who is a Jew is for me to decide!

Another person worthy of their attention was Bruno Lohse, Baron von Behr's assistant, young, blond, tall, and handsome. They must be warned against him, because he would lie to them. This would not be because he liked it, but because it was his duty. He was a true Nazi, and would remain one. That might be difficult for the Americans to understand unless they had read *Mein Kampf;* Lanny made them all promise to read it, for what was the use of going into a foreign land and wasting your time learning by costly mistakes when you could find it all clearly set down in a book that you could buy for two dollars?

VII

The P.A. saw a good deal of Margaret Remsen, called Peggy. She was twenty-one or two, fair-haired and fair-minded, and very agreeable company. Like Laurel she was a WAC captain, and looked natty in her new uniform. If Lanny hadn't been sent off to find out about the atomic bomb in Germany, and if he hadn't got wrecked in a plane and laid up in a hospital, and if Laurel Creston hadn't come aboard the yacht *Oriole*, sailing to the Far East—if all those things hadn't happened, it might well have been that Lanny would have asked Peggy to marry him. But the other things had happened, and that settled the matter; for whatever modern ideas this granddaughter of the Puritans might hold, Lanny was sure there wouldn't be any about sex. She was unmarried, and so far as he could find out, unattached; he hoped she hadn't been cherishing memories of him, and by way of precaution he talked about his wife and what she was doing, and about the little boy who was about to be brought to Newcastle to spend the summer.

Peggy's parents lived in Boston, in a fine home, and that was a pleasant place to come and meet the other "Monuments" people. (There just had to be some way of abbreviating "Monuments, Fine Arts, and Archives Section of Supreme Headquarters of the Allied Expeditionary Forces; so they called themselves the Roberts Commission or Monuments officers or outfit or people.) They would come for tea, or for the evening, and listen to the radio a while, and then talk shop. They were full of eagerness, like small children being put to bed on Christmas Eve to wait for Santa Claus. Lanny Budd, one-man "Intelligence," was asked to explain why it took so long to break through at Saint Lo, and did it mean that the Germans were really invincible, and how far would the Army have to get before they would come upon art objects to be salvaged and stored?

Nobody could have imagined the immensity of this job, and even Lanny was surprised by the thoroughness with which the Army had gone in for it. When the Commander-in-Chief—Cominch in the technical lingo—said "everything," he meant just that. The libraries and museums of America had been ransacked for catalogues of collections, both public and private, all over Europe. Individuals had sent in data —refugees and plundered owners, not merely at home but throughout the non-Axis world. The OSS had contributed the knowledge its spies and secret agents had brought in. There were photographs of every castle, and sometimes of its rooms; photographs of monasteries, caves, salt mines, and numerous other places where treasures might be hidden.

The young art experts of America were going into the most romantic adventure in the whole long story of art. What were the treasures of Captain Kidd and Sir Francis Drake and even of Aladdin's Cave compared with the gems of the Rothschild family and the crown jewels of a dozen monarchs ancient and modern, to say nothing of the altar pieces of the cathedrals of Ghent, Louvain, and Cracow, Michelangelo's statue of the Madonna and Child, and whole rooms full of paintings by Rembrandt, Van Dyke, Rubens, Velasquez, Raphael, Titian, and so on through a list that was like an index to an encyclopedia of the art of painting?

The Monuments people wanted to know, would the Nazis destroy all these treasures, or bury them underground, or carry them up into the last-stand fortress which they were reported to be planning in the Bavarian Alps? And which side would get to them first, the Americans or the Russians? Would the captured Nazis try to buy their freedom with information? And what would be the attitude of the ordinary Germans, would they hinder or help? The young experts thought Lanny was joking when he said, "Take along plenty of cigarettes and chocolates. They will be the currency."

VIII

Then there were the Alsos people, a quite different sort of learned folk. Many were young, like the Monuments, but they were less burdened with family and social traditions and dignities. Some had been farmboys who had got their education the hard way; without exception they were serious-minded persons, and growing more so every day under the pressures of this war. At first it had seemed a marvelous idea, to have all the world's resources at your disposal, to have A-1 priority on everything; but by now they had discovered several flies in this ointment. For one thing, you couldn't ramble, you couldn't follow strange ideas which might flash into your mind; you had to keep yourself pinned down to one special thing which had been assigned to you. And this business of secrecy, not being able to talk freely with anybody but a very small group whom you knew too well, not being able to publish, or to read other people's publications!

So far all scientific progress had depended upon the free and rapid exchange of ideas. A woman in Copenhagen made a discovery, and it was telegraphed all over the world, and within a few days a hundred different men in laboratories from Tokyo to Chicago were at work on the idea, testing it, and speculating as to its corollaries. But now all that was over; everything was hush-hush, and there was a man standing over you with the threat of a jail sentence if you dropped the least hint of what you were doing. Not even to your wife could you tell it, and some wives got cross about it and were harassing their men.

Worst of all was the realization that all your discoveries were being turned to ends of destruction. If you came upon some idea for the production of health and wealth and happiness, you were told, "Yes, that'll be fine, but only after the war." And then you began to wonder, Would there ever be any "after the war"? Suppose this one went on, and another got started, and another? Talking with these young physicists, Lanny discovered that a new and strange set of ideas was beginning to burgeon in their minds. So far they had been entirely wrapped up in their specialty, which they proudly called exact science, with emphasis on the adjective; they had thought that was enough, and some had even thought it was everything and would solve all the problems of mankind. But now they were beginning to doubt, and to confront the horrid idea that they might have to meddle in some of the sciences which were so far from exact that they were hardly worthy to be called sciences at all. Politics, and economics, and ethics, and even religion—for what was the good of giving men tremendous new powerful tools if the only thing they could find to do with them was to kill one another?

"So far in history," said young Professor Oppenheimer, "wars have been fought by soldiers, and it was they who died; the people at home went on working and living. But now war has been brought to the women and children, and we are providing the military men with the means of wiping out the human race."

It was the new weapons that were frightening the physicists out of their wits. Morse's phrase, "What hath God wrought!" had been changed to "What Satan hath wrought"—and the nuclear scientists were Satan, or at any rate his imps. They had gone and done it, by this summer of 1944 they were sure they had done it, and their minds were torn, one-half pride and eagerness to finish, and one-half horror at the thought of what it might do.

You had impulses to turn back and throw the whole thing into the middle of the ocean. But you couldn't, because the enemy might get it. You were in a trap; the brass hats had got you and would never let you go. You had harnessed the power of the sun for them, the power that had kept it blazing for a billion years and would keep it blazing for a billion more, at a temperature of twenty or thirty thousand degrees Fahrenheit. And now the brass was going to use it to shrivel up this pitiful little planet and make it uninhabitable for the rest of time.

IX

In a room of the Physics Laboratory of Columbia University the P.A. had a meeting with four of the Alsos men. They were not the top-flight physicists, but had been chosen because they were young and vigorous and had asked for the adventure. Washington had told them that Budd shared the most crucial of all secrets, so they talked freely in his presence. Like the Monuments people, they looked up to him because he was older and had been all over the territory they were planning to visit. Nobody ever expressed any doubt that they would go there—the only question was how soon. Lanny told them how he had spent two months at Princeton, being tutored by Dr. Braunschweig under the supervision of Professor Einstein, in order that he might know what questions to ask about nuclear fission in Germany. They were immensely impressed and did not lose this feeling even when he added that he had forgotten nearly all the formulas in three years.

The traveler told how he had made contact with Professor Schilling in Berlin. This very important man was just waiting for the Americans to come and get him: he was old and tired, but his head was full of knowledge, and he hated the Nazi gangsters. No doubt he would know others, whose names he had not been free to mention to a secret agent. Lanny told about Plötzen, another top man, whose home he had visited; Lanny had posed as an American traitor, a Nazi sympathizer, but it was possible, of course, that the physicist had guessed something different. Espionage and counterespionage made a complicated game, and you could never be entirely sure of the ground you were standing on. Plötzen was wealthy and elegant, and Lanny's guess was that he would know how to get along with his conquerors. Give him a laboratory and he would go to work cheerfully and make jokes about what had happened under the grotesque Nazis, the *Spitzbuben.*

Salzmann was a different proposition; a grim old Junker, and no doubt a patriot for any German government however barbarous. But he would be sure to hate the Russians, and if he saw he had to choose he would prefer the Americans. Nine-tenths of the educated Germans would, Lanny was sure—for the Russians lived near by, while the Americans lived a long way off and the habit of disliking them was not so deeply rooted. There would be a race for Berlin, and a hunt for scientists even more eager than that for the crown jewels of the Holy Roman Empire. The nuclear physicists had something that would melt all the jewels in the world to a glaze!

It was not only the atom bomb these Alsos men were after; they wanted every scientific secret in the Axis world, and every kind of scientist who might be willing to work for our side. And they were doing the same thorough job as the art people; they had every sort of catalogue and photograph and scientific record, index and card file and map and program. They didn't need Lanny to tell them about the Kaiser Wilhelm Institute, or Peenemünde, or Rjukan.

What they did was to ransack his mind as to every personality he had met and every hint he had picked up as to secrets. All about V-1 and V-2 and V-3; about Red Erickson and the oil refineries, and about Dr. Stoffel and the new process of making wood into sugar—had they heard of that? These particular men hadn't, but if the report had been turned in to OSS, no doubt somebody would be working on it. And then there was Bernhardt Monck, alias Braun, alias Vetterl, and half a dozen other names; he was now in Stockholm, and had once helped to smuggle out a new type of airplane supercharger for Robbie Budd; he had known a whole chain of anti-Nazi people in Germany, and probably most of them were dead by now, but you couldn't be sure. Monck was certainly a man who ought to be taken on by Alsos.

There was also the old watchmaker who had helped Lanny to escape from Germany the last time. He was a Socialist, and Americans had the habit of thinking of a Socialist as some kind of "nut"; but it would be well for the Alsos people to realize that the German Socialists had a philosophy a century old and were the people upon whom any democratic government would have to rest. No production or even scientific work could be carried on without workers, and these workers learned about what they were doing and often understood it better than the bosses. Lanny suggested that one of the first aims of Alsos should be to get in touch with the Socialists wherever they went in the Axis lands, tell them what was wanted, and see how quickly it would be produced. He had given this same advice to the Monuments outfit, for you couldn't move thousands of paintings without workers, and those workers might have no sympathy with the job or the masters and would enjoy revealing the secret hiding places of jewels and *objets d'art.*

X

Laurel wrote once a week as she had promised; and here was another person whose mind was torn. She was witnessing terrible scenes in the hospitals; her heart was wrung and it made her hate war worse than ever. But, on the other hand, she wanted this war won, and it couldn't be won except by fighting men, and they couldn't fight unless you kept up their courage and faith, and your own. Laurel wrote, "I hope the censor will let me say this," and the amused censor had written in the margin, "OK."

The letters came by a delightful new process, called V-mail; they were photographed on microfilm, which was shipped across by airplane and printed on this side. The addressee received a queer little envelope with the address printed on one side and the letter inside; it was folded and sealed by machinery, and the process was quick and saved an enormous lot of transportation. The same thing was done for letters in reverse direction, and it was a great booster of morale; nothing pleased a man in a foxhole or a hospital so much as to get prompt word from the people he loved.

Laurel sent her stories a few pages at a time and left it to Lanny to put together—a great mark of confidence. The most marvelous stories, and all true. She could never know whether somebody had got some particular episode and cabled it, so she asked Lanny to cut out anything he had already seen in print or heard over the air. Episodes both horrible and humorous, the way they are in war. There was one concerning D-day on Omaha Beach, the code name for a landing place where the invasion ran into severe German resistance. The swells were high, the confusion great, and the enemy fire incessant. One GI was clinging to something in the water and a landing craft came drifting by. "Throw me a rope!" he shouted, and the men on the craft shouted back, "You don't want to come on board, we're sinking!" The reply was, "I don't care what you're doing, throw me a rope! I'm sitting on a mine!"

Lanny wrote back and acknowledged every letter. He couldn't reveal what he was doing, only that it was useful and that he expected to return soon and would look her up if possible. He told about the baby and about various relatives and friends; that, of course, was the sort of thing the censors wanted you to write about. He could say that the war appeared to be going well and that he hoped she wasn't in any danger. It was better not to mention what the danger might be. Plenty of love and kisses—but don't make "X" marks for the kisses, for they might be code.

XI

Lanny got together with Jim Stotzlmann, and they talked war and then politics. The Republican convention had been held just after Lanny's return from England; they had nominated Governor Dewey of New York as their Presidential candidate—a cold, self-centered gentleman of whom it had been said that you had to know him well in order to dislike him. Jim said that F.D.R. knew him that well and would take great pleasure in thwarting his cherished ambition.

Now, the third week in July, the Democratic convention was due in Chicago, and Jim had been given leave so that he might attend. He urged his friend to come along, but Lanny said he might have a date with destiny. They discussed the prospects: there was no doubt that Roosevelt would be nominated for a fourth term, so the excitement centered about the vice-presidency. A great many persons, both friends and enemies, doubted that Roosevelt would be able to stand the strain of another four years, so it was possible that in naming a vice-presidential candidate the Democratic party would be choosing a future President of the United States.

The P.A. took in the show by way of the radio, which reported it entire. Nominating conventions are a curious and fascinating aspect of the democratic process; this one lasted three days and nights, with something over a thousand delegates and alternates attending, and an immense concourse of spectators who had come from all over the land, and who spent their time singing and shouting for four years more to add to their twelve. The various state delegations placed their "favorite sons" in nomination and then turned out and paraded through the aisles behind canvas placards bearing the names of their states. To one who had been brought up in Europe it seemed a strange method of determining the future of the richest and most powerful country in the world; but that was the way it was done, and if you didn't like it you could go back where you had come from.

The fight centered about the then vice-president, Henry Wallace, a man who had made for himself a host of friends and an equal host of enemies. As Secretary of Agriculture in the days of the great depression it had been his sad duty to order the plowing underground of crops and the slaughter of millions of little pigs; and millions of people took that as a sign that he was insane. They could not understand that they were living under an insane economic system, which produced enormous quantities of food but didn't give the people enough money to buy it; so farmers and merchants would go bankrupt, banks would close, and that would be called "hard times." After a few years people would regain confidence, they would borrow money and bid up the prices of goods, and that would be a "boom." Every boom was automatically followed by a bust, but you would be unpatriotic if you mentioned that historic fact.

Also, Wallace had said that it ought to be possible for every person in the world to have a pint of milk every day. His enemies took that as evidence of his impractical mentality; they picked out the Hottentots as the most unlikely folk they could think of and said he wanted to give a pint of milk—presumably American—to every Hottentot. The statesmen from the South bethought themselves how awkward it would be if every colored person got the idea of having a pint of milk every day, so they didn't want Henry Wallace to have a chance of becoming President of the United States. They were astonished and a little frightened by the clamor of the workers in Chicago, who did want Wallace and came to the convention hall and said so. All the same, the delegates cast their votes for Senator Harry Truman, whom they knew and liked, and of whom they could feel certain that he didn't have any eccentric ideas. In so doing they were making more history than they dreamed—something which happens frequently to humans, who are fated to live in the present, to forget the past quickly, and have no means of penetrating the future.

It was just at this time that excited reports reached America, to the effect that a bomb had been exploded in Hitler's headquarters, injuring him. How seriously no one could be sure. The man accused of the attempt was a Colonel Graf von Stauffenberg, a name not known to Lanny. He read eagerly every word he could get, fearing that the name of Oskar von Herzenberg might come up; but it didn't. Lanny couldn't even be sure if it was the same group of Army conspirators; it was entirely possible that separate groups were working to the same end. Many executions were taking place, and of course that would weaken the Wehrmacht and bring the defeat nearer.

XII

The break-through in Normandy came in the latter part of July. The British didn't gain much ground in front of Caen, but by constant pressure they held six out of the nine armored divisions which the enemy had, and that helped to make things easier for the Americans. Fifteen hundred heavy bombers saturated the lines in front of the latter—ten bombs to the acre—and after a couple of days of heavy fighting narrow gaps were opened up, and the tanks poured through. The Germans close to the sea had to fall back to avoid being surrounded, and the tanks got among them and cut them up. In a few days the German line had been forced back to a place called Avranches, at the entrance to the peninsula of Brittany. The Americans were out of the *bocage* country at last, and in places where freshly landed tanks could operate freely.

It was the American Third Army, headed by that war-loving old Episcopalian with the two pearl-handled revolvers. Georgie Patton was in his element now, doing the job for which he had been preparing all his life; he was wild with impatience, dancing with excitement, bellowing at his officers and men to keep moving, to get the supplies up, to keep hitting the enemy so that he wouldn't have a chance to recover his balance. The correspondents told about it over the radio, and the whole country listened, the non-Axis world listened, and saw that this was something new, this was the beginning of the end. American industrial power was at last making itself felt, and it was hard not to share the sense of glory—even though you had a traitor pacifist hidden in your heart!

The way of the public throughout this long war had been to alternate between depression and exultation. During the tedious periods of preparation you heard people say it could never be done, we could never conquer the whole of Europe; as for the business of "island hopping," had anybody ever taken the trouble to count the thousands or tens of thousands of islands in the South Seas and how many troops it would take to occupy them? They would watch the mounting public debt and talk about inevitable national bankruptcy; they would look at the casualty lists in the papers and make themselves ill with grief. But then would come a time of action, a landing in North Africa or Tarawa or Normandy, and everybody would cheer up suddenly and begin to figure out a timetable to Berlin and Tokyo.

Lanny had trained himself to resist those mass moods; he had realized from the outset that it would be a long war. But he had a map, and stuck little pins in it, and soon realized that this was a serious break-through. The armored columns, supported by planes overhead, were racing south across Brittany, to seal off that peninsula and its important harbors. Other columns were turning eastward, and that was the way to Paris, not more than a couple of hundred miles away. So Lanny called up the OSS man in Washington and said, "It looks as if it might be time for the first half of my job." The answer was, "Your papers will be ready tomorrow. Come prepared to leave at once."

He hadn't much packing to do: one suitcase, and he guessed he wouldn't take that any farther than London. He went out for a walk in the park to think things over. It was the beginning of August, and a warm day, but he walked briskly because he was so excited. Many times before he had taken trips when it was hard to have hope; but this one seemed like a holiday. He was going to take Bienvenu out of the hands of the Nazi despoilers! He was going to see the GI's with their heavy packs wading out of that blue water and onto the brown sand of the Juan beach, where he had played and swam and fished since the earliest days he could remember. At any rate, that was what he imagined, and it made his step light.

XIII

The P.A. phoned his father to send for the car and then took the midnight train to Washington and got his papers: a passport in his own name, authorizing him to visit Britain, France—we had some of France now!—Spain, Portugal, and North Africa; also a French *carte d'identité* in the name of Henri Jean Marie Girouard, a *permis de séjour* and a *permis de circuler*—all forged, of course, but so well done that they would convince any gendarme or SS-man who might inspect them. There were other papers for Lanny to have in his pocket: a receipt for payment of a grocery bill, a bill for payment on a life-insurance policy, a letter from the imaginary wife of this imaginary Girouard in an envelope with a French stamp and postmark; an entirely satisfactory job, and all Lanny had to do was to study them and remember who he was and the details of his affairs.

He was flown from the Patuxent airport in an ATC plane, a big one fixed up for the VIP's, with seats such as you found in Pullman cars and even an antimacassar where you rested your head. At night the berth was made up and you slept comfortably, if you were not nervous. Lanny's orders were to report to a secret address in London, and when he did so he was taken in hand by a couple of OSS agents who then proceeded to brief him, in a quiet businesslike way which seemed to imply that they had handled a dozen cases that day and had another dozen waiting. They told him that he would be motored to a near-by field, and from there would be flown across the Channel to the American sector. Beyond that they knew nothing and asked not a single question. They would take care of his suitcase, his passport, his American money, his watch, and other belongings; he must have nothing on him that wasn't French. One of them took him to the "wardrobe room" and saw him fitted with a complete outfit of clothing that had come from France and that had obviously been worn for a long time.

He had just time to write a postcard to Laurel and tell her that he had arrived and would be busy for a few days but would get in touch with her later. She knew enough to feel anxious, but to have no hurt feelings. He wasn't told where the airport was—so many new ones had sprung up it was rather hard on British agriculture. He was driven in a jeep, and put in a two-seated dispatch plane, along with some sacks of mail. He was flown westward and then south—this to reduce chances of encountering a German flyer. These came rarely now, the pilot said, but it was no good making things easy for them.

The course was across the Channel, and Lanny could look down and see the hundreds of ships of all kinds and sizes, which at a height appeared to be standing still. He could only hope that among their watchful gunners there was no one who would fail to recognize the American star and circle painted underneath his plane. Presently he passed over Cherbourg, and he observed the hulks of sunken vessels and the live vessels coming and going. There were the Army encampments, the trucks, the tanks on the roads, and many wrecks that had been dumped off the roads in a hurry. There were the smashed farmhouses, the whole panorama of war, seen in a bird's-eye view. Suddenly they were coming down, into a couple of pastures which had been made into an emergency field. Two or three bumps, and the plane came to a halt.

The sun was just going down, and the sky was golden and pink. Lanny got out of the plane, and a young Air Force lieutenant came up to him and said, "Bienvenu?" Lanny nodded, and was escorted into a tent sheltered by a tall plane tree. There was a folding table with a map on it and a couple of camp chairs. Lanny was invited to look at the map; it was one of those wonderful air maps, and there was a spot marked with a cross in red ink. The polite young officer said, "That is the place where you are to be set down tonight. Study it carefully and make sure it's the right place and that you will know where you want to go in the dark."

23

Outrageous Fortune

I

THE PLANE was tiny; it had to be, because, as the pilot said, it must be able to come down on a half dollar. It flew as low as possible in order to escape detection by enemy radar. To be sure, that made a danger of church steeples and tall trees in the darkness; but then, as Frederick the Great had said to his troops, "Do you want to live forever?" The main protection was that so many planes went out at different hours and to different goals that the enemy couldn't keep track of them all. The pilot had an automatic in his belt, but that was for possible use on land; in the air he was helpless and had to take his chances.

How would he find his goal, out there in the black night? He didn't say, and Lanny didn't ask. Obviously, the course could be plotted on a map; such a point of the compass and exactly so many kilometers, and there would be the pasture. But there was wind to be reckoned with, and wind is not reliable. Could it be that the Partisans had been provided wtih a sending set, and sent out a beam which the young Air Force lieutenant would get on his instrument board? Anyhow, they flew for something more than an hour, and suddenly ahead Lanny saw little pinpoints of flashing light, two rows, three on a side. "Right on the nose!" shouted the pilot above the noise of the plane. He dived, and down they came into the blackness. There were two or three bumps, and then the engine died and all was still.

Men came running from all sides. This was the crucial moment, for if the plot had been betrayed, these would be Gestapo men, and they might start shooting; Lanny would see the flash of guns, but might be dead before he heard the sounds. Or, worse yet, the inquisition and the torture chamber for the false friend, the double-dyed deceiver, the worst enemy the Nazis had.

But no, it was all right this time. The nearest man half whispered, "*Bienvenu?*" and Lanny answered, "*Bien.*" He had been carrying a package on his lap during the trip; he handed it out to the man and then climbed out himself. There were other packages stowed in the plane, and the pilot passed them out quickly. Only a few words were spoken, and these low. Half a dozen shadowy forms seized the plane and turned it about and backed it some distance—evidently it hadn't come the full length of the field. At the far end torches began to blink; no doubt there would be a hedge there, and perhaps tall trees. The pilot started his engine, then gunned it and bounced away out of sight; the sounds told you that he was rising into the air.

In the few minutes of turning and starting a hand was laid on the P.A.'s shoulder and a voice whispered, "Lanny!" A woman's voice, vaguely familiar, but he was too surprised to recognize it. "Who are you?" he asked, and the reply was, "Julie Palma."

Raoul's wife! How on earth had she got here? He couldn't refrain from asking, and the voice said, "I was ordered. Everything is OK." He guessed that possibly she hadn't told the others the identity of this secret arrival, so he said no more. She took his arm and guided him, and the others just melted away into the darkness. Obviously it wouldn't do for a group to be seen on any road or path at night. The coming of the plane must have been heard in the neighborhood, and enemies might be hurrying to the spot. Silence!

II

The last time Lanny had seen this old friend she had been working in Paris against the Nazis. Later he had heard that she had gone south to join her husband. Had she come back, or had she been sent especially for Operation Bienvenu? Lanny had told the OSS people that he would like to have the help of Raoul Palma at Juan; it was likely that Raoul had suggested his wife to help at the Château de Bruyne. Perhaps Julie herself might not know how it had happened, but had just been told to come. All day and night the BBC was beaming programs to France, and in them would occur strange sentences which seemed to have no meaning. "Violets are blooming," or "Cleopatra has a cold," or "Aldebaran has been calibrated." In secret places all over France men and women would be listening for the phrase or sentence which had a meaning for their particular group.

Lanny was walking on a dark night with a woman, and he knew that this was the safest thing he could be doing; it had been planned that way, and that was why the men had faded so quickly. A lovely warm night in August, with Aldebaran and several thousand other stars in the sky; there must be thousands of Frenchmen doing the same thing, and even some Germans, and they might all be disposed to let one another alone.

The couple walked. Lanny noted that they were on small footpaths, not roads; he soon became confused, for this wasn't the way he had planned to come. He whispered, "Are we going to the château?" Julie answered, "I have studied the way." He had confidence in her, having known her for more than twenty years. She was competent as well as devoted, and had kept the workers' school going in Cannes during the years when her husband had been helping the Spanish Republican government. She was risking her life every hour that she carried on these intrigues against the Nazis.

They came to a stile with which Lanny was familiar; he had often crossed it on his walks, and it was only a hundred yards or so from a side entrance to the château grounds. The woman said, "We are safe here," and they sat and talked in whispers. Julie told him, "I don't know what you are here for and I don't ask. The orders were to guide you; there will be two armed men in the shrubbery, and you can call them if necessary."

He answered, "I don't think it will be. I just want to have a talk with the family; it may lead to something important." It was then about eleven o'clock, as well as he could guess. "I may have to arouse them," he added. "There is one possibility that troubles me—there may be some new servant who does not know me and who might talk, or even telephone the police."

"There is no new servant, Lanny. Our people here know all about the place and have prepared for your coming."

"I was afraid the old gentleman might be in Paris and they would have to send for him."

"He is here, at least he was this afternoon."

"They used to have a dog."

"They have an old one and keep it indoors at night."

"*La vieille Fidèle!* She will make no trouble for me."

"How long a talk do you want, Lanny?"

"I can't be sure, but an hour or two ought to suffice."

"Make it short, for there is always a certain amount of risk. What do you plan to do then?"

"I was told that your friends would be able to send word, and a plane will come for me."

"That is true. It can come tomorrow night. But where will you spend the day?"

"I had the idea of letting them hide me in the château."

"We advise strongly against that. The reputation of these people is bad, and there are too many of them."

"I have a special relationship with this family, Julie—"

"I know, but I didn't feel at liberty to tell our friends about that. They object that there are children, who can hardly be kept from talking; the whole situation is unsafe, and they want you to leave as quickly as possible and let them hide you. Even if an alarm should be given, the enemy will not be able to find you, and the plane will come to a different spot."

"OK," Lanny said. "I'll come out as soon as I have got what I have been sent for. You will wait?"

"I will hide near by. *Bonne chance!*"

III

The P.A. walked quietly to the château, by the drive which led to the delivery entrance. The buildings were old, of red brick; they were not large enough to deserve any name but villa, but the neighborhood had seen fit to honor the family. Beyond the drive was a high brick wall with a solid wooden gate; it led into the garden, where Lanny knew every tree and shrub; this place had been one of his homes for the half-dozen years that he had been Marie de Bruyne's lover and a family friend, in the accepted French fashion known as *la vie à trois*. On the other side of the wall the apricot trees had been trained to grow like vines, and the fruit would be ripe now, each one carefully tied in a tiny paper bag—that is, if the old gardener was still alive. The peaches would be ripe, and the grapes would be ripening. The lawn would be smooth and green, and no doubt the grandchildren played croquet there, as Lanny had played with Denis junior and Charlot.

The gate was fastened, and it would have been difficult to climb over, on account of broken glass on top. He retraced his steps and came to the front of the house, where there was another lawn, shaded by ancient beeches. All the windows were dark, and he would have to rouse the family; so he lifted the brass knocker and gave three raps, which resounded like gunshots in the silence of the night. He waited; presently a window was opened in the second story, which is called the first all over Europe. A woman's voice asked, "*Qui est là?*" Lanny recognized it as the voice of Annette de Bruyne and answered softly, "A friend with a message from Denis *fils*." The voice said, "*Attendez.*"

He "attended," and presently a light was turned on and the little window in the front door was opened. Lanny whispered his name, and the bolt was shot back, and there stood young Denis's wife, wearing a peignoir; the light made a halo about her blond hair. Lanny knew her well—she had once telephoned him in distress when the police were about to arrest her husband for his activities with the Cagoulards. She had aged and had lines of care in her face, and, of course, a look of great surprise. "Lanny!" she exclaimed, and he said quickly, "I have an urgent message for *le beaupère*. Is he at home?"

The answer was that he was in bed, and Lanny said, "Let me go to his room." One would not have suggested that in a conventional French family unless it was urgent indeed; even so, the woman hesitated. "I have only a short time," Lanny said, "and it is important. Please don't say anything to anyone else until I have talked with *le beaupère*."

She invited him in, closed the door and fastened it, then led the way. "We have put him on the *rez-de-chaussée* now," she explained, and Lanny could guess that the aged man's health was failing and he could no longer climb stairs. They had no *ascenseur* in this old mansion, and couldn't get one in wartime even if they had been willing to introduce anything so modern, so *à l'américaine*. She tapped on the door of what had been the billiard room, and when a feeble voice called, "*Entrez,*" she stepped decorously back and let Lanny enter alone. She closed the door, and being the well-bred daughter of an old Catholic family, went promptly away.

IV

Lanny did not know exactly how old this French financier was, but he knew that he was in his eighties. Lanny had never before seen him in the state in which he was now, with his false teeth in a glass of water by the bedside, his sparse white hair in disarray, and a startled look upon his wrinkled face. It was taking an unfair advantage of him, but Lanny had planned it that way, meaning to jolt him into action and put the job through without a wasted moment. The P.A. had no desire to risk his life for the sake of a man whose ideas were repugnant to him and whose evil ways had wrecked the happiness of one of the sweetest and most loving women Lanny had ever known. A young American endeavoring to repair that damage had been scrupulously polite to the head of this household, but he surely didn't owe him anything, not even truth.

"*Pardon, mon ami,*" he began quickly. "I have come at great risk and dare not stay long. My father arranged for me to be brought here—a difficult undertaking, as you can imagine. It is because of his deep concern for your safety."

"*Mais, Lanny!*" stammered the other. "Who will wish to trouble a broken old man like me?"

"The American Army is approaching Le Mans; it cannot be many days before it is through the Orléans gap; the plan is to surround the whole Seine district, and all the Germans in it will be prisoners. The Partisans will rise, and those whom they consider *collaborateurs* will be in the gravest danger."

"But, Lanny, I have been out of politics for so long!"

"Memories are longer, Denis. You gave money to the Cagoule, and that fact is well known in this neighborhood. You have given support to the Nazis—"

"*Jamais! Jamais!*"

"Perhaps you didn't realize what you were doing; but the Partisans know, and my father is informed through secret Army sources that they have you on a list."

"*Nom de Dieu!* What does your father wish me to do?"

"He begs you to come over to the American side before it is too late. You must realize now that the Allies are going to win. I have had to reconcile myself to that fact and take steps to protect my own safety, just as I am urging you to do."

"But, Lanny, I am without any power. I am old and my health is failing. The Germans are still here, and if I tried to do anything they would shoot me."

"Robbie has a definite step in mind and has sent me to tell you about it. I was in Algiers a few months ago and had a talk with Denis *fils;* he is in a hospital, with a severe wound caused by a shell fragment in the thigh. His life was saved only by transfusions; he is recovering now and will not be lame. But he is dreadfully unhappy because of Charlot. He begged me with tears in his eyes to find some way to persuade Charlot to get out of his present position and save his life. I promised to do what I could; you know, *mon ami*, how Marie prayed to me on her deathbed to take care of them and help them. I gave my word, and I am trying to keep it."

"I understand that. What can be done?"

"Charlot is in the most dangerous position imaginable. All those Frenchmen who have helped the Germans with arms will be treated as war criminals, and either shot out of hand by the Partisans, or else court-martialed by the French Army that is fighting now in Italy. That applies especially to the officers, and Charlot has been one of the most active among them. He is a marked man."

"It is a dreadful situation, Lanny, and I have not failed to realize it." Tears came into the old financier's rheumy eyes, and his little white goatee quivered. His voice was muffled because of his missing teeth, but he was seemingly too agitated to realize it. "What can I do?"

"Charlot is a man with real power, and he is the one who must be induced to act. I tell you in strict confidence—the Allied Armies are about to land on the south coast. I do not know the time or the place, but the event is certain and cannot be more than a week off. The German defenses there are inadequate, and the entire Riviera will surely be in Allied hands. Charlot and his little force will be surrounded and captured. That is my father's judgment, and you must take his word that he knows."

"I have taken his word before and never been misled."

"Robbie has become one of the most powerful men in America. He is turning out planes by the thousands, and the Air Forces are dependent upon him. The sums that will be due you on your Budd-Erling stock when the war is over will be many millions of dollars, and that is a stake worth playing for."

"*Naturellement,* Lanny, but what can I do here?"

"You must use your authority and bring it about that Charlot comes over to the American side at once. You know how it was in North Africa—the men who joined us not merely escaped with their lives, but have kept all their property. I was present in Algiers when Darlan made his choice; and now there is exactly the same situation. It is the hour of decision for your whole family."

"Speak, Lanny, I am in your hands."

"I know how set Charlot is in his opinions, and how proud and stubborn. I am afraid that he would not heed my pleading. So I want you to write him a letter, not advising, but commanding. Use your authority as *père de famille* and tell him what to do. He respects you and will obey as a dutiful son."

The old man's hands were trembling so that he had to clasp them together to stop it. "*Mais,* Lanny! That might be suicidal for all of us here. If that letter fell into German hands, we should be taken out and shot."

"That is true, *mon ami*, and I wouldn't ask you to take such a risk. What I want you to write is that Charlot shall take my advice in the matter. Tell him to obey *me*, and I'll take the risks."

"You have a way to reach him, Lanny?"

"My father has arranged everything. I will get to him and put the facts before him. He won't like them, but unless he is entirely out of his mind he will see that he has no other choice."

"God grant that it may be so. But what are we here to do about our own situation?"

"Your helping Charlot will make all the difference. My father will tell the Army Intelligence people what you have done, and they will inform the Partisans. So, when they come to your door it will be to crown your heads with flowers instead of putting them on pikes."

V

With trembling hands the *père de famille* wrote under the visitor's dictation. Just two lines, on a plain sheet of paper, and with no names: "*Mon fils: Faites ce que notre vieux et cher ami désire. C'est un commandement de votre père.*"

Lanny pledged himself not to reveal the names to anyone, and least of all to the Germans if he should have the ill fortune to be caught. He did not stop to discuss his own change of front or any other news. He said, "It might help if Eugénie were to add her word," and *le père* assented. He got his skinny shanks out of bed—Lanny considerately looked away until he had put on his silk dressing gown. Seeing that he was a bit wobbly, the visitor took his arm, and they went out to the drawing-room, where the wives of the two sons sat in a dim light, waiting patiently for whatever the head of the household might see fit to tell them.

The doors were closed, and the agitated old plutocrat briefly told them his decision. Lanny wasn't called upon to say anything; he left France to the Frenchmen—it was the Army's program. To Annette, wife of the elder son, the announcement came as a shock, for she had political convictions of an intensely reactionary sort. If her signature had been asked, she might have refused. But Eugénie, the younger woman, was the old-fashioned sort; all she wanted was to get her husband back, with no bullet holes through his body. She gladly wrote under her father-in-law's words, "*C'est aussi ma prière.*"

So the P.A. had what he wanted, and he stayed only a few minutes to tell the agitated ladies what he knew about their husbands. They offered him food, but he said no, he was exposing them to danger every minute he stayed in their home. He folded up the paper and put it with the other documents of Henri Jean Marie Girouard, and pledged the three de Bruynes not to mention his visit to servants or children or anyone else. He went out by a side door, and they closed it silently behind him; he stood for a while, waiting for his eyes to get used to the darkness. Neither friend nor foe appeared, and he walked quickly by a path which he knew well to the stile where Julie Palma was waiting.

VI

When the former school directress came out of the shadows he told her, "Everything is done. What next?" She told him that a comrade would be coming soon. He had got through more quickly than they had expected.

They talked in whispers, a man and a woman in the darkness of a warm summer's night, but it was not the sort of talk that was to be expected under such circumstances. Julie told him that she had a job with an importing firm which had offices in Paris and Marseille, so she had a pretext for traveling and had been a sort of liaison officer for the Free French. She had made a score of trips, carrying messages, always in her head. She reported that Raoul was well and exultant over the events of the past two months. Apparently she did not know that Lanny was expecting to go south and to meet him, and Lanny didn't tell her that. He said, "I have been able to help a little, and I'm still trying."

What Julie wanted to know, most of all things in the world, was when the Americans were coming to Paris. He warned her, "Do not be disappointed if they pass you by. Remember, the goal of this battle is not Paris but Berlin. I have heard talk that we may go through the Orléans gap and straight across France to the Rhine."

This horrified the Frenchwoman, who exclaimed, "Oh, Lanny, Lanny! You mustn't fail Paris!" just as if he had been the head of the Allied Combined General Staffs! She went on to point out what the Nazis might do to that most beautiful of all the world's capitals; and how simple it would be to take it, just a few tanks and armored cars flying the American flag! When Lanny ventured to doubt if it would be quite that easy, she went into detail about the situation: three million people, burning up with hatred and ready to explode, just needing some one to give the signal, to speak the word. And they weren't helpless;

some had managed to save weapons from the days of their great disaster, and many of the young fellows had managed to steal weapons from the Germans or to get them from the Allies. All that was needed was to see the Stars and Stripes coming down the Champs Elysées, and Paris would rise to the last man and woman. But they must know that the enemy couldn't come back!

This nervous, high-strung little woman—she was at the age where women are like that—came near to forgetting the danger of her position and Lanny's at that moment. She couldn't accept his statement that he had no influence with the military authorities; she was sure he must at least know people who had. Hadn't he given Raoul and his friends proof of the fact that he knew President Roosevelt and was able to get to him? All right then, let him give the great President—hero to the French as well as to the Americans—this report from one who was living and working with the Free French in Paris and knew all the groups and the parties—the Gaullists, the Socialists, the Communists, and the plain humble people who had no one to speak for them.

They had suffered such indignities, such horrors, and above all shame, that they would be willing to die by the thousands in order to wipe out the disgrace of having had to surrender, and to live under the hated Boches and see them strutting in the streets, pulling wads of paper money out of their pockets and buying up the best of everything in the city. The Nazis had kept the Parisians down by the most abominable system of hostages, a thing that had not been known in Europe since the Middle Ages. Men and women would be seized, perfectly innocent persons, just because they were respected and beloved, and would be held in prison, and ten would be shot if some Frenchman lost his head and stabbed or shot a Nazi in the streets.

"Oh, Lanny, you must liberate Paris! Think of the prestige, the moral effect! All the world will know it, all France will rise up and go into action. For all the rest of our history they will tell how the American Army did it, and our gratitude will become a national tradition!" Raoul's wife became so excited over this chance to send a message to President Roosevelt that her voice began to rise, and Lanny had to whisper, "*Prenez garde.*" He told her he agreed with her and promised that he would find a way to pass on the information. She said, "We have comrades who can tell you exactly what strength the Germans have, and what we of the Resistance can assemble." Lanny answered, "By all means let them do so."

VII

There came a low whistle from near by, and Julie said, "We must go." She led the way, and presently there was a man walking in front of them, just near enough to be followed. They walked on cross-country paths and came to a patch of woodland, and in it was a hut. The man had disappeared, and the woman said, "This won't be very comfortable, Lanny, but it will be safe. You will find sacks to make a bed, and you can fasten the door on the inside. Food and drink will be brought to you, and the password will be Bienvenu."

"Fine," he replied. "How long do I stay here?"

"Until tomorrow night. Of course if a plane does not arrive you will have to wait longer. *Bonne nuit, camerade*."

By the light of the stars, to which his eyes had grown accustomed, Lanny could make out that this was somebody's wood hut and that it was nearly empty. He hoped the farmer had no dogs. He found a pile of sacks, and he wondered how many saboteurs and agents had slept on them in the course of four years. He locked the door and lay down and thought over his problems; he was just making up his mind to sleep when he heard footsteps. There was a tap on the door and the password was whispered low. He got up and opened the door. The form of a man was outlined against the faint light. The man held out a bottle and a package wrapped in newspaper. Lanny said, "*Merci*," and took them.

"Monsieur," said the man very politely, "I should like to talk with you if it would not be any trouble."

"Certainly not," said the P.A. He backed into the hut and sat down on his sacks, and the man sat beside him.

"Monsieur," continued the visitor, "I am a man of the Fighting French, a follower of General de Gaulle. I have two comrades, one a Socialist and the other a Catholic democrat. There are some things we think you ought to hear, and if it is not too late and you are not tired—" He stopped, and Lanny answered: "I am not at all tired, and I shall have all day to sleep."

The man whistled, and two others came in, closed the door, and fastened it. Evidently they knew the place and took seats on the piles of wood. Lanny never saw their faces; they did not strike any light, perhaps because they had no tobacco. They spoke politely, yielding to one another, and Lanny identified them by their voices as Tenor, Baritone, and Bass. Baritone was the one who had come first, and he was evidently an educated man, a doctor or lawyer. Tenor was apparently a slight and nervous person, and young; Lanny identified him with Montmartre and imagined a bow tie and a beret, except that he knew the Nazis had banned the wearing of berets, which was classified among "demonstrations harmful to the state." Bass had a country accent, and Lanny thought that he might be the owner of the property on which this odd *réunion* took place.

The P.A. guessed that Julie Palma had told these men that he was a person of influence, a friend of the great; their first concern was to defend the honor of *la patrie*, letting the outside world know that Frenchmen were daily risking their lives and many giving their lives in resistance to the hated foe. They had no means of knowing whether this fact had reached the outside world, and they hoped this important Monsieur Bienvenu might find some way to make their voices heard.

The world must not suppose that this Resistance had begun only since the Americans had landed; *non, pas du tout*, it had been going on from the first hour of defeat. Thousands of young Frenchmen had wrapped their weapons and buried them, and later had dug them up and taken to the mountains or the *maquis*. The French word for underbrush, *maquis*, had come to be the name for the men who hid in it and came out to carry on sabotage against the enemy. "Monsieur," said Baritone, "we have the enemy's own figures that more than forty thousand Frenchmen have been executed during the occupation, and a hundred thousand are in concentration camps in Germany. This in addition to the quarter million who have been deported."

Lanny assured them that the news of this heroism had not failed to reach America. He listened to dreadful stories of Nazi repression, and to figures as to the number of bridges which had been blown and trains which had been derailed in the neighborhood. Just now the whole population was holding its breath, expecting the arrival of the American troops. Evidently Julie had told them that Paris might be bypassed, for this was the subject they talked about most. They knew Paris, they knew the mood of the people, and that nothing but machine guns and grenades and tanks and artillery kept them in subjection. All that was needed was a small armored force at the city's gates, and the population would rise and barricade the streets behind the Germans and hurl building stones upon their heads. "Monsieur," said Tenor, "I was in Paris only three days ago, and I know on authority that there are now only two German divisions there; but one is armored, and that is our trouble."

No use for Lanny to plead that he had no authority, that the military would decide this question on military grounds. The three voices trembled as they plead: there were three million people in Paris, including the refugees, and they all wanted to work for the liberators. They would produce goods for the Army; they would restore bridges, rebuild railroad track, repair damaged vehicles, be a colossal force behind the armies. "Three million friends are not to be by-passed, Monsieur!" And Lanny assured them that Paris would not be forgotten, Paris would be delivered just as quickly as military security would permit. No use to drive the enemy out and then have him come back and blast the city in a siege.

VIII

The P.A. slept, and only the hedgehogs disturbed him. He slept through most of the day, and then thought about his plans, which had gone well thus far. He waited patiently, and after twilight had fallen in the woods he ventured to open the door and peer out; there was no one in sight, and he locked himself in again. It was about ten before he heard a step, and then a voice whispered the password. He opened the door. It was Baritone. Lanny followed him without a question, and they walked on country paths for perhaps half a mile. Then they came to a pasture, and on the edge of it they hid in some bushes—the *maquis*. "*Ne parlez-pas,*" the man whispered, and they made not a sound.

Suddenly Lanny's escort sat up and cupped his hands behind his ears. The sound of a plane. Instantly the *maquis* sprang into life, the flashlights began to wink up toward the sky and down again. The roar of the plane came near; it dipped fast and came to rest on the meadow. The flashlights went off; the men ran out, and there was the same business of taking off packages and turning the plane about and backing it to the limit of the field. It was one of those tiny cub planes, perhaps the same which had brought Lanny, but the pilot was different.

Baritone had escorted the passenger and given the password; now he said, "*Montez,*" and then, "*On les aura.*" The engine started up, and Lanny held his breath; it was truly a frightening thing in darkness—suppose the field wasn't long enough or the trees too tall? But no doubt the field had been measured and photographed, and possibly the trees had been topped; anyhow, the plane rose. The mysterious silent man at the throttle knew what was below him and what was in front; the passenger had nothing to do but sit there and hope that no wandering Heinkel or Junker night fighter would swoop down upon them, a hawk upon a carrier pigeon.

IX

Not that kind of bad luck, but another! They were flying west, toward the American sector. Black clouds loomed ahead, hiding the stars —one of those sudden thunderstorms which come from nowhere on summer nights. Lanny didn't hear the thunder for the noise of the plane, but he saw lightning flashes and realized that they were heading straight into the heart of the storm. The pilot swerved and shouted into the passenger's ear, "We have to keep out of that!" He began talking into his radio telephone, and Lanny couldn't hear what he was saying; he knew enough to be sure that the pilot of an unarmed plane would never call the ground except in an emergency.

The P.A. had been in a plane wreck once before and surely didn't want another. He had no parachute, and apparently the pilot had none; they flew too close to the ground to make such recourse possible. Lanny could only sit and wonder. Did the pilot plan to fly around that heavy black storm, or was he looking for a place to land? They were headed toward the south, and he guessed they were looking for that strip of *la belle France* which the American forces had taken in their eastward drive.

The helpless passenger thought that there must be some routine for situations like this; surely these little cubs couldn't stand heavy weather. The plane came lower, and suddenly bright lights flashed forth, directly ahead, and there was a field, with planes lined up on each side of it. The pilot dived, and down he came, and in half a minute they came to rest on the ground. The instant the wheels touched, the lights went off again. The glimpse Lanny got suggested another cow pasture but a bigger one; and so it was. The moment the Army made sure of a new district, their first procedure was to clear an "airstrip," so that "flying boxcars" might bring in supplies and fighter planes might be that much nearer to the enemy.

The pilot stepped out and his passenger followed, and in a jiffy the little plane had been run off the field into one of the waiting rows. The pilot said, "That storm will blow over in a few minutes, and we'll go on." Lanny replied, "OK." But then, as a field officer came out to get the pilot's report, another idea occurred to him. He asked the officer, "Where are we?" And the answer was, "Air headquarters of the 117th Division, Third Army." Then Lanny asked, "Are the general headquarters near?" And the answer was, "We don't give that information. What is it you want?" Lanny said, "I am an OSS agent, and I have some news that might be of immediate interest to your commanding officer. Could I have a telephone?"

The officer escorted him into a tent. There were several phones on a folding table. The officer took one and gave a number, just as if he had been calling in town; he reported what Lanny had said, listened, and then hung up. "This way, please," he said, and took Lanny outside and put him into a jeep with a soldier. "Take this man to General Young." Lanny stepped in, and they went bumping down a road without any lights; how it was done he couldn't figure, but presumably no one minded if the jeep turned over, because it was so light that you could set it back on its wheels, anywhere except on the side of a house or in the ocean.

X

They came to gates and turned in to what evidently was a fine estate, with a gravel drive and a double line of trees; unfortunately a number of the trees had been either shot down or cut, and pushed off to the side. They halted at a large mansion; many staff cars were parked before it. The mansion loomed high in the starlight, but large sections of it were missing and you could see the stars where the walls should have been. They went up some steps partly blocked with rubble; two sentries stopped them, but passed them when the soldier said, "The General's orders." They went into an entrance hall and then into what had been an elegant drawing-room. There were two or three candles burning inside, giving just enough light to see rugs and tapestries, upholstered armchairs and well-polished tables, and also that one corner of the room had been shot away and the wreckage dumped back against the wall.

Seated at a table, with maps spread before them, were two officers, one a two-star general and the other a colonel, both tired-looking overworked men who hadn't time for a bath or a shave. Lanny was aware that he himself didn't look like the glass of fashion; he was purposely ill dressed and had had no chance to wash his face or hands. The officers introduced themselves, and Lanny gave his real name and explained that he had been to the outskirts of Paris on a confidential mission and had talked with four members of the Resistance there, one of whom had just come out of the city. He repeated what they had told him about the strength of the German forces and the attitude of the population.

After they had asked some questions the superior officer said, "The

Chief ought to see this man." The other assented and remarked to Lanny, "General Patton is here on an inspection trip. He'll see you if he isn't asleep."

Lanny replied, "If necessary, I'll wait, because it's important. My plane can go on without me, and you can send me to England when you have a spare bucket seat."

The colonel rang for an orderly and gave him a message. The man went away and came back with a report that the General would see Mr. Budd. Lanny followed the orderly to a part of the mansion which the shells had missed and was escorted into a very elegant lady's boudoir, all fixed up in French fashion with ormolu and pink silk, double curtains at the windows, ruffles and lace on the bed, and perfume and rouge bottles on the dressing table. In the middle of these incongruous surroundings sat the khaki-clad warrior, on a gilt Louis Quinze chair with spindly legs, in front of a table of the same super-elegant period. He was reading, and the binding and shape of the volume told Lanny that it was a Bible; his quick eyes took in the fact that it was open at the last third, and he wondered if Georgie Patton was preparing himself for the conquest of Germany by reading the Sermon on the Mount.

XI

Fully accoutered, and wearing the two pearl-handled revolvers, the commander of four hundred and fifty thousand men looked up but did not rise. He was nearly sixty, and his hair was white and sparse; his face was long, and in repose somewhat melancholy. Without any preliminaries he demanded, "Well, what have you to say to me?"

He was one more tired man, and Lanny made allowances for him and came at once to the point. "General, I was sent on an OSS errand into Seine-et-Oise, close to the suburbs of Paris, and I have learned that the Germans have only two divisions in Paris, that the whole population is ready to rise the moment the first American troops appear."

"Who told you this?" snapped the commander.

"I talked with four active leaders of the Free French—"

"I don't pay any attention to those bastards. They are a bunch of Reds."

"The one who gave me the firsthand information, General, is a Catholic."

"It don't make any difference; they're all yellow. They quit cold, and we're not counting on them. We're winning this war with Americans."

"I understand, sir, that the French have been doing very well in Italy—"

"Goddamit, man, who sent you here to argue with me?" The warrior's lined and tired face took on the color he so intensely disliked.

"I'm not trying to argue with you, General; I'm telling you facts. I have lived most of my life in France and I know the people. The moral effect of taking Paris would bring you millions of allies—"

"Goddamit, man, I tell you we're not taking Paris, we're taking Germany!" Georgie was an old-fashioned cavalryman, and his every sentence contained a mention of either the First Person of the Trinity or the Second; Lanny observed that he never mentioned the Third—perhaps he had overlooked it, or perhaps he was afraid of it. He had a great variety of invocations and expletives, and two modes of speech, or dialects, one of which he employed in the presence of men and the other in what was called mixed company. Lanny had been about the world enough to know that this was supposed to be the way of a "he man," and he thought it rather silly. Also, he knew that he was poorly dressed, and unshaven, and that this declassed him.

"General," he continued patiently, "it would take an armored force not more than three hours to drive from Orléans to Paris; and Paris is nearer to the Rhine than Orléans."

"Jesus Christ, man! Have you come here to tell me how to run my Army?" The warrior hit the spindly table a thump with his heavy fist.

"No, General, I'm just telling you that if you don't send a task force to take Paris you will be making the worst blunder of your career."

Patton leaped to his feet. His face was purple now, and he called Lanny a very bad name indeed, and didn't smile while he said it. But Lanny smiled, for he thought he knew his man, and that it was essential to stand up to him. "Keep your temper, General," he said. "I am here as a friend, trying to save you from a humiliating experience. If you don't take Paris of your own impulse, you will be made to."

"You are an insolent dog and I ought to have you shut up in the guardhouse."

"No, sir, you won't do that, for you're not a Nazi, even though you try to appear one. I have risked my life going into enemy territory with false papers in order to get information, and I bring it to you free of charge. I make allowances for the fact that you are carrying a heavy burden, and perhaps are overstrained and short of temper. That is why I do not resent your bad manners and report you."

"Report me? Who the hell would you report me to?"

"You command the Third Army, General. Don't forget that there is

General Bradley, and General Eisenhower, and General Marshall, and finally a Commander-in-Chief."

Such were the steps in the military ladder; and there was something in Lanny's tone which caused this half-soldier and half-actor and whole-boy to stop and reflect. "Who the hell are you?" he demanded.

"My name is Budd, General."

"Budd, what Budd?"

"You have heard of Budd-Erling no doubt. I think some of our planes are overhead now."

"So you're telling me that you're Budd-Erling?"

"It happens that my father, Robert Budd, is president of that company and its founder."

"You expect me to believe that?"

"I don't know what to expect, General. I was surprised to discover that you had so little self-control. In the book you've been reading it is set down that he that ruleth his spirit is better than he that taketh a city."

"Now look here, Budd." The warrior's tone had changed with surprising suddenness. "How am I to know when a man comes in on me without any credentials and starts telling me my business—"

"I point out to you, General Patton, that a secret agent going into enemy territory does not carry credentials. I have none on paper, but I have some in my head. Suppose I tell you that on one of my recent visits to President Roosevelt I told him about a letter he had sent you to be delivered to the Sultan of French Morocco, and how you insisted upon revising that letter without the President's knowledge or consent."

"The hell you say! May I ask how you knew that?"

"It happens that I am a friend of one of our vice-consuls in Morocco, who brought the letter to you. I am sure you must remember the incident."

The blood had gone out of the warrior's face, and it looked even more drawn and tired. Lanny waited, with malice aforethought, to compel him to reveal the curiosity he felt. "And what did the President say?"

"He wasn't amused, General. But I think he will be amused when I tell him about this interview. Also, I haven't the slightest doubt that he will agree with me that it would be a grave error of strategy to leave the people of Paris at the mercy of the Nazis an hour longer than necessary. The city is like a boiler with the safety valve tied down; there is bound to be an explosion, and perhaps a frightful massacre, and not merely all France but the whole world will ask why we didn't prevent it when we so obviously had the chance. Be sensible, General, and listen for a few moments: you naturally think about military power, but the President has to think about moral power too—prestige, morale, whatever you choose to call it. He is playing a game of world politics and knows what it is to electrify our friends and to depress our enemies. Paris is not merely a center of romance, of beauty, *la ville lumière;* it is a great manufacturing center; the enemy is getting the products now, and we can have them for the taking. You will have to fan your armies out—they can't all move on one road—and if you fan a hundred miles to the north and go through Paris, that involves very little delay. Believe me, you won't have to hold the city or to govern it; the French are all ready to take over, as I saw them do in North Africa. And the road from Orléans to Paris is a fine highway; I have driven it scores of times from my home on the Riviera."

There was no more cursing. "All right, Budd," said the two-gun warrior. "I'll think it over. And no hard feelings, I hope."

"None whatever. Perhaps I was tactless in my approach."

"I like you, Budd. I respect a man who stands up to me." He held out his hand and they exchanged a clasp.

"Thank you, General," said the P.A. and started to leave. He was stopped by a word from the fighting man. "And by the way, Budd, do you have to tell the Cominch about the bad reception I gave you?"

Lanny was tickled, and a grin spread over his features. "Patton, I'll make a deal with you. I love Paris. I have a host of friends there, the real people, not those who live by preying on tourists. I hate to think of what those Nazi beasts might do to the city. You send a few tanks there and save it, and I promise to sing your praises for the rest of my life, and never say one word that isn't glory."

The whole-boy Georgie Patton had a sense of humor too. "Go to hell!" he said. "I'll do my duty, and you goddam highbrows can make what you please of it."

XII

The pilot of the cub plane had waited. The time was nearly up, for his orders forbade him to be caught over the Channel by daylight. But he had been told that Lanny was with the commander of the Third Army, and he was impressed. The storm had long since passed. The plane took off without incident and flew low toward the west, and then north, retracing the path which the famed Third Army had taken in its victorious rush. No enemy planes appeared, and Lanny was set down on a secret American field near London—we had built them all over the "unsinkable aircraft carrier," and when the war was over they would be a problem, because the English people would need potatoes more than planes.

The P.A. wrote out his report and entrusted it to the OSS men to forward; it would be in Washington in twenty-four hours, they assured him. Then there was another briefing; he was to be flown at once to the Mediterranean—he had barely time to telephone to Laurel and let her know that he was alive and well and sorry that he couldn't come to see her.

Since he was going back into France, the clothes he had on would serve; he wouldn't need his passport, because OSS would give him a special card that would save him questioning and would be taken up at Ajaccio, on the island of Corsica, the last Allied point at which he would call. He wasn't allowed to write his instructions down but had to learn them; and while doing this he had a chance to take a bath and shave. He was flown to the Bovingdon airport, and with an armful of newspapers and magazines he settled in a comfortable chair on a DC-4 transport, strapped his belt around him, and absorbed himself in the latest news of what the Third Army had been doing. Oddly enough, the news was two days behind what he had seen with his own eyes, for the Army never gave out the names of places until after the enemy had broadcast them. What the enemy didn't know wouldn't help him.

A wide swing to the west to avoid the perils of Francoland, and the plane came to the Rock of Gibraltar. It had once been a symbol for security, but now, with its crowded harbor and still more crowded airport, it would have been a "sitting duck." Göring had known that and had been ready to put it into his bag; the Führer had broken his Number Two's heart by changing his plans suddenly and attacking Russia instead. Most of the powerful guns which *Der Dicke* had installed on the land side, in Spanish territory, had been taken away and set up on the Channel coast, where they hadn't been good enough. The wild monkeys which hopped about in the trees on top of the Rock were still alive, so, according to the tradition, the British title to the place remained valid.

Lanny changed planes and was flown to Algiers, a hot and sultry spot in August, and a place for him of many memories. A wide ample harbor, ringed with tall white houses, and a background of green hills and high barren brown mountains, it was now a great Allied air and naval base, a distribution center for several fronts. Lanny had just time for a visit to Denis *fils*, who was now moving about on crutches, waiting for strength to come back into his damaged leg.

The P.A. was not free to tell Denis where he had been or where he was bound for; but for the *capitaine's* peace of mind he made up a story to the effect that *le père* had managed to get a letter smuggled out to Robbie Budd, saying that he and all the family were well. This, of course, did Robbie no harm and did Denis a world of good. He said, "You wouldn't tell me if you knew, Lanny, but I have learned from many signs that an invasion of France from the south is impending. I am praying God that poor Charlot may find some way to escape."

XIII

The plane that took the traveler to the island of Corsica was another bucket-seat job; it carried freight, laced tight with a spider-web of ropes, and passengers were a superfluity. Fortunately the trip took only a couple of hours. With Lanny there rode two other civilians, both young; one gave it out that he was a specialist in citrons, a sort of large thick-skinned lemon which was grown on the island, and the other said he was a specialist in the various disease-bearing parasites which interfered with work at the harbor. From the first moment Lanny had a different idea about them both, and he was not surprised when they turned up to continue the journey to the mainland.

The P.A. had never been to Corse, as the French call it, and knew only two facts concerning the island—that it was the birthplace of the Bonaparte family which he did not admire, and that its high mountains were inhabited by bandits. When the plane came over the harbor of the capital he discovered a well-enclosed bay, and a city crowded into a small corner of it. Amazing how human creatures like to pack themselves together! Here were buildings as tall as those in Algiers, and streets so narrow that Lanny saw two laden donkeys unable to get past each other. Ajaccio was a place of laziness and poverty, but like all other places in the war zones it was enjoying plenty now; there was a market for everything it could produce, and ships crowded its docks. There was a swarm of the new American landing craft, and the P.A. didn't need to ask anybody what that meant.

The new arrival was in the hands of the Navy. A wide-awake Intelligence officer took him into a small cubicle in an office building and informed him that he was to be taken in one of the fast motorboats and put ashore west of Cannes at approximately midnight. The distance was about two hundred miles, and they would leave an hour before sunset, the first part of the journey being in waters well guarded by American land-based planes. His further instructions were contained in a sealed envelope, marked "Bienvenu," which the officer gave him. When he opened it he found some well-worn French money, and orders to report to an address in the Old Town of Cannes with which he was thoroughly familiar—it was less than a block from where the labor school had been conducted in an old warehouse.

The traveler was free to take a walk and stretch his legs, and find himself a razor, a toothbrush, and a comb of French manufacture. He observed that the town was full of Allied soldiers. He got a bath, a shave, and a meal, and promptly at the hour specified, no standing around and attracting attention, he reported at the dock. The speedboat waiting there was about twenty feet long and had a one-inch gun in the bow, one that could be aimed either horizontally or vertically. Lanny was amused to see the two young "scientists" make their appearance; the three smiled knowingly, but talked only about the weather.

The little vessel pulled away from the dock, put on power, and shot out of the harbor. The weather had been delightful now for weeks, grand fighting weather for Georgie Patton's tanks and the planes which covered them, and the same for all operations in the Midland Sea. There was a breeze, just enough to kick up green and white waves, which the speeding little boat lifted up by its bow and scattered in showers over the deck. The passengers went below, for it wouldn't do for them to be wet when they came ashore. A member of the crew handed each of them a small can; he hoped they wouldn't need it, but his smile belied his words.

And sure enough, the wind rose, and the craft began to leap and buck. The three civilians became violently sick, turned a pale green, and lost their interest in helping to win the war. Sucking fresh lemons from Corsica did them no good, and the best the crew could do was to give them hard sea biscuits and candy to keep in their pockets, so as to restore their strength when they got ashore. Sea biscuits of French baking and candy of French manufacture—Naval Intelligence overlooked no smallest detail.

XIV

It was a miserable five or six hours, shut up in a tiny box with barely room to move their elbows; Lanny thought that the human race had never appeared more disagreeable; he would lean back and doze, but then somebody would waken him with violent retching. No wonder that seamen looked down upon landlubbers! These were very new seamen, but the weaklings had been weeded out. They knew that the passengers were going in on dangerous errands, so they tried not to patronize them.

Time passed. The violent heaving of the little craft died down, and a young ensign touched Lanny on the shoulder. Lanny followed him up the companionway, and when his eyes got used to the dim light of the stars he perceived that there was a still smaller craft on board the motorboat, one of those tiny kayaks which had set Lanny ashore south of Rome. It was made of wood and canvas, shaped like a bathtub and no bigger. The engines of the motorboat had been running slowly and softly, and now they stopped, and the craft drifted and came gradually to rest. The city of Cannes was blacked out, and so was the harbor, and Lanny could see nothing; but he had been shown a map with the spot marked where he was to be put ashore, outside the harbor, west of the mole. Now he trusted to a well-trained navigation officer who had secret ways of knowing exactly where he was.

Everything was still but the lapping of the waves. Not a word was spoken, and the men on deck wore soft overshoes; the enemy had his own secret ways of protecting his coast, and at any moment searchlights might flash out and a torrent of fire be poured upon the tiny craft. The officer in command gave a signal, and the kayak was laid down upon the water; a seaman stepped carefully in, and a paddle was handed to him. The passenger was helped down and took his seat, with his legs bent up and his feet packed out of the way of the seaman's. The kayak was pushed away by hand, and the paddler went to work. Lanny could tell by the sound of the surf that they were near to the shore.

When they reached it they did not touch the rocks. The seaman whispered to his passenger to lean to one side, to balance the craft while he got out on the other side. After he procured a footing on the slippery rocks, in water above his knees, he had Lanny stand up and take a piggyback ride, for Lanny must not be wet. After setting him ashore the seaman went back to the kayak, dragged it ashore, and dumped out the water which had splashed into it. He managed the feat in silence, then launched the kayak again and paddled away. Presently Lanny heard the engines of the motorboat start up, not too loud, and heard the sound fade into the distance.

Lanny was in France again, this time among the scenes of his childhood. He couldn't see them, but fond recollection presented them to view, and he enjoyed the wonderful sensation of being on something that didn't leap and buck and upset the tiny balancing apparatus in his ears and thus throw his whole nervous system out of order.

24

Tongue in the Thunder's Mouth

I

THE TRAVELER restored his strength by eating French biscuits and candy. He was in no hurry, for he was sure that no alarm had been given; the searchlights would have been used if such had been the case. He relied upon the Navy enough to think that he knew where he was, and there was plenty of time to reach his destination before dawn. When he felt stronger he got up and tiptoed over the rocks, away from the sea.

There were buildings, looming large and dark. Presently there was a path, then a highway, and then a railroad track; Lanny realized that the Navy had slipped up and put him too far to the west; he was close to that Villa de l'Horizon which had belonged to Maxine Elliott, retired American stage star. The railroad passed so close to her house that when a train roared by everything shook; you could hardly keep from closing your eyes, as if you expected to be hit. On the side toward the sea there was a swimming pool, and by it Lanny had sat and listened to Winston Churchill, clad in a red dressing gown and a big floppy straw hat. He had been writing his memoirs of World War I, and had declared that his political career was over, his party had put him permanently on the shelf. How little the cleverest of men understands his world!

Lanny didn't mind walking on the Route Nationale by starlight. He kept a careful watch ahead for flashlights, a sure sign of the enemy, for civilians could no longer get batteries. When he saw one he made a wide detour, and so came into the Old Town, with warehouses and small factories and whole blocks of tall tenements, ancient and ill cared for and packed with human beings. In times of peace, on warm summer nights like this, you would have seen people sleeping on doorsteps or with their backs against walls; but now they stayed indoors in spite of suffocating heat, and Lanny couldn't be sure whether it was because of a curfew, or because the Gestapo and their hired French agents were roaming the streets, picking up men of all ages, shipping them off to labor in Germany or on fortifications along this coast. The P.A. realized that his pocketful of papers wouldn't help him much, for the more he convinced them that he was Henri Jean Marie Girouard, the more certain they would be to give him a job. When he heard voices he crossed the street, and when he saw several people together he backed up and went along another street.

He knew the streets well. As a boy his Uncle Jesse had taken him into one of these dingy tenements and introduced him to a woman Syndicalist, his first contact with the labor movement. She had struck a spark in his soul, and he had grown up to become a young idealist, out of touch with the life of this Coast of Pleasure, the playground of all the wasters of Europe. He had met Raoul Palma, a clerk in a shoestore, and had helped him to start and keep going a workers' school, where Socialists and Communists and Syndicalists and all shades and varieties of these could meet and argue their ideas. Lanny had been the friend of all, and he wondered what had become of them, and which, if any, he was going to meet now.

II

The address given him was a tobacco shop, and it was shut up tight at this unlikely hour. There was a narrow alley alongside it, and, knowing the ways of the underground, he guessed that this might be the reason for its being a place of rendezvous. He groped his way into the alley and found there was a side door; he tapped on it softly, and it was opened so promptly that it startled him—there must have been somebody sitting right by the door, waiting. He whispered, "Bienvenu," and a woman's voice said, "*Entrez.*" The door was shut and bolted behind him, and he followed down a dark passage; the woman struck a match and lighted a candle, revealing a small storeroom with a cot in it, and a man lying on the cot. The slight sound awakened him; he sat up, and Lanny saw his old friend Raoul Palma.

This Spaniard had been in his youth one of the loveliest human beings that Lanny had ever seen; a painter had chosen him for the young St. John the Evangelist. He had delicately chiseled features, rich dark coloring, and an expression mild yet ardent. His dream was of a happy world order, to be attained by the co-operative working classes, and he had clung to that dream through a quarter of a century of disappointments. He lacked a sense of humor, but had loyalty and a quiet determination which shrank from no danger. Now when Lanny saw him it was a shock, for the bones stood out in his face and his coloring was gone; he was younger than Lanny, but he looked like an old man and one who hadn't had enough to eat for a long time.

That did not keep him from starting up with an exclamation of delight and two kisses delivered in French fashion. Lanny noticed that he didn't call him by name, and Lanny took the hint. The last time they met Raoul had been Bruges, but he might be someone else now.

The woman had left the room without a word, closing the door, and these two friends sat on the cot and spoke in whispers. Raoul said, "I have been so worried about you. You must not go out on the streets. They are picking up every stranger, and they are out day and night."

"How are you managing it?" Lanny asked.

"I am used to it and know the tricks."

Lanny didn't say how many tricks he himself had been forced to learn. He replied, "When I asked for your help I expected to take your advice. Have you been told what I'm to do?"

"I was told nothing except that 'Bienvenu' wanted me. I came from Toulon, and it was a difficult trip. Yesterday we got the code message over the radio that you would arrive tonight, so I was expecting you."

"Good service, I must say! You have a group here?"

"A strong one, and on tiptoe for action."

"You know that the Allies are about to invade?"

"We have known that for weeks; everybody knows. They say a hundred thousand people have left the Riviera in the past month; everybody who has the money, or any place to stay in the interior."

"How did they know it, Raoul?"

"Oh, there are reports of shipping activities in near-by Mediterranean ports; the assembling of landing craft there; the bombing of Toulon and Toulouse and military objectives all along the coast. Your planes have bombed out the radio-finding stations, and when you did that in Normandy the invasion came only a few days off."

"I see you are well informed, old man."

"There's the logic of the situation; everybody knows the defenses here are weak and that it's a long way from Germany. You will land here and march up the Rhône valley, join with the northern armies, and cut France in two."

"Just how weak are the defenses?"

"There's a lot of stuff on the coast, but it's a shell; there's nothing much behind it. The moment we rebels get the signal, we'll cut all the communications. What the Germans have here now is all they will ever have. If only you bring enough to get ashore and stay."

"I'm sure we have no other idea. That too is the logic of the situation."

III

Lanny knew that he could trust this friend, and, more important, he was authorized to do so. He told about the false papers he carried, his visit to Seine-et-Oise, and his meeting with Julie. Since her husband had not heard from her for several weeks, this was glad tidings. Lanny described the visit to the Château de Bruyne, the letter he had got there, and the use he planned to make of it.

The Spanish Socialist's voice was grave as he answered. "I thought of this as something you might have in mind, but I turned it down as preposterous. I must warn you that the man you have in mind is one of the very worst of our enemies. He is Darnand's righthand man, and Darnand is perhaps the most hated man in France, not even second to Laval. We know him from of old, because he operated here in Nice, where he was one of the leading Fascists. Now he's the Gestapo's French agent; his hands are stained with the blood of thousands of French patriots."

"I know all that; but we are trying to win a war and to save the lives of Frenchmen as well as of British and Americans. Don't forget that there are going to be French divisions among those which attempt a landing on this coast. If we can seduce Vichy Frenchmen away from opening fire on them, is not that what you call the logic of the situation?"

"I grant all that—if it can be done. But the idea sounds like madness to me."

"You must leave that to me, old man. I have been thinking about it for a couple of years, ever since we were planning the landing in North Africa, and I met Denis *fils* there. You must understand, both these brothers are honest men who sincerely believe in what they are doing. I have known Charlot since he was a boy, and I have a special hold upon him."

"You must realize that you'll be taking your life into your hands when you go among that gang."

"A lot of our men are taking their lives in their hands, and they'll be doing it on the Côte d'Azur very soon. If I can manage to have some of the guns badly aimed against them, it's surely worth the risk."

"Then what do you expect to do, Lanny? Convince our crowd that young de Bruyne has come over to them?"

"I expect to tell them the truth, and I expect you to back me up. They don't have to love Charlot—they can call him a timeserver and a double-crossing scoundrel—but they'll have to let him alone, as they did Darlan and Lemaigre-Dubreuil and the rest in Algiers."

"And let your Army put them in power over us as they did there!"

"That's something for the future; that's for the French people to decide, and you will be free to have your say and cast your vote. But you can't do it unless we win the war."

Raoul gave up. "*Bien*, you want to meet de Bruyne. How do you expect to do it?"

"That is something on which I seek your advice. I was told that he was living at Bienvenu. Is he still there?"

"So our people report."

"I might just go there and ask for him. But that might embarrass him, whichever way he decides. He would have to account for me, and it might awaken suspicions. On the other hand, if I sent a note to him, the messenger might be questioned, or the note might be read by someone else. I'm inclined to think the best way would be to telephone; he would know my voice and would come wherever I told him to."

"But if he came over to our side, the enemy would get busy on every clue. A telephone call can be traced."

"It should be from a public booth. And where shall I tell him to come?"

They both knew the city and discussed various places. In the end Lanny decided upon a program of boldness; he would go to the fashionable Hotel Métropole and register as Henri J. M. Girouard, order a room, go upstairs, and telephone Charlot to come there. Under police regulations Lanny would not have to report himself for a full day, and meantime he would be through and gone. Raoul objected that it might be suspicious for a man to arrive in Cannes when everybody else was leaving; but Lanny said that suspicions took time to crystallize, and he wouldn't stay long enough. Raoul said the *maquis* had friends among the hotel staff, and a guard could be set up to protect Lanny in case of trouble; but the P.A. vetoed that. He was relying upon persuasion and surely wouldn't take the chance of telling a number of persons what he was doing. If there were spies in a palace hotel, there would also be spies among the Partisans.

IV

Dawn was approaching, and Raoul would not let his friend walk into the fashionable part of the city. He asked for an hour's time and went away; when he came back, Lanny followed him out to the street, and there, dimly visible, was a small one-horse cart such as French market gardeners use. A woman was driving, and Raoul whispered, "Cover yourself up, and if anyone lifts the cover she will say that you are ill." Lanny could guess that he looked it, for the few bites of food he had had were a poor substitute for what he had lost.

"I will telephone the hotel tonight," Raoul said; and the P.A. climbed in and drew the canvas cover over him. The cart rumbled away at a walk, as French farm horses go unless violently disturbed. After half an hour of bumping the cart stopped, and the woman's voice said, "*Ici, M'sieu'*." He got out and saw that he was at the side entrance of the hotel. He said, "*Merci de tout mon coeur*." She deserved it, for she had risked the death penalty for him. He did not offer to pay, for it was not that kind of service.

He brushed himself off and walked into the hotel. There was no one in the lobby at that hour, and he was to discover later that there were few at any hour. The patrons of palace hotels had read accounts of what had happened to Cherbourg, Caen, and other places on or near the Channel, and they wanted none of it in their lives. Better to pack up a couple of valises and go and sleep in a wood hut in a forest, with only the hedgehogs for company.

Lanny registered and explained that his *bagages* had gone astray. Being a rather seedy-looking customer, he put the price down on the desk, and that made him respectable. He was escorted to the room, gave the bellboy the proper tip, and then locked himself in. His first step was to search the room for wiring and for peepholes; he even moved the bureau and crawled under the bed to make sure there was no listening hole into the next room. Then he took a bath, as well as a man could do with cold water and no soap; he shaved, under the same handicap, and then lay on the bed to rest and think and wait for daylight to make a telephone call less of an intrusion and an anomaly.

The number was that which he knew best of all numbers: the villa where he had spent his childhood, on the road which runs through the village of Juan-les-Pins and southward along the rocky shore of the Cap d'Antibes. As Lanny waited, he imagined the phones ringing—one in the drawing-room and the other in the long hall near the pantry.

He assumed that several officers would be quartered in the house, and they would have orderlies to wait on them.

When Lanny called, a man's voice said, "Villa Bienvenu," and Lanny replied promptly, "Capitaine Charles de Bruyne." He waited, and when he heard the familiar voice he said quickly, "This is an old friend. No names, please. I have just seen your father and your wife, and they are well. They have sent you an urgent message. I am at the Métropole and can't stay long. The room number is seven-fourteen. I have no means of transportation. Can you come to me at once?"

The answer was prompt, "I will come."

"Room seven-fourteen, the Métropole. I am staying with a friend named Girouard." The French pronounce it "Zheer-wahr," and Lanny took the precaution to spell it.

V

Two years had passed since Lanny had seen Charlot, and he was not surprised to discover lines of care in his face. The world had not been going the way an ardent and aristocratic-minded young Frenchman wanted it to go, and now, according to his point of view, it appeared about to slide over a precipice. But the *capitaine* was well set-up, his figure trim and well-corseted, his dark hair closely cut and his uniform faultless. His face was pale, and this brought out the scar which he carried as a badge of honor, having got it in battling with the "Red" mob which had rioted in Paris shortly before the war. He hated that mob and still burned to put it down.

They exchanged a handclasp, and Lanny took the precaution to look out into the hall before he closed the door. Then he said, "Charlot, I was at the château a few days ago. I saw *le père*, and Eugénie and Annette. They are well and told me the children were well. Having a garden, they are not doing badly. They begged me to get a message to you and I promised to try."

"Lanny, how on earth do you manage these things?"

"It was my father who made it possible. He was concerned about *le père*, as both a friend and a business associate." The P.A. signed his friend to a chair and drew up another. "*Cher ami*," he said, "I come as a herald of what I fear is bad news. I have taken a risk to come to you, and I have to pledge you to hold what I tell you in strict confidence."

"Of course, Lanny, you don't need to say that. What on earth has happened to you?"

"As you know, I continued to visit Germany and do what little I could on behalf of our cause. But on the last trip I was warned by friends that I was in an unsafe position. Both Hitler and Göring are surrounded by jealous persons who could not endure to see an American enjoying their trust, and these evil ones have been whispering rumors and slanders. I saw that my position was becoming impossible and made up my mind to withdraw entirely from this hateful civil war. That is what it is to me, for I have made my friends among Germans and French and British and Americans alike, and I cannot get any pleasure out of seeing them destroy one another. I decided to become once again an art lover, as your dear mother so often begged me to do."

"I can understand your decision, Lanny, and perhaps it is the wisest thing for a man of your gifts."

"I found that my father had entirely changed his position under the pressure of events. He likes the so-called New Deal as little as ever, but he has become convinced that the Americans are going to win this war."

"How can he bring himself to believe that Germany can be conquered, Lanny?"

"He is in touch with the men who mean to do it. He himself is turning out a fabulous number of planes—I have never seen anything to equal the mushroom growth of the Budd-Erling plants. There is no resisting airpower, Charlot. It gives the ability to land on any coast and to roll in any direction. From what I have been told I believe the last German soldier will be out of France within the next month, or two months at the outside."

"You may be right, Lanny," admitted Charlot humbly. "I have been unpleasantly surprised by recent events."

The P.A. got up and went to the door and opened it suddenly. He had left it unlocked, so that he could do this. Then he came back and resumed in a still lower voice. "Believe me, Charlot, my father has made it his business to know what is coming. He became greatly worried about your family. He says that between the time when the Germans withdraw and the Allies arrive, there will be a period of disorder in which great numbers of people who have aided the Germans will be shot out of hand; later, when a pro-Allied French government is set up, many of the Vichy leaders will be tried for treason and sentenced to death. You must know without my telling you that you are one of the most vulnerable."

"Certainly I know it, Lanny. It will not trouble me too greatly, for I have no desire to live under a regime of the rabble."

"Robbie sent me to explain matters to *le père* and urge him to change his position and make some contribution to the de Gaulle movement. I spent the better part of an evening with him and found that he had already taken this step. His one fear was for you, and he begged me with tears in his eyes to find a way to see you and transmit to you not merely his wishes but his command as *père de famille*. He wanted to write you an explicit letter, but I pointed out that if such a letter fell into the hands of the Germans he would be shot, and his property confiscated, and his grandchildren left in destitution. I persuaded him that it would suffice if he told you to follow my instructions, for I was sure you would not question my good faith in this matter."

"No, surely not, Lanny."

The P.A. took the letter from his pocket and put it into his friend's hand. Knowing the letter by heart, Lanny followed in his mind what Charlot was reading: "Do what our old and dear friend desires. It is a command of your father." And beneath it the words of the wife: "It is also my prayer."

VI

Charlot looked up from his reading and gazed hard at his friend. "Well, Lanny, what is it you want me to do?"

"It is not what I want, Charlot, but what your father commands and your wife prays. I am only their messenger. First, let me inform you, in the strictest confidence, that the Allies are going to invade this coast. It may be at any moment now."

"We know that well, Lanny. We have made all preparations to receive them."

"Do you think you can withstand them?"

"That is in the lap of the gods. My only concern is to defend my honor."

"You are aware, Charlot, that a considerable part of the force will be Frenchmen, under the command of General de Tassigny?"

"He is under the political control of the wretched de Gaulle, whom we consider a traitor to *la patrie*."

"I am surely not among his admirers, *cher garçon*, but it appears that he is the man the so-called Free French want."

"The Free French are a bunch of Reds and asssassins, and we do not consider them our countrymen."

"Let me assure you, I have talked with some of de Gaulle's supporters, men whom you were glad to call your comrades in past times. Whatever his faults may be, he surely has no trace of sympathy with Communism. If he has accepted the help of Reds, it is as any military man accepts the help of any ally in war. *Le grand Charlie* is a devout Catholic like yourself; a graduate of St. Cyr, and they do not train social rebels. If he should gain power he would quickly divorce himself from every trace of radicalism and proceed to make France the kind of country you desire. Yet you are fighting him!"

"It is he who began it, Lanny, by setting himself up against the legitimately constituted government of France."

"I cannot debate those questions with you, Charlot, because they seem to me metaphysical, and I am no abstract thinker. No words can alter the fact that you are going to fight an army of Frenchmen, and an army that is bound to win. You remember, we Americans had a revolution in our country; if George Washington had been defeated, he would have been a traitor under British law, and he might lawfully have been hanged. But he won, so he is called the Father of his Country."

"That is a cynical way to look at it, Lanny. I have heard you quote some American philosopher about the worship of 'the bitch-goddess Success.' "

"Yes, but you are a military man, and that means that you accept the arbitrament of arms; you consent to have the issues of history decided that way. Surely there could be no other reason for a Frenchman to fight on the side of Germans against a French army."

"What do you want me to do, Lanny, run away?"

"Again I remind you, I am not telling you what I want; I am repeating a message from your father."

"*Bien.* What does *le père* wish me to do?"

"He wishes you to live. He points out that you are the heir-apparent to half of a great property. Also, you are the father of a family, and you owe it to them not to throw your life away and leave them in destitution. *Le père* wishes you to take part in the shaping of the new France which will emerge from this war. He wishes you to work by your brother's side for those ends. I must tell you that I have seen your brother several times, and he is in an agony of distress about you; his pleading was one of the reasons which induced me to risk this journey. Denis was severely wounded and in hospital, and is only now beginning to get about on crutches. He begged me with tears in his eyes to persuade you to come over to the Allied side before it is too late. I do not need to tell you what will happen to you if you fight the French Army."

"I have faced that issue, Lanny."

"You must know," continued the P.A., "that the moral struggle going on in you is no new thing to me. I saw it with one Frenchman after another prior to the Allied landing in North Africa. Hundreds of your old comrades came over to the Allied side, they risked their lives, and they do not have to feel that they besmirched their honor. General Giraud, General Juin, General Béthouart, Admiral Fenard, Admiral Battet—I could call a long roll of the men I saw making up their minds, and without any help from me, because I hadn't made up my own then. Now these men are commanding French divisions or French ships. The hour has come when you Frenchmen on the Côte d'Azur have to make the same decision. It seems to me it should be much easier for you, because in North Africa there were no Frenchmen landing and no Germans giving orders to Frenchmen."

VII

This was the beginning of an argument that lasted all through that day. As a man who did not wish to be convinced, Charlot took the argument back over the same ground again and again. *L'honneur*, which means so much to a Frenchman, and *la gloire*, and *la patrie*, and *la légitimité*. Who was this Big Charlie? A mere brigadier general who had dared to rebel against *le vieux Maréchal* and to vilify him to the world? And the boy who had shot the Breton admiral, Darlan, for his treason, was he or was he not a patriot and hero? And what were the prospects for France if it was set free and entrusted to the politicians, to democracy *à l'Américaine*—would it not become a Red satrapy? And what would have happened if Vichy had had its way—would Hitler have ever kept his promises to withdraw?

Lanny had the advantage of having come fresh from the Allied lands; he could tell of the colossal preparations being made for Operation Anvil. What were the defenses of the Midi compared to those along the Channel? What was the roughness of the Mediterranean compared with those northern waters? Raoul had told Lanny there were few reserves back of the Riviera, and Lanny now pretended to know this, and Charlot admitted that it was true. The big battleships would pound the shore installations to pieces, the planes would do pinpoint bombing on what was left, the parachutists would seize the bridges, power plants, and airfields, and the tanks would be coming ashore in a few hours and racing everywhere. The Germans who stayed to defend the towns would be surrounded and made prisoners, and the younger son of the de Bruynes would be tried and shot. And what good would it do to his *honneur*, his *gloire*, or his *patrie?*

Charlot had four persons against him, his father, his elder brother, his wife, and his near-godfather; and that was about all a Frenchman could have in the way of family authority. Lanny had an especial hold, because up to recently he had believed as Charlot had. It did not occur to Charlot to doubt that such was the case, and when Lanny described the steps his conversion had taken, he was preparing a path for the younger man's feet. When Lanny had come to Vichy, his job had required him to buttress the *capitaine* in all his convictions; and now that he had changed, his example was equally convincing. He had recently been in London and could knock out the Nazi propaganda that the city was in ruins and the population in a panic. Of course the buzzbombs were nasty, but could anyone imagine that the killing of a few thousand more civilians would cause Britain to give up? It was just a question of digging out the launching sites, and already the British armies had broken out of Caen and were forcing their way eastward along the coast.

And then—the Germans! Had Charlot been able to get along with them? Were they kind masters? Did they respect the honor, the dignity, of their French partners? Just as Lanny had guessed, the high-spirited young *capitaine* had been ill pleased with his comrades-in-arms. They had become more and more exacting and less and less patient. As things went against them, they demanded more of France, and when it was impossible to meet the demands they became insolent. Would it be too unbearable to see a French army come in and knock them off their perches?

And then, Charlot's colleagues, the former Jeunesses Patriotes, now evolved into the Francs-Gardes—were they all patriots and heroes? Their *capitaine* was forced to admit that some of them were blackguards and others of low intelligence. In short, Lanny dragged out of him the fact that for a long time he had been unhappy in his occupation and in despair for the future of his country. Once started, he poured out his confession, and Lanny gathered enough information to make his journey worth-while, even if he did not win the soul of his friend.

But he meant to win, and he kept on until evening. The argument which clinched the matter was Lanny's statement that by coming over in time Charlot might be saving not merely himself but his whole family. Lanny would bear witness to the part which *le père* and *la femme* had played in Charlot's conversion, and the Partisans would know of it. Charlot bowed his head to hide the tears that welled into his eyes. "All right, Lanny," he said, "I will do what you advise." And suddenly it seemed to his near-godfather that Charlot turned back into the shy and sensitive lad whom his mother had introduced to Lanny at the château more than two decades ago, in that quiet garden, with the apricots and the grapevines in blossom, the jonquils and the narcissus filling the air with fragrance. Lanny thought, oh, God, if children knew what was going to happen to them, would they consent to stay in this world?

VIII

The younger de Bruyne was not the sort of man to wish to run away. If he was coming over to the Allied side, he would take an active part, and Lanny talked to him on that basis. Who was there among his associates who might be open to persuasion? What strategic places were there which might be occupied at the critical moment? The German garrison in Cannes greatly outnumbered the French group, so there could be no outright revolt; but saboteurs might blow up munitions dumps, set fuel stores on fire, put guns out of commission, render vehicles inoperable. Above all, a mass of information might be turned over to Allied agents, so that they would know when to strike and where to meet their Partisan friends and give them support.

Lanny reported what he had seen in North Africa. At Casablanca the conspiracy had failed, and as a result there had been two or three days of fighting between the French on the shore and the British and American invaders; General Béthouart, who had tried to help the Allies, had come near to being shot as a traitor. But in Algiers the conspiracy had been more widespread and there had been little fighting. Unfortunately the conspirators had gone into action too early, and their opponents had had time to rally; if the opponents had been Germans, great numbers of the conspirators would surely have been shot.

The next step was for Charlot to meet the Partisan leaders, and this was a matter of some delicacy. Lanny warned him that he would meet some he did not like and hear ideas which were anathema to him. He had to make up his mind to work with any and all who were willing to fight Germans. Lanny was expecting a telephone call from Raoul and told about this old friend who was in contact with the Partisans here. Charlot had been hunting these people and might have a hard time convincing them that he had come over. In all probability some of them had known Lanny in the old days and believed that he had become a Fascist enemy; they would feel sure that Raoul was being led into a trap.

They got some food delivered to their room—Charlot had a card which enabled him to order what he wanted. Soon after dark came the telephone call, and Lanny told Raoul to come to the room. In spite of the fact that Charlot and Raoul were old friends of Lanny's, they had never met, for Marie de Bruyne had been out of sympathy with Lanny's political opinions and he never introduced her boys to his socially undesirable acquaintances. In those days the grandson of Budd Gunmakers had lived in two idea-tight compartments, the world of Raoul and Rick, and the world of his mother and his *amie*.

Now these two worlds met and mingled, and if the occasion had been one of less deadly seriousness Lanny would have been amused. The scion of the de Bruynes was very stiff and correct; he was "St. Germain," which is the same as if you said "Beacon Street" in Boston or "Berkeley Square" in London. When Charlot met his social inferiors, they were servants or common soldiers with whom he did not shake hands. Now he was meeting a peasant's son who had fled from the police of the Spanish monarchy and who might on some occasion have fitted a pair of shoes on Charlot's feet in this city on the Coast of Pleasure. Whether or not not that had happened, it was certain that if the *capitaine* had caught him twenty-four hours ago he would have had him shot forthwith. The distinction between Red and Pink was vague in Charlot's mind, and he took it as wholly fraudulent, a camouflage.

But Raoul had his own form of dignity and thought just as well of himself as Charlot did of Charlot. They were like two Indian chieftains smoking a peace pipe—only Raoul did not smoke. What they did was to talk business, and soon they forgot everything else. Lanny said that Charlot was a man of honor and that when he gave his word he could be trusted to the death. That was enough for Raoul, and after a while he offered to go back to the hideout where he had met Lanny and try to persuade the leader of the Resistance in Cannes to come to the hotel for a conference. Raoul himself had been working in Toulon and had in Cannes no contacts which would enable him to transmit information to the Allies.

IX

The one-time school director went away, and the *capitaine* and the presidential agent talked about their families and about the war. After an hour or so Raoul returned in the company of another man, swarthy and dark-haired, who spoke with a strong Provençal accent. He was stocky and had once been powerful, but now, like nearly everybody on the Riviera, he hadn't had enough to eat for some time. Raoul introduced him as Ribault, which might, of course, be a name for the occasion. His manner was guarded and suspicious, and he did not offer to take the hand of this hated policeman of the Vichy gangsters. He spoke directly and to the point, and the substance of what he said was that the lamp still held out to burn and the vilest sinner might return. (Not that a leader of the *maquis* had ever heard the hymns of Isaac Watts!)

The *capitaine* replied with dignity that hitherto he had seen no possibility of getting rid of the Germans, but that now, when the possibility appeared, he was ready to do his part. Actions would speak louder than words, and if Monsieur Ribault would make notes, the *capitaine* would tell him everything he could. Raoul volunteered to do the writing—perhaps the other man's heavy fist was not adapted to the task. Charlot proceeded to pour out information about the number of troops in the garrison and near by, who commanded them, and what weapons they had. He gave the facts about fortifications, the number of the guns, their caliber and range; the location of oil and other stores, and of radio-ranging stations not yet bombed. He said that the Germans had seven divisions in Southern France, two of them armored; only three were at the coast, but others were on the way. He said that all the best troops had been taken to the north; many of those left behind were badly trained divisions, older-age groups, and convalescents; the way to deal with them was to attack boldly and push on, not worrying about your flanks. He answered every question promptly—and Ribault was in a position to judge the answers, for it had been his business to gather such facts and no doubt he had many.

When the session was over he got up and shook Charlot's hand. "*Monsieur le Capitaine, vous êtes un camarade,*" he said, and that was meant to settle it. The leader took the paper and hid it in his jacket, saying that he would get the information to the Allies before the night was over.

What were the others going to do? Raoul wanted to return to the neighborhood of Toulon, his post of duty, and he had a way of getting there. Lanny's problem was more complicated; not knowing how long his job in Cannes might take, he had made no arrangement with the OSS to be taken out of France. He had told them that he knew where he could hide out in the hills and wait in safety until the invasion was over. He asked Charlot to drive him to the neighborhood of this place, and Charlot agreed.

First the Provençal left the hotel room, followed by the Spaniard. Then Charlot went down to his car, telling Lanny where it was. After a short interval Lanny put his razor, his comb, and his toothbrush into his pocket—all he had in the way of luggage—and slipped out of the Hotel Métropole unobserved. He had already paid for his room and for the food. It was then after midnight, and Lanny could have used some sleep, but he dared not stay longer in the hotel without registering with the police. He stepped into the car, and after that he was safe, for not even the Germans would have held up the car of a captain of the Francs-Gardes.

On the way Lanny explained that his destination was the home of a peasant family, several of whose members had been servants at Bienvenu in past years. He didn't want to be driven there, because the sight of Charlot's uniform might trouble them; all peasants fear all authorities. Charlot agreed; he didn't want to be seen with Lanny any more than Lanny with him.

They drove on a road which led up into the mountains; it was lined with the gates to fine estates, and after they had gone a considerable distance Lanny said, "I think this is far enough to be safe." Charlot assented, saying that he must get back to his duties so as not to excite suspicion. They exchanged a warm handclasp and words of friendship and trust. "You were right," said the Frenchman, "and I am sure I shall never regret it." They were the last words that Lanny was to hear from his friend.

X

The P.A. climbed for a while, and then his breath began to come hard, and he realized that he was short on food as well as sleep. Bordering the road was one of the forests of pine trees which cover the slopes of the mountains, and he found a smooth place and sat down to rest. It is chilly on the Riviera as soon as the sun goes down, and when you climb it grows even more so; but he didn't wish to approach his destination in darkness, so he curled up into a ball for warmth and with one arm for a pillow fell fast asleep.

When he wakened dawn was spreading, and he was stiff with cold. He listened to the tinkle of sheep bells, then got up and started climbing again. But presently came another sound, one that stopped him. Thunder? No, bombing! He had been hearing it off and on for some eight years—the first time having been in Barcelona. He was an expert and could tell the difference between big ones far off and little ones near by. These were distant, but not very.

He looked about, and as the light grew brighter he found a spot on the mountainside that was clear of everything but brush. He pushed his way into it and stood looking down upon a scene veiled in early morning mist. Through the mist were flashes of orange-colored fire, quick and sharp, like the gleam of fireflies. Here, there, all along where Lanny knew the coast would be, he saw these firebursts, one after another, so many that the sounds were incessant. He stood fascinated while the light spread and the sun came up. He knew the view from boyhood: beautiful white villas below him, their grounds planted with ornamental trees from all over the world; orange groves of dark green and olive groves of silvery gray; and beyond them a rough and rocky coast with white stretches of sand here and there, and the Midland Sea, green in the shallows and deep blue all the way to the horizon's edge.

The mist lifted, but its place was taken by a cloud of smoke, so Lanny could not see the coast. What he saw was a swarm of planes, flying high, and diving down, dropping their deadly loads and then turning out to sea. He had expected to observe ships, but this was an air bombardment; so he knew that D-day wasn't yet. The fire flashes extended from Cannes as far to the westward as his vision could reach, and this told him, as it told everybody in the world, the general location of the coming invasion. His heart ached for the beautiful city of Cannes, which he loved in spite of its corruptions. He wondered, was it getting an area bombing, like Berlin and the other German cities? Hardly likely, for this was France, and the Air Force was doing what it could to spare the civilians; the planes would be spotting military targets, and Lanny wondered, had they received the information from Ribault in time? It was possible, for a radio-sending set didn't take long to work, and everything in this war was faster than ever before.

XI

Lanny watched for the smoke to rise; but there were fires, and more smoke from them. The sun came and warmed him, and he waited for hours before he was sure there were no fires on the Cap d'Antibes, and that the familiar buildings which stood out in Cannes were apparently undamaged. Then he climbed into one of the small side valleys, where lay the little farm of Leese and her family.

This capable Provençal woman had been the cook at Bienvenu when Lanny was a child, and she had risen to the post of *majeuse-dome*, a word which the playful Lanny had coined for the occasion of her twenty-fifth anniversary. Now she was old, and might be dead for all he knew; but her numerous relatives would be at the place, and the Budd family held royal rank in their eyes. In the early days of the war, before Beauty had fled from Bienvenu, they had been her bootleggers by exclusive appointment, keeping her supplied with every sort of farm produce. No doubt the money she had paid them was still hidden in mattresses or buried in some pot at the foot of a tree on the farm.

An unpaved road led into the little valley where the farm stood on a steep slope. Tiny gardens had been terraced, every cupful of soil was saved, and vegetables grew in plots no bigger than your handkerchief. The house was built of rocks—so plentiful, alas; the house was mainly kitchen, having a great fireplace of rocks, made tight, like the house, with plaster. There was the inevitable French manure pile, but reduced in size because the Boches had left them only one old cow and one tiny donkey. But the ancient olive trees stood, and the apricot and peach trees and the vines; everything perfectly tended despite the fact that there was only one old man left in this family, and one middle-aged man with his right arm and part of his shoulder lost; there were three women, two of them with husbands at war, and half a dozen children, all of whom worked.

They had heard the bombing; but would they stop work for that? No indeed! They had been hearing such sounds from the Mediterranean off and on for almost five years. Such sounds, in their view, concerned the people in the cities, the great and powerful who lived by collecting taxes and drafting young men into armies. What peasants did was to keep alive and get the highest prices they could for what products they could spare. Every hour there was work that had to be done, and no time to think about matters that were far away and beyond understanding.

The arrival of a stranger was no novelty just now, and they hardly looked up from their labors. But when this city man smiled and said, "Don't you know me?" they looked, and then cried, "Monsieur Lanny!" Everybody came running, and shook both his hands, and patted him on the back, and introduced him to the children, most of whom were too young to remember him. They wanted to hear about

Madame Detaze—so they called Beauty—and Monsieur Dingle and the little boy, where and how were they and would they come back? They took him in, and there was Leese, shrunken but still alive, bed-ridden but propped up, doing the family mending and knitting, and giving all the orders for the place. He kissed her toil-worn hand, just as if she had been a *grande dame*, and she patted him, as if it had been the good old time when he was a little boy, racing about the estate or learning to pound the piano.

So much there was to talk about, and so many people! He had a little daughter, a big girl now; he had a new wife and a baby boy, and when would he bring them to Bienvenu? When *les Boches* were gone, he told them; the Americans were coming to drive the evil ones out. So that was what the shooting was about! Well then, they would be glad; they knew how the Americans had come last time, and had paid for produce with good money, whereas *les Boches* paid with money that lost its value fast. But they came and made you take it and you didn't dare to say a word, but hid all the produce you could, and ate as much as you wanted. You got fat to spite *les Boches!*

Lanny said, "Don't say a word about my being here. It would be very bad for me. I came up to hide until the Americans have got ashore." They all promised, even the children promised, *pas un mot!* They had hidden some of the Maquis now and then, their own sort of people, fighting the harsh-voiced foreigners who came to search the peasant's huts and storerooms and carry off his grain and olives and fruit and poultry, all the means of life he had laid up for the coming winter.

That was what war meant to peasants all over Europe, to those fortunate ones who happened not to be in the line of march of armies or on the ground chosen for battles. It meant lugging your produce out into the forest and hiding it in caves, or in hollow trees, or in pits dug and bricked in. It meant the children keeping watch, and when the alarm was given, the women fleeing into the mountains and being hunted like wild animals by lustful men. It meant paper currency that presently became worthless, so that peasants learned to take only hard money, and change it into gold, and put it in a sock and bury it under a loose board or hearthstone.

XII

Also, it meant refugees, pitiful people fleeing from towns and villages, from battles and bombardments. That was what it would mean this very day; they knew it and discussed it with somber resolution. *Les pauvres gens,* of course one was sorry for them, but there had been too many of them, and farm people had to survive if farms were to continue to be worked. "Thousands have come, Monsieur Lanny, and we have given more than we can spare. What good will it do if we starve in the winter and are unable to work the fields in the spring?" It was a cruel world, and perhaps only the hardhearted were fit to survive in it.

The flood began to arrive late in the morning. People had leaped out of bed, for city people do not get up with the dawn. Some wore pajamas; they had not even stopped to put their clothes on. Others rolled bundles in baby carriages or children's carts. One woman had nothing but a gilded cage with her pet canary. They had toiled up the foothills and spread into the valleys, and one and all seemed to think that farm people had nothing to do but take care of them. They were exhausted, terrified, helpless; they begged and pleaded, with tears in their eyes. Surely they could sleep in the barn, in the half empty storeroom, or with the cow or the pig! Any place but out in the wild forest among the rocks, and only *le bon Dieu* knew what sorts of wild beasts! They held out money, the paper money printed for *les Boches;* the peasants had no idea how that money had come into existence, but they knew it would buy less and less, and they wanted less and less of it. "*Non, non, madame, monsieur, rien, rien! Il faut partir!*" The wretched ones didn't want to go, for where was there to go to?

These scenes went on, day and night, all the time that Lanny stayed on the place. There was an incessant stream of refugees, and they had to be scolded before they would move on. They wanted water, and you couldn't refuse water, but you tried to make them understand that wells in these hills often went dry and that water was as precious to a farmer as food. They begged to sleep under shelter, and would swear that they had no matches or tobacco. But you couldn't believe them; the old man declared that many a farmer who had done so had lost his barn for his kindness. Lanny observed the deeply rooted mistrust of the peasant for the city person. The city was a parasite upon the farm; the bourgeois slept late and wore fine clothes and did no real work, but charged the peasant high prices for tools and clothing and all the things he had to have.

Against this would be the claims of common humanity. A mother wept and pleaded for a little milk to save her baby's life. They gave her a little milk, even though their cow was going dry and there was not enough for their own children. And then, of course, the mother wanted to stay; she had found kind people, she had made a dent in the hard crust of this cruel world! An old man, apparently a gentleman, fainted from exhaustion, and what would they do about him? Who was to tell if he had really fainted, or if he was only pretending, as so many of these clever folk had learned to do?

Lanny's food choked him, but he ate a little, because he too had to survive; each person thinks there is some special reason why he should do so. To these Provençal peasants Lanny was a privileged being, an old friend, besides being heir-apparent to the Bienvenu estate. He had climbed here as a boy and a youth, loving these mountains and the country sights. He had come to the festivals and learned the songs and danced with the girls to the music of fife and drum and tambourine: a quick little waltz, and a jerky polka, and the farandole. He had sung "*Oh, Magali, ma tant amado,*"—Provençal being a cross between Italian and French. He had learned a lot of their words and had not forgotten them now; he would amuse them by exclaiming, "Name of a good little man!"

They locked him and themselves inside the house so that others might not see them eating. They cut him a slice of wholewheat bread, and put on it a slice from a large onion. With a handful of dried olives that was a meal for any farm worker, and it was a meal for Lanny. A cup of wine went with it, and they drank the wine exactly as the sun crossed the meridian. He didn't know why they did that, and they couldn't tell him; it was a custom. They kept him out of sight, for there might be spies among these refugees, or there might be Boches running away from the Americans. Later the Boches would be licked and would surely come then—and the peasant women would join the refugees and sleep in the forest. *C'est la guerre!*

25

Le Jour de Gloire

I

EVERY morning Lanny would hear the sounds of bombing, and walk out to the mountainside and look for ships. But he saw only planes and the line of shell bursts and clouds of black smoke ascending. Three days he watched that sight and noted that the most numerous bursts and the heaviest smoke were to the west. He decided that that was where he wanted to be, and he made a bargain with the one-armed peasant to escort him to the farm of one of Leese's nephews, who had worked at Bienvenu as gardener and would surely be glad to welcome his former employer. The one-armed man, a son-in-law, didn't want any of the paper money, but was glad to take Lanny Budd's check on a New York bank; that would be good for dollars, and he knew the day would come when he could cash it.

The mistral had started blowing, that cold wind which comes from the north and spoils the joy of tourists on the Riviera. The pair set out early and took the whole day. The streams have cut their way down to the sea in gorges, and it is not always easy to cross them; but a man who has lived here all his life knows the trails and the fords and how to keep out of sight. The mountains had suddenly become full of people, and how they were going to subsist was a mystery. Lanny and his guide walked all day toward the west, and spent the night safely in a cabin in the forests of the red Estérel mountains, behind which Lanny had seen the sun set all through his boyhood and youth. The owner of the cabin was a cork worker, small, black-haired, and swarthy, his features recalling the fact that the Saracens had many times invaded this land.

Before sunrise Lanny again sought a view of the sea, and there, looking down from a clear spot amid a forest of rugged cork oak trees, he saw at last the sight he had been expecting. The ships! The whole sea was spotted with them as if they had been sprinkled out of a pepper pot; they extended in all directions as far as the eye could reach. He did not try to count them, but later he learned that there had been more than eight hundred. And all headed toward the Côte d'Azur!

Ahead came the tiny PT-boats and destroyers, darting here and there, on the lookout for the subs. Then came the majestic battleships and heavy cruisers; they turned in lines parallel to the shore and at once opened up with their big guns, the mightiest cannonade that Lanny had ever heard or imagined. He saw the tongues of yellow flame shoot out, and saw the shells burst on the shore before he heard the report from either explosion. But it was only a few seconds before all the reports had become a blur, a roaring as of all the thunder in the world. All the warships of all sizes were bursting with flames, and swarms of planes over the shore were adding to the racket. Even through the smoke Lanny could see that the shell bursts were bunched at certain spots; he was glad he was not on any of those spots, and wondered how many of them had been listed in the information which Raoul and Charlot had furnished.

This bombardment went on for so long that the observer couldn't guess the time. Here and there through the smoke he could see other kinds of ships coming in from the sea and knew that what the Armed Forces called H-hour was at hand. The transports and other vessels came in and halted, and the swarms of landing craft set to work. Some that were big came to the shore with the loads they had brought; smaller craft were let down from the transports and the men came swarming down on rope nets on which scores could move at the same time. Lanny knew that everything had been rehearsed over and over, so that every man who took part in the enterprise knew exactly what he had to do.

The mistral which was still blowing made no trouble for them because it was a lee shore. Very soon the swarms of boats were moving in toward the beaches, and when batteries on land which had survived the bombardment opened up on them, the guns of the warships opened on the batteries, and planes overhead dived down on them with bombs. Surely an unusual sight, and worth crossing an ocean and climbing a mountain to see; Lanny hoped that none of the spotter planes would call the attention of a battlewagon to two civilians sitting on a mountainside!

II

The P.A. kept count and observed seven waves of men coming ashore in the space of a couple of hours. They were entering a little bay, full of fishing boats. He said, "That is St. Raphael, is it not?" The guide confirmed his guess. Lanny knew the town; a lovely place, especially favored by the art lovers who wanted to live cheaply and away from the fashionable atmosphere of Cannes. "The GI's will like it," he remarked.

He was joking, for he knew they wouldn't stay long. The other man replied, "They may be driving the Boches this way, Monsieur." Lanny took the hint, broke off his sojourn, and went back to the cork worker's hut and spent a night among the fleas and the refugees. The latter were nearly as thick as the former; the cork worker didn't mind their sleeping in his back yard, for he had no farm and nothing that would be of use to them. They wanted to keep out of the cold wind.

Early next morning Lanny got up and listened. There was still a lot of shooting, but not so much as on the previous day. He decided that it was time for him to move and said good-by to his friendly host. He went out to the place of observation and saw that there was resistance in the direction of Cannes, and some toward the west, but in other places the ships were shooting into the hills, doubtless at enemy tanks and transport. In front of him there was no sign of trouble; the ships were not bothered by the offshore wind, and the landing craft were gliding to and fro like ferryboats. The wonderful Navy put a hundred thousand men ashore in two days, on a seventy-mile front between Cannes and Toulon.

The cork man had pointed out an obscure path which led down along the mountainside and would take the traveler into St. Raphael. Lanny started down; there were refugees toiling up, and he was no longer afraid of them. He asked some of them for news, but found that their only idea was to get away from news. There came German soldiers, laden with their packs, and Lanny stood aside respectfully and let them file by. No Gestapo any more; nobody requiring French civilians to show their papers. He observed a baby carriage standing by the path, empty; somebody had found the going too steep, and he or others had emptied it of contents. Farther along was what had been a gun emplacement; its concrete had been knocked to pieces, and one gun was standing on its nose, the other sticking up at a crazy angle. The traveler got by that spot as fast as he could, lest one of the hovering planes should not be entirely satisfied with the job.

III

The nearer he got, the better he could see that show, and it was one to remember and tell his grandchildren about. The big LST's came up to the beach and opened their huge jaws; tanks came rumbling out, or tractors towing heavy guns. Pack-laden soldiers looked like waterfalls pouring down the sides of ships. Every sort of little boat was bringing them in, and the tiny harbor of St. Raphael appeared to be solid with craft. Lanny would stand and look for a few minutes, and then descend to a lower level and a closer view.

Presently there was some sort of structure on the slope that he took to be connected with the waterworks of the town; there were several men guarding it, and, glory hallelujah, they were GI's! Lanny stopped and spotted their leader, a private first-class. "Hello, soldier," he said.

It was a little dark fellow, sprightly of mind, and Lanny guessed that he was from Brooklyn. "Hello," he replied. "You American?"

"Happily, yes."

"Seen any Jerries up where you come from?"

"A dozen or so, getting away as fast as they could. Tell me, where shall I find your command post?"

"What's your business, Mister?"

"I'm an OSS man."

"What the hell's that? They dish up so many of these initials."

"Intelligence Service."

The "pfc" appeared suspicious. "What's your name, Bud?"

"That's my name," said Lanny with a smile, "Budd."

"Yeah?" The tone indicated that this was taken for fooling. "Any relation to Budd-Erling?"

"My father is president of the company," said Lanny, amused.

"Zat so? My name is George Washington, and this guy here is Abe Lincoln."

"Pleased to meet you, George and Abe. But tell me where to find your commanding officer, because I have information that I was sent to get."

"Abe, take this Mister Budd-Erling to the Captain; and make sure he ain't Benedict Arnold."

IV

So Lanny went on down the path to the highway, and, glory hallelujah again, here was the Army! All over the place, and none waiting around to see what was going to happen; all moving out into the countryside to make it happen. Dispatch cars, trucks, and jeeps all along the Route Nationale; wicked-looking tanks and motorized guns—everything loading up and starting after the Jerries. By the roadside, under a pepper tree, on the ground covered with its berries, were several folding tables and camp chairs with officers sitting in them, studying maps, reading dispatches, listening to telephones. The command post, no doubt, and Lanny prepared to tell his story in the fewest possible words.

But he didn't get to it, for on the way he ran into another kind of Jerry; ex-tutor, ex-lieutenant, ex-*pension*-manager, ex-travel-bureau-manager, ex-OSS agent Jerry Pendleton! Jerry in uniform, a second lieutenant again! They were so glad to see each other that they hugged and almost wanted to kiss French fashion. "What on earth are you doing here?" asked Lanny, and the answer was, "Franco appears to be on the shelf, so they took me for an interpreter. What are you doing?"

"They sent me to Cannes on an errand, and after it was done I decided to get up into the hills. A lot of other folks, including Germans, had the same idea. Tell me, has Cannes been taken?"

"No, the garrison is holding out."

"That's bad news for my friends. I tried to arrange for an uprising. When are we going in?"

"They don't tell things like that to interpreters, Lanny. Let me introduce you to our Intelligence man."

The P.A. was led to one of the tables and introduced to a Captain Harris, who heard his story and inspected his forged papers. Since Lieutenant Pendleton vouched for him so emphatically there was no question as to his good faith. The Captain said he didn't know the plans concerning Cannes; since Lanny was urgent, he called his superior on the phone and told the story. As a result, Lanny was put into a jeep and whirled down into the fishing village and tourist resort of St. Raphael.

He had a chance on the way to observe an Army in the process of getting itself in order. Already an airstrip had been cleared, and scout planes and small fighters were coming back from pursuit of the enemy; no doubt the site had been picked in advance and everything needed had been rushed to the spot. Gasoline, packed in square tins to save space, came ashore by the ton as soon as combat troops had cleared the beaches. Thus planes could be flown from carriers, and refueled and worked at short range; and thus a jeep could hustle an OSS man into the headquarters of the Thirty-Sixth Infantry Division of the Sixth Corps of the Seventh Army, Major General John E. Dahlquist commanding.

Lanny talked with the General, who looked very handsome in a uniform belted with a gold buckle and a trick scarf around his neck on which was printed a map of Southern France. Lanny talked fast, urging the importance of Cannes as a harbor and prestige point; but he couldn't insist, as he had done with Patton, because Cannes was not Paris, and the life of one French captain was surely not as important as the lives of many American soldiers the Army's strategy meant to save. The General didn't say why he hadn't taken Cannes or when he would take Cannes; he just said politely that Mr. Budd's information was of interest and that full use would be made of it. Lanny was free to go off and worry about Charlot all he pleased; he couldn't do a thing in the world to help his friend.

V

The P.A. had promised to return and have lunch with Jerry on the outskirts of the village. A cloudy day, and the mistral was still blowing, but they sat outdoors; they were leaving in a few hours, and it wasn't worth while to put up shelter. An orderly brought hot soup out of a can, and then pork and beans, and while they ate Jerry asked, "What are you going to do next?"

The answer was, "I have finished my assignment, and I suppose I'll go back to Washington and report."

The ex-tutor had a better idea. "Why don't you come with us? The Army's always looking for interpreters, especially one who knows French and German and a bit of Provençal. You'd have a grandstand ticket to the show."

"What would they do with me, Jerry?"

"Give you a temporary rank and put you in uniform, as they did me. I've already spoken to the Captain about it. You know how it is, they all think it's rather wonderful to be the son of Budd-Erling. They'd make you a captain, and you could boss me."

"Don't be foolish, Jerry. I'd need you to tell me what to do."

"My own briefing was short and sweet. They wanted me because I know French and a little German—you learn everything in the travel business. Think about it seriously, Lanny. We have the idea this is going be a parade; we have the stuff, and the Germans down here are third-raters. We're going up the Rhône valley—we'll be on our way this afternoon. Unless I miss my guess, you could be in Paris in a month, and there'll be nothing to prevent your getting word to OSS meantime, and if they have another job for you they'll let you know."

"Would the Army let us stick together?"

"Sure they would. I've told them how we worked together on the job before the Casablanca landing. This is a tiptop outfit, and you are the very guy to interview German prisoners, the *maquisards*, the peasants, and all the other sources of information."

That was the way the next stage of Lanny Budd's life was determined. The procedure was unusual, but the need for interpreters was extreme; the bag of prisoners was so heavy, it suggested the complete collapse of the enemy. So a man who had come into the camp with only a safety razor, a toothbrush, and a comb, was fitted with a brand-new field uniform with various objects in its many pockets and a holster which contained, appropriately enough, a Budd automatic; Budd Gunmakers was still working for the Army, even though Robbie and his family no longer owned it. They gave him a physical examination, which took only a few minutes because he was sound. They gave him some shots against disease, which soon made him feel as if he had all the diseases and more. They put a "dogtag" around his neck with a number on it—a number up in the ten millions. They gave him identification papers, and let him keep his forged French papers on the chance that they might come in handy. So far he hadn't had to show them to a single enemy person.

They also gave him time to write several letters: one to the President's man, saying where he was; one to OSS in Washington, one to Robbie, and one to Captain Laurel Creston in London—she would exceed him in seniority, which would give pleasure to a feminist! The letters would go by V-mail—that is, assuming that the censor approved them. By that time Lanny would be—he didn't know where, but the Army would know, and the answers would find him.

VI

The new captain had been told that he would move out immediately, but the orders were changed. There were so many prisoners, and so much to be learned from them! He and Jerry were escorted to separate rooms in a commandeered inn, and Germans and a few Frenchmen were brought to them one at a time; a stern GI stood guard and a male stenographer took notes in English as Lanny told him what to put down. The Army had been taken by surprise by the suddenness of the enemy's collapse; ten thousand prisoners had already been taken with losses of only five hundred. The "shell" had been broken, and it appeared to be empty. Everybody had to improvise, and an interpreter was put to work with not more than half a dozen sentences of briefing.

The son of Budd-Erling, who had said that he didn't like to give orders, had to put on all at once a stern and terrifying look. He remembered the *Feldwebel* he had seen, the Prussian drill sergeants barking orders, ready to kick the lout who failed to respond fast enough. He had a threat as alarming as any *Feldwebel* had ever employed: "Do you want to be turned over to the Russians?" Of course that wouldn't be done, but the prisoner wouldn't know it until later. On the other hand to "Do you want to be sent to America?" they would answer eagerly, "*Ja, ja, mein Herr!*" He would say, "If you tell me the truth I will have you sent to America, and if you lie to me I'll send you to the slave camps in Siberia."

He would start asking, "Where do you come from?" and "What is your unit?" and "Who is your commanding officer?" and "Where has the rest of your outfit gone?" and "How many tanks have they?" and so on. Generally the prisoner would tell what he knew, but now and then one would say that it was *verboten* to speak. Lanny would look his grimmest and reply, "*Im Gegenteil, jetzt ist es Befehl*"—now it is commanded. Incredible as it might seem, that would work in case after case; orders were orders, regardless of who gave them. This was true especially of the peasant *Burschen*, most of them from Bavaria; Lanny knew their dialect—it had helped to save his life and now it helped the Army. The soldier's face would light up, and he would talk eagerly.

The Prussians were tougher, and Lanny didn't waste much time on them; there were so many more, and time was racing. Now and then came an intelligent man who really knew things and would tell them. "I hate the Nazis," he would declare, and Lanny would ask, "*Sind Sie Sozial Demokrat?*" If the man answered that he was, Lanny would say, "*Ich auch*"—me too! But he wouldn't tell that to the stenographer. He would add, "There is going to be a democratic Germany. Help us with everything you know."

An amusing circumstance: Lanny was permitted to question enlisted men, noncommissioned officers, lieutenants, and captains, but under the Geneva Convention he was not permitted to question anyone of rank higher than his own. The German officers were always informed as to their rights and would refuse to answer. After a few days Lanny's own officers realized that his knowledge of languages was exceptional, and so they put him in a colonel's uniform; thus he was able to deal with majors and colonels. But no generals—it was against regulations for him to wear any stars!

He was not invited to be present when the high brass digested the data he had collected; but he could see for himself what the conclusions would be. The enemy had known for weeks that the invasion was coming but had not been able to prepare. Whole divisions had been drawn off to try to stop the attacks in the north, and there was no way to replace them. Fortifications had been begun but not finished, and few of the guns had enough ammunition. A good part of the troops were Poles, Czechs, and even Russians, and these had no stomach for the fight. One and all, they desired not to fall into the hands of the Partisans, who were infuriated and might shoot them; what they wanted was to be politely taken by the fabulously wealthy Americans and given hot coffee that wasn't ersatz and three meals a day of American canned food. Lanny mentioned these things frequently, and he could see the light in dark Bavarian eyes and sometimes even in blue Prussian eyes.

VII

The Army wasn't sitting and waiting for the result of such inquisitions. As fast as tanks and jeeps and armored cars got ashore, the men would pile into them and they would go off, by one road or another, to find out for themselves where the enemy was and how eager he was for a fight. When they found groups assembled by the roadside with their hands in the air, waiting to be captured, they would radio word, and ground forces would come in trucks to disarm the prisoners and keep the Free French away from them. Two divisions of American paratroopers and airborne troops had been dropped at strategic points, and these had seen some fighting, but now most of them were guarding prisoners and waiting to be relieved of the burden.

After darkness fell Lanny and Jerry were treated to a meal and then told to be ready to move. Hours were irregular in the Army, and surprises frequent. Jerry had been sure they would travel up the Rhône, and that would mean first going westward, across the delta lands of that great river. But they were put into a car and driven to the north, into the mountains from which Lanny had come. These roads were mere shelves along the sides of precipices and the cars were using only dim parking lights. There was nothing Lanny could do to help, so he leaned back and closed his eyes, and when he fell asleep he dreamed that he was shut up in a concrete mixer, one of the modern sort that turns round and round as the vehicle moves along the road. Perhaps it was the guns which he heard up ahead, echoing among the mountains like thunder; but thunder sometimes stops, whereas the guns went on and on. There would be few hours of the day or night when Lanny wouldn't hear them during the next month.

He had become a camp follower of the Army. He would follow just close enough to get all the backwash; to hear the shooting but not to be in danger from it; to see the ruins and the wreckage; and to hear the groans of wounded men, but not himself to suffer anything worse than discomfort. He was a part of the Army brain, which had to be kept safe; they told him that, and it should have satisfied him, but sometimes he tried to help where he shouldn't, and gave his food away to women and children for whom he was sorry. When the discomfort became too great he would recall the ribald song he had heard the recruits singing on route marches at home, in which they told one another that they were in the Army now, they were not behind the plow, they would never get rich—and they called themselves a bad name which happened to make a rhyme.

VIII

This "flying column" came to a town where there had been fighting, but it was over. Lanny was put up in a second-class inn—the Quartermaster Corps had a squad car which followed behind the troops and picked out the best for the higher brass and the second and third-class for riffraff such as translators. Anyhow, there were bedbugs, and Lanny wasn't surprised or shocked, for he had taken walking trips through Provence and knew what goes with the romance and picturesqueness of the Old World. After two or three hours he was glad to go to work again and get his sleep while riding in a concrete mixer.

Here were not only more "krauts" to be interrogated, but also the Free French, the *maquisards.* They came down from the mountains, on bicycles, in horse carts, in wood-burning busses which sometimes gave out and had to be pushed up the small hills so that they could coast down the long ones. They were for the most part young fellows, of draft age, high-spirited and unwilling to be enslaved; they were tough and inured to hardships, the sort with whom Lanny had hidden out in the mountains of northeastern Italy. They were enraptured to meet a comrade, and they told hair-raising stories. They were armed for the most part with hunting rifles and some had old-fashioned pistols fit only for museums; with these they had fought Germans armed with machine guns, and had not done so badly. They had wrecked the railroads and most of the bridges in this mountainous land, and perhaps they had made a mistake, they said, laughing, for it would slow up the pursuit.

What they all wanted was to get a Garand rifle and a bandolier of cartridges, and be allowed to go after the enemy. The Army took them on as scouts, paying them the French equivalent of two dollars a day, which was magnificent. They had to swear that they would not kill the German stragglers or the French *collaborateurs;* both were to be made prisoners, the former to be shipped off to the prisoner camps which had been built for the fighting in North Africa, and the latter to be imprisoned and tried under French law. After that the Partisans would go happily off, and the Army would be kept well supplied with facts about the Ninteenth German Army it was pursuing. Wherever the enemy stopped to resist, the Army would radio the location to the nearest airstrip, and the planes would come and make his life hardly worth living.

Such was the P.A.'s life for the next month. He learned, as men do, to accommodate himself to rough circumstances. He learned that the Army had a marvelous new insecticide called DDT; it was made into bombs, and you turned a little screw and it shot out a fine spray; a few seconds of that over and in your bed and you could sleep; it also came in the form of a powder, and you dusted your clothing with it to ward off lice. You learned to help work your car out of the mud when it rained, and when the earth dried you learned to eat gray dust and like it. You learned to carry some food with you, and to heat it with a little gasoline poured into sand or soft ground. You had a warm overcoat and put it on at night—for the high Alps, covered with snow, lay only a few miles to the east. You learned to sleep whenever you were not working or eating.

IX

The route led straight to the north, through the towns of Valensole and Castellane. It was famous as the road which Napoleon had taken on his return from Elba; the French had flocked to him then as now they were flocking to the Americans. The modern French have divided the province into departments: Alpes Maritimes, Alpes Basses, Alpes Hautes—that is, Sea Alps, Low Alps, High Alps. In the first group the rivers flow to the Mediterranean, and you travel along the sides of gorges. When you get farther north, the land drains into the Rhône, to the westward; there you climb through one mountain pass and go down into a valley, cross a swift stream and then climb into another pass, each higher than the one before. When you came to a bridge that had been blown up, you had to wait while the combat engineers who boast of having hairy ears put a new bridge together out of ready-cut sections of steel. Watching that sight you could be proud of your country.

Indeed, Lanny Budd was proud all the time. Surely if you were going to have war, this was the right kind to have: war in which other people had done the job of tiring out the enemy, and all you had to do was to chase him three or four hundred miles, for which purpose you were provided with an increasing swarm of vehicles. Lanny didn't see much of the infantry—they didn't have time to catch up. The motorized men considered themselves the crack troops and would do the job and let the "dogfaces" clean up and collect prisoners.

The "old man" who directed this chase was a Brigadier General Butler, and Lanny never saw him. Later he got a glimpse of General Patch, commander of the whole of Operation Anvil; a tall, nervous-appearing man, who bore the nickname of Sandy. A couple of days after the landing he issued an order which was read to groups of the men wherever they could be reached, telling them that the enemy was stunned and that they should "press on, regardless of fatigue and possible shortages of food and equipment." Thus the team of Lanny and Jerry occasionally had to forage for their grub. It was no trouble, for the peasants came out with chickens and eggs and all the kindly fruits of the earth, ready to swap them for American luxuries or even give them for love.

Lanny recalled Browning's poem: "It was roses, roses, all the way, and myrtle mixed in my path like mad." The people in the villages put out bedsheets in token of surrender, or the tricolor, or crude imitations of the Stars and Stripes as tokens of joy. They had waited so long for this day, and they hadn't expected it so soon. They stood by the roadside and cheered; they tried to drop peaches and pears into the men's laps, and the girls climbed onto the running boards and hugged and kissed their deliverers. "This is the damnedest ever," the men said, and it made them feel proud of themselves; they tried not to think about the buddies who had missed the show by getting drowned in the surf or shot while storming the fortifications. This was still going on—there were always gunshots ahead, and men coming back on litters, often with a blanket over their faces.

As a rule men at the front know only the tiny sector where they march and fight; but Lanny, being in close contact with other officers, could ask questions. He had told them why he was so concerned about Cannes, and they reported that the city was being pounded by sea, land, and air. It held out for ten days, and of course that meant that whatever Charlot had tried to do, he had failed. Lanny had no way of finding out what had happened to him. Jerry Pendleton was also on tenterhooks, because his wife and children were in Cannes. After the surrender he could hope to find out what had happened to them and to the *pension.*

Marseille, the great port which the Army had figured to take on D-day-plus-fifty, was taken in eight days, and Toulon in twelve. In the former city there had been a revolution, and the Germans and their collaborators were hunted like wild beasts. Both those ports would be put to immediate use; their capture would mean supplies not merely for Operation Anvil, but for the armies in the north via railroads and highways.

X

And what about Paris? Lanny, who had risked being put in the guardhouse in the effort to get help to that city, learned that it had been liberated on August 25, the same day as Cannes; but he had no way to learn what had happened to the de Bruyne family or to Raoul's wife and her friends. By that time his flying column had come into the department of Isère, a high land of forests and vineyards, pastures for cattle and horses, fields of wheat and rye, and mulberry trees for silk culture. It was harvest time, and the peasants were hard at work in the fields; they stopped to wave to Americans and let them know that they had come at the right moment—to keep the Germans from sending all the food away. In the middle of Isère, on the river of that name, is the ancient city of Grenoble, with a famed university, and factories that made twenty million pairs of gloves every year. The workers told Lanny that they would have to change their models now, American hands being longer and thinner than German.

From there were roads leading westward, downhill into the valley of the Rhône. The strategy of this bold dash became apparent; it wasn't to take a lot of mountain scenery and glove factories; it was to outflank the enemy who had been putting up stubborn resistance all the way up the Rhône. Fast columns rushed down the valleys of two rivers, the Isère and the Drôme, that empty into the Rhône. They posted themselves on the heights which overlook the narrow valley, and their artillery fire wrecked the enemy vehicles and blocked the roads. The enemy forces, raked by machine-gun fire and bombed incessantly from the air, had to fight their way through a twelve-mile stretch of death and destruction. It was a badly shattered Nineteenth German Army which got through and fought its way on up the river.

The team of Lanny and Jerry stayed with the column which rolled northwestward and came to the Rhône at Lyon, a great manufacturing city, which welcomed them with a fervor they would never forget. More roses and more myrtle! After that the route was northward, a main highway over which the son of Budd-Erling had motored times beyond counting. There was enemy resistance all the way, but only what the military men call delaying action. Back where the translators worked there was the sound of guns, but no steel or lead. The Allies had command of the air, and only twice during this long anabasis did Lanny and his pal have to dive into a ditch.

Most of the time it was routine business, asking the same questions of unshaven and exhausted, dust-caked and stinking Germans. Some were frightened and some surly; by long practice Lanny had learned to recognize different types and what technique would work best with each. By comparing one statement with others he could be sure which were lying. There was nothing he could do to the liars, and he didn't want to; poor devils, they were trying to help their country. The easiest way was to tell everything, and perhaps get a cigarette as a reward.

Some of these unfortunates were gray-haired old men, and some were boys of sixteen. They had endured incredible sufferings on the Russian front, the Italian front; they had lost fingers and toes, noses and ears, by freezing. One old man had had his legs run over by a tank, and had survived, as he said, because the mud was so soft. One boy, tending an anti-aircraft gun in Berlin, had been deafened by a bomb burst and recently had been wounded because, being deaf, he did not dive into a ditch as fast as the others. All had been promised an easy time ordering Frenchmen about; now they told with horror of American planes which had chased them on the roads and made life a nightmare. To the last man and boy they had swallowed Dr. Goebbels' propaganda, and they talked about the "Wuwas" that were going to save Germany. One boasted that all South England was already in ruins and that twelve million people had been killed. Another talked proudly about the "V-4," of which Lanny had never heard mention, which was designed to blow up the entire main island of Britain!

In the course of a month of such service the P.A. interviewed several thousand men, and only once did it happen that he was recognized. A sturdy SS sergeant had been in Hitler's Leibstandarte at the Berghof, on duty at the gate, and had seen the Führer's American friend arriving and departing several times. The days of Lanny's posing as a Nazi were over forever, so he didn't have to worry. He knew that he wouldn't get much out of that fellow, and he didn't. Let him go back into the horde, and be shipped to North Africa, and from there to America; he would be well fed in a stockade, and in due course would come back to Germany to make another try at world domination. Lanny had no hope for the men who had grown up under the Nazi discipline, but he thought that something might be done with the German children, if anybody was willing to take the trouble.

XI

The route followed the River Saône, which flows into the Rhône at Lyon. Straight north, and it was more of a picnic than ever. The enemy was in flight, and didn't have far to go, for at points to the eastward troops of Georgie Patton's Third Army were waiting. At Dijon some twenty thousand of the enemy were caught between the two forces and brought to surrender. That meant a respite for the translator team, for when a whole army has surrendered what it knows becomes of interest only to historians; the military men move on to new fields. Lanny had time to beg a couple of Paris newspapers from Third Army officers, and to read them and learn what a lot of history he had been missing in one fateful month.

The General with the two pearl-handled revolvers had been having a joyride wilder than had ever been dreamed by any Napoleon or Alexander. His armies had romped all the way across France and into Luxembourg, and he was now defending bridgeheads which he had established across the Moselle River, between Luxembourg and Germany. Whole divisions had been surrendering to him. At the same time the British had broken out of Normandy and had been making an equally spectacular dash, getting across the Seine and rolling along the coast of the Channel, thirty or forty miles a day, surrounding and investing one small port after another. This included Dunkerque—and what pleasant news that must have made for Rick, who had been there with Lanny! More important yet, it meant taking one after another of the launching sites of the buzzbombs which had been making London so miserable. The newspapers reported a partial lifting of the blackout in that long-suffering city.

Other items had been left out of the papers, but Lanny gathered them from officers whose friendship and confidence he had won. The sudden and unforeseen gains had put a tremendous strain upon the American Army's transport. Their artificial harbor had been pretty much wrecked by storms, and the enemy garrisons were still holding on to the principal ports. Le Havre had only just been taken, and Boulogne and Calais were still under siege. To carry supplies the long distances to the front the Army had set up a system called the Red Ball Express, an endless chain of trucks rolling eastward on one highway and coming back on another. New York City had got used to one-way streets, and now Europe was being taught about one-way streets three or four hundred miles long! So great was the demand for gasoline that pipe-lines were being laid on the bed of the Channel, and also across France. Patton's Army was being supplied by air, and had come to a halt because it couldn't get enough.

XII

Lanny had given his family the designation of his unit; you didn't give an address, for you never knew where you would be, and even if you had known you wouldn't have been allowed to tell. It was the business of the APO, Army Post Office, to find you wherever you had been sent; and soon after Lanny's Seventh Army made contact with Patton's Third, he received a letter from Paris. Captain Laurel Creston was there! She had managed at last to get permission to cross the Channel, and now was completing an article about how the French had welcomed their liberation. She wanted so much to have Lanny read it and was sending a carbon copy, taking the precaution to put it in a separate envelope. Lanny received the letter, but not the manuscript, and he never knew why—it was the way of things in war.

Straightway the P.A. made application for a week's leave to visit Paris. He wanted to make sure that Washington knew where he was, and that there was no call for him; he promised to come back and work for another month unless there was a call. His Seventh Army had been taken into what was to be the Sixth Army Group, and it was heading eastward, presumably for the Belfort Gap, a wide valley leading into Germany just north of Switzerland. Jerry was going along; he was a very happy lieutenant-translator—having received a letter from his wife. Cerise had boarded a lot of German officers during the war, but they had not molested her—they had been trying to win the friendship of the French. She added that they hadn't looted the *pension* before their surrender, the reason being that they had been surrounded.

Lanny managed to wangle permission to be flown on a transport plane which was taking permanently incapacitated men home via Paris. "Sad Sacks" they were, but the very thought of home gave them new life. The P.A. chatted with as many as he could, but he only had an hour or so before he was set down at Le Bourget.

Laurel was quartered in a WAC hotel, and he couldn't visit her there. He had no trouble in getting a suite of rooms, for half the hotels of *la ville lumière* were empty since the Germans had gone. The telephones were working again, and he arranged to see her after he had got a bath and a shave—with cold water because there was no fuel in Paris. When she came, they ran to each other's arms, and then held each other off and took a good look to make sure there was nothing missing. Such a lot of adventures they had been having, and such fun it was to tell them! Ladies first, of course; Laurel narrated how one of her editors had pulled wires and had got her the chance to come to Paris only three days after the Germans had left. She had witnessed the parade of the American forces through the Arc de Triomphe and the frenzy of the massed inhabitants, the most thrilling sight of her lifetime. It had been dangerous to be an American that day because everybody, men and women, wanted to kiss you!

She had made a story out of it, and Lanny pleased her by asking to read it right away. An enthusiastic story, a little bit hysterical, like Paris itself. Four years of shame and suffering, of hatred and loathing pressed down by terror; and then had come the landing in the south, and the news of uprisings among the Partisan forces everywhere. The Germans in Paris and its environs began rounding up the Resistance leaders, and that had brought matters to a head. The Paris police declared a strike, and an insurrection of the whole city followed. The Free French seized the central portions and the government buildings; barricades were thrown up in the streets, and for four days there was fighting. This forced the hand of the Allies, just as Lanny had told Georgie Patton it would. Georgie wasn't the one to act, being far out to the east. It was General Ike who made the decision, and he politely picked out a French armored division to have the honor of making the first entry.

Supported by American forces, General Leclerc had fought his way up from Orléans. And what a story that made for a writer of fiction! His real name was the Marquis de Hautecloque, and he had been twice captured by the Germans and had twice escaped. He had made his way to Lake Chad in Central Africa, and there had organized an army of Senegalese troops, and had led them across the Sahara Desert to take part in the fighting in Libya. Now, a general of division, he had been landed across the Channel, and French history for all time would celebrate him as the man who had delivered Paris from the Hun.

XIII

Lanny's leave in Paris was spent mostly in beauing his wife around and watching her work. She wasn't satisfied with what she had got, but wanted to collect more details and spend a lot of time weighing them and deciding which were the most effective. She wanted to walk in delightful autumn weather and savor the taste of the most elegant of cities in the midst of one of those great convulsions for which it is famous. She had learned her French from books, and wanted to hear it spoken. She wanted to see the sights of war before they were cleared away:

the burned-out tanks, the broken walls, the proclamations posted everywhere, first by Nazis and then by patriots.

Lanny introduced her to Julie Palma, who wasn't hard to find; all the Partisans had come out of hiding now, and in most places had become the government, replacing the Vichy masters who had fled with the Germans. The various Resistance groups had come together—the Francs-Tireurs et Partisans Français, the Front National, the Mouvement de Libération Nationale, and Ceux de la Libération. Now they called themselves Comac, for Comité d'Action Militaire, and had set up staffs to direct the struggle all over the land.

Julie, who had been in the thick of things from the beginning, told inside stories about the conduct of the struggle and about the supposed-to-be truce of which Lanny had heard reports. There had been a crucial debate in the headquarters of Comac, at which Julie had been present. The Consul-General of Sweden had been in negotiation with the Germans for several days, and he had pleaded with the liberation chiefs to be patient. General von Choltitz, the German commander, had wanted a truce and threatened that if it were not agreed to and kept he would wipe out the city. Many of the Partisans had wanted to agree because they had so few weapons.

But the fighting men had argued that the way to get weapons was to take them; to form small squads and raid the German stores, to capture German cars and tanks and turn them against the enemy. That was the way the Partisans had been getting weapons all over the country, and surely the capital city must not lag behind. If Paris let this German garrison get away, they would merely be condemning the smaller cities and towns to destruction by the same foes. So the vote was for fighting, and the barricades went up, and the German squad cars discovered that they could no longer race here and there to put down trouble the moment it started.

For four years Laurel's husband had been declaring that the realities of this war were exceeding anything that fiction writers had thought up, and here was the proof once more. Julie took her two comrades to the place where the historic debate, so vital to the future of *la ville lumière*, had taken place. The underground fighters had made their headquarters in a fortress built literally underground, and in which surely no fiction writer would have asked his readers to believe. Eighty-five feet beneath the city's surface, protected by a layer of limestone sixty feet thick, with steel doors, gas-proof, and a ventilating system pumping fresh air through it; with its own lighting and heating plant, telephone connections, and tunnels running to every part of Paris and even to distant suburbs—such was the military hideout which had been constructed by the French Minister of War in the critical year of 1939. And that secret had been kept from the German occupation for four years.

The tunnels were for the most part ancient, for through the centuries Paris had been mined with a vast network of quarries, catacombs, sewers, and finally the *métro*, the city's underground railroad. The whole thing made a labyrinth in which you might have lost yourself and never come out. Julie's friends were taken in by way of the *métro* station at the Place Denfert-Rochereau; because the elevators were not working, they had to go down a hundred and twenty-eight steps to the fortress doors. She gave the password, and they were admitted. Later they were introduced to Colonel Rol, the onetime sheet-metal worker who had been the active head of the Resistance all through the war.

Blond and blue-eyed, precise and elegant in manner, this man would have been taken for a poet or a scholar, and his age would have been guessed at no more than thirty. Laurel tried to get him to talk about himself, but did not succeed; he wanted her to write about the army of school children, so he called them, trained under the very noses of an enemy who thought he had the last word about youth training and also about secrecy. Colonel Rol showed them one of the textbooks which had been used in this liberation school, an innocent-looking little pamphlet with a cover showing a peasant plowing and a happy boy waving his hat. When you opened the book you read: "Chapter I: German Weapons. (A) The German Pistol. (B) The Automatic Rifle. (C) The Machine Gun."

XIV

The next day Julie took them to the scene of one of the battles, the Préfecture de Police. It is situated on the Ile de la Cité, an island of the Seine in the heart of Paris. The grandson of Budd Gunmakers had a most vivid recollection of the place, inside as well as out, for just after the Peace Conference in the year 1920 he had fallen under suspicion of the Deuxième Bureau for having in his possession some Communist literature belonging to his "Red" uncle, Jesse Blackless. They had made Bertillon measurements of him, and a commissaire with a black spade beard had put him through a severe interrogation. Then it had seemed amusing, but during the days when Lanny had been playing a Fascist role it had caused him many a qualm to know that his identification was in the possession of both the Paris police and those of Rome.

Now Paris was in the possession of the Reds and the Pinks, plus General Charles André Joseph Marie de Gaulle. How they were going to get along together was a problem about which there were as many opinions as there were Frenchmen, not to mention women. Julie discussed it on the way to the Préfecture. When they came to the Boulevard du Palais she stopped to tell them how, at this very spot, she had had to throw herself on the ground to escape German machine-gun fire. Then she had run to the Préfecture, and the door of the courtyard had been opened to let her in. The place had been full of trucks and weapon carriers captured from the enemy; and up in the windows had been men with English, French, American, and German weapons, all clamoring for more ammunition of their special sorts.

That had been a day which a former schoolmistress was never going to forget. She had gone to the place to make a report on the activities of her group and had been caught by an attack of the SS upon the ancient building. She didn't know about shooting a gun, but had worked a switchboard at the school now and then, so she took that duty while the fight was going on, knowing all the while that if the place were taken she would be stood against a wall in the courtyard and shot. The German tanks had come in the afternoon, and their guns had blasted the door leading out to the cathedral square. The opening was blocked by trucks and sandbags, and the fighting men were filling bottles with gasoline to use upon the tanks if they tried to force their way in. The enemy infantry didn't dare come up because of the fire from the building.

As a result of such activities Raoul's little wife had become quite military in her conversation. She explained that city buildings, made of stone, and with windows, stairways, and roofs, are surprisingly good places for ambushes; you can shoot quickly and get away unseen. Street barricades slow up traffic, and a car going one way can shoot up a car going the other way and make its escape while the shot-up car is trying to turn, assuming that the driver is alive to try. As a result of such factors, and of careful rehearsing and "dry runs," the losses of the Partisans during the ten days of fighting were surprisingly small compared with those sustained by the enemy. The German trucks and cars just couldn't be protected against the numbers who were setting traps for them, and when the Allied armies arrived ten thousand of the enemy were surrounded and forced to surrender. Hitler had given orders that Paris was to be destroyed, but the orders had not been carried out, and Lanny had a guess as to the reason; General von Stülpnagel, Military Governor of France, had been active in the plot against Hitler's life, and had managed to see that the Paris garrison was commanded by officers who shared his hatred of the Nazis.

The result of these days with Julie Palma was that Lanny's wife fell in love with the ex-schoolmistress and wanted to put her into the magazine and perhaps into a book. It was inspiring to meet people who had lived their faith and held on to it in spite of all disappointments. So many turned into tired radicals and took to living off the movement, or quit and lived by denouncing the movement. So many human organisms were unequal to the strain of being heroes, or martyrs, or saints—whatever name you chose to give to people who accepted new truth, spoke it boldly, and stood by it regardless of consequences.

Laurel voiced that sad idea, and Julie said, "We are having a flare-up of hope and excitement now; but there is a long stretch of privation and struggle ahead of us, and maybe we shall split up into factions as we did before. People who hope for a peaceful and co-operative world have a long job of education to do, and perhaps we shan't live to see the end."

The literary lady from *outre mer* put her arm about this nervous, high-strung little Frenchwoman. "Come and let us feed you at least one square meal," she said with a warm smile.

BOOK NINE

Feats of Broil and Battle

26

A House Divided

LANNY had the de Bruyne family very much on his conscience, but he put off communicating with them, hoping that he would get some definite news of Charlot. He had written to Raoul at the Toulon address, asking him to write to Ribault in Cannes to inquire what had happened. Presumably mail service along the coast was restored; the trouble was, Lanny had left his military unit, and how prompt would they be in forwarding a letter? He had written also to Jerry Pendleton's wife, asking her to find out if she could; but the same trouble applied there also.

The news reached him by a different route. Julie Palma came with a letter from her husband in Toulon, telling how his group had blown up the bridges and railroad lines in a semicircle about that city, and had received the surrender of many groups of Germans. He added, "If you see Lanny Budd, tell him that Charlot gained the support of several officers in Cannes, but their movement was betrayed, and several days after the Americans landed Charlot was taken out behind the ice house at Bienvenu and shot. Poor fellow, he changed his mind too late. But I suppose it will help his family up north."

So Lanny had to go as the bearer of this sad news. He took Laurel along, because she was a writer and wanted to know the French people, and this *gratin* sort were not so easy to meet; also, she had a normal curiosity concerning a family that had played an important part in her husband's life. The hotel porter managed to find them a small Citroën car, with no questions asked as to the *essence*. They drove out into the country to the northwest, by the route which the American troops had followed in reverse, coming in under the Arc de Triomphe through the madly cheering throngs. Now those *jours de gloire* were over, and the highway was empty of everything except military cars and a few peasant carts bringing in produce. The autumn rains had come and the landscape was dreary.

When they got near to the place Lanny pointed out the landmarks.

Here was where he had stopped his car and Marie had joined him when they had gone away together for a summertime trip through Normandy and Brittany and the "château country." Just over there was the stile near which he had sat talking in whispers to Julie Palma a couple of months ago. And here was the red-brick villa called a château; here was the rear entrance with the gate into the garden, and here the front drive with a box hedge now permitted to grow wild.

And here was the family manservant, almost as old as his master; and the drawing-room which Lanny had so often described to his wife. While they waited to be announced she did not stand on ceremony but went straight to the fireplace in which a wood fire was burning. Over the mantel hung a portrait of a woman with delicate, rather pale features; a woman in a light summer dress, standing by a rosebush. Laurel stood gazing into her dark brown eyes; woman spoke to woman, and Lanny stood in the background, watching, but not interfering.

II

"So you are Marie de Bruyne," said Laurel. "And you loved him."

"I loved him as long as I had life," said Marie.

"I can see that you are kind," said Laurel. "You are lovely, and he was not deceived about you."

"Surely I never tried to deceive him," said Marie. "You do not have to be ashamed for him."

"I have tried not to be jealous," said the wife, with just a trace of a smile.

"He is a better husband for what I taught him," said the *amie*. "It was a long time ago, but he has not forgotten."

"No, he will never forget," said the wife. "I have given up wanting him to forget. It is a little hard, for sometimes I think that he loved you more than he loves me."

"There is no grading in love," said the *amie*. "No two human beings are exactly alike, and no two women can give a man the same thing. Let us be kind in our memories of each other."

"Oh, you are very sweet!" said the wife. "I cannot love him unless I love you too."

"I would have loved you if I had known you," said the *amie*—and did the portrait smile? "But you would have had to look for another man."

"Perhaps you are right," said the novelist. "I am thinking of putting it into a story. Would you mind?"

"Not at all," said the Frenchwoman. "But you would have to understand our customs."

"I have tried to," said the lady from the Eastern Shore of Maryland. "I am still trying. You will help me."

"Take good care of him," said the mother. "He is not a difficult man to manage, but you mustn't let him know that you are doing it."

"Oh, surely not!" said the wife. "It has been a great relief to meet you."

"Perhaps we shall meet again, somewhere in the next world," said the memory. "It will be a pleasure to compare notes."

"Yes indeed," said the living one. "I have the better of you now, but then, perhaps, matters will be reversed."

III

Laurel Creston, novelist, had been advised by her husband to read one of the great American novels, *The Ambassadors,* by Henry James, whom Lanny described as the leisure-class historian. The central figure of this story is a young American of independent means who has chosen to reside in Paris. The members of his strait-laced Boston family wonder why, and after some years have passed they send over two of their number—the ambassadors—to find out. They meet a charming and cultured married lady, somewhat older than their young relative, and after they have come to admire her they make the shocking discovery that she is the young man's *amie* in the French significance of the word; she has made the young man over into an urbane and cultivated person, and the dilemma of the family as they come to realize this fact is presented with the quietest possible humor by a shrewd observer of the well-to-do and well-pleased-with-themselves. Henry James has been described as a novelist who wrote like a psychologist, while his brother William, the psychologist, wrote like a novelist.

It was a picture of two civilizations, the puritan and the hedonist, confronting each other. The teller of the story took no side, he told you what happened, and left it for you to understand if you could, and to draw what conclusions seemed proper. To Laurel, reading it, the story seemed like a paraphrase of the one which Lanny had told her from long ago—only a little more than two decades, but what a cycle of history had intervened!

As a wife, she had perhaps not been wise in asking for all the details, but as novelist she had not been able to resist. The story had not been in accord with Maryland mores, but she was trying hard not to be or seem a provincial person; she wanted to know all there was to know about the world she lived in, and not merely America, but Britain, France, Germany, even Russia and China. Her husband adored the memory of the woman who had been his friend, his guide, and his guardian for a matter of seven years; he had assured Laurel Creston that she was a happier wife because of that aid he had received.

The situation had been dominated by two facts: first, Marie's husband had cherished a secret vice; and second, the family was Catholic and therefore divorce was unthinkable. Laurel had heard much about that old man who "had to have virgins," and had wondered about him, and now here he came into the room, and she had to steel herself to meet him, telling herself that she was going to be a woman of the world. She had asked Lanny if she would be supposed to shake hands with him, and Lanny had told her that that was, for ladies, a crude American custom, and she would simply bow.

Whatever he had been, he was now a poor pathetic figure with a sparse white goatee, a skullcap on his head, and trembling hands. His face revealed intense anxiety, for he had had no news of his younger son and could guess that Lanny was bringing some. The two women followed him, and poor Eugénie could hardly wait to acknowledge the introduction to Lanny's wife, so great was her suspense.

There is no sadder duty than to be the bearer of news of a bereavement. Lanny had copied the words from Julie's letter and he read them without delay. For once the customs of France and America were the same, and the young wife burst into uncontrolled sobbing; her sister-in-law came and put her arms about her, and the old man hid his face in his hands. The two visitors sat in silence, for there was nothing they could do or say. Lanny knew they would wish to hear the story of his meeting with Charlot, and what the *capitaine* had said and promised to do; he waited decorously until the first shock of the disclosure had passed.

There was no longer any reason for secrecy, so he told all that had happened. They told him in return that they had received a letter from Denis *fils*, who did not know anything about his brother's fate, but reported that he had obtained a leave and hoped to be home soon. Lanny pointed out what the elder brothers' attitude would be toward the tragedy—he would consider that Charlot had saved his honor and the honor of the family by what he had done. Lanny refrained from adding that Charlot had also saved his father's life and the family fortune. The old man would know that many of his friends and associates had been jailed as *collaborateurs*, and that nothing had saved him from the same fate but the fact that the Partisans knew that Denis *fils* had been fighting with the Free French in North Africa and Italy; also, their leaders here in Seine-et-Oise had somehow been informed of what had happened to Charlot.

The present attitude of the three persons was something that didn't concern Lanny. He knew that Annette had been a Fascist without reservations; but no doubt she would find a way to adjust herself to her husband's career. Eugénie would put on full mourning and teach her children to revere the memory of their father as a hero and martyr. The old man's opinions would be determined by his property interests, as always, and no doubt he would be a loyal adherent of Budd-Erling. The internationalism of big business is a phenomenon with which Lanny Budd had been familiar since boyhood, and he was used to hearing it called law and order, honor and justice, free enterprise, individualism, and a lot of other good-sounding names.

IV

Back in Paris, Lanny wrote letters to his family and friends, telling them where he was and what he had been doing; he was going back to the Army, where new letters might come. He wrote to his father and his little daughter, and to his mother in Marrakech; to Nina and Rick in England, to Raoul in Toulon, and to Capitaine Denis in Algiers, taking the precaution to send a copy to the château. Laurel was staying on in Paris, for she wanted to see Belgium and Holland liberated and to get at least a glimpse of conquered Germany. How would that arrogant people behave in defeat, and what course would they choose when the Nazi yoke was lifted from their necks? Had they really loved and wanted that yoke, and what would they find to love now? Laurel Creston was another novelist who wrote like a psychologist—or, at any rate, desired to.

The night before they parted she asked very solemnly, "Lanny, are you going into Germany any more?"

"Behind the armies—I hope so," he told her.

"But not in front of them?"

"I couldn't, darling, if I wanted to. They know me too well."

"You must know I have guessed that you have been going into Germany. You didn't fool me."

"I was under orders, Laurel. This much I have a right to say: my orders are not to go into Germany any more."

"But you went into France while it was the same as Germany."

"Not quite the same, darling. I had a lot of friends in France, and they took care of me. But the Germans have found out about me, and not many would take care of me there. Put your mind at rest on that score."

"I'll put my mind at rest when this war is over, and when there is an international government with a police force to keep the peace."

"Just a little thing like that!" He smiled. He did not tell her any of his adventures, for he was sure they would disturb her sleep. Let her collect data from persons who were not quite so near and dear!

V

Lanny's time was up, and he was about to report and be returned to his division, which was at the Belfort front; but he was called to the telephone and asked to call at OSS headquarters in Paris, a top-secret address. He said to his wife, "That probably means I'm wanted in Washington." He went, fully expecting such a notice; instead, he was told that an Intelligence representative of SHAEF in Paris—Supreme Headquarters, Allied Expeditionary Forces—wanted him "for special interrogation purposes." That sounded intriguing indeed, and Lanny went to call upon a Major Hartman of General Eisenhower's staff. He received an order to report at once at G-2 of Third Army, whose headquarters were now at Nancy. The Major didn't tell him what he was wanted for, and it wasn't up to Lanny to ask. He was handed a pass, thanked the Major, saluted, and departed. He wondered how the all-powerful SHAEF had come to hear about him. Later he learned that G-2 of Third had asked SHAEF for him, and SHAEF had asked Paris OSS about him; Paris OSS had never heard of him, but had checked with Washington, and so had learned that he was with Sixth Army Group, and Sixth had given his Paris address. Quite a roundabout.

Lanny was driven to his hotel to collect his few belongings and say good-by to his wife. On the way he tried his best to imagine what this call could mean. Could it be that he had made such an impression upon Lieutenant-General Patton that that busy man had kept him in mind for nearly two months? Nothing could have seemed more unlikely. Or could it be that somebody at "topside" had spoken about him and awakened interest? Lanny, completely in the dark, was taken to a near-by field and put on board a "flying boxcar." Another bucket-seat trip, but it was only an hour or so; the front of the Third Army was from Luxembourg to Saarbourg, along the Moselle and the Saar Rivers, roughly within a hundred miles of the Rhine.

On the trip Lanny recalled what he had heard about Patton's forces and their present situation. In their astonishing sweep across France they had had casualties of less than thirty-five thousand and had inflicted four times that many upon the enemy, besides taking a hundred thousand prisoners. The Third had been brought to a halt early in September, but not by the enemy. Supplies had run out, and a motorized army couldn't move without hundreds of thousand of gallons of gasoline.

Who was to blame? There was a bitter controversy going on, and the G-2 officers of Lanny's Sixth Group had talked about it in semi-whispers. The shortage wasn't because the supplies couldn't be brought by air to rapidly moving troops, but because SHAEF had diverted them. Patton, wild with excitement, wanted to rush on to the Rhine and across it into Germany; he insisted that he had the enemy hopelessly demoralized and that the same thing could be done in Germany that had been done in France. Keep moving, and let the enemy do the worrying! At the outset Georgie had addressed his staff, "I don't want to get any messages saying 'I am holding my position.' We're not holding anything. Let the Hun do that. We are advancing constantly and are not interested in holding anything, except onto the enemy. We're going to hold onto him and kick the hell out of him all the time."

But SHAEF, which carried the responsibility, wasn't willing to stake everything on such a gamble. SHAEF believed that fighting in France, where the population was with us, was different from fighting in Germany, with the population against us. SHAEF knew that the Germans had immensely strong forces in the north, and that Patton's stretched-out line in the south might be broken and several hundred thousand troops cut off from their base. SHAEF considered that the Allied forces on the continent were in a bottleneck because of the lack of ports capable of handling the immense quantity of supplies required for a war that grew bigger every day, and also more distant.

The British, in their rush up the coast, had taken Antwerp with its port facilities intact; but unfortunately Antwerp lies some distance up the River Scheldt, and the Germans still held strong fortifications in that flat land which is the delta of several great rivers—the Scheldt, the Meuse or Maas, and the outlets of the Rhine, known as the Waal, the Lek, and the Yssel. In the effort to take that district the British landed an immense airborne force, some of it as far to the north as the Dutch town of Arnhem, across the Lek; but the weather was against them and they had to retire from Arnhem in the face of strong enemy attacks. That was a serious check, but the work of opening the port of Antwerp was going on, and when it was completed the advance could be resumed all along the line.

VI

Lanny's plane was landed in a rainstorm, with visibility close to zero. He knew about autumn weather in the Saar, wet and cold without limit, and had bought from Army stores a raincoat, boots, and gloves. He was taken at once to CP, as it was called—Command Post; there was a whole Army lingo made of initials, code, and slang, and you had to learn it or you were lost. This post was in an old barrracks which had been built by the French, occupied by the Germans, and bombed now and then by the Allies. He was introduced to a tall, thin gentleman, a G-2 captain; he was head of Interrogation and lost no time in interrogating the visitor. "Thanks for coming, Captain Budd, we had quite a hunt for you. Would you mind telling me if you have any friends among German generals?"

Said the P.A., "I have had opportunity to meet quite a number of them. It has been my job."

"Is there anyone whom you know particularly well?"

"Emil Meissner is the first who comes to my mind. I have known him since we were boys and I visited in his home."

"Would you mind telling me what you know about him?"

"I met his youngest brother at a dancing school in Hellerau, near Dresden, when I was thirteen years old. Kurt Meissner grew up to be a famous *Komponist.* I was invited to visit the family at Christmas, and there I met Emil. From then on I would run into him occasionally. In later years I had dinner at his home in Berlin. We didn't have much in common, but I liked him and had the impression that he liked me."

"He mentioned you as a friend, and that is why we sent for you. What sort of man is he?"

"Well, he's a professional soldier, highly trained; a Wehrmacht officer and a Prussian gentleman, which means that he is conservative and strict. His father was business manager of the Stubendorf estate, and that meant that he was an old-fashioned Prussian; not a Junker, which means an aristocrat, but completely Junker-minded."

"Is Emil a Nazi?"

"I couldn't say flatly because I never asked him. His brother Kurt is an ardent Nazi and a personal friend of Hitler. If Emil had been the same, I believe he would have expressed himself in my presence. The fact that he kept silent I took to mean that he was not altogether in sympathy with Kurt. You understand that from 1937 on I was acting as a secret agent, and it was my role to agree completely with Kurt. So Emil would have avoided discussing the subject with me, and he did. The

Nazi troops and the Wehrmacht officers did not see eye to eye, as you no doubt know."

"Tell me this: would you be surprised to hear that Emil was implicated in last summer's attempt to take Hitler's life?"

"I should be surprised, but not too much so. As a man trained in strategy, he would bitterly resent the Führer's taking over the direction of the war."

"I should inform you that Emil is our prisoner, and he tells us that he was one of the few conspirators who escaped suspicion."

"If he tells you that, I would feel certain that it is true. He is a very proud man and would not stoop to seek favors from the enemy or to increase his own importance."

"He has been treated with every consideration due his rank. We are being careful in conforming to the requirements of the Geneva Convention, hoping that the Nazis will do the same with our people. We have been working on Meissner in a polite and careful way; he has shown signs of coming over to our side, and of course that would be important to us, for we expect soon to go after Metz, and it seems that he has special knowledge concerning that fortress."

"It is very likely that he would, for he has learned all there is to know about fortification. He had little models in his home, and he also had a lot of toy soldiers and moved them around on a big table. He has that sort of mind; he likes to play chess, which, I gather, is a sort of miniature war."

VII

So Lanny understood what he had been brought here for. They wanted him to call on his boyhood friend and "work on him," try to persuade him to tell what he knew about the fortification of one of the great strongholds of the old Maginot Line. The Nazis had had four years and more in which to turn it around and make it face the other way, and maybe Emil had had charge of the work, or at any rate had been consulted about it. He had already become convinced that the German cause was hopeless, and Lanny might be able to convince him that the best thing would be to get it over before the last German city had been turned to rubble.

The P.A. said that he would be glad to try. Captain Morgan—formerly a professor of psychology at a Middle-Western university—took him to the officer's mess and gave him a good dinner, prepared by a cook from New York's Chinatown—"best damn cook in the Army," they called him. Then the officer took him to a room and gave him a couple of hour's briefing on General Emil, who had surrendered at Chalons in the course of the Third Army's mad rush across France. There was a dossier on him, including reports of conversations by various officers. Lanny was left in no doubt that they attached importance to the information this Wehrmacht specialist could give.

The P.A. had a choice of courses. He could tell Emil that he had been anti-Nazi from the beginning, or that he had been convinced by recent events that German defeat was inevitable. It was the latter course he had decided upon with Charlot, and it had worked so well that he was inclined to try it again. Lanny would tell Emil about Charlot—but not about his sad fate. He would tell what he had seen of American and British and French military power, and about industrial power as he had seen it in Newcastle, Connecticut, and Budd, New Mexico, and Los Angeles, California.

VIII

Emil had been separated from the other prisoners and was on parole; he had a room in a large villa occupied by American officers in the suburbs of Nancy, and his meals were brought to him. The place was guarded outside, but that would have been the case even if he had not been there. Lanny tapped on his door next morning; he found the officer sitting at his desk, writing; the visitor got a momentary glimpse of a long and pain-drawn face before it lighted up with recognition.

After that they had a pleasant time, for nothing can take the place of age in friendship, and the people we knew when we were young have a reserved section in our subconscious minds. This high Prussian officer, still in his uniform, sitting as erect and looking as alert as if he were still commanding an army corps, was to Lanny Budd the magnificent tall cadet who had walked into his father's home for a *Weihnachts* celebration. Rosy-cheeked he had been then, whereas now his cheeks were colorless and a bit flabby; but the scar on the left cheek which was the mark of his caste would be the same as long as he lived. He was fifty, and his close-cropped hair was gray.

How different now were their circumstances! Lanny apologized for his own. "I couldn't hold out, Emil. My father gave way, and then everybody I knew. The last time I met Hitler I was forced to realize that he was not the man I had believed him. Perhaps he had been once, but he had lost his character, his judgment, even his senses, I fear."

That made matters easy. "You are exactly right, Lanny," said the officer. "I saw a great deal of him and I decided that his self-esteem had run away with him. The handling of great armies is a science and requires a lifetime of study and the closest application. Excitement and fervor and raving cannot take their place. I cannot find in all history any calamity like that which has befallen Germany, to have so much power entrusted to hands which are incompetent to wield it."

Lanny might have said, "I am told that you had something to do with the effort to remove him," but he thought it better to talk about old times and re-establish their friendship before he approached the crucial subjects. First he satisfied Emil's curiosity, telling him that he, Lanny, had been acting as a sort of liaison officer for Budd-Erling, interviewing flight officers in the field to find out about the performance of the new models and collect suggestions for possible improvements. That gave him a chance to describe the mushroom growth of America's aircraft industry, and to add, "What a calamity that it had to be against Germany!"

He asked about Emil's family, and especially about Kurt: did he still cling to his faith in the Führer? The elder brother replied that he never discussed the matter; there had come to be such a tense situation in Germany that a man couldn't speak frankly even to his own brother. Lanny took that to mean that Kurt was still a Hitlerite; but he didn't say any more because he saw that Emil was heartsick on the subject.

They talked about old friends in the Fatherland, and it was a melancholy roll call. Emil's second brother, Fritz, was missing on the eastern front, and that almost certainly meant dead. The Berlin palace of Graf Stubendorf had been destroyed by bombs and fire. Lanny told how he had been in the palace of the Fürstin Donnerstein when the same fate had befallen it. He didn't say that he had since met Hilde in the Obersalzberg, or how he had got out of Germany. Instead he remarked, "I wonder if you ever met Oskar von Herzenberg."

"I have met him casually," replied Emil. "Poor fellow, he undertook to fight the regime, and he was unfortunate in his choice of confidants. Himmler had him shot."

Lanny didn't have to pretend to be shocked. "*Fürchterlich!*" he exclaimed, and added, "That concerns me greatly, because my half-sister, Marceline Detaze, was his close friend, and we have had no news about her."

"*Leider*, I can tell you nothing. I have heard people speak of her as a dancer, but, as you know, I am a family man, and I rarely went to night clubs. But the fact of my not having heard anything about her may be a good sign, because I heard the names of many who fell into disfavor for one reason or another. I knew practically everyone who was involved in the attempt on Hitler of last July, and it was a terrible thing. The SS went into action at the first moment, and it was enough to cause your arrest if you had ever been seen in the company of one of the conspirators, or if they had your name or number in an address book."

Lanny now thought it safe to say, "They tell me that you had knowledge of it in advance."

"I had been discussing the subject with a few friends for more than three years, ever since Hitler began taking control of the Wehrmacht and setting aside the decisions of the General Staff. One law that we had considered fixed was that Germany should never again become involved in a two-front war. The attack upon Russia seemed to us sheer lunacy, but we were helpless. Men who ventured to speak of tradition and experience were rudely shoved aside, and the plunge was taken."

IX

After that the P.A. had nothing to do but listen. A Prussian officer's dignity, his self-respect, were involved, and that of his caste, his profession, his people; the control of his country had been seized by a band of low fellows, gutter rats, frenzied malcontents born of the defeat and despair of World War I. They were criminals and degenerates, unworthy of the name of Germans; every nation had such creatures, but no nation with a civilization worthy of the name had ever before fallen into such hands.

The thing that made it hardest for Emil was the fact that his own youngest brother had been a supporter and even a friend of the head gutter rat. The elder apologized for him, saying, "Kurt is a man of genius, and they have never been distinguished for judgment about practical affairs. They mistake the intensity of their own desires for reality."

Lanny replied humbly, "*Unglücklicherweise*, I haven't the excuse of being a genius. I took my father's word that National Socialism was Europe's only recourse against Bolshevism."

"To me they are the same," said the Wehrmacht man. "And when you have won this war you will have another to fight."

The P.A. didn't comment on that, but asked about the conspiracy, and for hours listened to the details of a struggle which antedated the war, and concerning which he had picked up only a few hints during his visits to Germany. The anti-Nazi movement which Lanny had known had been that of the Socialists, the workers; but here was a movement of the aristocracy, the old masters of the Fatherland, and it had included some of the most highly placed personages, some whom Lanny had met without having the slightest idea of what was inside their heads.

There was, for example, Admiral Wilhelm Canaris, head of the Abwehr, the Counterespionage Division. Lanny had met him several times at the Berlin home of Graf Stubendorf. He was a nervous little man of Levantine appearance, and was known as "the little Greek." Lanny had taken him for a thick-and-thin Hitlerite; but now he learned that Canaris and his assistant, Major-General Oster, had been working ceaselessly upon the Wehrmacht officers, right under the noses of the Gestapo. One of their allies had been Colonel-General Ludwig Beck, Chief of the Wehrmacht Generalstab. Another was Colonel-General Werner von Fritsch, whose treason was detected; the Nazis shot him on the Russian front—or perhaps he shot himself. The story given out was that he had been killed in action. Emil called a roll of such personalities, and as Lanny recalled them it seemed to him that Adi Schicklgruber had been completely surrounded by traitors in his own home.

"It wouldn't have done any good to kill just the Führer," the General explained. "We had to get enough of his gang and to have a sufficient organization to act at once and seize control of the government; otherwise we'd merely have exchanged Hitler for Himmler. In the early years Canaris and Oster made the mistake of thinking it couldn't be done until the war had started. But then Hitler won so many victories that they knew it would be impossible to turn the German people against him. The opposition had to wait for defeat; which meant they had to sit helpless and see the country embarked on a two-front war."

The man who had approached and converted Emil Meissner was General-Major Henning von Tresckow, First Staff Officer of the Central Army Group. He had seen the tragic significance of the failure to take Moscow in the autumn of 1941; and when America was drawn into the war he knew that it would be the story of 1918 all over again. Emil told about the controversy inside the movement between the civilians who were afraid of making Hitler a martyr and wanted to take him prisoner, and the military men who insisted that he must be eliminated. They worked out elaborate plans for the seizure of control in Berlin and the other principal cities. They had won over General Kluge, who commanded the Central Army Group on the eastern front; but Kluge deserved his name, which means shrewd, and backed out at the last moment, after the conspirators had lured the Führer into a visit to Kluge's army.

"That was early in 1943," said Emil. "We tried to get Hitler with a time bomb as he was flying back from that visit. We had a special kind of English bomb, and Oberleutnant von Schlabrendorf, a young lawyer in uniform, made a bold effort and got it on his plane returning to

Berlin. But the thing failed to explode; and Schlabrendorf, who had wrapped it as a package containing two bottles of brandy, had to rush to Berlin by the next plane and try to get it before somebody opened it up."

X

The P.A. got many surprises in the course of this talk, the strangest being when Emil mentioned the name of Heinrich Himmler. Lanny exclaimed, "Surely you don't mean that *he* is involved!"

In reply Emil told him a strange story, having to do with a Berlin lawyer by the name of Langbehn, a man whom Emil knew well. Some years before the war this lawyer's little daughter had been invited to the home of a schoolmate, and upon the father's inquiry had said that the schoolmate's name was Himmler and that her father "had something to do with the SS." Out of this had grown an acquaintance, ripening into friendship; and after the German defeat at Stalingrad the lawyer had ventured to talk confidentially with the head of the SS about the tragic position of Germany, whose military affairs were in the hands of a man without military training. Herr Langbehn had made the discovery that Himmler, the ex-poultry grower, had become intoxicated by the power he was wielding and was convinced that he was better fitted to deal with the emergency than was his Führer. Out of that had grown a separate and smaller conspiracy with the aim of removing Hitler and putting Himmler in his place. One of the group was Dr. Popitz, a lawyer and Reichsminister.

"Emil, you take my breath away!" exclaimed the American. "Himmler came to the New Chancellery and put me through a questioning, scaring the daylights out of me. And now I wonder—maybe he was sounding me out, with the idea of taking me into his confidence!"

"Nothing is more likely, Lanny; but you would have been in just as great danger. The Langbehn conspiracy came to the ears of Bohrmann, who is Himmler's furiously jealous rival, and he reported it to Hitler. Himmler was able to persuade the Führer that he had been engaged in leading the conspirators on. Both Langbehn and Popitz were arrested and have been in prison for a year. Just recently I got word that they were being secretly tried; and the fear that they might mention my name was one of the reasons I decided to surrender my division. I much preferred an American jail to one of the SS."

The Junker-minded General went on to tell the story of his own efforts. After the failure of the airplane attempt he and his friends had spent another year winning over important officers and preparing plans for a new government. Another amazing thing to Lanny: among the men they had won to their support was Lieutenant Dietrich von Bose, an official in the Führer's field headquarters whom Lanny had met several times there and had despised as a timeserving Nazified aristocrat. Emil had twice been flown to that place, supposedly to interview Hitler, but really to get from Bose the details about the Führer's personal habits.

Said the General, "I volunteered to try to shoot him at the military conference which took place about noon every day. It would have been difficult because he kept himself so surrounded by SS men, and everybody had to be searched. My friends insisted that it must be done by a bomb, and I had moral scruples against killing all the persons who might be in that room. They picked another man, Colonel Klaus Schenck von Stauffenberg, who was Chief of Staff in the General Army Office; he came of an old Catholic family in Bavaria, and had been badly mutilated in the fighting in Italy. He carried the bomb into the conference room in a briefcase and set it by a table near the Führer's seat. Unfortunately it was in another man's way, and he moved it behind a pillar. That is why the evil genius of Germany is still alive."

Lanny remarked, "I know only the story the Nazis gave out, and one never knows whether to believe that."

"Half a dozen men were killed, and Hitler was deafened and had his right arm badly hurt. At first we thought he was dead, but then we heard him speaking over the radio, denouncing his enemies. First and last, about ten thousand men and women were arrested and questioned, many of them under torture. I thought that my time would come at any moment. Tresckow told me that he was afraid he couldn't stand torture, and he went out and blew his head off with a grenade. Stauffenberg and Olbricht were shot immediately, and Beck was allowed to take his own life. They are still trying people and executing them; a long list: Goerdeler, Oster, Hassell, Witzleben, Hagen, Oertzen, Dohnanyi, and Werner von der Schulenburg. If your armies are having an easy time in the invasion, Lanny, you must attribute it in part at least to the fact that a madman has shot out the best brains of the Wehrmacht."

"Yes indeed," said the P.A. "And we also understand why a number of high officers have surrendered rather easily." This was putting it tactfully and was balm to the wounded spirit of an extremely *korrekt* Prussian general.

XI

They talked about the war and how it was going and why. Lanny knew a great deal that Emil didn't, and he was free in pouring it out. He had been in London and could convince a military man that the new victory weapon had little military significance. The big ones, the rocket bombs called V-2's, had just gone into action; two had landed in English fields, and no doubt more would come. Many might hit London, level a few more blocks of houses and kill a few more hundreds of civilians; but they surely wouldn't stop the war and they couldn't be aimed at targets smaller than a city.

Emil said yes, but there was a V-3, bigger yet, and it might be better aimed. To which his friend replied, "You know, old man, my father has special information, and now and then he whispers something to me. Do not think that I am playing tricks upon you—I pledge you my good faith as a man and a friend. This is something that is probably not known to a dozen men in our armies here: American scientists with the help of those from several other countries, including Germany, are preparing a bomb upon an entirely new principle, never before known in the world. It will be capable of wiping out not a city block, but a city, killing hundreds of thousands of people in a fraction of a second."

Lanny waited to let that sink in; and after some thought the German remarked, "I suppose that what you are suggesting is the much-talked-about atomic fission."

"Don't guess, Emil, because I can't say yes and I can't say no, and it seems rude to say nothing."

"Can you tell me how soon this is likely to happen?"

"It may be six months, or it may be eight. If the war is still going on, some large city in Germany, or perhaps in Japan, will see the thing tried out. When I got my first hint of it I made up my mind that I wanted the war to end before that, because the power is something too awful to be trusted in the hands of the sort of men who rule our world today."

Again the other sat in thought. Finally he said, "You have come to urge me to give information to your side?"

"I came because I was ordered, Emil, and when I got here I was told that you had mentioned my name. I won't deceive you—I know that I couldn't anyhow. I came over to the Allied side because I found little by little how Hitler was deceiving the German people. He has broken every promise he ever made to them, as well as to the outside world.

Now I have only one thought, to get this horror of blood and destruction over with as quickly as possible. I am telling you facts and answering your questions as far as I am allowed to. I am not going to do any persuading—I leave it for you to make your own decision. You say you couldn't bear to plant a bomb that would kill some innocent men; well, both sides are dropping bombs on thousands of innocent men, women, and children every day, and that will go on until one side or the other gives up. I can assure you there isn't the remotest possibility of the American side giving up. We are going to clear out the Lowlands and turn the port of Antwerp into the greatest base in Europe; we'll restore the railroads, and bring new locomotives and cars, and unload billions of dollars' worth of ammunition and fuel and food. The men we have put ashore so far are not one-fourth of what we have in readiness; and, believe me, I have been all over America and know there is not the remotest chance of our weakening in the will to win this war."

"Our madman has done that for us," said Emil sadly.

"Exactly. We didn't want to get in, but Hitler declared war on us. Now every day a few more hundreds or thousands of German factories and homes and public buildings are being turned into rubble. It is for you to wrestle it out with your conscience and decide what you can do to save that part of Germany which hasn't yet been laid waste. Surely you know us well enough to know that we are not going to destroy anything after the surrender. All we want is to knock Hitler out and then give the people of Germany a chance to set up a decent government."

XII

The harassed officer wanted time to think, and Lanny gave it to him. He went out and entertained himself making the acquaintance of some of the staff of "Lucky"—such was the code designation of the Third. He had discovered that armies were a curious kind of one-sexed family; rent with factions, pulled and hauled this way and that by rival ambitions, greed for fame and promotion, jealousy and spite. There was a great war going on against the enemy, and there was a string of little civil wars within the organization.

In "Lucky" everybody was in a frenzy over the ill luck which had befallen, the "sit-down" which had been imposed upon a triumphantly advancing host. They blamed it upon SHAEF, which couldn't bear to see one army more successful than all the other armies put together. Ike, who bossed the show, was tender-minded, and under the influence of an evil spirit called Monty. This Monty, otherwise Field Marshal Sir Bernard Montgomery, was a Scot and couldn't bear to have Americans reap the glory. So he had persuaded Ike to let him have the gas and the guns, and had rushed his armies into the mud and mess of Holland, and got stuck there, just as at Caen. So "Lucky" had to sit down, chafing and champing, while the Germans in front of them got time to reorganize and to bring up reinforcements. They had forty thousand slaves working on the Siegfried Line, strengthening its defenses, and now it would cost thousands of lives to take what might have been had free of charge if Georgie had been allowed to have his way.

They all called him Georgie, and all swore by him, even while they chuckled over his foibles. He had infected them all with his cockiness; they all put on fancy dress, wore ties in the field, walked with a swagger, saluted smartly, and boasted of being the best damned army in the whole world. The rest of "topside" was afraid of their commander, because he hogged all the limelight, and now SHAEF had taken to censoring his utterances, claiming that his frank language might shock the folks back home. The real reason was that the correspondents took such delight in Georgie that they gave the impression he was winning the war all by himself.

Georgie was here, there, and everywhere; flying in a cub plane from one airstrip to the next, exhorting his men and blessing out his officers if they came down off their toes for a moment. Then he would fly to Group headquarters and beg and plead and scold. They were taking whole corps away from him and giving them to his rivals; they were wasting the precious hours, and the enemy was getting its courage back, even daring to conduct reconnaissance in Patton's territory, dropping spies by parachute all over it. Hot damn!—and add all the curses you know.

Lanny ran into the two-gun warrior once, in the corridor of the headquarters building. Georgie stopped, stared, and exclaimed, "Hello! Aren't you Budd?"

"Yes, General," said Lanny.

"What the devil are you doing here?"

"I'm one of you now, sir."

"The hell you say! What are you doing?"

"I'm interrogating prisoners."

"Well, go after them! If they don't answer—" Georgie's advice was that Lanny should apply his pedal extremity to the posterior of the illegitimate German, but of course he didn't say it in that Latinized language.

XIII

Lanny spent the better part of two days and nights with his special German target. He listened to the incredible story of how the German Army was being managed. Hitler, in Berlin, was growing every day more suspicious of all his old-line generals—and with abundant reason. He would send them elaborate detailed orders, from which they were not permitted to vary by a hair's breadth, on penalty not merely of their jobs but of their lives. He was insanely unwilling to withdraw from any foot of land he had taken, and would insist that the men must stand and die. In that way he had lost half a million at Stalingrad, and in the last three months twice that many in France.

Worse than that, he would keep his orders secret from everybody but the officers who had to carry them out. "The man next to me would be told to attack," said Emil, "and I wouldn't be told of his move, so we would lose contact and leave a gap for the enemy to plunge through. I had anti-aircraft units which came from the Luftwaffe and wore its uniform; Göring insisted upon keeping command of them, so I couldn't tell them where to go and they were never of any use to me. I was told that I was to get a new division, and when I sent it orders I learned that all that had been sent was a division commander, a medical officer, and six bakers. I got whole regiments that had had only a week's training and had never fired a gun. I got what were called *Magen* battalions, men who had been set apart because they had stomach ulcers and had to have white bread and milk—but I had no way to get either."

And always there was that insane raving, that cursing and browbeating over the telephone; there was the threat of being ordered back to Berlin, not knowing whether you were to be shot, and your family for good measure. Field Marshal von Kluge had wanted to withdraw from Falaise and Hitler had forbidden it; when the army was pocketed, Hitler had screamed that Kluge had done it on purpose, to prove that he was right. Ordered home, the field marshal had taken poison on the plane. General Rommel, hero of North Africa, had been reported dead in an automobile accident, but Emil said that he too had taken poison. Hitler had ordered it, partly because he had failed to stop the Normandy invasion, and partly because he was believed to have known of the plot against his Führer. "I am very well content with my fate," said Lanny's old friend dryly.

The P.A. did not push him, but waited until Emil himself brought up his problem of conscience. Emil did this many times, but still couldn't make up his mind. At last Lanny gazed into the eyes of his old friend and said, "Emil, you aren't being entirely frank with me. You have something on your mind that you haven't told me. What is it?"

The other looked away with a face of misery. Finally he broke down. "Yes, Lanny, there is something I haven't the right to tell you."

The P.A. shrugged his shoulders. "All right, old man. If that is so, I'm wasting my time and yours."

"If you would only let me tell you something in confidence—I mean, as one friend to another."

"You know I'm not here for social reasons, Emil. I am here as an officer in the American Army. If you tell me anything that has to do with the Army and its interest, I can't promise to keep it to myself."

"That is what has been worrying me. I want to put a price on my help, and I want your advice about it. I want to talk it over with you, as between friends and not between officers of enemy armies."

"I'd have to ask my superiors about that," was the American's decision. "If they give me permission, then of course I'll pledge my word."

"And keep it under all circumstances?"

"Of course I'd keep it, Emil. You wouldn't be talking to me unless you knew that." Lanny sat with knitted brows for a space, then said, "Let me ask you one or two questions, Emil. You may answer or not as you please. I've an idea that your concern has to do with someone other than yourself."

"That is true."

"Some member of your family?"

"Yes."

"I am guessing that it can only be Kurt."

"I'd rather not say, Lanny."

"Some member of your family has done something, and you want to buy immunity for him with your information. Is that the idea?"

"That is it."

"You want to ask my advice about it, and I am not to be free to mention it to anyone else without your consent. Is that it?"

"That is it."

"All right, I'll see about it."

XIV

Lanny took the problem to Colonel Koch, the G-2 of Lucky, that is to say, the staff officer in charge of its Intelligence Section. A quiet, scholarly man, as unlike his chief as possible, he listened to the life story of a German *Komponist* whose reputation was known to him. Lanny said, "Kurt is a metaphysician who has drugged himself with long words and mistakes them for reality. He was teaching me Hegel's formulas when I was thirteen and he was fifteen. He convinced himself that Adolf Hitler was the embodiment of all that lofty idealism, and now I suppose he thinks he has to die with his hero. Emil wants to try to save his life, at least that is my guess."

Said Colonel Koch, "The fact that Kurt Meissner has been a Nazi propagandist for the past couple of decades is known to all the world. There can hardly be anything confidential about that."

"No, and so I'm guessing it must be something that Kurt is doing now. I have not forgotten that after World War I he came to Paris as a secret agent of the German Army to stir up the French Leftists against the peace terms. I was young then, and swallowed the propaganda myself, and helped him to escape into Spain. I surely wouldn't like to have Emil put anything like that up to me now."

"You don't have to worry," responded the Colonel. "The hint you have given already is enough for G-2; we can very quickly get photographs and descriptions of Kurt Meissner, and if he is operating as a spy anywhere on this front we can find him."

"That's all right," said the P.A., "so long as you are acting on my guesses and not on what Emil may tell me. The question I should like to have answered is this: suppose that Emil reveals something of that sort and asks my advice, what am I to tell him? Would you bargain his life in exchange for the vitally important information that Emil could give you on the subject of German defenses and fortifications and troops?"

"That is a difficult point, Captain Budd. The Army has an over-all policy to avoid all types of immunities."

"So I have been told, Colonel. But everything has its price in war. Emil may be the means of saving many thousands of American lives; and surely they are worth more than the life of one spy."

"It is a problem I would have to refer to a higher authority."

"Let me point out to you that Kurt Meissner was a captain in the German Army at the end of World War I. Could he not be treated on that basis when we catch him?"

"He would be—provided that he was in uniform."

"Use your imagination, Colonel. Let us assume that OSS has a lot of uniforms of the enemy, taken from dead bodies. They must be using them in their business."

"That is a fair assumption." Colonel Koch smiled.

"And suppose that I went along when Kurt was to be taken, and I persuaded him to put on the uniform? I would take the responsibility, and it wouldn't weigh very much upon my conscience. A well-known musician would be sent to a prisoner-of-war camp instead of being shot, and we would get everything that General Meissner knows about the Metz fortifications. Don't you think that if that were put up to Georgie, he might consent to break one of the regulations?"

"I couldn't say, Captain Budd; but I'd be willing to ask him. Of course it would be conditioned upon General Meissner's coming through with the real stuff. He'd have to answer questions and his answers would have to be right."

"That goes without saying, Colonel. Let me urge you to get the decision as quickly as possible; the only difficulty I see is that Kurt might be captured by some other unit of the Army, and I don't suppose they delay very long about trying and executing a spy."

"Indeed not!" said the G-2 man.

XV

The deal was made, and Lanny went back to Emil Meissner and made the proposal. He saw at once that he had lifted a ton load off the General's shoulders. "You have guessed correctly," Emil said without hesitation. "Kurt was operating as a secret agent in my territory, and that is within General Patton's territory now. He didn't come to me for permission—he went directly to the OHK." (*Oberstes Herres Kommando*, the Army High Command.) "I was never sure whether they assigned him to watch me or to watch the enemy; the split in our Fatherland is that terrible. Two weeks have passed since I was captured, and I don't know where he is now, but I can tell you the name he was using and the place where he was staying."

"Was he operating alone or was he part of a group?"

"We Germans are always part of a group, Lanny. But he did not tell me the names of the others, and he will not tell them to you. He is posing as an art expert, representing a dealer in Berlin who has a way of smuggling German-captured art treasures out of the American zone. That, of course, is what he tells the Germans; what he tells Americans I do not know."

"He has taken a leaf out of my notebook," said Lanny, somewhat amused.

"Of course," replied the other. "He has heard you talk art on a hundred occasions, and it has become a second specialty with him. He has grown a beard as further camouflage; but he cannot conceal the fact that he has a crippled left arm."

"I understand that Hitler has the same, and so did the last of the Kaisers."

"I have not failed to note the coincidence, Lanny. We old-timers look back upon the *Kaiserzeit* as the happiest in all German history. I suppose that is a habit of the aged and a sign of premature aging. The world is going into something new and strange to us. Perhaps you can foresee it; I can't."

"I can foresee this much, Emil; either the Americans are going to get to Berlin first, or the Russians are. You have to make your choice between those two—and which will you say?"

"You hardly need an answer to that."

"All right then, get busy and tell our people what they need to know in order to break through the Siegfried Line and get across Germany before our bombers have knocked every last stone off the top of the next one."

27

A Friend in Deed

I

THE DEAL was closed, and Emil provided the G-2 Section with a detailed description of his brother; he was five-feet-ten and weighed seventy kilos, about a hundred and sixty pounds. His face was long and thin, with deep lines at the mouth; his eyes and hair were gray. He could move his left arm, but slowly and without much power in it. He had heavy scars on the left chest. In the library at Nancy they found a good portrait of him and made a photograph of it, and Emil drew in the beard and mustache as he had last seen them; these were painted in by an artist and then another photograph made, and all the G-2 agents went out with this. Emil knew that his brother's hiding place was in Toul, but knew only the general locality. "It won't take us long to find him," said Colonel Koch.

Meantime Emil was provided with an American uniform, for reasons of security, and installed in a villa with a G-2 staff. They brought him their wonderful photo-reconnaissance maps, and he sat at a big table poring over them with a reading glass; he put little numbers on certain spots, and then wrote out a list of emplacements, giving a detailed description of each, its depth, amount and kind of armament, and the forces it contained. He told its strong points and its weak, and how it could best be taken. He did this for all the fortifications of Metz, from Forts Kellerman and Gambetta on the north to L'Aisne on the south, from Bordes on the east to the row of defenses on the west: Guise, Jeanne d'Arc, De Vaux, Driant, de Verdun—a territory of some thirty or forty square miles. The American officers could check many details by their spies, and they said that Meissner's memory was beyond belief.

Emil, for his part, said that American coffee, candy, and cigarettes were *himmlisch*. He was particularly pleased with apple pie, and when the officers of the friendly enemy came to a party in the evening he served it to them proudly. When the time came for the jump-off, they had his German uniform newly cleaned and pressed; and took him into a large drawing-room with an immense map on the wall. The commanders of all corps and divisions of Third came in, and Emil stood, pointer in hand, and gave them a briefing, showing them where to attack and how. He spoke in excellent English for two or three hours without a break. Lanny wasn't there at the time, but he was told about it later, and how freely the American generals had expressed their admiration. They said that only one thing would have improved the occasion, and that was to have Adolf Hitler among the auditors.

II

During the P.A.'s sojourn with the Third Army it still had the Moselle River before it and was permitted to fight only for "limited objectives." But with Patton that meant a lot of activity, especially as the enemy seemed to be in the same mood. The front was "fluid"; each side kept stabbing at the other, and units found themselves now and then behind the enemy lines. The sound of gunfire was incessant; and as Lanny wasn't supposed to get into danger, they would pick him up and with other G-2's move them away. The rain was incessant, the mud was horrible, and men were in misery from head to foot—

head colds and trench feet. The airstrips were so soggy that planes couldn't get off, which gave the enemy a great advantage.

But G-2 went on working, and after a couple of weeks they reported that they had located Kurt Meissner. They wouldn't take him right away. That, they told Lanny, was the weakness of the Gestapo: they were so full of hate that they couldn't restrain themselves and would grab one man; but the Americans were calm and calculating and would watch their man for a long time and get all his associates. Lanny wasn't allowed near the place for fear of being recognized; he spent his time interviewing prisoners who were brought in every night from the raids. The officers had promised that they would let him be present when Kurt was taken; they wanted his help in handling this prize catch, soothing him down, and possibly getting information out of him.

The day came, and they put the P.A. in a staff car with two other Intelligence men. Lanny had his comforting Budd automatic in a holster, and by his side on the seat a large bundle, carefully wrapped and tied; it contained a complete outfit for a Wehrmacht *Kapitän*, five-feet-ten and weighing about seventy kilos. It had been taken from a dead man and was newly cleaned and pressed, and included everything except the arms and the insignia. The wardrobe department of OSS thought nothing of equipping a score of men every day with different outfits, each exactly what it ought to be. Some of the outfitters had come from Hollywood and had been doing that sort of thing for thirty years.

The party was preceded by two other cars and followed by two more, under supervision, with men specially trained to take particular prisoners and not let them get away or commit suicide. The amount of brain power and hard work which had gone into this war would have solved most of the secrets of the universe. Or so, at any rate, thought the pacifist son of Budd-Erling, as he sat looking out upon a rain-soaked landscape, shivering slightly, and wiping his nose now and then—for he had an undignified cold, like so many others of those who would never get rich in this man's army. The car skidded now and then on a slippery highway, and twice they had to get out and wait while the GI's lifted it out of the mud and set it onto the pavement.

But they were coming to the town of Toul, and Kurt was there, and Lanny had been waiting for this D-day a long time; so he perked up, and by the time that darkness fell and they were coming into the town, he found his heart thumping with excitement. However, the way things happened wasn't at all picturesque or dramatic; the caravan stopped by a sidewalk, and Lanny was told to sit there and wait, and he did so. He knew that the men were surrounding a certain house, but he didn't see that house, except later as a dark form looming. He had been told that the telephone wires would be cut, and that what was called a "surreptitious entry" would be gained; that is, they wouldn't ring the bell or batter in the door, but would pick a lock or cut a pane of glass out of a window, while having on one hand a sticky glove that would keep the pane from falling when it was pushed in. So many tricks there were—and so many unsolved secrets of the universe!

III

Lanny was prepared to hear shooting, but there wasn't any. A sergeant came and reported, "Everything is ready, sir." Lanny asked, "You have them all?" And the answer was, "All that were in this place." Lanny got out, took the bundle of clothing under his arm, and followed the man to the house, which was one of a block, only dimly to be made out. They went in by a doorway where two soldiers stood guard; they went up a flight of stairs by the light of an electric torch. There was an open door at the top and light pouring from a room. Lanny stopped in the doorway, and there, in the middle of the room, sitting stiff in a straight chair, was Kurt Meissner, and perhaps ten feet away a GI with a tommy gun at ready.

Lanny took in the scene at a glance. The room was somebody's study, and had bookcases against the wall, and a flat-top desk at which Kurt had probably been sitting, for there were papers scattered over it. He was wearing a dark gray business suit, and his beard and mustache were as the artist had drawn them. Lanny thought, he is thinner and paler. Poor fellow!

"Hello, Kurt," he said aloud.

The other turned his head. "Oh, so it's you." His voice was cold and said very plainly, no nonsense here!

Lanny set his bundle down, then spoke in German, very gently, "Kurt, an old friend wants to have a talk with you."

"You may talk as long as you please," was the reply, with no change of tone. "I am your prisoner."

"One thing I ask, Kurt. Your word of honor that you will not attempt to escape or to commit suicide."

"I am not interested in what you have to say, and I don't see why I should bother."

"Believe me, what I have to say is important to you, not to me. I am not going to ask you to betray anybody or to tell any secrets. I know you too well to expect it. I am trying to help you; take my word for that."

"All right," said the *Komponist* grimly. "You give me your word and I give you mine."

"*Richtig*." And then, speaking English, "Sergeant, you and this man may go downstairs and wait."

The sergeant looked troubled. "Are you sure, sir?" he asked.

"Quite sure," was the reply. "I have known this prisoner a long time."

The sergeant and the private with the tommy gun went out, and Lanny closed the door behind them. Then he went to his bundle, slipped the cord off, unwrapped it, and took out the uniform. He held it out, saying, "Put this on quickly."

The other could not conceal his surprise. "What is this for, Lanny?" It was the first time he had spoken the other's name.

"In the clothing you are wearing, you are a spy and would be shot in a few hours. In this clothing you will be a prisoner of war and will be sent back with the other officer prisoners."

"Who is doing this?"

"I asked for your life, and my request was granted. This was one time when it was good to be the son of Budd-Erling."

"And what is the price of it?"

"No price whatever, Kurt. I am paying an old debt of friendship. Be quick; I have reasons for haste."

Without another word the ex-*Kapitän* took off his civvies and dressed himself according to the rank he had held a quarter of a century ago. He had trouble with his bad arm, but Lanny didn't offer help, knowing the sort of perverse pride the German had. There was a cap and a swordbelt, but, alas, no sword. Lanny rolled up the civilian suit and wrapped and tied it—OSS would have use for it whether it was German or French or English. He tucked the bundle under his arm and said, "You understand, Kurt, you are still under parole?" When the other assented, Lanny led the way downstairs and out to the street.

To the sergeant he said, "Lend me your flashlight." He took it and turned it down the street, away from the prisoner. Some of the men might notice the change of clothing, but they knew it was G-2, or perhaps OSS, whose doings were frequently beyond comprehension. Suppose that this captured man had been an American agent posing as a German; suppose that now he was to be dressed in a German uniform and put with the other officer prisoners—whose business was it to inquire, or even to guess?

Lanny escorted his man to the car and put him into the back seat, with Lanny on one side and one of the officers on the other. Several more prisoners had been taken, and they were put, handcuffed, into the other cars. The cortege drove through the streets of this ancient town which had once been the capital of a Roman province. A great bulk towered up to the stars and Lanny guessed it was the cathedral. Presently they were out on the slippery roads again; as they couldn't afford accidents, they drove more slowly and got back to headquarters very late.

IV

Lanny had asked the privilege of interrogating his special prisoner, so he took the prisoner up to his own room. He was sure that Kurt would not reveal any secrets and that he would take such a request as an insult; Lanny had promised not to request it and he didn't. But he was curious as to his own affairs, and Kurt would know about some of them. How much had the Gestapo found out about the Führer's one and only American friend? How had they found out, and how had the Führer taken it? Above all, would Kurt by any chance mention Marceline?

"Well, Kurt," began the P.A., "this is a strange way for you and me to meet."

"I see you have gone into the Army," was the unpromising response.

"Yes, Kurt. There is a limit to the amount of pressure a man can withstand."

"You were always a weakling," remarked the other; and Lanny didn't mind—he had known for thirty years that this German man of genius held that opinion of him. It had been useful of late years; and maybe it was true, who could be sure?

"I should like you to know," said he gently, "that I have never done any fighting, against Germans or anyone else. I am here as an art expert to see that cultural treasures are properly cared for."

"And to ship them to America, I suppose?"

"You suppose wrongly. They will all be returned to their original owners."

"Even if they are German?"

"If they belong to German museums, they will be returned without question. If they belonged to private parties, it will depend upon who those parties are."

There was a pause. "Well," said Kurt, "what do you want to question me about?"

"The Army wanted to question you, Kurt, but I convinced them that you would never tell them anything that would do harm to your cause."

"Thank you," replied the *Kapitän*, but his tone was one of sarcasm, and there were no thanks in his soul. "Would you mind telling me how you came to be mixed up in my affairs?"

"A pure bit of luck, Kurt. A friend mentioned that you were in danger of arrest. I went to one of the higher officers and persuaded him that you belonged to a special category, and he gave permission for you to be changed into a prisoner of war. You will be treated according to your rank and, I presume, will be shipped to America. The officer prisoners who give parole are spending their time in comfortable summer hotels and have a money allowance. You will have no trouble in getting music paper and will be in a position to write that piece of music which the Führer commissioned."

This was a bait, but Kurt didn't take it. He sat in silence. Lanny could be sure he was recalling the scene in the air-raid shelter in the garden of the New Chancellery. Adi had promised to provide the funds for a new *Götterdämmerung;* and what a piece of irony if the funds were to be provided, not by the Führer of the Germans, but by his despised foes, the materialistic, the Judeo-pluto-democratic Americans! Bitter bread indeed for a German *Komponist* to eat while he did his work! He could taste it in his imagination, and he set his lips together tightly, refusing it.

V

The humble American made an effort to change the conversation. He said, "I want you to know the reason I left Germany, not to return. I learned that jealous persons in the Führer's entourage had lied to him about me, telling him things that cast doubt upon my good faith."

"And so you came and put on the uniform of his enemies!" This was a sneer, and the tone was bitter as gall.

"I did the best I could, Kurt. I could no longer help the German government, but I am helping German art and culture."

There was silence; the two men looked at each other, a duel of eyes. When the *Kapitän* spoke, it was with quiet contempt. "If there are questions which your duty requires you to ask me, do so. Otherwise I prefer to end the conversation."

"All right, Kurt. There is nothing else. Someday, perhaps, we can meet under happier circumstances." He rose, and Kurt rose. Lanny held out his hand, saying, "*Viel Glück!*"—which means, "Good luck to you."

Kurt's two hands stayed by his side. Facing his old-time friend, and standing close to him, he spat full into his face.

And so Lanny had the information he wanted. He stepped back a pace or two, took out his handkerchief, and carefully wiped his face. Then he took the Budd automatic from its holster and held it in his hand. He said, in the same cold tone the other man had employed, "Precede me downstairs."

Kurt said nothing but obeyed; and when they were down, Lanny said to the waiting sergeant, "Take charge of this man. Guard him carefully, because his parole is at an end. Have you other men with you?"

"Yes, sir, there are two outside."

"All right. If you handcuff him, be careful, because one of his arms is lame."

"OK, sir," said the sergeant.

Lanny went upstairs to his room and shut the door; he sat on the bed, and tears ran down his cheeks, and he did not wipe them away. Strange as it might seem, he had loved Kurt even while he was deceiving him. The deception had been for Kurt's own good, but Kurt had not appreciated it.

Lanny had his information now; he knew that Kurt knew that Lanny had been a false friend and a spy all through the years that he had been visiting Hitler. Lanny knew more than that—many things: what the Nazis were going to be after the war was over; how they were going to feel about Americans and how they would behave when they were let out of prison camps! He knew that the Nazis were Germans, the old, old Germans, the *Drang-nach-Osten* Germans of Wilhelm II, the *Blut und Eisen* Germans of Bismarck, the Pomeranian-grenadier Germans of Frederick, called the Great; yes, even those Germans who had poured out of the dark forests wearing bearskins, and helmets with cattle horns on them, and had burned and sacked the cities of ancient Rome!

Lanny had seen such Germans as a boy but had refused to believe in them. He had seen them in elegant expensive uniforms, strutting on railroad platforms, clanking their swords and twirling their upturned mustaches. He had seen them drilling on immense parade grounds, galloping on horseback or rolling in huge machines, raising dust that floated across the country for miles. Worse yet, he had collided with the spirit behind this drilling; in Kurt's home he had come upon it in a little song book prepared for children. "Now, brave sword, show honored your worth! Break, bare steel, our woe with flaming lightning! Crush to earth those who dishonor our horde! May the blood of the brute besprinkle our threshold!" So it went—iron and steel, saber, sword, and spear, flags and banners, trumpets and drums, defiance and hate, blood and death!

VI

Lanny made up his mind that he would not tell anyone about that painful episode. He would never let himself hate Kurt, no matter how much Kurt hated him. He told the officers that the prisoner had refused to say anything of significance; he did not suggest that they should put the civilian's suit back on him, but turned that suit over to the OSS, to be worn by some American spy. He told Emil that Kurt had been bitter, but he did not say how much so. It had been agreed that Lanny would give the younger brother no hint that he had met the older.

The P.A. forbade himself to brood over the episode. It was a small part of a war which was an infinite tragedy. Curious that Kurt himself had been a spy, yet he despised Lanny for being one! No doubt Kurt would say that Lanny had been spying on friends; but maybe Kurt had made some French friends in Toul; very certainly he had made some in Paris years ago. The real difference was that Kurt had been spying for Nazi-Fascism, while Lanny had been spying against it; also, perhaps, that Kurt had failed in his spying, whereas Lanny had succeeded. Let this be an omen for the fate of the two systems!

The son of Budd-Erling reported to his superiors, and they wanted him to stay with Lucky. It was the beginning of November, and the Army was about to jump off for the Moselle crossing. Then it would be view halloo to the Rhine; a good show for everybody, but best of all for the Patton mob. Lanny said that was all right with him, but he had promised to rejoin his old friend Jerry Pendleton with Sixth Group. The reply was that if Jerry was as good as Lanny said, he really belonged with Third, and they would try to find a way to wangle him, or maybe to kidnap him.

But before this plot had been worked out there came a message from OSS in Paris: Lanning Prescott Budd was to report at once for a return to Washington. Lanny knew that meant F.D.R., but he didn't say so. He was glad, because he was tired of rain and mud and of having a running nose. He packed up his few belongings, and said good-by to his new friends, and promised to see them again if it could be arranged. He got a seat in a fast plane and was set down in a Paris airport an hour later.

Laurel was still at the WAC hotel. He had been exchanging letters with her and had persuaded her not to return to London. The new rocket bombs were sudden death out of the sky, and there was no defense against them; why should a woman expose herself when she could write just as well in Paris? Now he said, "Why don't you go down to Cannes and get warm? There's a story there: the taking of the Riviera, and how it was under the Germans, and how it is now under the Americans; Monte Carlo in wartime, and the international refugees there, and the British and Americans who were interned and now presumably are liberated. People at home will want to know about those matters."

The writing lady said, "Fine!" And Lanny told her to go and stay at the *pension* with Cerise Pendleton, and gave her a letter to the authorities, both Army and civilian at Juan-les-Pins, authorizing her to take charge of the Bienvenu estate. Since the Vichy Armed Forces had had it, presumably the American Army would have it now; they would expect to pay rent, and could pay it to Laurel, who would forward it to Beauty. Laurel would send Beauty a report on the condition of the place. Incidentally she would find out about Charlot; and she might also get in touch with Raoul and have him come over from Toulon and tell his adventures. Wonderful to realize that France was free once more and that people could travel where they pleased—provided they had the price and could squeeze themselves into a train.

VII

OSS asked Lanny how he preferred to travel, and he chose the southern route; he would get warm for at least a few hours. Also, he would like time to have a chat with his mother; they routed him via Marseille and Marrakech, and from there direct to New York. He kissed his wife good-by, promising to write her often, and to see the baby as soon as possible. She didn't go to see him off at the airport, because it was a miserable rainy day, and anyhow it frightened her to see a plane rushing down a runway and perhaps not rising into the air.

But it rose; and Lanny was set down in the greatest of Mediterranean ports, where he would have liked to stroll and see the damage that had been done in the small civil war, and ask about how the new government of the Free French was making out. But he saw only the airport, and the harbor crowded with shipping; within an hour he was off again, across that blue sea which had been the center of his life—for swimming, for sailing, for fishing, for traveling in everything from pleasure yachts to armed motorboats. The rain had been left behind, and the wrinkled sea looked like a sheet of the fabric called seersucker, spread out below him as far as his eye could reach in every direction. Here and there a vessel cut a temporary path across it; the biggest looked small, and the small looked like tiny specks, motionless, with two little stripes sticking out, resembling the antennae of insects.

They skirted the coast of Spain, just far enough away to give Franco's guns no chance to practice on them. Then it was Africa: first a shore, and then plains, mostly barren, here and there flocks of sheep, and white spots which Lanny knew were *marabouts,* little round shrines. There were tumbled ranges of mountains on the left, and behind them the tall Atlas range, at this season mostly white with snow. Now and then a town came into sight, or an oasis with palm trees and herds of cattle mixed with camels. At last there was Marrakech, a great city, at least geographically speaking, spread out with gardens and orchards, and here and there tall pink mosques with gleaming domes, and the white villas of wealthy foreigners, and a great hotel famous for luxury. Two years had passed since the American forces had come here, and now the airport was one of the biggest and busiest in this war-busy world.

VIII

Cablegrams were slow and planes were fast, so Lanny dropped down unexpectedly out of the blue and surprised his mother and stepfather. How glad they were to see him, and what cries of delight and what bearhugs they gave! He had a night to stay, and spent most of it answering their questions. Kurt Meissner had been Beauty Budd's lover for a matter of eight years, and there was no secret about it; the story of what had happened to him was one that Lanny could tell, all but the climax, which would have caused Beauty too much pain. "Oh!" cried the mother. "Are you *sure* they won't shoot him?" Lanny could say that he was quite sure.

He told about Laurel, what she had been doing and what she was planning to do. Beauty hadn't been able to get any word about her home and of course was anxious. "Lanny, I suppose you've got just the sort of wife you wanted," she said, not for the first time, and Lanny assured her there could be no doubt about it. There would always be a little humiliation in this for a mother who had tried so many times to find her son the sort of wife that he really and truly ought to want. Irma Barnes had been the best of all possible guesses, and the fact that the marriage had fizzled was a wound in Beauty's soul that would never entirely heal.

But Laurel Creston was a fact too, and had to be accepted; so was her little son, whom Beauty knew only by snapshots. She had to be told all about him, and about Robbie and the fortunes he was making—colossal, only he had to pay an income tax of eighty-two per cent, and to pay it before he made it. This almost broke his heart every fifteenth of March—"Caesar, beware the Ides of March!" It almost broke Beauty's heart to hear about it at the beginning of November, and Lanny had to remind her that the money had been spent to take Bienvenu from the Germans and restore it to its lawful owner. That was something, of course.

Beauty had had no word from Marceline, and neither had Beauty's son. The Army was going in there soon, and they would find her. Lanny had to tell about his visit to Patton's Army; Georgie was the sort of man that Beauty Budd adored, and she had met him at a party in Marrakech; she had done her best to charm him and thought she had succeeded. Poor soul, she fought so bitterly against old age, and couldn't bring herself to face the idea that she was launched into her sixties. She was taking part in the social life of this community of millionaires in pleasant exile, and was full of chatter about who was who and who was whose.

Also, there was that lovely little boy, Marceline's son and Lanny's nephew, who was allowed to sit up late in order to renew his memories of his suddenly-coming and suddenly-going uncle. Half Italian, one-quarter French, and one-quarter American, he had lovely dark eyes and eager intelligence. War did not frighten him, for he had never seen it; to him it meant gay-colored uniforms, and airplanes flying overhead, and stories of dramatic and delightful events. He listened to Lanny's stories until he fell asleep and was put to bed.

28

The Paths of Glory

I

UP IN a plane over the Atlantic Lanny Budd busied himself catching up with the news. In Marrakech he had bought New York newspapers and magazines that had come by air and cost a dozen prices. He read about the unending British battle for the delta of the Rhine, and about the American landing in the Philippines. There had been a three-days' naval battle in Leyte Gulf, in which a good part of what was left of the Japanese fleet had been wiped out.

Very pleasant indeed to be warm after being so wet and cold; very pleasant to refresh your mind after the boredom and ignorance of war. A hot political campaign was near its climax at home. Lanny had heard about it in the Army, but it had been something remote and hard to make real. He had applied for an absentee ballot, and had cast it, giving the address of his apartment in New York. Here and there he heard men talking about the campaign, but for the most part they left it to the folks at home, who had time for luxuries. In the Army you thought about getting in out of the wet, and getting a chance to put on dry socks and rub salve between your itching toes; then maybe about getting a bit of freshly baked bread or an egg that was real. What you wanted from home was a letter telling you that your wife hadn't forgotten you, and that the baby had got over the croup, and that the interest on the mortgage had not been overlooked. Politics, hell! The politicians were getting themselves re-elected, and when the war was over they'd be helping the guys who had got rich out of the war and forgetting those who had been sitting in foxholes full of rain.

When Lanny arrived at the La Guardia airport he called Baker, guessing that the summons had come from him. He was told that Baker was out campaigning with the President; when Lanny gave the code name, Traveler, he was given a telephone number in Boston and called there. It was Saturday, three days before election day, and that night the candidates one and all would be closing their campaigns at the biggest meetings their managers could assemble.

The President's confidential man said, "The Chief didn't think you'd get here so quickly. He wants to see you right after election. He told me if you called to tell you to come to Hyde Park for supper on election night."

"Fine!" said the P.A.

"Come early, because the returns begin to come in at about seven. Tonight we're putting on a grand show in Fenway Park. All Boston will be here, except Beacon Street. Why don't you fly up and take it in?"

Lanny thought for a moment. "I'm just getting over a cold," he said, "and it will be a raw night. I'll take it over the radio."

II

He got a morning paper, so as to see how the campaign was shaping up. Then he took a taxi and was driven to the little ferry which crosses Long Island Sound. From this it was only a short ride to Newcastle; and there was the family, always glad to welcome him, and to hear his stories of the world of blood and terror. There was Baby Lanny, now running about on sturdy legs, and no longer in doubt about this tall smiling man who called himself Daddy. The little fellow had been here ever since summer, with Agnes to take care of him and a nurse to help her; it was much better for him than being shut up in a New York apartment. There was a governess for the grandchildren and also a music teacher, three ladies who had their meals together in the breakfast room. Robbie and Esther always had everything exactly right—in spite of having to pay eighty-two per cent of their income to the federal government!

When Lanny telephoned, Robbie left his office and came home in the middle of the afternoon to hear about the Budd-Erling planes in Europe and what the Army was saying about them. Incidentally, of course, he was interested in learning about Kurt and Emil, both of whom he knew; about Laurel and her writings; and about Jerry, and Raoul, and Beauty and her small family in Morocco. Lanny could talk more frankly now and told what he had seen and done in France; he still didn't say anything about Marceline or about having been in Germany.

Robbie talked about his family, and how things had been going. Robbie Junior had the flu, and Percy's wife was expecting another baby. At the plant, production had reached its peak, and it was something to come and see; but already the head of the concern was starting to worry, for fear they were beating Hitler too fast and there might be a cancellation of orders. That led to politics, on which Robbie had been spending a lot of the firm's money, listing it as advertising—imagine the Budd-Erling plane needing advertising with the news dispatches full of its exploits! Robbie said the election looked very close; the polls gave Roosevelt a tiny edge, fifty-one per cent, but that might not be enough. There was a still better chance of the Republicans carrying Congress, which would at least be a brake upon the insane extravagances of the New Deal. Under that head Robbie listed various kinds of "social security"; you could be sure that he wouldn't list any purchases of military planes.

Lanny remarked cautiously that he had been out of touch with politics for a long time. To that Robbie replied that Governor Dewey was making his closing speech that Saturday night at a mass meeting in Soldiers' Field, Chicago, and the family would assemble in the drawing-room to listen over the radio. That would give Lanny a chance to hear the issues of the campaign carefully explained; and Lanny said he would see what he could do about attending. It was pathetic—for just thirty years Robbie Budd had been hoping and scheming to bring his firstborn to a proper set of political and economic beliefs. He had never succeeded and never would succeed, but he would go on trying.

What Lanny did was what the schoolboys at St. Thomas's Academy had been wont to call a "dirty Irish trick." He saw Agnes Drury going out with the baby, and he went along. He explained to her that the family wanted him to listen to Thomas E. Dewey in Chicago, whereas he wanted to listen to Franklin D. Roosevelt in Boston. Did Agnes have her small radio set in her room? Agnes was slightly tinged with Pink sentiments—she could hardly have failed to be, having lived for years with Laurel Creston. She was tickled still pinker by the idea of committing this crime of *lèse-majesté* against the Budd tribe.

She whispered the secret to the other governess and the music teacher, and the governess was willing to join her; the music teacher was afraid and went obediently to the drawing-room and listened respectfully while the Governor of the Empire State told a hundred thousand people in the great Chicago Stadium and perhaps a hundred times as many more over the radio that this election represented an effort to turn America over to the Communists. Meantime Lanny and the other two sat in Agnes's room with the radio turned low, chuckling while they listened to the warm caressing voice of Lanny's Boss telling an equally great audience that Governor Dewey in one city had threatened that the victory of the New Deal would mean the establishment of Communism in America, and in another city that it would bring about a monarchy in America. The Governor should have made up his mind which he wanted, for surely he couldn't have both!

It had become a fighting campaign, and this was a fighting speech. Roosevelt had been roused to indignation by the falsehoods told about him, and about his family, and even about his little dog Fala. The President's four sons were all at the front, doing their duty, but that had not saved them from charges. The President himself had been accused of bringing on the war, and he answered that the war had been brought on by the Japanese attack upon Pearl Harbor, and by the declaration of war against the United States by the German and Italian governments. He said that he had been reluctant to run for a fourth term, and had not cared much whether he was re-elected; but "since this campaign developed I tell you frankly that I have become most anxious to win." The thunder of applause which this remark brought made it necessary for Lanny to turn the radio still lower.

To the son of Budd-Erling this speech was thrilling, because he knew the ex-Governor of New York State so well and could visualize him and every detail of the scene. He had discussed the issues with him—long ago, before the campaign had shaped up, before the war had begun. This was Lanny's fight, and had been since his boyhood, and he gloried in having a champion who could defend his cause before the whole world.

Yet at the same time his heart ached for the tired, overdriven man, the cripple who was carrying the burden of the future upon his shoulders, and who had been goaded by his enemies into coming out and "taking the stump" in his own defense. Lanny had been reading accounts of him, traveling about the east and the northeast, and as far west as Chicago, addressing outdoor mass meetings at night, and speaking from his motorcar and from railroad platforms—this man who could not stand even for a few seconds on his heavy steel braces without pain. Campaigning was the American custom, and his supporters expected it; he himself enjoyed it, or insisted that he did; but what a ghastly strain upon a man who was Commander-in-Chief of armies, navies, and air forces all over the world, and had to carry on diplomatic negotiations that might decide the future of the world for centuries.

III

Lanny rested, played with the baby, and wrote letters to Laurel and to all his friends abroad. On Monday Robbie loaned him a stenographer, and he dictated letters having to do with his long-neglected art business. The fond father wanted to send out a hurry call to all Rotarians in Newcastle and have them come to a luncheon and meet this traveler from overseas. They would give him a circular piece of cardboard with his first name printed on it, and he would hang it on his buttonhole so that everybody would know what to call him; they would feed him and then call upon him for a speech, and when he told them that Hitler was on his way out they would cheer him lustily and pat him on the back. But Lanny didn't want any publicity and wouldn't have had his picture in the *Newcastle Chronicle* for anything he could think of.

He had to face a reception of the Budd tribe; there could be no getting away from that. There were old ones—they lived to vast ages. Some were recluses, but they would come to meet Lanny in order to disapprove of him; some were quiet and scholarly, some were worldly and chirrupy; all were rich. There were young ones, male and female, and in-laws; some of these were modern and full of curiosity about a strange, left-handed relative who could travel all over the world in wartime and was full of evasions and suspected of unorthodoxy. Election eve, and he had already voted in the Army, but he wouldn't say how he had voted—he just smiled and said he had forgotten.

Election day morning he went and looked at the plant. It never stopped running, day or night, Sundays, holidays, even Christmas. There were three shifts of men and women, and enough in each shift so that one-seventh could be spared each day in the week; many of them slept in beds that never grew cold—one man got in as another got out. Some kind of aircraft rolled out of that plant every few minutes, and each one already had a load of high-octane gas in the tank; it went under its own power to the flight field, and after its engines had got warm it rose into the air and circled a few times and then disappeared, never to return.

Lanny came back for lunch, and then put his belongings into the little car which he was accustomed to drive, and set out up the Newcastle River. He didn't say where he was going—just a business engagement. It was a wintry day, there had been snow, and he was headed north into the Berkshire Hills, and then westward to the Hudson

River. He took his time. The scenery was beautiful, not so different from that of the Moselle country, except that it was peaceful and still; no rumbling of guns and no heavy transport rushing over the roads; only farmers going to town with loads of straw or cordwood. Thank God for the peace of America, and pray that it might endure! The sun was shining and the squirrels were out, and tracks of rabbits and foxes gave life to the blanket of snow on the hills.

So, towards sundown, Lanny came to the city of Poughkeepsie, the "Reed-Covered Lodge by the Little Water Place," and turned north up the Albany Post Road, now a broad, paved highway. He came to the village of Hyde Park, made famous by its citizen known as the Squire of Krum Elbow. The Squire had come in that morning and had cast his ballot. Scores of reporters had been there to see what happened, and cameramen and newsreel machines. They had wanted him to pose; everybody had to pose—this was America! The voting had been by a machine, and it hadn't worked the first time; an official had had to show the voter what was wrong. He didn't tell how he had voted, but nobody would have much difficulty in guessing.

The polls were still open, and Lanny stopped across the street and watched for a few minutes. There was an American flag on a staff before the old white frame town hall, the polling place, and a few people waiting in line—but no loitering, and no electioneering within a specified distance of the sacred spot. He had seen people fighting one another on so many parts of the earth's surface, and how he longed to teach them this dignified and orderly way of settling their problems.

IV

Lanny drove on and came to the sentry box which had been set up at the entrance to the Krum Elbow estate. He gave his name to the officer on guard and was given a nod. A long drive lined with trees led to the gray house, part stone and part brick, with a semicircular portico in front. Several cars were parked in the ample drive, and Lanny added one more. A Negro man opened the door for him, and a secretary led him down a passage to the President's study.

Eight or ten people were there ahead of him, and the Chief said casually, "Hello, Budd. Make yourself at home." It was "Budd," not "Lanny," and the P.A. understood that he was to be inconspicuous and semi-incog. If newspapermen asked about him, he would be "a friend of Mrs. Roosevelt." The First Lady had a host of friends, and many of them were odd fish; they were not supposed to have political significance, and the less said about them the better. Lanny's uniform did not make him conspicuous, for there were ten million in the Army now. He slid into a chair and sat watching and listening.

His first thought was of the Chief's appearance. His face was thin, and exhaustion was written in every line. He was playing the host graciously, as always, but what he did was an effort; he had put all he had into the battle with his foes. Presently he remarked, "We shall get all the answers tonight." And the P.A. wondered if, deep in his heart, he might be longing for the answers to be no, so that he could sink back in his comfortable chair and rest. He told his friends of his love for this place, and how happy he would be to stay in it and write history.

Seven years and four months had passed since Lanny had first sat in this spacious room and listened to the creator of the New Deal expounding his political philosophy: "Mr. Budd, I cannot go any faster than the people will let me." Lanny had never forgotten his simile of a man driving a three-horse team, what the Russians call a *troika.* The first job of anybody who wanted to effect social changes was to stay in power, and for F.D.R. that meant guiding his three wild horses, keeping them from balking and getting in one another's way; feeding them on patronage, keeping them in harness, and choosing a course they would consent to follow.

Every four years he had to submit to the whole people the decision as to his competence as a driver. He had done it three times, and received a verdict of approval; today was the fourth, and pretty soon he would be getting the answers from some forty-eight million voters, who would say thumbs up or thumbs down on his conduct of the war and his competence to make the peace. There could be no halfway verdict; either it was Roosevelt and his party or it was his opponents, who had falsified so recklessly about him, and his friends and family, and even about the little black Fala, who now lay peacefully snoozing at his master's feet, having no idea that this was one of the crucial days of history.

The dining-room with its big table had been given over for the night to men from the press associations, who received by telephone the telegrams which came from the President's friends all over the country. The guests were served a buffet supper of scrambled eggs, and Lanny sat next to his hostess, telling her a little of what he had seen in France. She was a woman of tireless curiosity, also of tireless kindness. She was busy all of every day doing services for other people, and the excitements of the campaign hadn't seemed to trouble her at all. She had set a new standard for "First Ladies," one they would have a hard time living up to. She watched over her husband, guided the conversation, got the important people next to him and the bores away from him. It was a lesson in social tact to watch how she got people out of the room while the handicapped man was being shifted from his seat in the dining-room to his wheel chair, and then how she showed them paintings and other objects of interest to keep them from entering the study until he had been shifted from the wheel chair to his seat in that room.

The radio was turned on, and the scattered returns began to come in, a precinct at a time. The President had a book in his lap, giving the votes of each city and state in previous elections, so that he could form an idea what the new returns indicated. Everybody was burning up with anxiety, but it wasn't good form to show it; the way the excitement revealed itself was in mid-evening, when the returns were pouring in fast, and it was evident that the Chief was doing a shade better than the sample polls had promised.

Presidential elections in America are conducted upon a system which would be puzzling to a foreigner. The people do not vote for candidates, they vote for a slate of "electors," who go through the form of choosing a President. Each state has a number of electors in proportion to its population, and the slate is elected as a whole, Thus Roosevelt or his rival might carry New York State by a very small margin, yet win all forty-seven of that state's electors. That was the way it was happening now. By midnight it was plain that Roosevelt was getting a little more than half of the popular vote in the whole country, and more than three-quarters of the electoral vote. That made it look like a landslide, and everybody in this Krum Elbow study chose to take it that way. Only the partisans of Governor Dewey were surly enough to point out that it was really a very close decision.

You could laugh at them, because a victory was a victory; the ins were in and the outs stayed out. Everybody laughed and cheered, and drank cider and ate doughnuts. At eleven o'clock there came the sound of thumping drums and tootling fifes—a red and white torchlight parade coming up from the village. It was a Republican village and a Republican neighborhood—the Squire of Krum Elbow had never once been able to carry his own Dutchess County. But there were enough Democrats to make a rousing hurrah. The Squire was bundled up and wheeled out to the semicircular portico and made a little speech, with the reporters taking notes and the newsreel cameras grinding. He told the crowd his boyhood memory of the election parade which had come here to celebrate Grover Cleveland's victory, more than fifty years ago.

The paraders cheered and shouted their slogan of triumph: "Four—four—four years more!"

V

Captain Budd had kept himself inconspicuous, and he was prepared to steal away and get in touch with Baker again; but the secretary came to him and said that he was to spend the night. His bag was fetched from his car and he was taken upstairs to an old-fashioned mahogany bed in which—so he was told later—the Queen of England had slept; also, he could guess, that ancestor of the Roosevelt fortune who had been a ship captain in the China trade, not entirely unacquainted with smugglers. The guest slept soundly, undisturbed by ghosts; and when he came down in the morning he had his orange juice and toast alone with the secretary, nobody else having appeared. He glanced over the delightful election news, magically provided in the New York morning papers; also he read that the Third Army had launched a heavy attack south of Metz and had taken a dozen towns. Lanny could feel that he had had something to do with that. Elated, he went for a stroll among the Squire's Christmas trees, soon to be cut for the market.

The host was busy in his study and did not appear for lunch. Lanny found himself a book and kept out of the way. When at last he was summoned to the presence, he made bold to say, "Governor, it's a lovely day. Why don't you let me take you for a drive?"

He didn't know whether that was protocol or not; but the response put him at his ease. "Fine!" exclaimed the Chief. "The only way we can escape the telephone!" He pressed a button, and Prettyman, his Negro valet, brought the black naval cape and the old fedora hat; the master was wheeled out to the portico, and Lanny tactfully talked to the Secret Service men while the Boss was lifted into the comfortable sport car and had a robe well tucked about his legs. It must have been someone's business to tip the operatives off, for there they were, and four of them in a car fell in behind Lanny's car and followed it as if the two had been connected by a cable. Those capable men, whose duty it was to guard the Chief's life, had the most elaborate training you could imagine. They boasted that they could shoot out a man's eyes at fifty yards. The President used to recite some lines from a children's poem by Stevenson:

> I have a little shadow that goes in and out with me,
> And what can be the use of him is more than I can see.

F.D.R. knew these roads as well as Lanny knew those about Juan-les-Pins. He indicated his choice with a movement of the hand, and they went up into the hills where the views of the river were glorious. A land of much history—for the New World—but they did not talk about it. The busy executive was plying his friend with questions about Europe: first, Lanny's own adventure, which hadn't accomplished very much, he was afraid. F.D.R. replied that Operation Anvil had been a whopping success, and there was credit enough to go round. Certainly General Meissner had given help—the President had already heard that story. As for Kurt, who could guess how much harm he might have done the American Army? Roosevelt had never met the composer or heard any of his music that he could recall, but he had been hearing about him from Lanny, and it was like the continuation of a serial story.

VI

"What are we going to do with Germany?" demanded Roosevelt, suddenly; and Lanny smiled a little and replied, "A lot of people would like to know, Governor—including all the Germans."

"We are going to have to settle upon a policy before long, and I am taking all the advice I can get. You know the Germans well, and that's why I called you home."

"I'll tell you anything I can, Governor; but don't expect me to pull a formula out of my sleeve. It's a tremendously complex problem."

"Henry Morgenthau wants to turn the industries over to the nations which have been plundered and make Germany into an agricultural nation. That way they would never be able to attack their neighbors."

"That's quite true; but the trouble is, you'd have twenty or thirty millions of the population as permanent objects of charity. They couldn't be fed from German soil and they'd have nothing to export. We couldn't very well let that number of people starve to death, and I don't know any place they could emigrate to."

"But if we let them rebuild their industry again, they'll start rearming. We have learned how easy it is to convert heavy industry to military purposes."

"We'll have to police the country for a long time whatever your long-range program may be; also, we'll have to supervise the educational system and try to raise a different sort of German. In the long run I don't think there is any chance of avoiding war in Europe so long as its big industry is in private hands. There are many causes of war, but in modern times the number-one cause is the race for raw materials and foreign markets."

"You are just as much a Socialist as ever, Lanny?"

"More so every day, Governor. You are going to have to move in that direction because of the state of mind of the new people who are taking over the governments behind our armies. The Partisans in Italy and France are Socialist or Communist almost to a man; even the Catholics have been brought to realize that the old masters of industry are nearly all *collaborateurs*, and that the days of wholesale exploitation are over. It is just unthinkable that we should turn industry back into private hands when the peoples are so set against it."

"Hasn't it occurred to you, Lanny, that a state which had all big industry in its hands would be more powerful for war than one in which the power is divided?"

"I have thought about it a lot, Governor. I think your picture is deceptive because you fail to realize that in prewar Europe both industry and government were in private hands. The steel and coal and armament industries in Germany were one strong combine, and they fixed prices and ran the country, under the Kaisers as well as under the Nazis. Hitler was their creature; they paid for the weapons which put him in power and he would never have got anywhere without them. To be sure, he ran away with them for a while; but notice he is shooting great numbers of his generals, but no members of the cartels."

"That is one aspect of the situation that has not been put before our public."

"It is true, I assure you. My father has dealt with these men and I have sat and listened ever since my boyhood. They hold the power, and they have no idea of giving it up. They are the same sort in France, and right now they are working on our top brass, wining and dining them, and persuading them that they are the people who know how to run the country, and that it mustn't be allowed to fall into the hands of a bunch of Reds. Imagine Georgie Patton, for example; can't you hear him snorting at the idea of letting the Partisans take power?"

"Yes, Lanny; and I can also hear our newly elected congressmen snorting at the same idea. It is from them that I'll have to get the appropriations to carry out any program."

"What you have to show those congressmen is that they have to choose between a parliamentary and democratic Socialism and a violent and fanatical Communism. There is no other choice. If we try to keep the people of Germany from socializing their industries after this war, we shall simply be putting our armies in the place of the Kaiser's armies and Hitler's, doing the same job of repression. Automatically we shall find ourselves in alliance with every reactionary force on the

Continent—and, believe me, you won't like some of them. They will like you only so long as they can get money and arms out of you."

"Oh, Lanny, Lanny," exclaimed the tired man. "I am trying to end one war, and you are trying to start another!"

Said the P.A., "The war I am telling you about has been going on in Germany ever since the Peasant Revolt, about four centuries ago."

VII

When they finished with Germany they discussed Italy, and then France, and at last Russia. Roosevelt said, "I am going to have a settlement with Stalin before many months. I have waited, to be sure I was going to be re-elected. Since he won't come here, I suppose I'll have to go to him. I'll take you along, as an expert on the subject."

Lanny smiled. "On the basis of a two-hour talk with Stalin! But, as it happens, I have known many Communists, and I understand their party line."

"I wish I did, Lanny. It seems to me they change it every week."

"That is because you don't distinguish between temporary situations and fundamentals. Lenin was an opportunist; he ordered the NEP, the New Economic Policy, but that was just until he had got production started after the civil war. What every Communist has as his fixed goal is a Communist world, and he counts on the discontent in every capitalist state to bring it into being."

"And what are we supposed to do about it?"

"We have a choice of two courses. We can cling to our competitive commercialism, through one depression after another, and repress our social discontent; in that case we'll get a revolution, sure as shooting. Or we can proceed to put our big industry on a production-for-use basis, and thus do away with the possibility of depressions."

Said F.D.R., "It seems to me, Lanny, that the Communists hate the Socialists even more than they hate the capitalists. So what good would it do us to turn Socialist?"

"It's puzzling, Governor, I admit. But the reason the Communists hate us Socialists is because they don't believe the changes can be brought about peaceably; therefore they call us betrayers of the workers' hopes. But if you once put industry on a co-operative basis, that attitude would dissolve. The attraction between the two systems would be irresistible and they would be drawn into a truce. With capitalism, of course, there is no possibility of a truce, because capitalism is forced by its very nature to expand. Within five years after this war is over we shall be producing twice as much goods as our people can purchase. We shall either have to take all the foreign markets in the world, or else face the worst depression in all history."

The President thought for a while and then remarked, "What I have to worry about is the immediate problem, whether Stalin will make a deal with us, or whether he is going ahead with a program of expansion after this war."

"I would wager that he will make a deal; but the question is whether he or any man can prevent the conflict between Communism and capitalism from increasing. There are countries all along the border of the Soviet Union which will be in collapse, and their Communists will be in a state of revolt, clamoring to join the Soviet system. The reactionaries will be putting them down. And what will we be doing?"

"You don't promise me much rest in my fourth term, Lanny." The tired man said this with a smile, but Lanny knew he meant it.

VIII

The P.A. kept quiet, waiting for the next question. None came, and looking out of the corner of his eyes he saw that Roosevelt had leaned his head back against the seat of the car and closed his eyes. Whether he was thinking or dozing Lanny didn't know, but in either case the Chief was the one to speak first; Lanny sat as still as was possible for the driver of a car. He thought about the problems his Boss had raised and what more he ought to say. Every man of power is surrounded by courtiers who make a business of telling him that everything is fine and that his judgment is perfect; but Lanny had never been one of these, and he knew that was why Roosevelt called upon him. The son of Budd-Erling thought that the world was in a God-awful mess, and he feared it would get worse because of the blind passions and the sheer ignorance of men. He couldn't say otherwise—and especially not to a man who might have the power to dispel some of the ignorance and allay some of the passions.

He decided that the President was asleep; but as time passed he became uneasy. Out of the corner of his eyes he could see his face, so pale and drawn, and he thought how people sometimes died in their sleep; propped as this man was, he might stay in position. But at last Roosevelt opened his eyes, smiled, and resumed the conversation without apology. "What are you planning to do next, Lanny?"

"I came for orders," was the reply; and the President stated his idea: that Lanny should follow the Army into Germany, meet as many people of all sorts as he could, and find out their attitudes, and what classes and groups could be depended upon for the building of a democratic government.

"I don't think you ought to spend your time interviewing prisoners, Lanny; that is a job for the military. What I need to understand is civilian opinion and how to organize it in support of a civilized regime. I don't care whether it is Socialist or what, provided it is willing to stand by democratic principles and the process of free discussion."

"All right, Governor," said the P.A. "I'll do the best I can. What shall I use for camouflage?"

"I leave that to your judgment. I think you had better continue in uniform, so that the Army will give you help without your always having to show credentials."

"There are two groups that I might work with nominally; one is the Monuments people, who are looking out for the art treasures, and the other Alsos, who are after scientific secrets."

"Which do you think would be better?"

"I might shift from one to the other, meet both kinds of people, and follow whatever leads they give me."

"OK," said the Boss. "Baker will arrange it that way. You should run down to Washington and report to OSS and tell them what you have told me. Doubtless they will have suggestions."

Lanny said, "I'll start as soon as you turn me loose."

IX

Having returned his charge to Krum Elbow, Lanny crossed the Hudson by the Poughkeepsie Bridge and sped down the west bank of the river, where the towns were fewer. He joined the Skyway and followed Highway One, and got into Washington well after midnight. Baker had telephoned a hotel reservation for him—he had to share a room with a genial salesman of metal pipe from Cleveland. In the morning he reported to General Donovan and spent the whole day and most of the night with various sections of the OSS.

Next morning, Friday, the President was due to arrive at Union Station at eight-thirty, having taken a night train from Hyde Park. Half a million people were expected to greet him; the opening of schools had been postponed, and all government workers were permitted to be late for their jobs. Unfortunately it was a rainy morning, which discouraged many; but Lanny had his waterproof coat and came early. He had watched French crowds celebrating victory, and he was interested in comparing an American crowd with them. Besides, he felt victorious himself and had some pent-up enthusiasm.

He did not join the throng at the station, but listened to the resonant voice from a loud speaker in front of a radio store. The President was thanking his friends, and especially the faithful government workers. Lanny walked on Pennsylvania Avenue; a heavy shower had come up, but the people stuck it out. There was a forest of umbrellas, and the rain from one man's umbrella ran down the neck of the next man; but they stood patiently, just to get a glimpse of the face of their new-old Chief. The residents of the District of Columbia have no votes, and perhaps that is why they wanted so much to use their voices. A vast wave of cheering rolled up the wide avenue as the little procession moved slowly by. In spite of the rain, the President rode in an open car, a long one known as a phaeton; he was wrapped in a waterproof, and let the rain run in rivulets off his head as he raised his hat to the cheering throngs.

His face shone, for he loved these demonstrations and the people who made them. He believed in the people, in their right to choose their own destiny, their ability to look after their own interests. He believed in the whole democratic process, by which he appealed to them and got their response. Three days ago he had won their endorsement in the greatest number of votes ever cast in an election in the United States, and very probably in the whole world. He was on his way to the Executive Mansion, from which he expected to carry out another four-year mandate, and the government employees who made up most of the crowd were the humble subordinates who were going to help him in the task. Eight moist bands shook the water out of their trumpets and tubas and played the Sousa marches which have become standard for American manifestations.

The procession passed, the crowd scattered, and Lanny strolled on into the business part of the city, which is very close to the White House grounds. The rain had slacked up, and he was meditating upon his experiences of the last three days and the conclusions to be drawn from them. The papers reported that Patton's Army was continuing its fierce drive south of Metz; it was the route which Emil Meissner had recommended, and Lanny could feel that he had had something to do with that. Everything was coming his way, and there was only one thought to disturb his peace of mind—the glimpses he had got of a harassed and exhausted man dozing in a motorcar. That face would light up with excitement for a victory parade, but afterward its owner would be so tired, oh, so tired!

X

Lanny came out of his unspoken prayer and saw that he was on a run-down business street; Washington is a mixed-up city, and in the very center of a block of handsome houses you will find the most abominable tenements, considered fit only for the Negro population. Lanny did not know the street he was on, but later he discovered that it was Tenth, and across the way he saw a dingy red-brick building resembling a warehouse. He recollected having had it pointed out to him; it was the old Ford's Theater, where Abraham Lincoln had been shot nearly eighty years ago. It was now the Lincoln Museum.

Lanny recalled the story of the frenzied Southerner, an actor himself and brother of a famous actor, who had sneaked past a drowsing sentry into the President's box and put a bullet into the back of the Great Emancipator's head. Then he had leaped down to the stage, catching his foot in a flag used as drapery and breaking his ankle. He had shouted his melodramatic cry, "*Sic semper tyrannis!*" and had made his escape on horseback. A dreadful story, and a dreadful calamity for a nation; for Lincoln, the Emancipator, had also been the Conciliator, the merciful man who had pledged himself to bind up the nation's wounds. He was the one man who could have allayed the furious hatreds of the period, and his death meant that the country had to go through the blunders of Reconstruction, and be set back by a generation of partisan strife and corruption.

Lanny had been riding with another President, and thinking about assassinations and death, sudden or slow. He considered Franklin Roosevelt another Emancipator, and an even more practiced driver of political mad horses. Once more the country was coming to the end of a cruel war, and once more the wise man, the man of mercy, would be needed to bind up the wounds, this time of the world. He was such a tired man—a sick man, as Lanny believed, in spite of all the optimistic pronouncements of his physician. Lanny stood at this scene of old-time tragedy and tried to imagine what would happen to mankind if Roosevelt went under—the confusion, the unleashed hatreds, the helpless drift to calamity in both hemispheres. Despair seized him; he felt himself growing dizzy and had to turn and walk quickly away from that haunted spot. Abraham Lincoln had been too good for the American people, a piece of blind luck; and that was exactly the way a presidential agent felt about his Chief in this world crisis. Where would they find another like him?

Printed in the United States
32943LVS00005B/148-150

9 781931 3132